CW01018745

Lovers' Knots

Marion Halligan was born in Newcastle on the east coast
of Australia and grew up by the sea. She has spent several
years intermittently in France and now lives in Canberra
with her husband and occasionally two children.

She has been nominated for most of the major literary
prizes. Her book *The Living Hothouse* won the 1989 Steele
Rudd Award for the best collection of short stories and
the Braille Book of the Year, and *Eat My Words* received
the Prize for Gastronomic Writing in 1991. She was also
winner of the 1990 Geraldine Pascall Prize for book re-
viewing and criticism.

Marion Halligan has published over sixty stories in
magazines and anthologies in Australia and overseas, as
well as articles and conference papers on food.

Other books by Marion Halligan

LOVERS' KNOTS

A hundred-year novel

Marion Halligan

MINERVA

Published 1993 by Minerva
a part of Reed Books Australia
22 Salmon Street, Port Melbourne, Victoria 3207
a division of Reed International Books Australia Pty Limited
Reprinted 1993 (twice)

First published in Australia in 1992
by William Heinemann Australia

Copyright © Marion Halligan, 1992

All rights reserved. Without limiting the rights under copyright
above, no part of this publication may be reproduced, stored in
or introduced into a retrieval system, or transmitted in any
form or by any means (electronic, mechanical, photocopying,
recording or otherwise), without the prior written permission
of both the copyright owner and the publisher.

Typeset in 11/14 Caslon by Midland Typesetters Pty Ltd
Printed and bound in Australia by Australian Print Group

National Library of Australia
  cataloguing-in-publication data:

Halligan, Marion, 1940–
  Lover's knots.
  ISBN 1 86330 159 3.
  I. Title.
A823.3

For my sisters Brenda and Rosanne

Contents

◆

Acknowledgements

———◆———

My special thanks to the Literature Board of the Australia
Council, whose grants have given me time and space in which
to write, as well as the encouragement to do so.
I would also like to thank Margaret Connolly for her
unfailing and cheerful support, and my family, who are
good to me.

Queer are the ways of a man I know:
   He comes and stands
   In a careworn craze,
   And looks at the sands
   And the seaward haze
   With moveless hands
   And face and gaze,
   Then turns to go . . .
And what does he see when he gazes so?

Thomas Hardy: 'The Phantom Horsewoman'

Fate is not an eagle; it creeps like a rat.

Elizabeth Bowen: 'The House in Paris'

To eat without being eaten is the first law of insect land. The second law is to lay eggs and provide for the young. There are no other laws but these.

The answer of the wise old ant to the tragic
riddle of life. In Cassell's Book of Knowledge.

THE TIN MISSION

◆

Ada Gray stepped down off the tram, landing with a thump as she always did because she was not agile. She launched herself off the step like a small blimp that might have expected to float up into the salty summer air, but always came down to earth with that teetering jar. The tram hissed steam, she sometimes thought sarcastically, and clanked down the line to the terminus at Merewether Beach. Ada gave a delicate wriggle to settle her stays; she was a stout woman, the bones of her breast well-protected by padding. There was quite a hill to climb to her house just round the corner from the Methodist church and she set out with small tired steps; so many would be needed to get her there. Her feet were tiny, pathetic; they looked like a Chinawoman's that had been bound since birth and had protested by bursting out in bunions. Bathetic, too, as a support for her bulk, and she had to sit down to see them. She never felt any friendliness for them, even when she washed them and powdered them; they were like hidden enemies darting sharp pains from ambush.

It was hot, too, and only September, the same as March at Home. The sun beat brightly on her eyes. She'd have been better off in a hat with a brim, but she wouldn't give up her toques. Somebody had once said that she looked like the Queen and whenever she stood in front of her dim spotted mirror and pinned the hatpin into the veiling-swathed felt, down under the butterfly-waved hair and out through the felt again, she held her head at the right proud angle. She composed her lips and lowered her lids coldly and regarded herself. There was certainly a likeness. Of course she was a more substantial figure than the dear Queen, but there was the same regal air.

Good afternoon, Mrs Gray.

Good afternoon, Mrs Cooper. Her hand came up in a brief wave.

Thinks she's a blooming duchess, Mrs Cooper muttered to the cocky, watching the slow plodding of Ada's flowered back up the street. Neat street, small square houses made of wood, two rooms in the front, two at the back, and a narrow hall straight through. With a facade like a face, door-nose, eye-windows, beetling brow roof, and a moustache of a verandah reached by whitewashed tombstone teeth. A tiled front path as straight as the hall, and a little square of green buffalo grass on either side. No trees. Ada Gray approved of that. Messy things trees. Always dropping leaves. Soaking up the sunshine. Here it lay thick and yellow on the ground and filling the air, pouring down, pouring down like honey; by the time the summer came you could drown in it.

A lot of the houses had names: Eothen, and Lucknow, Strathaird, and Malvern, Aberystwyth, Alexandria, Montrose. They tinkled from gilded glass plaques, and challenged; they were something to be lived up to. The demands of another world, left behind, rejected even, but not forgotten, spoke in those names.

Ada's front garden had the squares of buffalo grass that grazed on the sand and rooted and multiplied, and something more. A camellia tree, tall and woody. Its everlasting glossy leaves had a lot to do with the bedroom's darkness. Now it was covered with red flowers that browned and curled and dropped; the grass was ugly with rotting brown and red petals. When her tiny painful steps brought her to her own fence she stopped and bending from the waist picked up dead heads and carried them across to the gutter. While she was doing so several more flowers fell and broke in fleshy shards, silently, mockingly, staining the grass. Her gloves were marked with their stickiness.

She looked to the letter-box for comfort, but it failed her. Never mind, she had a reward in her bag: a thin envelope, an unknown hand, English stamps. She'd got it today, at the Mission. Simply addressed: Mrs Gray, Missions to Seamen, Newcastle Port. It had found her without any trouble; they always did. She put it on the table. She hadn't had time to read it all day; she always saved her letters to savour at home.

But first, the fire stirred up under the kettle, the toque unpinned and boxed away on top of the wardrobe, the cruel feet unbound and soothed with old slippers, the calico apron hoisted. Only when the tea was brewing brown and toothsome in the pot did she open her letter.

Dear Mrs Gray, it began, *God Bless You*. They often began like that. *I cannot thank you enough*. The tea nourished and refreshed, so did the words. It wasn't a very long letter, written by an unaccustomed hand with a scratchy pen that made blots, but it was enough. She cut herself a slice of sinker, such hunger always on Mission days. All that dispensing of tea and sandwiches and sinker to others. George would be pleased to see the sinker, he loved it. It was only a mush of stale bread with dried fruit and spices, moistened and pressed and cooked, cut into dense greyish-brown slabs with a doughy sheen, but it did taste good. The sailors loved it. Stockton has the best sinker of any port in the world, some of the boys said. Get away with you, she'd say, and give them a little push, but she believed them. She had another slice with her third cup of tea and went back to the letter.

It was from Jimmy Archer's mother. She didn't remember Jimmy Archer and had never met the mother (often the letters began, *You won't know who I am but I felt that I had to write . . .*)

but it was enough that the mother knew the son. So many
boys passed through her hands, such babies, twelve or thirteen
some of them, pretending to be tough little sailors and then,
when they saw a kindly motherly woman, not being able to
keep up the swagger of all those months at sea, breaking down
and crying on the soft padded shelf of her bosom, remembering
they were children still.

Have you written to your mother yet? she always asked.
And you've been away how long: six months? A year? Three
years? How do you think she feels, not hearing from you all
this time? Not knowing whether you're alive or dead. I want
you to promise me that you'll write today. And these born-
again children usually did, the very same day. They often
mentioned the nice lady Mrs Gray and often the mothers saved
from their worst fears sent back their gratitude. *You are a
mother, you know how I feel*, they wrote, and Mrs Gray proud
would show the letters and say the same thing: I am a mother,
I know how they feel. She would add this one to the collection
she kept in a cigar box, where they took on its faint perfume,
so that whenever she smelt the odour of unlit cigars she thought
of her mothers and their yellowing gratitude.

It's the first thing I ask these boys, she said. She wasn't
above bullying them a bit, all in a maternal way. The poor
things. They've always meant to. They just haven't. Sometimes
she gave them paper and pencil and envelopes, would even
offer to post them, and as time passed and more and more
mothers wrote gratefully to her she became more concerned
to inspire letters in remiss sea-going lads.

She would come back from Stockton, where the Mission
was, in the punt, and the gentle harbour waters would slap
against it a little, and she'd look at the rows of ships and
remember what it was like for that to be the pattern of your
days, and was glad when the punt docked (the voyage only
took a few minutes) and she was on land again. The three
months from England, fifteen years ago now, had finished her
for boats; she would never see Home again. But it was on
her lips a lot; ideas from Home, books from Home, especially
people from Home, were always welcome, and the fact that

home for herself and her family was now this often beautiful sunny bright seaport on the other side of the world was never regarded.

Do you know, it used to be the greatest port in the world, in the days of sail, said George. Not any more, of course. He had a photograph of the forests of masts, the ships lined up, four or five deep, at the wharves. He loved the water and the vessels and all the life of them.

She heard the whirr of his bicycle wheels along the side path. George home, and no meal started. Still, he could have a piece of sinker, and there should be another cup of tea in the pot. She was pouring it out when he walked in the back door, still wearing his grey dust coat. He put his arms round her, bending down, giving her a hug.

Hullo, little mother. Had a good day?

George was comfortably tall, a healthy lad, heavy chested and sharp ankled. It was hard to believe they'd fled the old country to save his life.

He was drinking the tea and smacking his lips over the sinker. Mm. You know what a fellow likes.

Ada often felt damp prickles behind her eyes and in her nose when she looked at him. He was so substantial, and such a good son. She liked to walk out with him at weekends, when he was dressed up, and the creases of his flannel trousers fell sharp and fluid to the shining toes of his shoes; she wanted to hold on to his arm with her nose close to his shoulder and sniff the faint fumes of the spirit with which he cleaned his jacket and feel his strength and imagine all the old dears in the street thinking, What a handsome couple, isn't she lucky to have such a good son.

Salmon at work today, he said.

Pink?

No, red. Nothing but the best for your boy.

George worked at a customs agents, which handled all sorts of goods, including tinned salmon, sardines, crab. Quite often they had to open several tins in a shipment and weigh the contents, in order to estimate the quantity and quality of the whole, whether it was true to label, and what duty was liable.

Then they could eat the delicacies themselves. They had to test the very best things.

Pity it's not the whisky, said George. This was a good joke, because he never touched a drop, rarely even a shandy; his father was enough to put anybody off. He'd had to leave the Mission because of his problem, though that was the job he'd come to the country to do; he was in the railways now and it was not nearly such a nice position. When Ada walked out with Albert she never took his arm. He might take hers, timidly, but more often he walked a pace or two behind, a small man in a dusty navy suit, silver watch chain drooping over the waistcoat that hid his narrow ribs. His mien an apology for the shortcomings he understood very well. A consort.

Whereas George was the heir. The second heir. The first, her dear little Albert, had died at the age of two, of pneumonia, one terrible dark damp winter. Daisy had been a tiny baby at the time, but healthy enough, and then had come Rose, little toughie, and George, chesty like his poor dead brother. Winter after winter George spent in bed, coughing his little heart out. At the seventh the doctor, solemnly unhooking his stethoscope, had said:

If you want that boy to last another winter you'll take him away from this God-forsaken climate. Emigrate. I will not guarantee him another year in this country.

George celebrated his seventh birthday on a small sailing ship in the middle of the Indian Ocean. He got a penknife and a piece of chocolate. His baby sister Lily nearly fell overboard. His mother said, I do not know how I survived that voyage. I expected each moment to be my last. But she was a strong-minded woman. Newcastle seemed a place of possibilities, and since there could be no going back there was much to be made the best of. Three years later, when the War came, she knew they had done the right thing. She rejoiced that George was too young, and as the years passed and little Albert would have been old enough for the conflict, she took her first grain of comfort in his death.

George's sisters spoiled him and he grew to like his own way. But he was a good boy, and gave his mother no more than the usual doses of motherly sorrow, except that he nearly broke her heart when he insisted on leaving school at fourteen. He was clever, she wanted him to be a doctor. She could see him, sitting on the edges of beds, solemnly prescribing healthy futures, like the doctor at Home who had saved his life. She still reproached him with this picture. But George had been sick of school. He wanted to go out into the world.

All topsy turvy. There was Rose and her fancy notions. Wanting to stay on at school. Wanting to go for a nurse. Full of wants.

Ada had put a stop to that. You've got your living to earn, my girl. And Rose had worked, first of all in houses where the wife had had a baby, cooking and cleaning so the new mother could stay in bed and rest, a job she was good at because she'd had a lot of practice at home, and then as a maid in a very nice family, a doctor's, who lived on the Hill. Every week she brought her money home and made three piles: one for mother, one—tiny—for her own expenses, and one to save. Last year she'd put by enough to buy her uniform and begin her training. She's stuck at it, I have to admit that, said Ada. But it's a terrible life. She has to do terrible things. If you ask me, not at all the sort of thing that a nice young girl ought to do. Rose was happy. She was going to become a triple-certificated nurse and then a sister and then a matron, preferably of a maternity hospital, in one or other of the flourishing Australian cities. Though she still and all her life called England Home, she had no desire to live there.

Rose remembered the old days, and going with her mother charitably visiting in the small sickly cottages down the road, and the nappies taken off the babies and dried in front of the fire, to be used over and over again, without being washed, so that the sharp stench of urine was always in the air, mixed with the thin crying of angry red flesh.

In this country the nappies crackled and snapped in the sea winds, warmed and whitened in the suns of summer and winter. Next door but one, in a tiny cottage held together with morning glory, lived the midwife, whose buxom daughters kept her in practice, in between pegging out the childbirth sheets and hoisting the long lines of washing on the clothes props. They boiled and scrubbed with their fat pink arms and sang and afterwards made love in the dark folds of the sandhills and got babies of their own. Every day while the new mothers were resting and girls like Rose cooked and cleaned for them, the midwife's daughters collected the dirty linen and nappies and returned them fresh, sweet and sun-dried, and the babies smelled milky and powdered and delicious enough to nibble. Rose had learned the shape of babies, how to hold them and soothe them, and been much in demand for lying-ins. She was kind and efficient, and never minded putting the babies down when it was time to go.

Now that she lived in the nurses' home Ada missed her. She'd been handy round the house. George refreshed the pot and they had another cup. Plenty of time for a meal later.

You're the only one I've got left, sighed Ada. Neither considered the omission of old Albert, he was not significant. When she finally got around to frying up some liver and bacon, with slices of bread to soak up the drippings, his would be left over a pot of hot water at the back of the stove against his return from the shift. The food would wrinkle and harden, go crisp or soft where it ought to have been the opposite, but he wouldn't complain.

She leant over and stroked her son's face, the smooth cheek and the prickle round the jawline. The only one. And you'll be up and leaving me soon, getting married to some silly girl or other, I shouldn't wonder.

She said this indulgently, conversationally. She knew no girl was good enough for him, and expected him to know it too. She didn't even demand denial of him, a laugh was enough. In fact, George was working himself up to proposing to Alice, a pretty gentle girl who was the sister of Rose's best friend, Nell. Last Sunday he'd decided that she was the girl for him, as they walked along the railway tracks beside the beach. He saw again her shyly smiling face, rosy just as a rose is, pink and cream and golden, peeping up at him from under her hat with its tiny brim at the front swelling out over her ears, over the shining brown shells of hair that covered them. He thought of her gleaming stockinged calves and her small feet. She was so prettily made and delicate that he, usually cocksure and demanding, had been happy just to look at her.

Alice had been to tea at the Grays' one Sunday night, with Rose and her sister. Ada had demanded in her loud duchessy tones: And what do you do, dear? When Alice had replied that she stayed at home and helped her mother, she'd learnt dressmaking at the Tech but, well . . . Ada had said, Oh? in a very chilling surprised voice, and there'd been a lot of noisy conversation, and Rose in her bossy way had talked about her work at the hospital and George had argued loudly about the mistakenness of women having careers, and Lily who was still home then had argued back and everyone had begun shouting and Alice hadn't said another word all evening. And ever since George had thought about her face like rose petals and the dark lashes that so often fluttered down over her eyes and her shining silken shells of hair. This Sunday he would see her again; the thought filled his chest with pleasure. He liked the clothes she wore, fluid mysterious dresses that she made herself. When he pinched a corner of her skirt between his fingers so as to touch something belonging to her she said words like *crêpe-de-chine, eau-de-Nil*, tussore, ninon, tea rose, that made him feel he was being invited into a female world with queer new territories to be explored.

George?

Oh . . . yes . . .

Well?

What?

I said, two slices of bread, or three? Ada was waiting at the stove, irritable as the sputtering fat.

It's nice and cosy, just the two of us, he said when they were sitting at the table, he with his plate mounded up with piles of liver, and four rashers of bacon, and three slices of crispy fried bread, golden and succulent. Ada was keeping her boy substantial.

I wonder how Tiger's getting on, he said after a bit, taking a breather from eating. He meant his sister Lily, his favourite ever since she'd been his baby sister and he'd felt responsible for her, had been tried and not found wanting on that birthday on the boat out, had grabbed at her skirts as she toppled over the rail when the boat heeled, and had learnt in the force of the fury and relief with which he'd shaken her till her teeth rattled how much he loved her. He'd nicknamed her Tiger and never called her anything else. Now she was nineteen, big and shapely, a dark girl with a deep voice and a swelling brown throat and skin spotted with moles, pollen dusky, seeming to promise secret places full of honey. She was alternately stately and lively, duchessy like her mother or a tomboy doing everything her brother did. She'd written only one brief note when she'd first gone up north: the life was fun, the children were brats, she was hoping to learn to ride a horse. They'd heard nothing since.

Oh, I'm sure she's all right, said Ada.

Victor'll look after her.

Mm.

Victor and Lily were courting. Vic was a carpenter and had a good job on the railways. He'd been sent to Moree and shortly afterwards Lily had got herself work as a governess on a property just out of town. Ada thought little of this; Lily was about the business of life, for a woman: getting married, with its inevitabilities of child-bearing, child-rearing, hard work, difficulties, unhappinesses. With the possible reward of a good son. All husbands were the same: unsatisfactory.

Ada put men into two categories. There were the children women bore, and loved fiercely, and cosseted with all their power, which often wasn't enough. They could be wild and difficult and break their mother's hearts, could sail the seas and ignore them for years, but they were doted on. And there were the men women married. These had nothing to do with sons, were feckless, hopeless, uninteresting, disappointing. Vic was likely to be as good as most, perhaps better, and if not, why should Lily's lot be different from anybody else's? The eldest daughter Daisy had been married for ten years, to a cook off a boat, a fat pale man who looked like a boiled pudding. They lived in Wollongong and had no children; Ada rarely saw her.

George was delighted by the connection between Lily and Vic. Vic was his friend, a quiet young man who smoked a pipe and rode a good motorbike. The salt of the earth, George called him. Solid as a rock. Utterly dependable. And sensitive too; he copied out poems for Lily, read them to her, even tried his hand at writing them himself, and brought her presents of wild flowers that he picked on walks in the bush. George missed him now that he had gone to Moree. He was a person you could have a serious talk with. He was glad that he was going to have him for a brother-in-law. And he considered Vic was a very lucky chap to have got his sister.

George thought of a future with Tiger and Vic back from Moree and married, and him and Alice married and how jolly it would be. He had prospects at the customs agents, he would save up and buy a car, perhaps like his friend Norman's, very long, with padded leather seats and a hood to pull up when it rained. They could drive out on Sundays and have picnics, Alice would make cakes, such good cakes as she made, and sit close beside him in the front seat, her cheeks blooming rosier than ever in the wind of their passage.

♦ ♦ ♦

When Albert came in, cold and dirty, George was reading and Ada crocheting in front of the fire. His gladstone bag clattered when he put it on the table. He ate the dried-up liver, the stiffened bacon, the soggy bread. Ada refreshed the teapot again.

Bit of excitement at the depot tonight. Albert watched them sidelong from eyes like sad oysters. George still read, Ada grunted. One of the shunters. Went under. The idea rose in his chest, hot and familiar, threat and talisman—somebody else. Every somebody else a horror, and welcome; keeping up the statistics. He took a mouthful of tea and sucked it round his dentures. Wagon went over his leg. Took his other foot too. Should have heard him scream. It's a sound you'd never want to hear again.

The kitchen was quiet save for Albert's mournful shuddering tones. Ada's mouth curled but she said nothing. If Albert expected a little reflected doom he was disappointed. Neither

Ada nor George was responsive to the dangers of his situation.
They were his own doing. He'd had a nice gentlemanly job
at the Mission; if he hadn't got drunk once too often he'd have
had it still. When Ada tossed her letter on the table in front
of him she knew he would hardly look at it, not wanting to
be reminded of what he'd lost, now that he lived in the dangerous
dirty world of trains clashing and shunting in the night.

◆　◆　◆

George had his portrait taken, by a photographer in Hunter
Street. He brought it home in a stiff paper envelope for Ada,
who was amazed anew at how beautiful he was. The picture
showed just his head, sloping slightly at an intelligent and
pensive angle across the page, against a background of pleated
satin, not more flawless than his skin. His slightly open lips
were carved with marble clarity, and his pince-nez were the
elliptical ornaments of genius. It was a work of art. She liked
it so much he bought her a frame for it, and she stood it
on her dressing table, where it gleamed quizzically at her in
the dim light. She thought he'd had it done especially for her;
he didn't tell her it was on account of Alice. He intended to
give her one that weekend.

　　After a while he realised that he was carrying two things
in his head at once: the Sunday afternoon walking out with
Alice, perhaps persuading her to risk her pretty shoes along
the stormwater pipe that made a useful path round the headland,
past the baths, to where there were few people, where the
beach stretched yellow for miles and the mesmerising sea rolled
in, when he could give her the photograph and perhaps pop
the question. When in fact he would be walking along this
pipe, but not with Alice, and not stopping to sit against a
warm rock and murmur futures together, but keeping on
tramping down those miles of yellow beach as far as the next
headland. For the other thing in his mind which he was
remembering perfectly well was the cubs camp at the lagoon,
from Friday to Sunday. Twelve small boys, Bill Stretton the
cubmaster, and himself the assistant. Certainly no Alice. She
liked to walk; she and Nell and Rose would take long tramps

along the beach and up into the bush, they knew the tracks
to find their way through the miles of unpeopled country,
coming back with blackberries or tender-fleshed gumtips to
arrange in vases. But the cubs were a male enclave. Alice would
have to wait for the portrait.

◆ ◆ ◆

The scout camp was on a ledge of the hill above the lagoon.
The lagoon itself was a large brown pool of water that changed
shape, fed by a creek that ran down from the hills in a series
of waterfalls. A rim of sand separated it from the ocean, but
occasionally the waves washed that away and then the sea
water got in, and the river water got out, and the pool was
a mixture of salt and fresh. Always the waves washed the sand
back, the lagoon never disappeared altogether. Part of the charm
of walking out to it was seeing what state it was in, what
shape. Some people swam in it; the cloudy water was warm
from lying in the sun, sybaritic, even decadent, compared with
the bracing surf just by it. Other people thought it was
unhealthy, lying still and breeding germs. The cubs were not
to swim that weekend, though the September sun was heating
it up quite comfortably. George and Bill took them for a long
walk instead, way up the creek, which was called Flaggy Creek,
perhaps because of the large flat stones like flagstones which
made its bed and which it ran over and between in hundreds
of little rivulets that chuckled and wandered in the sunlight.
Or maybe it was named after the rushes that grew in its pools.
The broad creek bed of big flat stones was a marvellous place
for campfires, and for boys to play; they cooked sausages and
romped about, jumping and chasing and building dams.

It was on the way back from this tramp that George saw
something he never forgot. It stayed in his mind and for a
long time he would take it out and think about it again, with
a warm feeling of wonder. The trek was rough going in places,
especially at the waterfalls, where there were great boulders
to climb down, and the boys who hadn't been still for a second
all day, not even when eating hot sausage sandwiches, were
taking a rest on the broad warm flagstones, drinking the creek

water and splashing it on their sweaty faces. It was very quiet, the boys were too tired even to chatter and laugh, there was only the deep noisy silence of the bush, the faint clicking of tree bark in the sunshine, the endless splashing of the waterfall, the distant Caark . . . Caark . . . of a crow. George thinking that all the pain and sorrow and loneliness of men was in that cry, feeling it drop into his heart like a stone, walked to the lip of the falls and looked over, down into the next valley of the stream.

Below him on the warm flags a blanket was spread and on it lay a couple, naked. They were not making love, but they were lovers. They lay a little apart, on their backs but turning in towards each other, just gazing, very still, except that the man's hand reached out and touched the girl's breast and stroked it with dreamy slow pleasure. Her hand rested on his thigh. Their bodies lay pale and delicately made on the grey blanket, the girl's hair fanned out across it and gleamed in the sunshine. They were beautiful. George stood and looked. He'd never seen a woman naked before, not like this, whole and clearly. He looked for a long time. When he turned, and bellowed much louder than was necessary: Very well boys! Enough lazing about! Form two lines *over there*! he felt as doomful as the archangel barring the gates of Eden.

They scrambled down beside the waterfall. The couple were completely covered with another blanket. When the twelve curious little boys filed past they were lying all tucked up with the covers over their ears, as respectable as parents in a double bed.

Out of earshot, Bill looked sidelong at George.

That's pretty rum.

Mm.

◆ ◆ ◆

It was late on Sunday afternoon when he got home, the small boys all accounted for. The gnarled branches of the camellia tree still dropped their handfuls of browning petals, in the corner of the eye, not quite flaunting, and the cocky down the road cried, Come back. The fire was well alight when he got inside, and Ada was unexpectedly bustling about with a cake. Lily stood at the table shredding lettuce.

Tiger! What're you doing home?

Her dark red lips curved. She kissed him, smack, on the cheek. Jog, love. I'm back.

But the job. Moree. Vic?

Oh, got sick of it. She laughed. Her head tipped back, and her brown throat swelled. Like a bird's it pulsed with the notes of her laughter. A man came through the door. Lily turned and looked up, put out her hand.

This is Joe, she said. Just saying the name took all her breath. She gasped. Joe Sullivan.

From Home, said Ada. The two women stood beaming, offering Joe to George, proudly, as though they had just made him, moulding him carefully to be perfect in every part and now trusting him to go forth and charm. He seemed very large—as if they'd got the scale wrong.

George looked up at Joe, who squeezed his fingers hard in the handshake, hurting him. Joe crinkled up his eyes, curling his lips, booming out in an Irish voice as full of plums as a pudding, Hullooo, hullooo. He went on squeezing his hand long after the reverberations of the greeting had died away, and George felt cold shivers in his knees and had a moment's mad notion that a giant had stepped out of a legend and was putting him to a test. Mad Cuchulain in person.

I came down with Lil, he said, with such a lingering emphasis on the *i* George was surprised when he got to the *l* and didn't instantly know who he was talking about. On Friday.

Ada spread mock cream over the cake. George would have liked to give his attention to that. He was on a minesweeper, she said. In the War.

Joe shrugged, smiling deprecation in a way that emphasised the significance of such a past. He had taken Lily's hand again, and raised it to his mouth. The gesture took a long time, and all the while Joe looked at her with glittering eyes. George thought of the lovers in the glade; there had been such innocence, such gentleness about them compared with this violent glitter of Joe's.

He's come down to look for a job, said Lily. There's nothing in Moree. Not for a man like Joe. Her brown eyes, which had always seemed to him velvety and soft, had caught the same hard sparkle. George didn't want to look.

What about Vic? he asked.

Lily shrugged. He's gone bush, she said.

It was a very good meal, with ham as well as the lettuce, and tomato, and raspberry jam, and the cake, but George didn't really enjoy it.

Do have a cup of tea, said Ada in her fruity flutey voice that made people think that she was putting on the dog, though it came naturally to her. I always say there's nothing like a good cup of tea. She passed Joe one of the best flowered cups.

Indeed, said Joe, there is nothing like a good cup of tea. His voice had so many notes he seemed to be playing a musical instrument. By contrast George's, which cultivated the local accent, seemed flat. Albert said nothing. He would have to go to work soon, since he was on the late shift, and he sat quietly enjoying the good food, eating unwisely of the raspberry jam. He sucked the tea round his dentures trying to wash out the seeds.

Joe was talking about his minesweeper. He pushed his plate to one side, dismantled the cruet, and with the help of his knife and fork made diagrams of its activities. Ada and Lily thrilled to their dangers. The terrible German mines lay in wait for the mustard pot, the salt cellar might explode at any minute.

But Joe, said Ada, you must have been so young. Far too young. We shouldn't have to depend on children to defend our shores. She put her hand over his, there were tears in her eyes. Her baby sailor boys were cosseted in comparison.

Joe laughed, playing new variations on the wonderful instrument. He leant back, both hands on the table, his head thrown back, laughing.

Ah, dear lady, he said, and Lily shivered with pride, dear lady, life is all a game to the young.

I thought the Irish refused to fight with us, said George.

I joined up in England, said Joe. In Liverpool. That's where I was living at the time.

With your parents? asked Lily.

Liverpool is very close to Ireland, said Joe. And it's a great port. He talked about Liverpool, its wharves, the rows of ships berthed. What a triumph of man's skill it was, the dredging needed because of the River Mersey constantly casting shifting sandbars across its channels, difficult ports these estuaries.

Newcastle's an estuary, said George. It's a feat of engineering, too.

Oh yes? said Joe.

And what about your mother? asked Ada. What did she think of you going off like that, that dangerous life?

Joe smiled, a wet curved gleaming smile in his brown face. I am here. I survived.

George was annoyed to have this tea with its unusual cake and luxurious ham spoilt by Joe. Ada pressed delicacies upon him and flirted. She kept turning her head and patting her bun into place and making small pleased mouths. Tiger whom he hadn't seen for months was taking no notice of him, apart from inviting his admiration of Joe, rolling her eyes round to make sure her brother missed nothing of his brilliance. He wanted to talk about his camping trip, and the cubs, but all conversation led to the visitor, and cubs were child's play compared with a minesweeper in the late Great War. George wished he'd go so he could have Tiger to himself, and ask about Moree and Vic.

Where're you living Joe? he asked, hoping the fellow would take the hint and remove himself there.

The women looked at him. Here, said Lily, he's staying here, smiling at him as if she expected him to be pleased.

Where?

Well, we've fixed up a bed in your room. It seemed the best place.

His room. George's face became very red, he could feel his skin prickling and burning. He'd only just got that room, with Rose gone nursing and Lily governessing; before that he'd had the glassed-in back verandah, a narrow draughty dusty place, and he still felt the pleasure of a real room to himself, with a lowboy for his clothes and shelves for his books and a washstand with a large oval mirror for shaving in. Now he had to share it with somebody whom he already disliked. He couldn't think of anything to say that wasn't rude. Lily and Ada stared at him critically.

Just till he gets settled, said Ada. Finds himself a job and somewhere to live.

Joe and Lily turned their glittering eyes on one another and it was as though sparks jumped across the spaces between. George thought to himself that the fellow was disgusting. Why didn't Lily, let alone his mother, see that?

Should try the railways, said Albert. Plenty of good jobs there.

Yes, well, there's plenty of time for that, said Ada. When he gets sorted out.

George felt like stamping off in a rage and going to bed, but he couldn't escape like that, the fellow would follow him. He had a book he was looking forward to reading, about Lost Atlantis. A book of mysterious things. Perhaps offering explanations. When he rode his bike to work he looked at the sea and the landscape so open to the sun and the Chinese gardeners hoeing their glistening flourishing rows of vegetables and the small groups of people waiting at the tram stops and wondered what they all meant, what the pattern was, why the tram was steaming along its tracks, the sea heaving, what was the power that kept these things so exactly fastened on to a globe spinning in space? Sometimes he thought himself into a daze at the mystery of it all and his bicycle wheel would catch in the tramlines, which was very dangerous, it could pitch you forward over the handlebars into a nasty accident, and then he was jolted back to the simple outward significance of trams and cars and iron tracks set in the roadway.

He went to the library at the School of Arts and borrowed books; whenever he could he bought them. He read Wordsworth for the meanings and gave a copy to Lily when she went up north, he read Mary Baker Eddy and G. B. Shaw and Edgar Cayce and Bertrand Russell and Havelock Ellis and the teachings of the Buddha, and learned a lot, but did not feel any closer to understanding. Ada was not impressed with all this reading; she liked to sit at night and crochet intricate flowers that grew into doilies without her even looking at them. You should go to church, she said, when she saw him reading *The Hidden Doctrine Beyond Karma*, but he had tried that all through his childhood, waiting bored and mischievous until it was time for the choir to raise its angel voices in the anthem. He often sang a solo part, having as a boy one of those soprano voices so pure that sinful men can perceive heaven in them, and when that broke, a charming tenor. The singing was a pleasure, but it was a decoration, its meaning as mysterious in the scheme of things as the tram, or the sea, or death. The vicar had never offered elucidation, only a morality of *don'ts* that couldn't satisfy his desire. Pelmanism seemed more useful.

◆ ◆ ◆

Monday morning was bright and gritty with a tweaking twitching tetchy wind that gave no rest. Joe was still asleep when George wheeled his bike out the gate and pushed it along the footpath, reluctant to begin riding through the westerly. Mrs Cooper's bird called, Hello cocky, hello cocky, and one of the midwife's daughters waved at him as she heaved the recalcitrant washing line on its long wooden prop. His thoughts nagged and teased his insides as the wind did his outside. Tiger had been maddeningly vague: she'd hated the job, the woman was mean, the children brats, the town a dump and the property miles from it. She said all this in a glib way, it was a kind of chant, and he couldn't tell whether it was true or not. She had nothing to say about Vic, except that he'd gone bush. George and Vic wrote to one another, but George hadn't had a letter for a while. Tiger had lowered her eyelids, looking at one leg twisted round the other, sitting hunched with her hands on her elbows and her arms tight against her chest. It was dull, she said. I didn't like it. Vic fussed.

But Tiger, you two are getting married.

Who said?

Well, it's one of those things. Everybody knows.

They shouldn't. Not until they're told.

I thought you were really sweet on him.

I'm fond of him. He's your best friend.

The glib words came out of her mouth all slippery, he couldn't catch them, hold on to them, hold them up and show her what she'd said.

Poor old Vic, he said. I suppose he's not very happy.

She said nothing. George thought, perhaps all this means nothing, perhaps she just got sick of being in Moree, wanted to come home. Then he heard Joe's dark laughter; it made his stomach turn. He tried to tell himself he was being illogical; perhaps Tiger was infatuated with Joe, but that was all it could be, a brief dazzle and then she would see clearly, see again the solid worth, the essential value of Victor.

When he got home from work, a dreary day checking rice, sago and tapioca, no pleasure in them and on top of it the bills of lading lost, Ada and Joe were sitting in the kitchen drinking tea. He heard the rise and fall of Joe's dark deep voice before he opened the door. He was already bad-tempered from the wind, which blew hard as ever. Ada sat solid and stolid in her chair. She had a tendency to immobility; her heaviness and small painful feet made her want to stay put once she'd sat down. For years her daughters had looked after the house, so the last couple of months with none of them at home had been hard work for her. George did certain chores, but they were masculine ones, she did not expect him to involve himself with housework or food. Now Lily was back and looking after such things, and even more delightful had brought her an amusing companion.

I can't remember when I laughed so much, she said. George took his tea and sat in the opposite corner of the room reading *Lost Atlantis*, trying to lose himself in its theories of a race of supermen, talented and beautiful, who destroyed themselves by their misuse of science, of which their knowledge was greater by far than contemporary man's.

Thus it happened every afternoon, it seemed, Ada and Joe drinking tea, endlessly chatting, with sometimes Lily, and

Albert insignificant and silent, if it happened not to be his shift. You're a terrible old gloom, George, said Ada. Always got your nose in a book. I used to think you enjoyed a good talk.

I've heard all your talk before, he said. But usually he liked to hear her stories of the old days at the Mission as much as she liked to tell them.

You should have seen the place when we arrived, she would say. The old Tin Mission it was called. The floor was awash at high tide, the roof leaked. And the rats! The boldest and cheekiest rats you ever saw. They'd sit on the altar in the chapel and wink at you. Gambol round the pulpit during prayers. The apprentices'd be really tickled.

It must have been really pioneering, said Joe.

That came to an end with the great storm of 1912. We had eighty men for tea and service. All our usual ladies helping. The whole floor lifted. The water was knee deep. A raging torrent. We had to abandon ship! And then the most charming thing. Each sailor chose a lady, just as though he were securing her hand for a dance, swept her into his arms and carried her to safety.

Ada laughed, hand on bosom. Her lace handkerchief patted damp eyes.

Wonderful days. Wonderful days. Of course Albert was a lay reader then.

I wish I'd been there to rescue you, said Joe.

Oh you. Mind you, I was a bit lighter at the time.

But no less handsome.

We've got a new building now. An equipment equal to any in the world, they say. A chapel with stained glass windows. And the apprentices' room the gift of the boys' mothers. I'll take you one day, if you like.

At the sign of the Flying Angel, said Joe. I know the Missions, of course, from my own sea-faring days.

Albert was a wonderful reader. You should have heard him do the bit from Revelations. *Then I saw another angel flying overhead, sent to announce the good news of eternity to all who live on earth, every nation, every race, language and tribe.* That's where the Flying Angel comes from, you know. He read it so beautifully. But that was in the good old days. He won't do it now.

Ada patted her eyes again, and Joe patted her hand.

There seemed no hurry about his finding a job. When he gets settled, said Lily, who'd been to see the midwife and was doing a bit of housemaiding for the new mothers. Joe'll be all right. These things take time.

♦ ♦ ♦

In the meantime the odour of his presence filled George's room, making it smaller, stuffy. It didn't go away when Joe did. At night he snored; the resonant instrument produced awesome sounds.

On Saturday George hurried through his customary chores—chopping wood, polishing the boots (ignoring Joe's on the bench by the back porch), cleaning the knives, which were carbon steel and needed a lot of scouring—and rode down to see Alice. He found her at her front gate, buying rabbits from the old man who sold them for ninepence a pair and skinned them on the spot. Being able to spend a few minutes alone with her seemed a good omen. And it was; she agreed to go for a walk with him on Sunday afternoon. He went inside to say hello to the family; her parents were there, and the married sister with her baby. The boys were out and Nell at work; she was a milliner, in a shop. George liked visiting Alice's family because there were always people busy and enjoying themselves.

He bicycled home, thinking of the next day's walk, picturing her holding his hand as they walked gingerly along the pipe, round the headland, finding a sheltered sunny spot, sitting, talking. And then he remembered the lovers lying on the warm stones of Flaggy Creek, and imagined they were himself and Alice. He'd never thought of her naked before, she wasn't that sort of girl. This was the gift of the lovers, that he could do so now, without feeling dirty, in a sacramental sort of way. *With my body I thee worship*. He felt an enormous grave excitement, as though he'd understood a mystery. Not that he intended to entice her behind a rock and out of her clothes on the morrow, not at all, but one day they would be together, like that, and he would know a secret of life.

In the event he held her hand and kissed her cheek and gave her the photograph and didn't ask her to marry him. But he did invite her to go to *The Gondoliers*. He liked lively music, and himself played the cornet in a brass band. He thought that if Joe stayed much longer he would get up half an hour earlier and practise it in his bedroom. Trouble was, Ada wouldn't be too happy either.

That night out was the cause of a row over Joe. He'd come home to wash and change before picking up Alice. Ada was there, but not Joe or Lily; they'd gone out, she said, to the pictures. When he came to get dressed he couldn't find his best tie, which astonished him. He was a methodical person, always putting things away (A place for everything and everything in its place, he would admonish the careless Tiger) unlike Joe who was very untidy; the only thing that saved George being driven out of his mind by Joe's messiness was the fact that he owned almost nothing, hardly even a change of clothes. And of course that was the answer: Joe would be wearing his tie.

That beast has stolen my tie! he roared, stamping out to the kitchen.

Oh, just borrowed, said Ada. He'll give it back. He just wanted to look nice to take Lily out.

I'm warning you, if he so much as touches any of my things again I won't be responsible for my actions. The beast will be using my toothbrush next. Eeugh. He stamped back to the bedroom and put on a tie that was not half so nice.

They caught the tram into the Theatre Royal. Alice enjoyed *The Gondoliers*, and the chocolates he bought, and then they caught the tram home again, and he walked her to her gate. She didn't stay talking long, the spring night was chilly, but she stood for a while, her sweet face upturned to his in the moonlight. He felt he wanted to look at it forever. He told her so, and she hung her head and shortly went inside.

Ada was alone in the house when he got home. He was

delighted with this, they could settle down into a good cosy chat, and he could tell her about the night out, and how she misjudged Alice, who wasn't at all the feeble person she thought; she might not be a strong forceful woman like her and his sisters but she wasn't stupid, she had amusing things to say. But Ada straight away began to talk about Joe, and how amusing he was.

And it's so good to have somebody straight from Home to talk to.

But he's from *Ireland*.

Oh, he's not really Irish . . .

With that voice?

. . . not vulgar Irish, he's the English landowning class sort of Irishman, quite different, and besides he's lived in England quite a lot, I gather.

You certainly have to *gather*. He's certainly pretty secretive about himself. Got something to hide, I shouldn't wonder. Probably a criminal. On the run from the law.

George! Don't you dare talk like that about a friend! Anyone can see Joe's a good man. Ada's duchess tones brooked no contradiction. George was irritated; he could see that it was Joe's outrageous flattery that got her in. Flattery to the music of that flowery voice and in the regard of those explicit glittering eyes, oh he might be courting Lily but that gaze upon Ada offered an admiration more titillating than simply a motherly vicarious satisfaction. You're a handsome woman, Mrs Gray . . . It's so good to meet with a really intelligent woman in this country . . . Ah, here is our Lady Bountiful. And how are your sailor boys today, Mrs Gray? Her hand was kissed and her chair brought and her tea poured and in George's ears he as good as said, Ah Mrs Gray, if only you were free . . . What upset him in all this was that since his mother didn't see it as flattery he couldn't point it out without insulting her, making her think her son didn't care for her as much as this stranger. He'd done it once and had to talk very fast to get out of it. Hadn't, he was afraid, managed to undo the damage; she'd stayed offended. He tasted the bitter rage of his impotence to save her, and Tiger, Tiger the threatened one.

Lily and Joe came in, hand in hand. Lily's brown face was flushed duskier than ever, her hair wildly curling.

Bit late to be coming home from the pictures, isn't it?

We've been walking along the promenade, looking at the moon shining on the sea. Making a silver pathway right to our feet.

A sparkling silver causeway to heaven. We thought of taking a walk up, but decided to come home and have a cup of tea instead. Joe's eyes glittered as though they'd snatched up the sea-broken moonlight and he towered down on them with his strange smile that turned his lips down rather than up. Ada glowed.

Oh Joe. You're quite the poet.

Ah, it's this lovely Lil. She'd turn any man into a poet.

Every time George heard this morsel of his sister's name succulent as a fruit in the man's mouth he imagined it was her flesh that he was nibbling. And the mockery in the man's eyes knew it. Tiger was Tiger only to George, to everyone else she was Lily except to Joe who'd made her his own with his own name for her.

George took his tea to his room with a book. But all those deep fruity voices booming away in the kitchen, laughing, echoing, spoiled his concentration. So he went to bed and lay in a contrived unsleeping dream of Alice. Making up simple possible stories, fantasies that could happen. Walking to the lagoon. Playing tennis. Going to the pictures . . . *If I had a talking picture of you-ou, I'd play it every day all way through-ough* . . . Riding on his bike: she would sit on the bar and he'd have to hold his arms quite firmly around her so that she wouldn't fall off, and push his head forward over her shoulder, or perhaps she would lean back, sort of curl up, under his chin, so that he could see where he was going. He would need to concentrate very hard, not like riding to work and the risky tramlines, to keep her safe, and she would be fearful and need his comfort. He could imagine how monstrous a speeding flimsy bicycle would seem to his gentle love. The simple bare event of Alice on his bicycle grew and flowered in his mind; he didn't think he'd ever been so perfectly happy before. It was quite surprisingly sufficient; he no longer felt any urgency to ask her to marry him; wooing her was enough. He decided to join the tennis club at the Glebe, which was nicely situated, well out of the way of the tram route, a bit far to walk, just a good distance for doubling her on his bike. He was asleep and truly dreaming by the time Joe crept noisily to bed.

Time passed, and Joe got a job. Wonders will never cease, said George. He'd followed Albert's advice and tried the railways, been taken on as a shunter. I'm just a boy at heart, he said. I've always liked playing with trains. It's no game, said Albert. It's dark and dirty work and men die, men are killed, men are maimed, but the monsters don't care, no, the monsters go on, inexorably, in the night. Nobody, not even ardent Joe, took any notice of him, any more than they bothered to listen to the maundering of the sea. When Joe got his first pay he brought a bunch of roses and an enormous box of chocolates tied with red silk ribbons, for Ada. Whenever she ate one, which was often, she remarked that never had she seen such beauties, or tasted. She ate almost all of them herself; Joe and Lily rationed themselves and George, though he loved chocolate, refused them. They'd stick in m'throat, he muttered. Ada shrugged. You'd cut off your nose to spite your face, you would, she said, and ate another with ostentatious sensual slowness.

For Lily he bought a feather boa, going in to Nell's department store and getting her to help him choose it. Lily was thrilled; she danced about the house, the feathers lifting languidly in the breeze she created.

Tiger thinks she's the bee's knees in that thing, George said grudgingly, unable to dismiss his sister's pleasure. She did look beautiful, with her dusky throat rising out of the creamy feathers, her eyes huge and shining as she challenged Joe.

Now all I need is somewhere to wear it. She began to Charleston, swinging her hands across her knees.

George also admired the feather boa because it was evidence of Joe's job, which meant he could move out. Ada didn't tell him that he had offered to pay board, or that she was asking less than George paid, so that he could get himself established.

When the weeks passed and there was no sign of his going, George's complaints intensified.

When's the beggar going? Doesn't he know when he's not wanted?

But he is wanted, said Ada. Joe continued to bring her little presents and amuse her.

Not by me he isn't.

We should give him a chance to get established. It won't be long. And he is a sort of war hero after all.

So he says.

You can tell truthfulness, said Ada.

And in the meantime he's eating us out of house and home.

Then Ada admitted that he was paying board. That made matters worse. George thought he would never go if he was paying. Fortunately he was so angry he didn't ask how much and she didn't have to prevaricate. Instead she talked about Lily and how happy she was to have him around.

Don't encourage her, said George. He's no good to her. She ought to have a decent chap.

Ada sighed. She and George seemed to argue all the time now. She tried to cheer him up by showing him her latest mother's letter from a woman in Plymouth who had three sons at sea but he didn't seem to care. He had such a one-track mind these days. Such a stubborn young man. She said to herself smugly, George takes after me. When she put on the Queen Mary toque in front of the mirror, regarding herself with a regal eye, contented enough with her lot, though clearly a woman of her character could have ruled in a much wider sphere but it did no good to repine, she sometimes thought of George, her son, her heir, and was proud of his fineness, his beauty, his strength. She hardly recalled the despair of his childhood; he was too substantial and stubborn for coffin breaths of mortality. The sense of his preciousness remained, but she was still the reigning monarch, she was not going to let him take over power yet. All in good time. She dipped the hatpin through the thin scalloped waves of her hair and thought, George is getting a bit too big for his boots. All in good time. All in good time. She leant her weight on Joe's arm when they walked down the street, arched her chin and minced along on her painful feet, gleefully inviting the neighbours to eye another favourite. To observe handsome young men as a fact of Ada Gray's life. Good afternoon, Doris, she said to the midwife's unsuitably curvaceous daughter— Sunday and still she wrestled with the lines full of cracking nappies—and wondered if she should take them some soup. Probably not. She never made it these days anyway.

George coming up the street, disconsolate in fine cream flannels, watched them making for the tram stop. He'd gone to see Alice and she'd been out, visiting her grandma. The old lady was a bit of a shocker, from all accounts, offering her visitors nips of port, even when Alice was a child she'd done it, not when anyone else was there of course, giving her a little glass, saying, Drink up, it won't make you tight, it won't make you tight, Alice told a good story of it. And now she was planning to get married again, the fourth time, and her son, that was Alice's father, didn't think she should. The old lady wanted Nell to make her a veil to wear to the wedding but her father had forbidden it.

He'd stayed talking to the family for a while, but it wasn't the same thing, though he liked them. It was a pleasure to see them together. Especially at Sunday night tea, when they might be eleven or twelve at table, with the married daughter come home, and the married son, and Nell, and the boys and their girlfriends, the table loaded with good food, tomatoes and lettuce and beetroot and hot new potatoes grown by the father, and a great array of cakes and scones and biscuits and slices cooked by Alice and her mother. George's sweet tooth made a future with Alice a delicious prospect. One Saturday he'd sat at the kitchen table and watched the two women mixing Christmas cakes, moving gracefully round the room together like dancers who are long familiar partners. Looking at her mother was another thing that made him feel good about Alice; at fifty he imagined her just like this slender woman, fresh-faced and nimble. He watched Alice as she picked over raisins with slim skilful fingers, her head with its shells of hair over each ear, her rosy cheeks, her eyes intent on the job in hand.

And the great bowl of raw cake, brilliant yellow with eggs
from their chooks, heavy with fruit and brown sugar and butter,
almost too much for her to stir. Here, he said, let me do that,
that's a job for a man, and manfully he turned the unctuous
batter. Life could be like this for ever. You could make a song
of it: *Let me mix your cakes forever, Always I will stir for you.*
He made up a little tune for the words, hummed it, then daringly
sang them out loud. She blushed, and smiled, and turned away,
with a slight saucy consciousness, he thought.

He liked watching her doing things, mixing cakes, putting
food on plates, even playing tennis, though she was an awful
duffer at it. She would swing at the ball fiercely and almost
never hit it. She would end up with her elbow bent and her
racquet at a funny angle, and look so baffled that he would
laugh. Hole in the racquet, he would say, and she'd frown.
Once she almost burst into tears. I'll never be any good, ever,
she said sadly, and he replied heartily, Of course you will,
it's just practice. It's like anything else, it comes with practice.
He'd stand behind her and, holding his arm the length of hers
and gripping her wrist, try to show her how to get the right
easy swing. He'd feel her stiff with doubt and squeeze her
waist and say, Never mind, it's just a game, it's fun when
you know how. He jollied her along; when she got over her
nervousness she'd be all right. And above all, don't worry.
Stopping worrying is half the battle. Fiercely and desperately
she would swing with that queer awkward movement and come
closer to hitting her own head than the ball. There was a
kind of grace in her clumsiness that was endearing, and despair
and effort made her prettier than ever, all rosy and glistening,
with small curling tendrils of hair flying out from the neat
coils, which sometimes came down altogether, when a long
brown plait would bounce across her back as she made her
mighty missing lunges at the ball. Her white dress would flare
round her knees. Anybody who looked so charming couldn't
possibly be having a miserable time. She would watch him
playing singles, and smile with admiration at his skill, and
sometimes clap. When it came to supper her cakes were always
the best, though the compliments made her as nervous as the

game. And any fool could see that she was the best looking girl there. He loved taking her to tennis.

He slowed down, not wanting to catch up with Ada and Joe, off to a band concert in King Edward Park, where they'd meet Lily; he'd been going to suggest it to Alice, it was a good brass band from Lismore, but now he didn't have the heart, though he didn't want to go inside either. He loitered along, stopped and talked to the cockatoo in its cage by the fence. Hello cocky, hello cocky . . . it would cackle away forever. Cocky want a biscuit . . . cocky want a biscuit. But George hadn't brought any biscuits. The bird cracked a seed, and put its head on one side to see him better. When he walked away the bird cried, Come back, come back, and George echoed, Come back, come back.

♦ ♦ ♦

So the long wooing summer wound on. The sun poured its light over the shadeless landscape, man and beast and plant gasped for breath in the honey-viscous heat that flooded all its spaces. The sea was too bright to look at. George and Alice played tennis in the evenings, they went on picnics, and to the pictures, and sometimes to a show, they had Sunday night teas at Alice's place. Nobody doubted they were courting. Ada stopped making gibes about that mouse of a woman, not because she'd changed her mind particularly but because the idea of George's doing something foolish preoccupied her less. Lily and Joe were considered to be courting too. George came home one night and found them sitting in the front room, with the light out, but the moon and the streetlamp were illumination enough to show the long bent-back arch of her neck and Joe's hand creeping inside her shirt. He couldn't talk to Tiger anymore, not seriously; whenever he mentioned Joe she became furious and refused to listen. He irritated Ada too. For goodness sake leave him alone, she said. Joe's all right. He's a good man. She dipped her fingers into a box of his chocolates. George no longer brought such things. He refused to compete.

He'd finally heard from Vic, just a short note which told

nothing save that he hadn't forgotten how to form letters on a page.

George, looking in his drawer for fountain pen and pad of paper to write back, found a photograph of himself and Vic taken by Lily. Ready! she'd called, bending over the box brownie, and the two young men had grabbed one another about the waist, tipped their heads sideways and stuck out a leg each, in a pose perfectly symmetrical even to the wide carefree smiles they beamed at the camera. George looked at it, remembering Tiger's singsong, Ready! and the quick simultaneous spontaneity with which they'd struck the pose. At Vic's thin, rather pointed face, his own squarer and solider, both the faces of happiness. He felt guilty; he was all right, he had his Alice. Vic was far away and miserable, gone bush somewhere.

He wrote to him and worried about him, in moments of his busy life. As well as Alice there were the cubs, and the band (he wasn't practising his cornet as much as he should, the conductor had been sorrowful about it at the last rehearsal) and his reading: he'd moved from *Lost Atlantis* to *The Secrets of the Great Pyramids*; it was fascinating to perceive the degree of civilisation among such primitive peoples. There was so much to know about so many things.

❖ ❖ ❖

Christmas came. Ada cooked a goose and thought of England. No mean feat given the temperature in her kitchen. She got a letter from the bishop thanking her for her work at the Missions to Seamen. Doing the right thing by our lads. The stuff of Empire. Ada, or the boys? George wondered. It was typewritten and signed in a handsome scrawl of purple ink quite simply *Newcastle*. Ada showed everybody she could find, even one day getting into conversation over the fence with the midwife and just happening to have it in her bag. It was the best Christmas present she could have had, she said. She wasn't one to go on about what she did, but it was nice to be recognised. Anybody liked a bit of recognition. George said, Now there'll be even less escape from the horrors of letter-writing for those poor little blighters, and Ada wasn't amused. Joe had not needed to make sarcastic remarks, he'd simply kissed her hand and said, It's no more than you deserve.

The Christmas puddings were consumed, the cakes almost. George conspired with Tiger to have a festive Sunday night tea and invite Alice, but not Nell, so he could walk her home on his own. Joe would be there but nothing could be done about that. It turned out to be Rose's day off at the hospital and George, thinking of the big happy gatherings of Alice's family, was pleased. Lily made brawn, and a Victoria sponge with mock cream and apricot jam, there were cheese and pickles and celery and raspberry jam and scones and rock cakes, quite a spread assembled under an embroidered muslin throwover to keep the flies off. Ada hated the flies. She couldn't get used to them. Soon after her arrival she'd cooked a roast and just left it on the carving dish for a moment to rest while she made the gravy; she couldn't have turned her back on it for more than a minute, and there it was, suddenly, flyblown, crawling with maggots. She'd sat on her chair and covered her face with her apron and cried. Home was a long way away.

◆ ◆ ◆

George called for Alice and they wandered up beside the beach, walking along the tracks of the little railway line, whose engine was called the old Coffee Pot because of the curious wide angle of its funnel. It ran all the way to the lagoon, parallel with the beach, threading its tunnels through the headlands, to pick up coal. It didn't work on Sundays, so they were quite safe walking along its tracks. Even on weekdays it wouldn't have mattered much. It pottered along the suburban streets, blowing its whistle, crossing the tram tracks, bisecting the market gardens. Children could easily run faster than it. They walked slowly, in mincing steps from sleeper to sleeper. Even at five o'clock it was very hot.

When they arrived at George's place it was quiet, no sign of anybody but Ada, in her favourite chair with the afghan, her heavy body somnolent, her fingers quick at their crochet. He sat Alice in the sitting room, and went to his bedroom to get the book he was reading, called *The Logic of Reincarnation*, because she'd seemed interested when he'd told her about it.

His fury rose sudden and huge and black when he went into his room. The basin on the washstand was full of grey scummy water. One of his cut-throat razors lay hairy and unclean in a greasy puddle. George had three such razors, the precious beginnings of a collection; he intended to achieve at least seven or eight. They were beautiful objects. One had an ivory handle, two were of black bone, one with silver chasings on it. Each had a little curving silver loop to rest the finger, and the blade was a wicked shining silver swoop of steel, ground wide to hair-splitting sharpness. He kept a leather strop hanging on the back of the door and sensuously sharpened them before each shave. He would use one for several days, then put it to the bottom of the pile to regain its temper, resting. Three wasn't quite enough, they couldn't remain out of use long enough. But they were a start, and he was fanatically strict in his care of them, drying and polishing them and sliding them into their cases with the meticulous pleasure he always took in keeping things orderly.

He rushed out of the room, shouting. That beast! That beast. This's the last straw. He's been using my *razors*! This is the end. He was so angry he was stuttering. He pulled himself together, to a dangerous calmness. It's the end, he said to Ada. Either he goes or I go. Twenty-four hours. If he's still here after that, I won't be. He went back to get the book for Alice, who sat timid in a corner of the couch.

Then Rose came in, and Lily and Joe, and they went into the kitchen to eat. Lily pulled off the throwover with a flourish. The flies buzzed into the air.

What, no sinker! cried George. Tiger! Where's the sinker?

Oh George, you great goop, she cried back. Who wants sinker for a nice smart tea?

When they sat down it was noticed that Albert wasn't there. Lily went to the back door and yelled, and in a few minutes he shuffled into the kitchen. He didn't look at all well. His eyes were more sadly oysterish than ever, and he seemed unsteady on his feet. He stood beside Alice, and patted her shoulder. He smiled vaguely at her. The pats were more like holding on.

Dad! said Lily and Rose, sharply, simultaneously.

What have you been up to?

What about your promise?

Albert sat down, sheepishly, clumsily. Ada stood up, pushing her chair back from the table, pushing herself upright. Everybody watched her weighty progress across the kitchen, out the back door, down the bare garden to the shed.

Do have some brawn, said Lily. Alice disliked brawn, but took some.

Ada came back with a bottle three-quarters full. She stood with it for a moment, holding it like a kind of trophy, then she went over to the sink. She paused again; now she looked like a witch, about to embark on a spell. She raised the bottle, and slowly began to pour, very slowly, so that the brown liquid dribbled from the bottle, filling the room with a smell of alcohol which might have recalled Christmas cakes and flaming puddings. Then she turned it abruptly and the last bit came glugging out, into the sink and down the waste pipe and into the slop bucket underneath, so that it was twice poured out, once out of the bottle, once out of the sink. And there did seem to be some magic in the act, because as the liquor drained from the bottle so did his spirit drain from Albert, and he sat wizened and sad at the kitchen table, eating almost nothing, though the girls more vengeful than kindly piled his plate with brawn and lettuce and tomatoes and beetroot.

Rose began to tell her stories of hospital life, how Wharton did this and Saunders did that and the duty sister ticked off Morgan for having her cap on crooked, and McTavish painted her knee with black ink to hide the hole in her stocking but it shifted and she got found out; she made them sound like silly girls at a storybook boarding school. She described in great detail Saunders giving this old man an enema, and not being sure how to do it, and forgetting to have a bedpan handy, and Ada shrieked with laughter and held her hand on her bosom as though with all the heaving it might fall off, and George said primly it was not a very suitable subject of conversation for the tea table, and Joe said tommyrot, nothing wrong with a bit of good clean fun, ha ha ha, and under cover of the hilarity Alice wrapped the brawn in her handkerchief and put it in her pocket.

Then there was an argument about Vic, and what was happening to him, and whether his life was being ruined, and Joe said, well if he was fool enough to let it be ruined then he deserved everything he got, and George said perhaps there were things he deserved that he wasn't getting, and Rose said what would George know about it, and Lily said it was her life, she knew what she was doing, and George shouted did she really, he jolly well wondered about that, and Ada said that Lily knew full well that she'd have to lie in any beds she made, and Joe said as long as he was in them too he'd be happy, and half the table shrieked with laughter and the other half stayed black as thunder in the argument, except Albert who sat sadly shrinking, and Alice whose face was stiff in a small foolish smile of false enjoyment.

This is a bit dry, said George, munching on a piece of Christmas cake, changing the subject.

Well, it is the end of it, said Lily. I just thought we'd taste it.

Nonsense, said Joe. It's superb. Lil's cakes always are. I've never known a better cook than Lil.

I have, said George very meaningfully, and looked at Alice, as did everybody else. She wished she was anywhere but there. The brawn was squeamish in her pocket.

Alice didn't drink tea, or coffee, though there was no chance of the latter being offered. Ada pouring said, Good heavens, fancy anybody not drinking tea, and Rose said Alice'd never make it as a nurse, it was the only thing that kept them going, and Lily tossed her curly head back and showed the long dusky speckled column of her throat gurgling with laughter, and said in stage Irish, Ah, tay, 'tis the most beauthiful drink in the world, and Joe pretended to strangle her, holding his hands round her neck a second too long so that a fleeting breath-stopped terror crossed her face, but she began laughing again as soon as he stopped, taunting him, daring him, calling him her great bully. Alice stared at the brawn wobbling on its plate.

She said she had to go early. George didn't mind, since he intended to walk her home very slowly. They took the train line path again; Alice demurred, but there was a moon George said, bright as day, they would be able to see perfectly well, should look at the moon on the water, he would look after her. He put his arm round her waist; she was afraid he'd feel the brawn.

The sea was dark, more sound than sight, except where the moon still low in the sky made a pathway across it, very wide where it began, just at their feet, stretching and narrowing far across the water.

It looks like silver cobblestones, said George. As though you could walk across them and get somewhere, somewhere . . . significant. The mild air, the breathing of the sea, the mysterious pathway: he was overwhelmed by their beauty, their meaning. Let's walk out on it, Alice, you and me, together, for the rest of our lives . . .

She looked at him. He squeezed his arm around her.

Let's get married.

She refused him. She said no. He couldn't believe it for a long time, he kept saying, *Why, why*, he'd thought she liked him, he'd never doubted that she would marry him, he was quite sure they were made for each other.

That's the trouble, she said.

What?

You're so . . . arrogant. So high-tempered. All your family. There's so much violence. I couldn't live with that.

But it's *me* you'd be marrying. I thought you loved *me* . . . He grabbed her by the shoulders, his fingers pressing through her flesh to the frail bones inside. He shook her, very faintly, as though he would transmit some of his force to her, but she was wooden in his hands. As when she tried to hit tennis balls.

You see, she said. Everybody's so rough. You frighten me. I couldn't marry you.

Nothing he said could move her. Gentle Alice, invincibly gentle to the end, irrevocably choosing gentleness. His strongest arguments were baffled by it.

He walked around all that night. He walked along the railway tracks and through the tunnels, whose dripping clammy darkness was an extension of his unhappiness. The first one was quite short, but the second was long and he couldn't see the end. He was very frightened, alone inside the blackness. He wondered if he existed any more, if his mind which had been so passionate to understand the meanings of his world would ever be able to perceive light again. He thought of the dark night of the soul; in the mindless beingless blackness he had nothing to believe in that could draw him out of it.

He stood for a long time thinking of hell. He held his hands in front of his face and they weren't there. He had no idea how long he stood, trying to see his hands. Then he took a step and fell over a sleeper. His hand struck the rail, hard, and he pushed himself upright and began to walk, feeling his way with one foot against the rail. Even going very slowly, with small steps, he tripped often. Finally the arch of stars at the end of the tunnel gave him his self back, and his unhappiness, and led him out into the airy murmuring night.

He stumbled down the embankment to the beach. The moon had gone, but he could see the foamy white edge of the waves. He followed it to the lagoon. He thought of the waterfalls dropping down, and Flaggy Creek, and the naked lovers. Walking back along the sand he watched the dawn. The sea was grey and unfriendly. The tide was up, cutting off the last headland, and he had to wade, his trousers rolled up. Even so they didn't escape the splashings and stainings of the salty water. They would never be the same again.

When he rode his bike to work and home again it was the misery of the universe as well as its mystery that put him in danger from the tramlines.

Joe's things were still strewn round his room; he grew messier as he acquired more of them. The razor was cleaned and put away; he knew that the beggar had been using them all along, and had always hidden the fact.

When's he going? he asked Ada.

Oh George, you know we can't throw him out. He's Lily's friend.

He got his bike out again and rode over to Vic's mother's house and arranged to live with her. She was very happy to have him use Vic's old room, she was lonely with her son away.

I'll never forgive you for this, you know, he said to Ada.

Of course you will, she replied scornfully, she could easily match him at that, and though she was worried about his behaviour, not letting him see it. Of course you will. You'll see.

She was partly right. George did, in a way, forgive her, but he never lived with her again.

BOXES OF
SNAPSHOTS

———— ◆ ————

Prologue

◆

If your house was burning down, what would you save? The money, the silver, the compact disc collection? The original Dali print? The last plate from your great grandmother's dinner set? Standing like a spectator on the lawn, hearing the greedy eating of the flames at your possessions, smelling the noisome smoke of your belongings, suddenly you disobey. You bunch up your skirt or your shirt in a mask against the heat and run inside like a footballer ducking detaining hands, to save your precious ... what?

The boxes of photographs ...

◆ ◆ ◆

And then one day your granddaughter or possibly your great granddaughter comes to you staggering under the size rather than the weight of one such box, in stout white cardboard and marked as having contained 2500 sheets of A4 computer paper, and you say, yes of course you can look in the box, sweetheart. What's in it? Take the lid off, carefully . . . see? Yes. Photographs. Hmm. That's Mummy when she was a baby . . . and Father, Grandfather, wasn't he handsome when he was a young man? Look at his gold watch chain. No, you can't see that it's gold, but I know. That's me. Do you really think it's a funny hat? But the dress, it was lovely. I made it, all those pintucks. *Crêpe-de-chine* it was, and the colour, let me see, *eau-de-Nil* they called it, pale green like water, water of the Nile. The lady with the cat? I'll have to work it out . . . she's your great aunt. And that's Grandma, your great-grandma, or is it great-great, in a hat like Queen Mary's, oh she was a queen a long time ago when we had queens, yes she is rather fat, stout we called her. That's me and my sisters at the lake, look at the car, it used to be a hearse, that's for carrying coffins to funerals. No, little children often don't go to funerals. We just drove in it like a car. Mummy with a bunch of Christmas bush. Yes, and that's her wedding. Very quiet, it was. The rocking horse, isn't it beautiful? It's your cousin riding it, a birthday party, before you were born. That's grandfather on his bike . . . and your grandma up a tree. Who's he? I wonder . . . maybe he was a friend of . . . no, he's a mystery. Quite handsome though. There's the twins when they were babies, and your father, in his little red car, you can see how pretty it was. And who's this? Ah, let me see, who can it be . . . I know . . .

Yes, of course, sweetheart, it's you.

◆ ◆ ◆

Some of the photographs have names and dates and places written on the back, some do not. You may be the last person in the world able to identify them. You are Alice, or Lily, or Veronica, or Robyn or Jade or Elinor, not because you believe in the interchangeability of women but rather in their community of experience. You look at all the lives shuffled in together, all the generations, all different and all the same. And all happy. Mostly. Occasionally a child is glum, or squints, a baby howls, a teenager cultivates a mournful look, I'm hideous when I smile, but despite the odd gloomy face the occasions are happy. *I count only the hours that are serene*, says the motto on the sundial. And so does the family photograph. At all the important daily moments of human intercourse, there it is. Except at funerals. At parties and picnics and trips to the beach and overseas, at christenings and births too these days, at weddings though not so far copulations, there the camera is, clicking away, but never at funerals. You know; at your age, you've been to a lot. Only one man ever took photographs at funerals, that you know of, and he couldn't see without his camera.

The child has got bored by now, too many unknown faces, dead, disappeared, never there, what does she care? Names without stories are not interesting. She begins to treat them not as information but as objects; she picks them up in handfuls and lets them fall from her fingers like water. You are about to say, Don't do that sweetheart, for after all they're almost as frail as the people they picture, may bend or crack, go greasy or fade, then you look at her, a little girl, concentrating, and streams of snapshots running through her fingers, cascades of snapshots, rivers, and you think, what a photograph Mikelis would have made of this!

◆ ◆ ◆

What a photograph Mikelis would have made of this. Maybe he would, maybe he wouldn't. One thing he did know, almost never, when people said that to him, was it true. His camera was his eye, and it did its own seeing.

Grass than concrete

———————◆———————

He found a place in the pitted skin and pressed the needle home; he pushed the plunger slowly down until the syringe was empty, then pulled it out quickly and pressed his thumb against the tiny hole. The skin hung like a shabby sack around a proffered bone, the flesh worn away and the skin wearing, fragile and age-spotted. When Dane first saw Mikelis do it, he said, How can you bear it? And Mikelis looked at him with long dislike and said, I used to think that, at the beginning; I used to think I can't bear it, and then I realised that to say you cannot bear a thing is to recognise that you can.

Now Dane gave Mikelis the injections. The first time the old man mocked him: Can you bear it? Now he turned his melancholy milky gaze with love upon him, and smiled.

Fifty years ago, he said, thirty, twenty even, when I was a man in my prime, a long prime and fruitful, people used to talk about the miracles of technology. Old people said, In my lifetime: flight, and cars for everyone, and radio. A man on the moon. Where will it end? What they did not realise was that they'd seen it, that end, that technology would not continue its mechanical marvellous flowering, that what looked like ever more burgeoning was actually the blowsiness of decay, superb but already over the hill. So that when people said, I cannot imagine where we'll go from here, what more science and technology could possibly have to offer, they were right, there was nowhere to go, nothing more to offer. Just a slow quiet falling of petals. And grass still stronger than concrete.

Mikelis's eyes stared, contemplating, but the pictures he saw were all in his head. Dane stopped the tape recorder, finger at the ready to start it again should the old man continue his talking. He, too, saw the terrible wrenching green strength of the grass, the concrete flaking and frittering, cracking and buckling, and the green grass running all through it like greedy flames. Sometimes Dane thought the old man projected his own pictures into his head, into Dane's head, as though they were both watching the same movie, as much as two people ever can watch the same movie. He supposed that the pictures in his head came out of Mikelis's; he knew of no other source for them.

There were no more words. Just the pictures, the grass gobbling the concrete and on to it the silent scented falling of rose petals.

Dane made tea thick with milk and sugar. It's late, he said. I think you should go to sleep now. When Mikelis was settled he climbed in beside him, offering him closeness and youth-warmth to keep the night at bay. The lightness of the old man's bones always saddened him; he imagined death as an ultimate weightlessness, and Mikelis getting nearer it by the day. He wondered how long a lucid mind could survive in an ever-lightening body.

A lucid mind, and agile, still with the energy to pounce. Dane has used the phrase, the guardian of memory: you are the guardian of memory, to Mikelis, and been jumped on. Guardian . . . guardian? I guard nothing. I invent. I make it up out of what remains to me. Memory is not the event. It's what remains, ten, twenty, fifty years later, with all the glazes of the intervening days. Like varnish on brown old masters. Or, even better, like drops of gum, slowly hardening, encasing a small mosquito creature with gauzy wings and a bent proboscis, once alive but so no longer. No longer available as itself. A quite other substance. An artefact.

Memory isn't an instant fax from the past, you know. We should try to ignore technology—remember it has no more to offer. The intervening glazes of the years, gum, or varnish, they're much more true than the naked fact of the coloured video. And do not self-destruct, but preserve themselves.

Yes, thinks Dane, even with the scolding, and glad he's recording this. Technology has its place.

He had come to Mikelis, Ballod he knew him as then, because of some photographs in a folder in a dusty box on the top of a cupboard in Newcastle, and their fellows in the National Gallery, an early series of a woman, his wife, naked, her body abstracted into shapes that were still flesh, and more. He came to him as disciple to master. Let me be your apprentice, he begged. Mikelis ignored him. Dane persisted, he was there, so Mikelis got into the habit of giving him jobs, menial at first and then gradually as his disease took hold he learnt to depend on him. So Dane was not just apprentice but assistant, and amanuensis, this Dane's idea entirely, and he not sure how much the old man was aware of it, and nurse and finally bedfellow.

But most important of all was the listening. To Mikelis.

Christmas bush

◆

Newcastle, 1966

Mikelis Ballod met Veronica Gray when he took her photograph in Hunter Street. It was the morning of Christmas Eve, fresh still but holding the promise of heat as it did of Christmas, a breathless excited waiting. Veronica's feet felt the celebration, they carried her springily along, swirling her skirts. She was wearing a new sundress she'd made herself, white with little red flowers and tied with red shoestring straps on her shoulders. She had red sandals too, and her hair coiled on the top of her head, with lots of tendrils escaped and fluttering in the breeze that curled in from the sea. At the end of a side street, across the railway line she could see the harbour, indigo-coloured and glittering, with a green and cream ferry sailing across it. The gates were down; a train clattered through, offering the glamour of the capital its destination, Veronica as always for a passionate moment wanting to accept. But perhaps it was only going to Maitland, or Toronto on the lake. Not Sydney. Real city Sydney. She got there quite often these days, but still found the promise of the train irresistible.

She'd finished her shopping and later would have lunch with Martin at Oliver's. Oliver knew them and though sardonic as with everybody always gave them a good table in the window. Always at Oliver's they ate his Italian icecream, with toffeed nuts in it and a strange red bitter liqueur poured over. Everybody did. Afterwards Martin would drive to Sydney to be with his family, but wouldn't stay long. It wouldn't be a glamorous trip but a dutiful home visit.

A man with a camera rose like a pigeon in front of her, moving backwards, his fingers flickering on the shutter. She was a little girl again, walking down this street with Daddy, and the man with the camera saying, Smile, smile, his fingers flickering. Just keep walking, her father said. Don't take any notice. But Daddy, he's taking our picture. No he isn't, he's just pretending. He won't take our picture unless we pay him. So they kept walking, Veronica twisting in her father's hand to look over her shoulder at the man jumping out in front of people, apparently ardently shooting pictures of them. She hadn't seen such a thing for years, hadn't remembered it happened, had forgotten the idea of street photography. She smiled, nearly laughed. Don't take any notice, just keep walking. This time she didn't look back; she was sure that the young man had turned and was following her with his camera. She felt her hips sway.

She went into the Café Continental and drank a cappuccino, and afterwards put lipstick on again. The café was airconditioned and when she went outside the street was hot and dusty. She stopped at a barrowman and bought two big bunches of Christmas bush, and walked along with her arms full of them. It was looking through bunches of starry red flowers, with the sharp dry scent of the bush in her nostrils that she saw again the young man with the camera, moving backwards, fingers flickering. When she stopped at the bus stop he spoke to her, a little bow, polite words.

If I might have your address, I will send you the pictures.

You haven't taken any photographs. You were only pretending.

Of course I have. He held the camera a foot from her face. This time she heard the shutter click. He showed her the film winding on. He took two more shots.

You mean, you'll sell . . .

Of course not. Not at all. I would like to give them to you.

Why do you want to give me photographs?

Because I think they'll be good.

Out of the corner of her eye she saw her bus arrive. People were getting on. Clumsy laden people. She looked at the young man. He had a nice face. What might that mean? The last old lady was lumbering up the steps of the bus. 24 Bennett Street, Merewether, she gabbled, and launched herself across the pavement. The driver had to open the doors again and was cranky.

There was a sporting chance the young man had heard. She wondered if he had.

♦　♦　♦

He turned up four days later, on a Saturday afternoon. It was embarrassing to have to introduce a young man whose name she didn't know. Her parents gave her odd looks. George, she said, she was trying to learn to call her parents by their Christian names, this is . . . Mikelis offered his hand and his name, so did her father, they carried it off quite well. The photographs were an excuse, a refuge, a gift, and there he was sitting in the dining-room passing them round and her parents were giving her even odder looks. This mysterious girl with the springing step, the swaying hips, gazing big-eyed through bunches of Christmas bush (they looked at the original come to rest in a white vase on the sideboard as though they didn't believe it), and one of those same eyes larger than life and framed in kiss curls, and a nose turned up and a laughing mouth; they looked at her and the girl in the flesh beside them wearing the same red-sprigged sundress, and said, They're very good, aren't they. And her mother made tea and cut Christmas cake and her father talked about man's role in the scheme of things and when he went they invited him to call again and see them, he could be sure of a welcome. He comes from Latvia, they said; he seems a decent type. Very polite. They liked foreigners, and being kind to them; interesting people it was a pleasure to do your duty by. Other places, other manners; they might have looked askance at an Australian boy behaving like this. Maybe not; it was easy to underestimate parents.

That was when Veronica began to fall in love with Mikelis, when he showed her the photographs he'd taken of her; she fell in love first with the self he showed her, that she didn't know she was. But she didn't realise it. Martin was her boyfriend.

Watch the birdie

———◆———

Mikelis said: When Eva's baby died, do you know what I thought? I thought it was a pity she was living in Rome because I couldn't take a photograph. I wanted to say wait and I'll come. I telephoned even.

Oh, of course I wanted to comfort her. My child, half-orphaned, now losing her child. Before it even had time to live. But I wanted first of all to photograph that lost baby.

He spoke softly, offering this like a gift to Dane, trusting him with this knowledge. And on the other hand, it was a test, a dare; Mikelis was trying out Dane's friendship. Can you stand knowing these things, he was asking him. Dane wondered what he could give and demand in return.

Your daughter; has she had more children?

No. Her marriage didn't survive that grief. When her husband came back from Rome she stayed. If I have time, I'll send for her. I'll tell you, you'll have to do it; not yet.

Mikelis took Dane's hand, pressing his nails into its flesh. That meant he wanted him to take particular notice. You could marry her, when she comes, he said. Dane wondered if this was what could be given and demanded. Marry, he said. She might have something to say about that.

Dane knows what Eva looks like, from photographs. Not taken by Mikelis, snapshots in an album, a woman's record of her family, herself hardly there. Pages of meticulous coloured oblongs: Eva as a baby, Eva on a tricycle, with a cat, starting school, with her cousins, graduating. And picnics, with friends: Black Mountain, the Cotter, Brokenback Range, Bermagui, Provence. On rugs or at tables, with wine bottles, loaves of bread, bowls of food, cherries in a pile, in shade from the summer sun or warming themselves in the winter, by barbecue fires and mountain streams and distant views, people, friends, relatives, turning to the camera, smiling, recording the fun they are having. Watch the birdie, they used to say, and there it is in their eyes, about to descend.

String of pearls

◆

Newcastle, 1967

To grow up in a town is to learn it. While you're at work getting educated in and out of school, its maps, its shapes and landscapes and the intimate physical details that only lovers know become a part of your mind. Veronica left Newcastle at the age of twenty-three; it was some decades later when her parents had both died and the family home had to be sold that she realised she was losing the city too. She would become a tourist, a person who visited not lived there, not a native as always she'd felt when she went to stay with her parents and then her mother: an interrupted dweller in her home town but still its inhabitant, owning it by right of birth and knowledge and affection and the possibility of residence whenever she wished. And now she would lose it. The final orphaning—for her father's death had not prepared her for the loss of both parents—hard enough to bear without losing her home town as well. By then she'd lived in Canberra longer than in Newcastle, and was fond of her new home, but not as of the place of her growing.

That summer Mikelis was learning to love it too. He got into the habit of calling to see the family, sat and drank tea and talked to her parents. Mrs Gray kept the cake tins well filled. Sometimes they went for walks, just the two of them, up to the beach, along the promenade, past the baths. They took off their sandals and walked about the rock shelf and Veronica told him about the life of it, the deep rock pools always full of water, the shallow ones drying out, waiting for the tide to come and renew them, and the different creatures that had adapted to these environments. They both liked to wander and talk. Mikelis had a special avid way of listening that made conversation an action. All her growing years Veronica had seen the sea as something to plunge in, had loved the violence of swimming in Merewether's long unsheltered surf, with rips to drag you out and breakers to dump you. Suddenly at the age of about eighteen she discovered that she liked looking at it just as well. Mikelis never wanted to jump in. He wanted to walk along beside it, look at it, close up or far away, and talk.

Her parents never came on these walks. It occurred to her that living so close to the sea they took it completely for granted. They walked the other way, to shops and town and work, and unless something spectacular happened, such as the great storm that whipped the water so ferociously it left foam like dirty meringue waist high even on the farthest promenades, they didn't bother to go and look at it, let alone touch it.

At five o'clock the beach emptied of people and the light changed. The sea mist blew in and hazed the land, the late sun shone low and it was very quiet, like walking through a nimbus. One of the things Mikelis liked to talk about was the Baltic, to speculate on the ways it would be different from the Pacific. They walked through the dry sand, dragging their feet like ploughs to see what they could turn over: old seaweed, worn shells and polished glass, occasionally a bit of coal. In the Baltic there would be amber, he said. The wind blew fresh and damp, fitting their clothes to their bodies, depositing salt on their skins and hair; Veronica would have to wash hers before she went out.

Usually on these Saturdays she had to get home in time to get ready for Martin to take her out. She was going out with Martin. Once this preparation would have taken her the best part of the afternoon but now she was refining her time like a record seeker. After one of the Mikelis walks she showered and washed her hair and dressed and painted her face, all done and perfumed though a bit breathless in thirteen and a half minutes. Her hair was still wet but she wore it like a cape spreading over her shoulders and it dried in the warm summer night. On that occasion Mikelis was having a glass of the sherry kept for cooking though of quite good quality and talking to her parents; they introduced Martin to him. Afterwards Martin said, Your parents know some quite young people, don't they? He admired this, he thought his own were stuffy and dull. Veronica said it was because she was the youngest of three daughters; her parents had had lots of training in being with it.

Martin was an engineer and already had a good job. BHP had paid for his education through a traineeship and now his future was assured. He always brought something when he came to take her out, usually chocolates, or if it was a ball or a dinner dance a corsage, orchids were his favourite, octopoidal mauve-tinged creatures in nests of fern. The chocolates piled up, Veronica hardly ate them because of spots and fat, and her parents didn't get through them. He had a sports car, an Austin Healey; it was long and gleaming black with high curved mudguards, not new but he kept it in good running order. She knew he was coming from the dark animal roar of its engine along the street, a svelte and vigorous roar, wellfed but predatory.

You're looking gorgeous tonight, Vee. As usual, he said, shutting her in the car. He said it softly, with a little quirky smile. It was his word: You're gorgeous, Vee; holding her hand, leaning over the table, bending to her ear. It always made her tremble, secretly. She liked being the girl in the Healey, liked getting out of it in front of busy cinemas, liked walking down the stairs at Oliver's to its long black shape waiting at the kerb. Liked sitting cosseted inside while the rain fell and the wind blew, feeling sorry for woebegone people at bus stops. Or driving with the hood down, wearing a chiffon scarf over her head, so her hair streamed only behind.

Martin opened the door for her, walked always on the outside, necessitating a bit of dancing about when they crossed streets, took her arm. He wore Veronica like a flower in his buttonhole. She was like the car, a badge of distinction.

One Saturday Mikelis didn't call. Veronica saw the time spread too empty for merely dressing. She started to make a blouse, but got bored with the fiddle of it. Instead she cut eight inches off the bottom of a pale blue linen shift. Now it was two inches above the knee; she looked like Jean Shrimpton at the Melbourne Cup. With some of the cut-off bit she made a wide head-band for her hair. She painted her fingernails pale pink, decided it was dull, took it off and did them crimson. It made them look long and sharp, as though they'd drawn blood. Martin liked pale pink.

When her mother saw the dress she was appalled at the danger and the waste of the cutting. It's a dress ruined, she said. Her father said, You're not going out in that, are you, it's not decent. Martin said, Crumbs, Vee, you look gorgeous. Getting in and out of the Healey she showed a great length of leg, and walking down the street; people turned to look.

For her birthday Martin gave her a pearl necklace. Real pearls, real cultured pearls, very milky and fine against the pale brown skin of her neck. She looked in the mirror and hated them. It was like a dog being owned with a collar, all that was missing was an engraved tag with the name and address of the owner. Everything else, legality, respectability, propriety, organisation, all the bourgeois virtues, was there. Worse, they suited her, their lustre brought out the sheen of her skin. She fumbled taking them off, for a moment she imagined there was some secret to the catch that she couldn't know, that she was stuck with wearing them forever. They would tighten about her neck and she'd never escape.

She held the unclasped necklace in her hands. Pretty milky

things and harmless now. Aunt Rose who was a royalist had made a scrapbook of the Queen for her nieces. In it there was a picture of her as a little Princess, on her birthday, with a caption saying that every year she was given a pearl. When she was grown-up they'd make a complete necklace. Veronica could hear the years of pearls dropping one by one, plink, plink, plink. Like a knell.

Elinor said Ladies with pearls used to get their cooks to wear them in the kitchen. The steam was supposed to nourish them, or something. Or perhaps it was the sweat. You should wear them doing the washing up.

Veronica did a lot of washing up, now that Elinor had left home. You're just jealous, she said. None of your boyfriends give you pearls.

Thank God, said Elinor. I couldn't bear to be so bourgeois.

Sisters are good at the weak spots.

So was Mikelis. He took photographs of her wearing the pearls. Close up; there was one that showed the curve of the necklace, the rise of her neck, another curve of jawline, and one eye, a wide and rolling eye like a frightened animal, and just a corner of her mouth, opening. Another was from further back, the pearls and above it her head, lightly bowed, downcast: image of a virginal bride. Yet another had her looking at the camera, stern, sharp-eyed, mouth pinched. She looked thirty years older. Mikelis had photographed all her fears.

One afternoon she ran into him in town, after work. She wished it was one of the days she was wearing her own clothes instead of the uniform. They sat in the Café Continental and had several cups of coffee. Mikelis talked about being a photographer and his job at Neville of Newcastle doing studio portraits: babies, and kids posing in front of painted backdrops, simpering little girls in ballet dresses and small boys in bow ties. Neville wouldn't let him do the weddings yet, he didn't have the clothes. Neville thought he was saving up to buy a suit so he could. The way he told it was funny, she couldn't stop laughing. When she got home tea was over and the washing up done and her parents crabby now they saw she had come to no harm. Next day at work Jan said, Who was the bloke

I saw you with last night, and at first she couldn't think what she meant, then said, Oh, just a friend of the family, remembering Mikelis in his ancient cords and daggy jumper. Jan giggled. I thought maybe you were trying to make Martin jealous.

Martin and Veronica were invited to the Bachelors' Ball. John, another engineer, was one of the Bachelors; each invited half a dozen couples, who didn't have to pay. Veronica got the dressmaker round the corner to make up some rose silk taffeta, crumpled like petals into complicated elegant drapes. She had her hair done; it took all Saturday morning and wasn't what she wanted, piled up on the top of her head and spilling out curls; instead she thought it looked like a row of cream horns on a plate. Don't be silly, said her mother. Martin whistled. Wow. You look *gorgeous*, Vee. He'd found out the colour of her dress from her mother and brought a corsage of pink roses, a large spray of buds already tiring of the wire that bound them and the silver paper that hid it. It was heavy and pulled the neck of her dress askew, and the pins needed to hold it would mark the papery silk.

It was a good ball, not crowded, in the town hall; very classy. Dr McGovern one of the junior radiologists in the practice she worked for fell over during the last Charleston; he keeled over flat on his back, twitching his legs like a beetle. His partner stood and giggled. Several of his friends came and helped him up, helped him stagger away, his white tie under one ear, his tails covered in dancing dust. She thought he must be hurt. He's drunk! she realised, and Martin said, Of course, and then she noticed that quite a few people were. She told Mikelis about it on one of their beach walks; he laughed and said, You're shocked because they were so dressed up. After that whenever she did X-rays for Dr McGovern she thought of him sprawled like a beetle in a smart carapace of white waistcoat and tails.

After the ball they went to John's for coffee and then straight home, the sky was paling, and said good night in the car. On earlier nights they went to Martin's flat, put music on, made coffee, danced sometimes, lay on the bed and necked passionately but never below the waist. Once her hand strayed and he moved it. Nothing was ever said. She understood they were keeping themselves. He was keeping them. It was getting her down. She wanted him to touch her below her waist. So much for motherly warnings; it was only Martin's chastity that kept her safe. After these sessions he drove her home, dishevelled, lips swollen with kisses, desire unfulfilled. Creeping through the lightening house listening to the throaty animal roar of the car driving away she wondered how he could stand it.

He called in the middle of the week with photographs of the ball taken by Neville of Newcastle who, dinner-suited, had mingled with the guests. She looked goofy in all of them, the roses pulled the neck of the dress askew and her hairdo looked like a row of cream horns on a plate. Martin seemed to like them, he'd bought two copies, one for each of them. She got out her photograph album, her own, not the family one, and stuck them in. Regard Martin in a frilly shirt, said Elinor, *très* classy. Fabulous dress, but why the row of sausage rolls across your head? Veronica decided to give up hairdressers.

Babushka

George found Mikelis inter-
esting because he thought he'd seen great suffering in his
childhood. Mikelis said, Not really. I can't remember much
before New Zealand and that was quite happy. But he quite
enjoyed talking about exile. He sat at the dining table which
Mrs Gray had set with her tea cloth embroidered in roses,
large blowsy blooms in a multitude of reds and pinks, and
ate buttered date loaf. He frowned as he stirred his sugary
tea, putting the spoon in the saucer with a click.

The thing about Latvians, he said, is that our migration
wasn't ever something we wanted. It wasn't ever a matter of
choice, as it was for you English.

Choice, said George. I don't know about choice. Is it much
of a choice for parents to be told that their second son will
also die if they don't get him away from the climate of their
homeland? Of course, they did choose Australia. There was

some talk of New Zealand, my mother had people there. I don't know what it was that made them come here. But the actual going wasn't a choice, not really. He dropped a saccharine tablet in his tea, as a countermeasure to stoutness. The girls told him he looked just like Mr Menzies, portly double-breasted suit and eyebrows and all, which irritated him because he hated his politics.

I suppose not. But it wasn't persecution that made you leave. I've got an uncle whose family migrated to New Zealand in 1905, when he was a child, because of what the Russians were doing to them; they went as far away as they could to the other side of the world. He still considers himself Latvian.

But so do lots of English people. Consider themselves English.

But not you Dad, said Veronica. You always reckon you're Australian. And anyway, it's different, this place was a colony, you could always look on it as an extension of the old country.

It's the language. Mikelis stirred his tea again. That was my mother's great worry. You English could keep on with your native tongue. People like that old uncle of mine had to make sure that their little Kiwi kids never lost the old language. They started up schools to keep it going through the generations.

The really ironic thing, the thing that makes it sad, said Mikelis, is that culture preserved like that, well, it's not very dynamic. It's like creatures set in amber, intricate, beautiful, all their marvellous detail there, and very very dead. Not dead just now, long ago in the past. In Latvia itself there's danger and the country's full of energy and a kind of mad hope, it has to fight for itself. Well, what I mean, it's alive, isn't it? Whereas over here it's dead, preserved and dead. Like bees in amber.

Are you saying repression's a good thing? asked Veronica.

No, not at all, it's terrible. That's why I said it's ironic.

What about the food? That's important, isn't it? I expect your mother was a good cook, said Mrs Gray, passing the plate of mushrooms, little crisp tarts with jam covered in nutmeg-sprinkled cream, and a stalk of pastry sticking out. Did she make special Latvian dishes for you?

These are so good, said Mikelis, who'd already eaten three. No, no, she was a hopeless cook. Didn't like it at all. It was always a chore.

Mrs Gray nodded. Well, I suppose it is. But it's just one of those things. It has to be done.

My mother didn't think so. She always had much better things to do. That's how she saw it. She resented the time it took.

Mikelis thought of the dining table at home, the oil cloth that was wiped down with a dishcloth, the pepper and salt, the jams, the sauce, the dish of butter never put away between meals. Why bother? his mother said. Why bother to put things away when you only have to get them out again a few hours later. But other people did, he knew, they cleared and bared their polished wooden tables every time they ate. His mother's was spread with dictionaries, papers, books, even at meal times they were there, piled beside her plate. Eating meals was almost as much a chore as making them, except for the conversation, in Latvian and serious. Without that she preferred reading her dictionaries. She'd sit, only occasionally remembering to put something in her mouth, turning over the pages, her eyes shining when she found the things she wanted. Sometimes she'd read bits out, a definition, a poem. Your mother is an intellectual, his uncle said to him once; it was not something he'd been able to repeat to anybody.

Scones, he said to Mrs Gray. She made scones like stones. It is difficult to live in New Zealand when you make scones like stones.

I know how she'd feel, laughed Mrs Gray. I'm not too hot on scones myself. I can never manage to get them as fluffy as you should.

Not bad at mushrooms though, said George, taking another one.

Father's ruin, said Veronica, patting his stomach as though it were a small round creature she was fond of.

So, said George, Latvian is really your first language.

Not really. When I was a kid I wanted to be like all the other boys. I hated that terrible foreignness. I rejected it as much as I could. Still, quite a bit stuck, and I'm quite grateful for that now. At the time; well, I regret to say how much I upset my mother. When she talked to me in Latvian I replied in English. And look at me now, at home in neither.

Oh no, said Veronica. That's not true. Your English is superb.

Superb; maybe. A fine accomplishment. But does it really belong to me?

Veronica would have to change her image of Mikelis's mother. Throw away the dumpy smiling Babushka woman stirring her bubbling cabbagey pots, and construct in her place a scholar thin and angular, grey-haired perhaps, with round metal glasses, sadly speaking the difficult syllables of her native tongue to a small rejecting boy.

Is she still alive? she asked.

No, neither of my parents. I was the child of their later years. A surprise, I imagine. Not an intention at all.

She had got that bit right. The woman she'd sat at the dim oil-clothed table, stooped over dictionaries, wasn't young.

I should bring a picture to show you, said Mikelis. She was very beautiful. There was something about her, somehow she never stopped looking like a girl. Even when quite elderly, and her face lined. And her hair never went grey, it simply got paler and paler, like . . . like flax; flaxen-haired she was until the end of her life.

The Bearslayer

◆

A good place to start thinking about Latvia is the Baltic Sea. The Mediterranean of the North people called it, in the same way as its river Daugava was known as the Northern Hellespont, at that place where its estuary widens and shifts and changes places with the sea. Alfred Bilmanis, exiled historian of his beloved country, names it *element*, *provider*, *poetry*, and *betrayer*. A boisterous sea it is, but it moderates the climate of this latitude. The autumns are stormy, the summers cool and rainy, the winters set in slowly and do not stay too long. Bracing is its sea air, and silver the light that bathes its neighbouring lands. One of them, Latvia. A country of water, of swamps and marshes, of long straight rivers that link the sea to the Slavic hinterland, and lakes, 3000 lakes there are, nearly. A country of mists, and peat bogs, and sandy beaches, pale yellow beaches that slip gently under the water, where the shallow shelf is full of shoals of tiny fish, and the sea washes up shells and pebbles. Perhaps, for a lucky one, a tiny nugget of amber.

Inland are undulating plains and forests and rolling hills, full of riches. Look at these for lists:

1   Forests: white pine, fir, birch, aspen, black alder, maple, ash, elm, chestnut, walnut, linden, oak. There are several huge oaks preserved from pagan times, when they were believed to house the souls of ancestors. Religious rites centred on them. And the linden is the symbol of womanly grace: see the ancient songs, 36 000 of them, or 650 000 if you include the variations.

2   The fauna inhabiting these forests: squirrel, fox, hare, lynx, badger, ermine, deer, elk, nightingale, oriole, blackbird, woodpecker, owl, grouse, partridge, finch, tomtit, quail, lark, heron, stork.

The children at Latvian schools write these lists in notebooks. Doubly strange: the objects (with unhelpful exceptions) are as foreign as the words for them, in this other watery country on the opposite side of the world, where the light may sometimes be silver but nobody thinks to call it so.

The Latvian people appear on the scene of Western civil-isation when they are discovered to possess amber. Though they were around for a millennium or more before that. Amber: northern gold. You can't blame the Latvians for all this equivalating; it's the southerners who insist on it. Of course the people of Amberland as they named their country may have described the Mediterranean as the Baltic of the South, but they didn't succeed in making anybody else notice.

Amber is the fossilised gum of an extinct species of pine tree, native to low-lying swampy ground, now submerged by the sea. It's washed up on its sandy shores in storms. Taci-tus says, This substance lay long neglected until Roman luxury gave it a name and brought it into demand . . . The Aestii gather amber into rude heaps and offer it for sale with-out any form of polish, astonished at the price they receive for it.

This is ethnocentric of Tacitus. All the Mediterranean societies prized it more highly than the gold they likened it to (though it is brittle, not as hard as marble or glass, and not malleable like a metal). They used it as medicine, as incense, as jewellery. Baltic amber beads are to be found in pharaohs' tombs. The Greeks attributed mysterious powers to it because it becomes electrified when rubbed and attracts light (in the sense of not heavy) bodies: their name for it, *elektron*, gives us electricity. A Phoenician merchant, Pytheas of Massilia (now Marseilles) sailed to 'the island of Baltia' in 330 BC, in order to acquire amber. The Etruscans went overland through Germany. There were routes from Byzantium, and the Orient. Arabian geographers describe the wonders of the Latvian tribal kingdom, from the tales of returning Persian merchants. So though Tacitus may have named these people, calling them Aestii, short for Aestorium gentes, after the estuaries of the amber fishers, may have first described them in detail, he didn't discover them. The trade in amber had long flourished, with a little help from furs. The inhabitants of Amberland acquired much gold and silver from the trade, and no good it did them, in the end.

Geography and hydrography determined Latvia's fate, says Bilmanis. These fishermen, amber-gatherers, bee-keepers (honey, they were famous for their honey: the solid and the liquid gold of the north, preserving for now or forever), these horse breeders and forest-clearers, led too pleasant a life to escape the notice of their neighbours. Christianity was the original excuse to convert and massacre in the name of the Lord. The Swedes, the Poles, the Muscovites, the Germans (as heavyweight a bunch of nations as you could fear to see), they fought for Latvia, worse, they fought in Latvia. East faced west, demanding Windows on the Baltic, the *mare clausum* as the Latin ambition of certain countries would have it. Greed is a neat summary of all that. And that is how the Baltic betrays its countries: by making them coveted by all who see them.

We are a people with the luck of history against us, Mikelis's mother would say to him.

In the youth of his parents Latvia achieved independence after seven centuries of foreign domination; for the first time since her medieval tribal age she possessed her own soil. Sent home the Russians and the Germans. Set about governing the democracy that poets and philosophers imagined for her.

Not for long.

◆ ◆ ◆

You can't imagine how good it was to be speaking our own language again, said Mikelis's mother. Openly, freely, *officially*. Halina Ballod spoke in this same native tongue which was perfectly legal in their new country, just irrelevant. The boy mutinous did not pay attention and it was only later that the burden of her words came back to him. You have to remember, she said, we'd kept it alive against enormous odds.

Her husband had worked in the state printing office. Thirty thousand books in twenty years. Creating a literary canon from scratch. Halina had worked for the philologist Endzelins on the 1932 edition of the Dainas, and on the encyclopaedia that came out in 1938.

Women have always been highly regarded in our country, she told Mikelis. I had no problem in working along with your father.

When he looks back on his parents at this time he imagines them like figures on a monument, sculpted out of some warm golden stone, standing tall, larger than life, eyes wide and lifted to the better world ahead. He sees them as impossibly young, as children almost, though they are near enough to forty, and have been on the job for two decades and more.

Of course, things weren't perfect, Halina said. By the end we did have a kind of dictatorship, even if it was benevolent. But it was necessary, and we were prospering. And yet that didn't save us. The old story: betrayed by our prosperity. Mikelis hated these bits, when his mother's grey-blue eyes would shine with sadness. He imagined himself drowning in them as though they were lakes, watery, brimming; he wanted her to smile and be happy. This wasn't the time, she said. He had to know.

We were invaded by Russia. Remember that, Mikelis. It was all absolutely illegal. They simply sent in troops, and just dismantled the whole country. They tried to make a show, pretend it was what the people wanted. They said they'd held elections. All false, of course. They allowed no campaigns, no time for programmes, not even for candidates to say, Here I am. The Minister of Information forbad the printing of election material.

Your father . . . he wouldn't accept. He printed leaflets. The Russians arrested him. He was deported. I don't know what happened to him.

This is where Mikelis comes into the picture. Posthumous Mikelis. Last-minute offspring of those child-like idealists who almost left it too late. Did you have me on purpose? he asks, and Halina says, Of course. This isn't exactly true. His conception wasn't intended. After so long they believed they couldn't. That was sad, but there were other things to be done. They'd forgotten about the possibility of a child. Their sudden fertility surprised them. But Halina doesn't see herself lying to her son; his advent was accepted with delight, and that was a kind of choice. Welcome is a choice, and so is joy. People said, How awful for you, pregnant at a time like that, and she answered, A time like what? You don't know it's a time like that till afterwards. Even when Janis was deported, she didn't know she would never see him again. You just get on with living. Eating and washing and doing what has to be done. Somewhere, a lot of places, it's always an awful time to be having babies, but people go on doing it.

The labour was hard. She was strong and healthy, but she was forty years old and her body was set in its ways. Not easily did bones and muscle and gristle and skin spread and stretch to allow the passage of this offspring of a statuesque pair. Two nights and a day passed and still he was not born. There was danger. Halina's strength was gone. She would not be able to keep going any longer. He does not want to be born, she heard an old nurse whisper. He has understood what this world is like, and he does not want to be born into it. He will go back to the land of the shades and take his mother with him. Don't be stupid, Halina shouted, of course she didn't have the strength to shout but she always felt that she had shouted, and her body gave a great heaving shudder to repulse this fate of death so drearly stated, and that was the mighty push that began the series of pushes that finally and still not easily expelled the baby into life. But no end to danger. Halina's blood followed in a silent heavy stream. The baby was bluish and cold like porcelain. Both were exhausted with the effort of getting him born. There was still a possibility that he would slide back to the land of the shades and take his mother with him. The old nurse seemed set on it and the others feared she was right. But Halina's will saved them, that was what her family always said. Good health and strength there may have been once but no longer enough, not after such hardship and grief and the long labour; it was the sheer force of her desire that kept them in the world of the living. When she was at last able to open her eyes and look at this small person with the soft round head that had caused them both so much pain and he opened his eyes and with his slow pink tongue tasted the air, she did not believe that Janis would never see his marvellous child.

The years passed, the Russians were pushed out by the Germans, the Gestapo came. Halina joined the mass of refugees fleeing to Sweden. Crossing the Baltic in a small boat with her nephew and his wife, the treacherous Baltic kinder to them than to others; a lot of their countrypeople drowned. The war ended, Russia invaded again. *Hunger, isolation, fear, helplessness, death . . . escape is the only hope*, wrote Bilmanis.

Halina Ballod went with her boy to New Zealand. We can't be sure your father is dead, she said to him. People disappear into Russia, oh yes, that is certain, but that does not mean that they cannot come back. The regime is oppressive, its measures are draconian, but he may well have survived all that. To herself she wondered whether she ought to hope for this, that he was surviving whatever horrors he was living through; maybe she ought to hope that he had met an early swift execution at the hands of his tormentors. When men wanted to marry her, for in her fifties she was shapely, tall, handsome, with large blue-grey eyes and dark blonde hair wound in plaits round her head, a candid woman and with a charming childish gravity, she pointed out that her husband might still be alive, the statutory lapse of time didn't count where the terrible mysteriousness of disappearance into Russia was concerned; he might still be alive. She taught the children at Latvian school, citizens of this new country, many unwilling like Mikelis to believe themselves exiles whatever their elders told them, perceiving that the language their parents spoke was a foreign tongue. Halina reminded them that their country-men had preserved their language through seven centuries of oppression, keeping the words alive in the mouths of the people even when they weren't written down. She would not accept that prosperity is more destructive than tyranny.

She taught them as many as she could of the Dainas, the folksongs that she had helped to edit back in 1932, fairytales, epics, proverbs, even sorcery formulas, sitting at the piano playing for them. Pretend you're taking part in one of the great National Singing Festivals, she'd say to them; they didn't really but they liked singing, they put their hearts into it. At least they are Latvian in that, she said to her contemporaries.

A typical folksong tells the story of an orphan girl, not a boy, the boys are always away fighting with the men. There is little to eat. Often there is a wicked stepmother, always it is very sad. The children sang them and did not really think what it was they were singing.

When Mikelis was small his mother would tell him stories, which he loved; at this time he was too young to make any judgements about the language she told them in, he just listened. His favourite was the Bearslayer legend.

Once upon a time, said his mother, a prince was riding through the woods, hunting. A she-bear crossed their path, and his men shot her full of arrows. But she didn't fall, she kept going, staggering, bleeding, but not giving up. The men followed her to a cave, and then she fell down and died. Inside the cave was a human child, the she-bear's nursling, a wild boy with sharp nails and savage manners. The prince took him to his castle and taught him his noble ways, so he grew into a boy who was wise and kind as well as strong and cunning. Lacplesis, for such was his name, one day inherited the throne and ruled with brains and heart. He made good laws, and a strong army. He set up a council of wise men to advise him, called the Burtnieki, because they were the guardians of sacred scrolls kept in the Castle of Light on the shores of Lake Burtnieks. But one day the Black Knight stole by treacherous means the key of the Castle of Light from Lacplesis and this glorious edifice sank back into the waters.

One day, said Halina, Lacplesis the Bearslayer will return from the depths of the Daugava, where he continues his struggle with the Black Knight, and restore the Castle of Light, and Latvia will be her own nation again.

Mikelis loved this story and his mother told it to him over and over, coming up with more details about the bear and the forest and what the savage boy had for breakfast. Calling him my little Bearslayer, brave and true. The Bearslayer looked just like him, he had hair like his, brown and straight, he had big grey eyes the colour of a Latvian lake, he had broad cheekbones with fine skin stretched over. Strong you are too, she said, and cunning. You have brains and heart. And you can learn to be wise, my little Bearslayer. He liked this identification with a person in a story, a hero, to feel his mother's love for him in the wobble of her voice as she told him these tales. Until one day he realised that she meant it, she was actually casting him in the role of Lacplesis. He was to be the hero who would get back the key from Black Knight Russia and summon up the Castle of Light, and make that faraway country itself again. After that he didn't want to hear the story any more. Not that one. Not that one. He didn't want to spend all his life at the bottom of an icy river fighting a horrible black man for a stolen key. However would he breathe?

Truth talents

◆

$\mathbf{D}$ane was not just amanuensis and assistant, apprentice and nurse, he was secretary too. He fended off importunate requests with polite refusing letters on the grounds of his master's failing health. He always told Mikelis, who said, Yes, yes, go ahead, not really listening. When the invitation came to talk to photography students at the art school the old man quite surprisingly decided to go.

Dane helped him to the lectern and he hung on to it sideways like a child clutching his mother's leg and stared unseeing at the clotted groups of students. He was a bit breathless, so his words came out in little runs with pauses which gave an odd mysterious emphasis to them.

A lecture, he began. An address to the troops.

He held up his hands, making a square shape (his elbow still on the lectern), a container perhaps, or maybe he was miming the action of a photographer, indicating an imaginary camera.

Here is a box of truths. Take one, take several, go out and multiply them. Like the talents.

You know the story of the talents? In the Bible? No? Well, you wouldn't. Nobody does these days.

Here. Listen. This is the story of the nobleman travelling abroad, giving his servants his talents—that is, his money, the Bible makes puns too—giving them his talents, so weighty and so valuable, to mind, in amount according to their abilities. Two used the money, that is, the talents, and increased it, doubled it, in fact, and the Lord said to each of these, *Well done thou good and faithful servant. Thou hast been faithful over a few things, I will make thee ruler over many. Enter thou into the joy of thy Lord.* The third brought the same one talent back; he'd been afraid and hidden it in the earth; he was rebuked, wicked and slothful, and his talent given to the first. *To him that hath shall be given, from him that hath not shall be taken away.*

The unprofitable servant is cast into outer darkness, with weeping and gnashing of teeth.

So, here's the box of truths—again, the finger-squaring gesture. Take them, use them well, cause them to multiply, for the day of reckoning will come. And the weeping and gnashing is better avoided.

Mikelis paused. Even breathless he had a deep voice, a resonant intoning cathedral voice, a pleasure to listen to, so that sometimes people listened to its sound and not what he was saying.

I hear you ask: Did *you* do so? Did you multiply them?

Oh indeed. Not just doubling, but many fold. Hundreds of truths. Far more than would fit in this basket—he put his hand on the back of his neck; it bowed him down—this shoulder basket deep and wide such as convicts used to carry coal in. A plethora, an embarrassment of truths. A myriad illuminations. But the outer darkness remained. And think of the inner darkness, blacker than ever.

Nevertheless, illumination must be laboured over. The talents of truth must be multiplied. It is up to you.

He turned away from the lectern. The students clapped

politely. Dane didn't think they'd listened. Though they had apparently offered attention, their eyes were like stones. Hadn't listened, hadn't heard, hadn't understood: they were young. One day they would recall having heard Mikelis speak to them, and maybe one would remember what he'd said, and at that later time make sense of it. But most would be the third servant with the talent, unable to make any use of it. Worse, not even return it as received.

The rector invited them to take afternoon tea. Dane declined for reasons of tiredness. When he got Mikelis home he wondered if he had given this as his last speech; if he was the nobleman about to travel abroad and never come back. He gave every sign of embarkation. But he didn't in fact set off, and after a day or two was back to work again.

Dinner at Oliver's

◆

Newcastle, 1967

Elinor came home for a week-
end and brought a man with her, a tall black-haired newly
arrived Englishman named Ivan Spenser. George was a bit
prickly to begin with; his own Englishness was something
he'd put away in a box in the back of the cupboard of his
mind, never looking at it, even forgetting it was there
sometimes. Perhaps he supposed the box would be empty now,
containing only a pinch of dust perhaps, or a withered
unrecognisable shape. His sister Rose called England Home,
still, though she had only ever made one visit, in the slow
late languorous summer of 1939, whence she'd hurried back
to enlist as a nurse in the Australian army, and being refused
on account of flat feet escaped the fate of her intended
companions, who were massacred at Banka Island by the
Japanese. His parents and other sisters had never gone back.
George no longer even had the accent, he'd carefully divested

himself of it. He didn't want to play 'we English' with a stranger.

But Ivan charmed him. Ivan had a courteous listening manner and settled back into a conversation, where his daughters sat on the edges of their chairs, waiting for a gap to escape through.

On Saturday night the two couples went to Oliver's. Veronica and Elinor juggling their faces in the bathroom mirror putting on make-up were just like the old days, critical and needling. Veronica wished that she and her sister were close friends, that she could say, are you sleeping with Ivan, do you love him, do you like him? Talk about Martin and his chastity; why struggle with such difficult problems on your own? Two sisters could work out the world between them. She said, El, are you sleeping with Ivan? and Elinor stretching her lips to outline them with a lipstick brush replied, Oh my dear, we are prurient, aren't we, in a glottal voice produced by not moving her lips at all, and Veronica wanted to push the lipstick so that it made a great smudge across her face. If she couldn't pierce her armour, then mess it.

When the men were introduced to one another Martin said, You're a historian. Ivan said, You're an engineer. Martin said, What kind? Ivan said, Modern French. And you? Mechanical, said Martin. They eyed one another with the wariness of men brought together by women.

George thought they were silly to go out for a meal when there was perfectly good food to be had at home. None of that junk'll be a patch on your mother's cooking, he said.

It does seem foolish, said Ivan, and appeared ready to stay, which alarmed Mrs Gray because they'd already had their tea and the washing up was done and she didn't want to start again. Ivan noticed and went on, But looks like we're stuck with it. Too late to do anything else. Too late she cried and waved her wooden leg.

Whatever does that mean? asked Veronica.

I don't know. My mother says it. You must admit it does marvellously convey the idea of too-lateness.

Martin showed Ivan the car in great detail while the women stood around on the footpath, turning their faces to the sea-breeze so it wouldn't muss up their hair. Then they all went in Ivan's VW, Veronica and Martin reluctantly, though not showing it in the face of Ivan's keenness for them all to go together.

Oliver paid his usual sardonic attention. They sat in the middle of the room; the tables in the windows were all for two. Elinor looked round. The place hasn't changed at all, she said.

Well, you've only been gone for a year and a bit.

True. But it seems like another life.

I'd like another life, said Veronica.

You haven't even started this one yet, said Martin.

Oh yes I have. I'm twenty years and more into it. I've only got two-score and ten to go. Almost a third of the way there.

Women live longer than that.

They mightn't by then.

Should I have the icecream? said Elinor. It might not be so good as I remember it.

Now there's a philosophical dilemma, said Ivan. Should we attempt to recover remembered pleasure? Perhaps memory has increased the pleasure and tasting it again will destroy that marvellous extended sensory recollection, all for a moment's gratification. It's a dreadful risk to take. I of course have no problems, since I have no memories to be disturbed. In fact, with a bit of luck, I'm about to create a few.

Veronica had already worked out that when Ivan talked like this he was joking. She and Elinor both laughed.

I don't think the icecream's changed in the last couple of years, said Martin.

Afterwards they went to a café where there was jazz, and then back to Martin's flat, which was really just a big room with a bathroom and kitchen, part of somebody's house, and played records, and danced. Veronica looked at Elinor and thought, I bet she is sleeping with him. If she and Martin were on their own they'd be lying on the bed now. Refraining. She wondered if she were sorry or not. Then they all went home, Martin too because he had to collect the Healey.

Ivan and Elinor said they'd go for a walk and look at the

sea. They went along the road above it, down the ramps to
the lower promenade, as far as the baths. The night air was
sensuous against their faces and they walked entranced by the
dreaming movement of their bodies side by side. On the way
back, in a corner by the steps leading down to the beach where
there was a heap of grey rocks, she noticed a luminous
movement; they were almost past when she realised it was
a white bottom moving up and down, catching the light on
its round pale surfaces. Good morning, said Ivan in a voice
of great gravity.

He was sleeping in the lounge room, on the night-and-day.
Elinor helped him to unfold it, and together they made it
up with the sheets and blankets her mother had left out,
laughing awkwardly under their breaths. It was the first bed
they'd made together. Elinor crept into the room she was
sharing with her sister, to make sure she was asleep, put her
nightgown on, then back to the lounge room where Ivan naked
waited. They made love on the floor because the night-and-
day was too noisy, half-kneeling in an awkward way and very
intense and still because the floor wasn't too quiet either and
afterwards turned into one another's arms and lay wrapped
together until the prickliness of the carpet underneath and
the chill of the night air sent them to their separate beds.

A month later Elinor rang her parents and said she and
Ivan had decided to get married. But you hardly know one
another, said her father.

Veronica wasn't going to tell Martin, but her mother mentioned it one night. He was very excited, he kept looking at
Veronica and asking questions: where, and when, and how?
Saying how marvellous, what a terrific idea, weren't they
thrilled? I thought it was women who were supposed to be
interested in weddings, she said. Why? he asked. Men get
married too, it takes both kinds. And anyway, men start it
off, they do the asking.

Not necessarily. I'd ask a man if I wanted to, said Veronica.

Gingerbread men

◆

Canberra, late 1970s

Elinor and her daughters were making gingerbread men. She rolled out the brown sticky dough, they cut out the people and stuck on sultanas for eyes and buttons, bits of candied peel for mouths. Run, run, as fast as you can, you can't catch me, I'm a gingerbread man, sang Elinor. But the fox gobbled him up in the end. A case of hubris, she can't help thinking.

Blanche says, Was Dad your first boyfriend? Was there ever anybody else? Isabel joins in. Did you ever think of getting married to anybody else?

She understands what they're getting at. They know the facts of life, the biological ones. As told in Picture Puffins. Dad's sperm and Mum's egg. Mating and splitting, a new joint being. What they are doing is flirting with the fragility of their own identities: if Mum had married X, where would they be?

Elinor remembers herself at much this age, looking at

Granma's album and the photograph of Steve, handsome young man in puttees, playing with her mother's Persian cat Peter, who died of furball long before Elinor was born; yet another actor in the drama of the photograph album. That's one of your mother's old boyfriends, said Father. Chased him off pretty quick she did when I came on the scene. Elinor looked at Steve, his crinkling eyes, his wavy light hair, his face so young, so different from Father's. She leant against her mother and said I wonder what would have happened to *me* if you'd married *him*. Astonished when all the adults roared with laughter. Elinor remembers because it was the most successful remark of her childhood.

She knows the answer now. If her mother had married Steve, she wouldn't exist. She wouldn't be older or different, she wouldn't be.

Her children know this but don't yet realise it. They are teasing themselves. So: did Mum nearly not marry Dad and leave them in the lurch?

Oh yes, she says, helping the *frisson* along. Lots of times. There was the athlete, the architect, the Jewish intellectual. Alex the older man. And the Chinese student from Sarawak.

It's a list, a blazon, a chant, it has the formal incantation of a fairytale. And it owes a little to art. Oh, they all existed, all these men, boys, youths, but they weren't all suitors. Though they might have been, given the chance. Men were keen on marrying in those days. The architect and the athlete were short-lived, displaced by time and circumstance. Alex the older man made her nervous, he was so courtly, so European, so middle-aged and correct; she couldn't imagine what he saw in a green girl. If she'd been less green she would have. Foolish, farouche, she ran away. Better to be an old man's darling than a young man's slave, her mother used to say, but didn't often believe it.

But Roderick the Chinese boy from Sarawak. Roderick was a different matter.

◆ ◆ ◆

Elinor likes to think of Roderick. For the *frisson*. How different her life might have been. She could have married him and gone to Sarawak. He asked her often enough. And not just Sarawak. He wrote to her from London, where he was an executive of the Hong Kong and International Bank; teaching at the Dragon School hadn't satisfied him for long. She could have had oval-eyed golden children with straight black hair instead of these grey-eyed rosy cheeked girls whose father is not just the same race but the same class as herself, their fathers both petty clerks though in different countries, they the clever, the upwardly mobile, the sky their limit and the world their oyster. So it had seemed once. Before the sky clouded over and the oyster shell snapped shut. She doubts her children will ever irritate into pearls.

Would they have had a better life, whoever *they* would have been, cosmopolitan children of a Chinese finance man?

She rolls out the gingerbread, sticky spicy brown, Isabel cuts, Blanche decorates. She's put his mouth on upside down; he's not smiling.

He's unhappy.

Perhaps she should consult the Tarot, see if the card she chose from the handful shuffled her was a good choice or not. Does she want to know? The children don't; they need a bit longer to believe in their own inevitability. But Elinor; for her there's the dangerous entertainment of looking back at the Lady in the Tower whom suitors called upon, offering odd chunks of the world.

Who am I kidding, she asks herself. Apart from my children. The girl in the weatherboard cottage in the suburbs, it was . . . Yet the chunks of the world were real enough.

It makes a good story too, so come closer my lucky-to-be-alive little daughters and listen to the tale of your mother's wooings.

◆　◆　◆

Roderick was a Colombo plan student. She met him at a summer school at the Old Rectory in Morpeth. A painting course, residential, a fortnight long. That was in her would-be polymathic days. She wasn't much good, but the courses were fun. The group was eclectic, old people, odd people, people working for a living, not the predictable youth she went to university with. And a bunch of Asian students. They painted in the morning and devoted the afternoon to cultural trips and walks. The Asians enjoyed themselves greatly and it was catching. Shoved in a drawer somewhere she has a pile of photographs to recall that time; all the Asian students endlessly snapped one another and everybody else and every change of scenery, as though without camera to eye they could see nothing. When the fortnight was over and the pictures developed they sent her copies of all the ones they thought would interest her. Maybe she could show them? . . . no. Better to leave it up to their imaginations.

Roderick had smooth yellow skin and black hair, his face was rather flat and his features were slightly and delicately moulded so as hardly to disturb the flat plane of his face. He had a habit of narrowing his slender eyes even further when troubled or confused, when he did not understand something that was said, or he saw. As though he were shutting out all further stimuli in order to retire inside his head and concentrate on the problem already in it. And then he would smile with pleasure, or embarrassment. He had a great desire to know things. This narrowing of his eyes touched Elinor. She wanted to help him understand. His intelligence, his vulnerability, his sensuousness were irresistible. He smelt deliciously of a certain scented soap made by Coty called L'Aimant; he gave her a box of it. The box she still has, still faintly scented with the odour of his presence. L'Aimant: the magnet. Not ultimately strong enough.

After the fortnight they returned to their separate cities and Roderick wrote long enthusiastic letters and sent a present and a poem (the first of many) for her birthday. In May she went to a reunion of the summer school in Sydney, which was where Roderick lived. Elinor stayed with an elderly lady who wanted to reward her for finding her lost watch, though she protested that it was quite accidentally she had found it, had kicked it in fact, in the long grass near the pottery kiln. Miss White and her sister lived in Bellevue Hill and ran a secretarial school for young ladies; they treated her like one of them, politely, distantly, and expecting acquiescence. Their habits and manners and even their conversation had the undeviating strictness of ritual, and a visitor in the house however kind their intentions was an interloper, the coldly stared at unwitting breaker or at least buckler of sacred conventions.

Elinor describes the small tight ladies coloured and corseted into strutting plump pouter pigeons with kindly malice; she thinks of the rows of typewriters in the front room of the old family house, musty with the odour of decaying gentility, of the Bed-time I think sister, at ten o'clock, the small economical meals, and forgives them. The children shiver and laugh. It's hard to believe in their mother not having her own way.

She hardly saw Roderick at all. She was obliged to play the nicely brought-up young lady and attend her hostess, especially since she provided the transport, in a brown Ford Prefect upright and prim as a tea party, which meant home early to bed. They managed some conversations, desperate disappointed conversations, brief and superficial. But perhaps Miss White did them a favour, provided the difficulties that made love flourish. (The love of Elinor and Ivan was never unrequited. Perhaps it ought to have been. They were consenting adults; when passion got strong enough they gave way to it.) After the reunion they wrote letters, tender, passionate, and chaste. Letters of lovers pitifully parted. She sent him a tiny leatherbound copy of Shakespeare's sonnets, bought second-hand, with pressed rose petals to mark appropriate ones. *Let me not to the marriage of true minds/Admit impediment* . . . And she invited him home for the weekend.

Her parents were intrigued by all this. They expected their daughters to make life interesting. She wondered what they thought was happening. Perhaps they looked on him as an exotic penfriend occasionally incarnated. Nice to correspond with people from other races and countries, broadens the outlook. And such interesting stamps. Or there would be when he went back to Sarawak in July. They enjoyed being broadminded.

◆ ◆ ◆

Late at night. Elinor and Roderick on the kitchen floor. The corner by the back door. She can't remember why now. Perhaps the farthest place from her parents' sleeping bedroom. But she remembers the kissing. His fine smooth scented skin. The strong curve of his teeth. And his murmurings. Words of love that wreathed in her brain and made her dizzy. Neither had glasses on, both sat gazing beatifically and myopically into each other's eyes. He asked her to marry him and she said yes.

Straightaway he began to take off his clothes. Shall I unzip your dress? he said. He meant to consummate the engagement immediately. On the kitchen floor, on a strip of coir matting, with her parents a door away across the dining-room.

What she thought of was the coir mat. In the kitchen, by the back door: daily footwiper. No fun to bare your bottom to a coir mat. At the time she said, Oh no, we can't, not here, fright instantly undizzying her brain. He didn't seem to mind. He looked at her, his eyes narrowed, he smiled. Buttoned up his shirt, slung his narrow black tie round his neck, did up his shoelaces, quite calmly, though perhaps ruefully, but maybe he liked the idea of a virginal bride. He certainly had excellent manners. He went back to kissing and stroking and murmuring words of love. When he'd gone, she tidied away her refusal in neat distinctions: their love was romance, not sex; poetry, not copulation. She didn't believe them. She blamed the prickly presence of her parents, embodied in a coir mat.

Mum, Mum, did you have a party? When you got engaged to Roderick? And a diamond ring?

Well, no. It was a secret, you see.

Why?

We were very young. I was. It was going to be a long time . . .

And the coir mat their last chance. Elinor went to Sydney the weekend that his ship sailed (the *Neptunia*, bound for South-East Asian ports) and didn't this time stay with the secretarial lady but at the YWCA: some improvement. She could stay up late, with a pass, and the knocking up of the night porter, though Roderick could not come in beyond the foyer, its purplish marble and solid echoing space a kind of chaperonial air-lock to the virtue of young women. He had treats planned:

a trip on the harbour, a play, dinner at Prince's, one of Sydney's two classy restaurants. What a waste, thinks Elinor now. She was so miserable at his departure and so nervous of the splendours of the place that she remembers almost nothing of it. She has tried, but can only call up an impression of red velvet banquettes and huge quantities of starched white linen and rudely attentive waiters. The food: what was it like? Glamorous and bad, she guesses.

Afterwards they walked through a park—Hyde Park? Misery seems to have destroyed the details—arms around heavily coated waists, sometimes sitting on a seat and kissing but it was really too cold, pretty subtropical Sydney really quite cold in winter, and anyway too public. And so they wandered sadly through its comfortless spaces, bearing the burden of their imminent separation.

They were so miserable, so miserable. Her eyes could fill with tears as she tells it. Blanche squeezes her hand with sticky gingerbread fingers. And yet there was a certain pleasure in it. Though only hindsight names it. They were lovers about to be cruelly parted. The classic romantic situation. So they wandered in this perfect beautiful misery. Elinor had never felt so intensely alive before. He kissed the tears on her cheeks, she pressed her nose in his neck, they felt the pure pain of loss, their despair was unbearable. He spoke Romeo's words of Juliet softly in her hair: *It seems she hangs upon the cheek of night/Like a rich jewel in an Ethiope's ear*. Glorious words in the mouth of her beautiful Chinese lover.

Afterwards she remembered that Romeo and Juliet had enough sense to go to bed before parting.

How innocent they were. They survived. She saw him off on the *Neptunia* next day; had dinner on board, foretaste of his feasts to come. She can't remember that either. A quick affectionate embrace, no courage for passion. So many friends, other students, his landlady, summer school people. Neither abandoned enough for a real goodbye. Though they longed for it ardently enough in letters afterwards. Too late she cried, and waved her wooden leg. As your grandma used to say.

The boat moved away from the wharf. They threw ineffectual streamers. She never saw him again.

• • •

The Chinese student. The athlete. The architect. Shuffle the pack of tarot cards. Futures meted out. Retrospective futures.

She met the athlete at a dance at the union. He was a geologist. He took her to watch him in field and track events. He was tall and lean and bony and fast. They went to a ball; there's a photograph of them, he cropped and craggy headed, she slightly bemused behind a barrage of orchids, flattering to the ego but not the appearance. He took her to the cinema as well, and to supper afterwards in little coffee shops to drink fashionable espresso and eat raisin toast, and he wanted to kiss her in the car when he brought her home. She left her glasses on. She had a notion of faithfulness to Roderick, still passionately letter writing, though she did write and say they ought not to be any more formally engaged (which she supposed they weren't really since nobody knew), so far apart and the future so uncertain. Not for him though; he was already plotting his ambition. She was to go to Sarawak and marry him as soon as she finished her degree. No, she wrote, no, we must wait, work and wait until the time is ripe. For a literature student she was rather heavily into clichés.

Symptomatic perhaps of a general failure of the imagination. She couldn't quite picture herself in Sarawak either, silly consti-pated fool, thinks middle-ageing Elinor. The failure of the imagination is the only sin.

The athlete told her he thought they made a good team. He tried to get round the glasses, but they made their point. Looking back she can smile at the figment of their life together; herself sitting on the sidelines of it bringing up cadaverous stubby-haired little boys in the tracks of their father. Or little girls. Not long after he married an old schoolmate of hers, a curly blonde socialite—what's a socialite? asks Isabel—and they went to Western Australia; the minerals, she supposes.

The architect was more amusing. Once he carried her across a puddle (she was quite light then) and his conversation was good. She wondered if he was frigid. He didn't seem to be interested in sex. (Now she thinks gay, maybe.) Sarawak was a long way away. The letters of anguish and despair had turned into catalogues of doings.

The athlete, the architect, the married man. Oho. She doesn't tell the children about him. She wishes to appear a virtuous woman. A victory for the flesh, finally, and the demise of love by letter. A spacious ledge on a cliff-face over the sea, and love in the sunshine, and Elinor saying again, again, and he, men can't, not all that often. They were to be married as soon as his wife left him, which would be any day now, he said.

He wrote skilful elliptical poems that needed a gloss on practically every word. They showed her what she had always known in her brain, though her heart had tried to ignore about Roderick's: that the sentiments were impeccable but the poetry pretty clumsy.

Ivan has never written her poems. But poems come of pain, and separation, and loss. Is a man naked in your bed every night, even if he snores, more important than a poem?

It is impossible amid the solid fleshly presences of Blanche and Isabel and Ivan coming home soon to imagine that she could have married anyone else. And the solid fleshly presence of her married lover had been too much for Roderick then. His face was there in the grey of the photographs, his scent ghostly in the old soapbox, but Elinor was no longer at the end of his letters. Was he of hers? She comforted herself by thinking he could not possibly any longer be. He wrote once or twice more, the last time from London and the great adventure of the bank, but by that time Elinor had stopped answering, in fact as in spirit. She didn't even tell him she was getting married.

She fells more guilt now than then. Then she was too busy living. Cramming in the Jewish intellectual and the lawyer before feet-sweeping Ivan, life a prickle of possibilities. And the present guilt; even that might be a cheat, might be regret. A present settledness enjoying intimations of what might have been . . .

She wonders who he did marry. A Chinese girl? An Englishwoman? For marry he would have, she's sure. His ambitions were too strong for one body, would have flowed through into children.

◆ ◆ ◆

The athlete, the architect, the married man. The Chinese banker, the intellectual, the silky lawyer. The men your mother might have married. They make a good chant. Say them over, weave a spell. Choose a name and make a future.

But only retrospectively is it like that. At the time it just happened. With doubt and mistakes and fear. And a bright bland minute-by-minute making of minuscule choices, with no more than the next hour, day, week, in mind. Only now is it the pattern of a lifetime. Only now is it a tale ending *happily ever after*.

◆ ◆ ◆

So there, dear children, is the story (a bowdlerised version indeed, indeed) of how your mother nearly married a clever young man with a career in international banking ahead of him. And one or two other people.

They smile, smugly. They know that all along she had no intention of letting them down. That the past is a fairy story, a pseudo-shivery tale for children, in which the heroine their mother moves inexorably (all alarms are false) into destiny's only proper choices. Safe in their own existence, sure that it is inevitable, they only flirt with the idea of non-being. They cannot conceive how accidental it's all been.

The gingerbread men were a great success. Mm, said Ivan, said Daddy, the best gingerbread men I've ever eaten. Though the last batch got a bit burnt down one side.

Rock platform

◆

Newcastle, 1967

The cliffs at Bar Beach fall roughly sheer to a rock platform, which stretches a hundred yards from their foot to drop in steps some fifteen feet to the sea bed. This is the littoral, divided into five zones: the supra-, upper-, mid-, lower-, and infra-littoral zones. It is the water that makes these distinctions; they indicate a range from the mainly dry to the always wet.

The littoral is an ecological community inhabited by plants and animals depending on one another for energy, food, shelter. Though it is not their own doing they all have names. There is tough-tunicked cunjevoi, the only marine animal to have kept its aboriginal appellation; coralline algae branching red; chiton coat of mail shell, *Cataphragmus* the many-plated barnacle. There is Sedentaria the tube worm; and the molluscs: oysters, and the limpets and periwinkles that browse on the algae. There are Crustacea, crabs, which may masquerade as speckled pebbles, and Porifera, sponges, in purple, red, yellow, orange, grey-brown. Coral, which is Coelenterata. Galeolaria, small white skeletons full of worms, and the blue Melaraphae, little molluscs hidden in crevices for the dampness. The algae are Hormosira, named Neptune's Necklace because it looks like beads on a string, the brown striped fans of Padina, the velvety green fingers of Codium, and Ulva the sea lettuce. There are anemones and sea stars many coloured, spiny sea urchins, and fat brown *Scutus* the sea slug under rock ledges. There are little fish with long feathery gills.

Their constant concern is to prevent desiccation. All have different methods. Some depend on limey shells, or a tough thallus, others have a thick mucous covering. Barnacles like to be splashed, so their presence shows where this happens. Others herd together, or hide among seaweeds. Crabs survive provided their gills are wet, fish must have pools with an outlet to the sea. And because the necessary waves wash over them, the violent storms, the high tides of spring, they have perfected means of attaching themselves to rocks, by a hold-fast, or encrustation, which are permanent, or with a muscular foot, or tube feet, or a limey secretion, which allow ambulation.

All these creatures are linked by the energy flow. Algae and phytoplankton absorb the radiant energy from the sun, turning it into potential and eventually kinetic energy. Zooplankton feed on phytoplankton, and herbivores like the periwinkles graze on the algae. Carnivores eat the herbivores. Sea stars and anemones gobble up their edible fellows. All die and decay, releasing nitrogen and phosphorus into the water, thus in turn nourishing the green plants. But the potential energy in their bodies is lost during decomposition. As is the kinetic.

So the cycles turn around for this multitude of named creatures all perfectly adapted to their environment. And what does perfect adaptation mean? That the organism is able to reproduce in that environment with maximum efficiency.

It is often difficult to see much of the infra- and lower-littoral zones, and indeed of the mid-, because of the sea. At high tide it is impossible, but even at its lowest the water may surge and splash and threaten to swirl away large human bodies who have no hold-fast, or muscular foot, or secretions, or capacity for encrustation, and maybe dash them against the rocks which are never so smooth as diagrams make out. In fact this problem needn't arise except for fishermen cutting cunjevoi for the juicy red animal inside its gnarled green plant which likes to be kept awash by the breakers, since that hundred yards or so of supra-littoral is pitted with pools, many of them deep and the water always there, which repeat exactly the five-fold zonation of the rock platform. So people can squat in comfort and observe in microcosm the ecological community of the littoral.

Like Mikelis and Veronica one sunny autumn Saturday, bending down to a deepish pool. Mikelis sat on his feet with his face between his knees, intently examining the contents. Gently he brushed his fingers across the reddish and grey-blue sponges that lined it; he rubbed barnacles on the shallow lip where the waves would splash, waited for an anemone to suck at his finger. Some blue and red starfish wandered across the bottom, perfectly visible through the wavering clear water, and a speckled pebble turned out to be a crab in camouflage. Veronica told him the names and he stayed still a long time gazing at the pool. She watched him watching it. It was as though he were memorising it, not that exactly, imprinting it on his brain, as though his large light blue eyes gazing could store all this tiny detail, and that the process could work the other way, that somehow the crystal of his eye would one day project what it saw with unimpaired accuracy. Is it because I know his profession that I think this, she wondered. Would I think it of anybody else? She couldn't imagine anybody else looking and storing so intently. She regarded his round face with its taut fine skin and the complicated crystals of his watching eyes, and after a while felt like a woman who reads a letter not addressed to her, found in a book perhaps, or dropped on the floor; excited, intimate, prying but enjoying doing so. She wondered what his skin would feel like, and the round curve of his eyelid.

They were both so entranced with their watching they didn't notice the turning of the tide, until a rather large wave splashed over them, and then wet they realised that the hot autumn day was declining into cold evening, and when they got back to the house Martin was there. Veronica had forgotten that he was coming early; he wanted to drive to a restaurant fifty miles down the Pacific Highway, a place that specialised in fancily cooking its own chickens. That way they could have the fun of driving as well as dining out.

Veronica liked being in the car at night, the hood up and the noisy rushing dark shut outside, the car speeding down the road like a clever hunting animal after its prey and its own throaty bubbling roar making conversation difficult so that they were together yet inside their own thoughts, but tonight this feeling shifted sometimes and the car became the prey fleeing and its noise a wail of fear; but only sometimes. Martin put his hand on her knee and squeezed it, resting it there briefly whenever he changed gear. She was in a car and they were off on a pleasure trip. Whenever she thought of life with Martin it was as a series of outings. What about the bits in between?

Lenses in the garden

———————◆———————

Mikelis and Dane were sitting in the garden in April sunlight. Mikelis closed his eyes and held his face up to the sun. Dane did the same, but only for a moment; the intense velvet red of the blood against his eyeballs became unbearable. He lowered his head and half-opened his eyes; his lashes made prisms of light that fluttered iridescent butterflies against his vision.

Mikelis lay back in his chair, face still tipped to the sun. It is curious, he said. The warmth of the sun's rays is also light, we believe. And light is vision. Yet here is warmth and no vision.

The garden sloped down to the bush, a little tongue of it amid main roads. There was no fence to separate the cultivated from the wild. Mikelis pointed. There are snakes in that bush. There used to be. One day, soon after we came to live in this house, our cat killed a snake, and died to do it. A big black cat he was, like a panther sleek and padding. His mother was a Burmese; he had an air of the jungle. And the snake a monstrous long thing. We came home and found the two bodies lying side by side, in the evidence of a heroic struggle. Like Beowulf killing the dragon, and dying himself.

Dane knows this story. He has heard it often, and always enjoys it. Family stories are like glasses of wine from good old bottles in the cellar, not to be refused because you've drunk the vintage before. Expecting the richness you can savour them more.

There's no cat in this garden now, only an old man with his face to the sun, and a young man who listens. The old man touches his eyelids with his fingers. Lenses, he says. They're lentils you know. The same word. Little round objects like the humble pulse that fed Europe. The invention of the lens gives us telescope and microscope. And camera. We can see far away and close up. And believe we record what we see. Do you know who was the finest lens-maker of his time? The man who polished the lenses of Galileo, inventor of the great and little scopes—Spinoza. The philosopher. No accident that. Philosophers are obsessed with light. And poets. And so are we who write in light.

He lies back in his chair. His thin chest quivers with the weight of his breathing. Dane knows he hasn't finished, is only pausing, and after a while he goes on.

We say our eyes have lenses but not like that. This little lentil in its humours aqueous and vitreous is not susceptible of grinding; not even Spinoza could polish away its opacity. However mathematically perfect the curvature of his surfaces he could not polish away the dark.

Mikelis smiles. Once Dane was bothered by the melancholy of the old man's meditations, but now he understands them differently. Understands the pleasure they give him. First in the seeking and finding of words and the ordering of them in his own way, and second in the offering of them to his friend. Third is Dane's listening. Sometimes the old man holds out his hand as though he can feel the intensity of this. Dane thinks of himself as a kind of radiant listener, warming the old man's murmurings. Warming and recording. If he's not powerful enough they'll fade away.

On the other hand . . . Mikelis spreads his palm. Here's a thing. Two distorting lenses give a true picture. So, consider the *simple* visual difficulties. The curable ones. If the eye is distorted by astigmatism, it can be corrected by a spectacle lens distorted in the opposite manner: the combination of the opposed distortions produces a normal image on the retina.

Ah. The combination of the opposed distortions. It's a life's work.

Distortions, he says again. Distortions. The word twisted by his repetitions becomes the image of itself.

The sun leaves early in April. Even the frail gum tree shadow is beginning to cool the garden. They stand up to go in.

When I was a boy, says Mikelis, and naughty as most, we used to use magnifying glasses to set fire to things. Focus the sun's rays on a bit of wood or paper, and set fire to it. And girls' necks. You'd creep up behind them when they were sitting over a book and narrow the rays down to a spot on the backs of their necks. Of course it didn't get time to really burn. They'd swat at it like a mosquito, and then see it was the work of one of the awful boys. They banned burning glasses at my school because the girls got upset.

Even a bit of bottle glass can start a fire like that, in the bush in a dry summer, and burn down houses and burn out forests and burn up people, all from one bit of glass.

Mikelis shivers. The blue shadow of the mountain is over the bush at the bottom of the garden. Hard to believe in a fire down there. It's chilly enough to set the snakes hibernating. Were the scrub to glow red and the flames to leap from crown to crown of the gum trees and all their scented oils conflagrate, Mikelis would still be a thin old man, and cold.

Inside Dane lights the fire which he has set with pine cones for kindling. They burn up brightly, small branches catch, the flames roar. Mikelis sits close, holding out his hands, his face reddened. Warmth without light, he says. But not without sound. Not for me. Sight and sound, so easy to lose them both, but feeling remains. You never lose that. Not even freezing to death. Did you know that Dane? The dangerous thing about being lost in the snow is when you stop being cold, and begin to feel warm and comfortable. At least I feel cold enough to be sure I'm alive.

After dinner he says, Read Eva's letter again. Dane gets it out of the file in the crimson-coloured cabinet. *My dear Papa, It's the spring and everybody's happy. So it seems. I wonder if there's a kind of chemical in the air, making everybody just a little bit high. Maybe the new flowers and leaves and blossoms exude it—it's clearly very strong for it reaches even into the stony streets of Rome. There is plenty of work, everybody wants translations. And the payment is princely. So I have no problems with money; please don't worry. I can eat and drink and pay the rent and even clothe myself—I have glamorous plans . . .*

Dane pictures Eva dressed like an Italian beauty in lush curving clothes of fur and fluid patterned wool. He wonders if she would write different letters if she knew he read them. He imagines writing to her, telling her that he is the medium, that her letters come and go through him, that he now is her father's spectacles. *Dear Eva*, he would write, not this time at the old man's dictation, using instead of the word processor a fine ink pen and onion-skin paper, forming the curving letters of the greeting with full-bodied affection. *Dear Eva, I am writing to say that I am your father's spectacles. It is through me that he must look to see things . . .* Of course he can't do this. Mikelis is protecting her from the knowledge of his failing sight, he does not wish her to be told. So Dane goes on being the go-between of the love of father and daughter, and preserver of her ignorance. He sits at the machine. *My dear Eva*, Mikelis dictates. *Your spring, and our autumn. Remember the yellow lines of poplars in the valleys? The fire is crackling; try to smell the pine cone scent 12 000 miles away . . .* When it's finished Dane shows the old man's hand the place, and it writes a flourishing strong black *Mikelis* with thick and thin strokes and curves as complex as a drawing. It would trick anybody into believing in his vigour.

Naples

◆

Newcastle, 1967

Everybody knew that George
had dearly desired a son, but he didn't make any of his daughters
think she should have been him. There'd been a miscarriage,
once, somewhere between their births; maybe the boy was there.
Maybe he'd have been the next one, if the parents hadn't run
out of time. Veronica thought about her own birth, and
wondered how sharp a stab of disappointment it had been.
But only intellectually, long after the event and sure that he
loved her. He made jokes about living in a houseful of women
and never getting a word in. He claimed to be hen-pecked,
which made everybody laugh. He loves it, said Elinor. He's
waited on hand and foot. He revels in it.

A boy could have been much harder to get on with, rebellious,
competitive, wanting Oedipus-like to defeat him. His daughters
fought for their own way but on different terms, and with
them there could be the necessary giving-in, the conflict didn't

have to be mortal. They couldn't loom over him physically, as even a young boy might have done, like a growing animal whose bristling body says, Move over, old man, I am the fresh and the strong here now.

Didn't you say you were the youngest sister? Mikelis asked Veronica.

Yes, she said. There was a freezing southerly blowing, so they were walking along streets where a little sun-warmth collected, instead of the windy beach front. Yes. Three daughters. Three sisters.

You and Elinor . . .

And Diana. First of all, Diana.

Diana our eldest sister, and maybe the closest to the boy who never came. A tomboy, anyway, mad keen about sport. A terrific swimmer. Lean and broad-shouldered. You know what shoulders girls get from swimming. Always tanned, with downy blonde arms. Played hockey, too, and tennis; she was school tennis champion, and later for the district. You can imagine how popular at school; she was sports captain and vice-captain; the younger kids thought she was marvellous. Didn't do a stroke of work, or hardly; she and Dad had terrible fights about her marks, he reckoned she was too clever to get such mediocre ones, but all the while he was really proud of these other things she did. Anyway, she got into Teachers College, and that was just like school, sport and popularity and barely enough work to scrape through.

After that she got posted to a little school at Port Macquarie which she enjoyed because the sporting–swimming life carried on, and the popularity. And boys like energetic muscular pretty girls with brown skins and streaky blonde hair, they're good fun. So she had plenty of boyfriends. Never any doubt that she'd get asked to the right things, or that once there she'd dance every dance with those strange eligible boys who everybody recognises, though you don't know how, are the most desirable.

Like Martin.

Oh no, not like Martin. With Martin you don't see the rough edges rippling under his skin, all polished on the surface but the roughness underneath, the way you do with the really important boys. Martin's nice and quite good-looking and does the right glamorous things but none of those are what I mean, they're not what the boys round Diana were.

And I'm not either.

Of course not. You're not the slightest bit eligible. She laughed.

Now, you probably don't know this, Mikelis, but there comes a moment in the lives of girls. A magic moment. Or a fatal moment. For girls like Diana, it's about twenty-two. School's over, and training: nursing, uni, Teachers College, whatever, and you've been out working for a year or two. Suddenly everybody's getting married. It's like a biological clock, saying, Now! If you're not getting married, you go overseas. The Old Country. The working holiday. Australian girls are in great demand for jobs in England you know. London's full of them, all living in Kangaroo Valley.

Men too, said Mikelis. We go overseas too.

I suppose so. Well, Diana wasn't getting married. She didn't fancy any of the Port Macquarie boys, she said, and I expect that was true. So she went overseas. Went with a friend from Teachers College who also wasn't getting married. Sailed on the *Galileo*, we went to Sydney to see her off, a beautiful tall white ship it was, though in her letters she said it bucketed about terribly and most of the passengers were seasick all the time, but the surgeon told her beer and apples was the best cure and he was right. Lots of handsome Italian officers, and dances all the time. And wine out of a tap in the middle of the dining tables.

Imagine Diana playing deck games, very fast on her feet; those strong shoulders and muscular arms, catching the quoit, throwing it, her skin glowing browner and browner, and her hair, it was shoulder length you know, swinging blonde in the salty sunshine. And swimming in the pool in her black Speedos; she said it was too short to get into your stroke.

The boat was going to Genoa, and they were taking the train to London. But there were lots of other stops on the way. Exotic ones, the Suez Canal, and the Mediterranean ports; Malta, and Messina, and Naples.

Do you know Naples? No, neither do I. It's a place people say you should see. See Naples . . . It's one of those cities whose names have a kind of magic. People sing about them. Imagine a song about Newcastle. Anyway, liners pull in there. There's a long concrete dock out into the bay, I've heard. Maybe it's called a mole. That makes you think of burrowing away, but of course it's above the water. And buildings jumbled up the slopes. Diana sent a postcard, she bought it on board and wrote it sitting on the deck, watching the ship berth. She wrote that she loved the way it went sideways into the wharf, at the last minute, she always watched it if she could. If only her little car could have parked itself like that, zip, sideways into the gutter. The postcard had a fat sort of castle on it, I remember, and a lot of shiny blue sky. The passengers were all going ashore, to Pompeii, or the old town, or the castle. Diana and her friend were going exploring on their own, she wrote, they hated guided tours and being organised. She said she might buy some boots, Italy being famous for its leather. So Diana and the friend, she was called Judy, took a taxi . . .

Veronica shivered. This southerly's so cold, she said. She rubbed her hands up and down her arms. The wind blew straight through the warm woollen threads of her jumper.

That's the end of the story. There was an accident. Nobody seems to know what happened exactly. A collision. Narrow streets, sharp bends, steep: speed, probably. People say those Naples taxis go very fast. The collision pretty violent. The taxi rolled over and Diana was thrown out and killed. Hit her head on the cobbles.

Somebody from External Affairs came and told us. Pretty garbled message. Mainly that Diana was dead, and what did we want done with her?

It's funny. It took a long time for us to . . . believe it. There was the fact, this death, but it didn't make any sense. As though a mistake had been made, and it was somebody else, not Diana. Even when her ashes came home, in, well, they called it an urn. Though there was never any doubt. But somehow, so far away and so surprising . . . so unlikely, so out of character for Diana. I'd never thought of people dying in character before.

My parents have never got over it. Oh, Dad thinks positively. After all, he does believe in reincarnation. Each life's a stage in the progress of the soul to perfection, Diana must have done all she could in this life and been ready to move on. Exciting, in a way. Sort of being chosen for promotion. That's what he thinks. That's what he says. But it's not easy for him. And Mum. All she knows is she's lost her. She's always been a bit more interested in bodies than souls. She listens to Dad and I think she believes him but the loss doesn't go away. Of course it's five years, it's a habit by now. But still not very easy.

Hard for us two as well. I was thirteen when she went to Port Macquarie. I don't suppose I knew her very well. We didn't have much time for each other. Different lives. Same with her and Elinor; El was always happy sitting round reading a book, Diana thought she was pretty hopeless. But sisters, three sisters are a unit. I'm still the youngest.

Do you know the poem by Wordsworth? Awful poem. He goes for a walk and meets a little girl and asks her how many brothers and sisters she's got, and she says, We are seven, though it turns out two are dead and the poet keeps trying to get her to see they can't be seven if two are in the churchyard and their spirits in heaven, but the little girl just goes on saying, We are seven. I feel like her, just keeping on saying, We are three, against all evidence.

Mikelis took her hand. When she looked at him she saw there were tears in his eyes. She was surprised. Diana was their story, their sadness; aunts saying, Poor Diana, such a lovely girl, hardly impinged. Now Mikelis was sharing it. Her eyes were tearful too in the stinging wind.

Your Diana, he said. She's like her namesake, the goddess, isn't she? In a skimpy dress and sandals, running fast as the wind. Suntanned. And unmarried.

And a bit of a myth, too, you mean.

No, I didn't mean that. Just beautiful, and still going on.

I suppose she is a bit of a myth, in a way. In the family. We talk about her sometimes. My father believes it's important to talk about people's lives, not forget what there was of them.

His parents would never mention his brother, who died before he was born. He doesn't think that was fair. Like killing him twice over.

People don't like cultivating pain.

It's not the pain, it's the good bits. He'll tell his grandchildren, you know, about the aunt they never saw.

They'd come to the part of Watkin Street where its two sides were divided by a little cliff. Veronica pointed to the high side, to an old house with a verandah across the front.

My grandmother lives there.

Does she? Your grandmother! Mikelis looked amazed. You're really a local.

Mm. And she was born in a house only about a mile from here. On the corner of Bull Street. It's a Spanish restaurant these days, called El Toro. Then after she was married they moved here. It's quite a grand situation, you know, looking across the whole valley. And a large piece of land. My grandfather sold some of it to the people next door to build their house, and you can see there's room for another between. That's a loquat tree in the middle. I used to eat them. I like bitter fruits.

Mum says that when Grandma moved in there were rats. She was very shocked. The house had been lived in by the minister before they bought it. Grandma couldn't believe a minister would have rats in his house.

They picked their way down the little cliff. At the bottom were stone outcrops, and puddles; it looked as though it might have been a creek.

Along here's where the railway used to go. The one out to the lagoon, to get coal. And all around here, when my mother was a girl, were Chinese market gardens. My grandfather used to say, when I die, I'll come back as a Chinaman's horse.

Why?

Because they were so well-treated. That's a surprise, ay?

Did your grandfather believe in reincarnation too? It sounds Pythagorean.

Oh no. No. It was a joke. And a kind of compliment, I suppose. He used to buy seedlings from the Chinese market gardeners.

Walking along the creek-like slimy stones Mikelis slipped. His foot turned and he started to keel over. Veronica grabbed his arm, then held him tight around the waist, supporting him. He put his arms round her shoulders, and hung on.

Hello Veronica.

She looked up. A woman was watching from the higher bank.

Hello Mrs Price.

Mikelis standing on one foot turned to see who it was; they swayed dangerously, each tightening grip on the other.

How's your mother, Veronica?

She's very well, Mrs Price.

The woman eyed the embracing couple.

I think my friend's sprained his ankle, Veronica said. She and Mikelis turned, still clutching one another, and limped along until they came to smoother ground. He sat down and rubbed his foot.

That's not good. You want to watch yourself, said Mrs Price.

It's all right, really, said Mikelis. Just a twist. He hobbled a bit, but wasn't badly hurt. He walked with his arm round her shoulders, not really leaning on her.

You really are a local, he said again. We can't even sprain my ankle in private.

Of course not.

When they got home the fire was lit, most unusually early. Let's make toast, said Veronica. But it was too soon, the fire was still flames, not red coals. You really have to wait till supper time, she said. I know, come for tea tomorrow night and we'll make toast for supper. She wasn't asking him for that night because of going out with Martin. She insisted he wait and get a lift home when Martin came for her, because of his foot. The Healey was a two-seater, but she sat half on Mikelis's lap and half leaning on Martin's shoulder as had often happened before.

Next night they made piles of toast, thick white bread held out to the coals on a long iron fork, charring a bit, smokey, doused in butter.

Isn't it good? she said. Diana used to love it.

The Order

◆

Newcastle, late 1940s

George went into his study and shut the door. It was a long narrow room that had been a laundry before he built a stout wooden shed in the backyard to get the steaming copper out of the house. He paused in the dark, waiting for the room's quiet habit to take him over. It was necessary to put all preoccupation out of his mind. Not think of the flat look in his wife's eyes, Diana's disappointed smiles; at least Elinor and the baby were already in bed and couldn't look at him as he went to shut himself away. The room smelled of the incense he sometimes burned there. It was cold.

Man has only three questions to ask: *Where do we come from? Why are we here? What is our destiny?* He repeated them as he lit the candles, watching the flames waver into life, straighten, burn sturdily. Destiny made him think of his little girls. That morning he and Elinor had stretched out on the couch reading the Sunday comics; she could read pretty well herself now though she hadn't started school, but the Sunday comics were a ritual, for him and Elinor; Diana couldn't stay still long enough. After the comics she'd stayed resting in his arm while he read the paper. Examining the political cartoon she'd asked him what it meant, and when he said, It's a picture with a double meaning, she'd got up and climbed round to the other side of the newspaper to see what it was. Bright and full of life are his daughters, and little he'll be able to save them from in this world.

He stared at the candle. Such thoughts he had to clear out of his mind, make it empty so that it could be filled. *To become mystics we must mentally disrobe.* He imagined slipping off grubby work-stained clothes, stepping out of them, reaching out his hands for other fairer raiment. *We must not try to know God through intellect or reason, but must enter into a state of contemplation and meditation, and permit ourselves to be absorbed into the absolute.* He went through the exercises. *In the beginning was the Word. At one stage all things were inchoate conditions of the Word. It is a vibratory undulating energy in which the basic essence of all things exists. Man once possessed the Word but has lost it.* Lost it? What carelessness. How could he have become dispossessed of so great a treasure? *It is possible to believe he may redeem himself, may recover the lost Word, or at least certain efficacious syllables of it.* George pronounced the potent vowels so far revealed to him. The candle flame grew in his eyes, its colour changed from yellow to rose to purple. The Sumerians believed that the breath of God was a warm flood of light.

He took the new week's monograph out of its envelope and unfolded it. The particular smell of the ink—the paper wasn't printed, exactly, perhaps it was stencilled—flared his nostrils, promising answers. After all the years of trying to find them, here they were in the smell of this ink. The Order did not expect belief. That would mean lack of knowledge. *A mystic should have no beliefs, but should supplant them with knowledge or a frank admission that he doesn't know.* What a relief, after so many exhortations to have faith, only believe, trust. Here were facts.

Death is not only inevitable, it is a necessary element in the cycle of life. Death and birth are synonymous, for so-called death is birth into another plane, while birth is likewise a transition. The transition of soul into a body is considered just as strange and fraught with unknown possibilities as the transition of soul from a body. Both constitute the Great Experience. Both are a form of Initiation affording an opportunity for greater advancement.

When Veronica was born he looked at her lying in her crib and said, She has been here before. Her milky blue eyes gazed serenely, her little pink tongue tasted the air. She looked as though she knew what she was about, was prepared for getting on with this new life. She knows, he said, she knows. The Order held that babies and small children were highly spiritual because of the closeness of their souls to the pre-birth state. That was why Wordsworth saw them trailing clouds of glory. As Veronica grew he could see her separating from it; he fancied that the changing of her eyes from that serene milky blue, heavenly blue it was, to sparkling mischievous world-conscious brown, was a sign of this separation.

Both death and birth are looked forward to by the soul without guilt or fear. So what brainwashing made man fear death? *Whether we consider the transition from a natural or a spiritual viewpoint, there is no death; the term is not only erroneous but absolutely contradictory. Matter is indestructible, that is a fundamental law of matter, and it is in constant change; that is another fundamental law.* For the millionth time he wished he'd taken notice of his mother and stayed at school. *The soul is immortal and cannot be destroyed, lessened, increased, or otherwise modified, except by experience . . . neither body nor soul ever dies, and there is no death.*

When he'd finished his study and exercises for the evening he came out of his room, which he thought of as his sanctum, his head full of light. Diana was in bed by this time; he crept in and watched by the dim lamp in the hall his three little girls asleep. They had survived their birth into this life, there they were, perfect of body and lively of mind, mysterious souls waiting. Their transition into the next, not death but another birth, need be no more terrifying.

He went back to the room where his wife sat embroidering white daisies on a blue linen dress that she'd made for Diana. Fair-haired Diana, brown as a berry—why a berry, he wondered —thin and strong and never still. He thought of water when he thought of her, quick flowing, gleaming with light, an endless murmur of sound. How's my little babbling brook today? he'd say, when he came home, sitting her on the bar of his bike for a ride up the path to the back door. From his port he took his lunch-time book, he was reading Hegel's *Doctrine of Becoming*, and a small white paper bag of coconut ice; they would eat a couple of pieces each while they sat on either side of the quiet fire, he reading, his wife sewing, and the sandy rain spattering on the windows.

The studio

◆

Newcastle, 1967

Squalls of rain burst out of the sky; the headlights of the buses lit up their wild flurry. The ground was splashed with stains of red and blue neon; however hard it rained they didn't wash away. Tyres slicked on the road and the brakes of buses squealed like animals. On the harbour a boat wailed. Veronica stood sheltering in a shop doorway waiting for her bus. It was only five thirty, but dark as midnight.

Hello, said Mikelis. It was the week after the toast.

Veronica was glad she was wearing her new overcoat, cherry-coloured wool with a collar she could stand up round her neck. She smiled. Hello, what are you doing here?

Mikelis didn't speak the truth, which was, Waiting for you. I'm at work, he said. Just out for a breath of air. Veronica looked out at the eddies of rain. Air? You could drown in that. She shivered, holding the collar of her coat against her cheek with a black-gloved hand.

Would you like to see the studio?

Well. I better not be late.

Won't take a minute.

He took her elbow and steered her round the corner, into a side street. The wall of the building was covered with glass cases full of studio portraits. Here her mother had brought them to eat icecreams on their trips to town because she didn't approve of eating in the street. They stood with hankies tucked in their necks and looked at the brides, solemn women or toothily smiling, with layered skirts of tulle and sweetheart necklines, spotted in dots of pink and blue—eyes, mouths, flowers, ribbons—where the black and white photographs had been tinted. At that time it was a great sorrow in Veronica's life that her mother had no such photograph; there was even no such dress, just a pink drapey crêpe now in the dress-up box along with a sad-eyed moulting fox and some battered hats. There wasn't any time for a proper dress, said her mother. And it seemed a waste of money somehow. The photographing appeared to have been forgotten.

Elinor and Veronica (she couldn't remember Diana who must have been at school) and then just Veronica ate icecreams and trained their eyes on the wedding clothes. There were dresses and dresses, they could see that, some a dream of beauty, others a disaster. Not all the pictures were of brides, but the rest, men in suits, or women in twin-sets with small organdie collars, the children red-lipped and rosy-cheeked against the grey, didn't interest them.

Veronica hadn't noticed this display of wares for years. They still looked the same, except that the twin-sets had been replaced by straight shifty dresses. Mikelis took her in a door between the cases, up dingy stairs lined with more portraits and into the studios of Neville of Newcastle.

A warren of rooms, round a large space, with cameras certainly but mainly objects. The light for ordinary seeing came through parchment shades yellow and tasselled, giving things a double presence, as themselves and shadows. There was a streaky patterned marble table with heavy gilt mouldings for sitting babies on; the mothers had to squat behind to make

sure they didn't fall off. We've got a picture of Diana on one
of these, she said. There was a rustic seat that looked as though
it were made of very spiky twigs but was actually plaster—
very popular with engaged couples. The girl could let her hand
rest on the arm and show off the ring. Her soft hand on the
twiggy branch. As with the wishing well, heads twining together
to look through the frame of it, the girl's ringed hand lying
lightly on the rope. There was a rack of screens to pull down,
on rollers like blinds, to make backdrops: casement windows
overlooking fields with cows, or a river, or a distant Tuscan-
type villa; slatted venetians glimpsing a perfect branch of peach
blossom; French windows balustraded before some imaginary
Mediterranean. There were rods with curtains, heavy brocade
bunching on the floor, bobbled velvet, dreamy chiffon. Urns
and garlands and sheaves of plastic gladioli lolling. An enormous
red velvet *chaise longue*, a bit bald, for spreading a lacy dress
or train to show the pattern. In a corner a Gothic arch with
gargoyles and purple carpeted steps for brides descending into
a new life; a fake door with a horse-shoe; a dovecote; a small
papier-mâché tower with bells. Best of all was what Neville
called Hymen's Bower, a kind of grotto covered in long pannicles of wistaria made out of purple crêpe paper. Any dampness
and it stained white dresses with indelible dye. All these were
for the wedding parties that came between church and reception
to be posed in all their combinations amid the scenery of their
choice, while their guests got drunk waiting for them.

And not just brides. There was a short wall of painted books
for graduation studies, a carved wooden chair for judges and
captains of industry, dolls and a marbelised ball, tin soldiers,
a wooden pull-along duck, a spinning top, a hoop large enough
for an acrobat to jump through. In pots were a round bay
tree made of green felt, and two orange trees studded with
fruit of painted wood.

You could be anything here, said Veronica, pulling off her
black kid gloves. You could create a history for yourself and
make a landscape to fit it. Except it's so tatty.

Not in a photograph. It looks quite perfect in a photograph.
Not real, but charming and bland. Who wants reality in

weddings? Though now there is a trend to the outside world. Brides wanting photos in real parks with real ponds, peering at their not yet real hubbies round real trees. A dangerous business, to get away from the artificial so soon.

The studio was very hot from a gas fire, to stop the clients getting blue and goose-pimpled, so she took off her coat as well, even though she had her uniform on underneath, skimpy white cotton because her doctors' rooms were heated too. Mikelis took a piece of yellow brocade and wrapped her in it, binding it with a long garland of frayed white silk roses, sitting her in the carved chair. He set up a camera. Silk filters, he said, to hide the tat. You'll gleam and glow. Open your eyes. Don't smile. You'll look as glamorous as Garbo.

He took a lot of shots, then unwound the strings of roses, let fall the yellow brocade. She stood still. He kissed her. She kissed him.

He unbuttoned her uniform, not stopping at the waist. She helped him take her clothes off, then his. The *chaise longue* was in front of the fire. They lay on it and touched one another, feeling a kind of peace that all these months of walks and conversation had come at last to a logical end. Veronica remembered the first photographs he had ever taken, thinking I knew then that I would love this man. I just didn't know I knew.

Afterwards they lay together, the gas fire hissing ceaselessly and unheard, in the thick yellow light of the tasselled parchment shades. Veronica could think, so this is desire fulfilled. The pleasure and the sadness of it. And the wanting it to keep on happening.

She missed the last bus and had to go home in a taxi. This time her parents didn't seem too worried. At least they'd gone to bed. If we had a telephone I could ring you up, she said next day. George's daughters never missed an opportunity to point out how miserable he made all their lives by refusing to have a telephone. They could put up with no television and were used to no car, but they reckoned no telephone was turning them into old maids.

Any man worth his salt wouldn't let that put him off, said George. I courted your mother without a phone.

Nobody had one then. Everybody does now.

Mr Right will find you, said her father. I thought he had already.

What makes you think that? said Veronica, pushing her parents out of her private life.

Jack Hawley's gift

◆

Paris, early 1960s

Men go overseas too, said Mikelis to Veronica, because that was part of his experience. Leaving school, going to work, saving up: not getting educated, not going to university, as his mother wished, but turning the casual teenage present of a camera into a hobby, then a job. He took ship via Panama to Southampton, among the economy class crowds of young people going Home, just to have a look, not to stay, not for long, though among them were a number of potential expatriates. He wasn't going Home, having promised his mother that he would not go to Latvia in its present state of travesty. He went instead to Paris, taking a room in a small hotel in the Rue Cujas. It was very cheap. Its wooden stairs narrowed at the balustrade edges in a vertiginous but classical manner, and the *minuterie* always went off in the middle of the flight. Even if he pressed it on each landing and ran, he never made it to the next before the darkness clicked out.

In a nearby café, called L'Ecritoire, he came across Jack Hawley. He'd go in early in the day and drink a *grande crème*, strong coffee and hot milk, standing at the counter because it was cheaper and at that time of day he didn't need to rest. Jack sat in a booth, writing in a notebook. Every morning he was there, writing. Mikelis noticed him but didn't realise he wasn't French until he heard him asking for more coffee. He didn't speak to him; he didn't think that both being foreigners was a reason for claiming acquaintance. One day he was walking along the Boulevard Saint Michel and had stopped to read the menu outside one of the big brilliant corner cafés, the Cluny, when a voice behind him said, You can't afford it. Jack stood at his shoulder, mocking.

I wouldn't, even if I could, he replied angrily.

Well, of course you wouldn't.

And yet, it's front row seats for the spectacle. Mikelis pointed to the chairs on the terrace, glassed-in for the winter. They were arranged in rows, facing the street; customers at the tables didn't sit around them but in lines, looking outwards. I wouldn't mind being part of the audience for a bit.

Not a hope, said Jack. You're part of the show, here; it's you they're sitting there looking at. We need a different stage to be audience to, you and I.

Mikelis didn't consider then that it was odd that they should begin having this quite prickly conversation from the first. Jack engaged his attention and he responded; they went on from there.

Jack knew of a cheap place where you could get a lot to eat, and very good; they turned off the glittering boulevard where Mikelis had walked with his leather bag tucked tight under his arm and went through narrower darker streets to a restaurant whose yellow lights shone on thick glassware and paper tablecloths and brown jugs of wine and the bread baskets never got empty.

I'm a writer, said Jack. It was clear from his accent that he was American.

What do you write? Mikelis asked.

You've seen me, in the café, often enough.

Yes, said Mikelis, and was about to say, But, when Jack went on.

Are you going to tell me that you'd like to write a book one day when you have the time?

No. I haven't the slightest desire to write a book. Why should I? I've got much better things to do.

Jack shrugged. It's what people always say. I've hardly talked to a single person who wasn't going to write a book one day when they had the time. As though it were easy, normal. Like having children, something that everybody expects to do.

Well, I'm a single person, and I'm not.

Another thing people are always saying to me, said Jack. They say, here's a good story for you. And it never is. That'd make a good story, they say, but it never does.

What does, then? asked Mikelis.

That's my trade, knowing what does. Things you'd never guess at. Queer things. Ordinary things. A woman in a car with a brown paper bag of courgettes in her lap. Not anecdotes. Not the sort of funny things people tell you about. Fancying themselves raconteurs.

Mikelis thought of people telling him about scenery, saying to him it would have made a great photograph, and how they were always wrong. I know exactly what you mean, he said.

Jack sat in the café with little black cups of coffee and wrote in his notebook, which was small and black too. Mikelis stood at the counter drinking long milky ones. He'd have liked to know what Jack was seeing, scribbling so diligently. He would nod and tip his finger to his head, but never in welcome, and Mikelis knew enough about work not to interrupt. Once he went into the café in the afternoon and sat in a booth, being cold and tired; Jack was in his usual place, writing in his notebook; Mikelis could see that he used a fountain pen filled with pale brown ink, forming the letters with voluptuous care. It occurred to him that it was a small notebook, not offering much scope, but then he thought that he could have a number of them, could fill three or four a day, in fact, that of course it wouldn't be the same one all the time.

They often ate together; Jack knew a lot of good cheap

restaurants. He talked about his work, but always the process of it. The shape's the thing, he said; the world's full of stories, but it takes a writer to see the shapes of them. What about the words? asked Mikelis. Well, of course, said Jack. I need the words to write down the shapes.

He lived at the top of a thin mouldering building, in an attic sloped back in the roof so it couldn't be seen from the street. He never invited Mikelis up. Six floors, without a lift, he said. And the *minuterie* always goes off in the middle. Did you ever see *Kidnapped*? Scared me to death when I was a kid. There's a young boy and the wicked old uncle sends him to bed without a candle. Lucky, as he goes up the stairs there's a flash of lightning and he sees that they just stop, there's a bloody great yawning chasm in front of him. That's what I think, when I go up the stairs in the Rue des Fossés Saint Jacques; maybe there'll be a yawning chasm and no lightning flash to show it to me.

Are you going to write a story about it?

No, but you can take a photograph. Be my guest.

I'd like to, said Mikelis. He walked up his own stairs in the Rue Cujas and when the light went off felt the cold air of chasms at his feet. Against his will they hesitated, wanting to be sure the steps were solid before their weight went down. He held his hand against the wall, where the steps were wider, and thought about Jack and the shapes of stories. It seemed logical to suppose that photographs were about shapes too, but somehow the idea didn't move him; he couldn't say, firmly, as Jack did, it's a matter of perceiving the shapes, it just sounded dull, not important, and anyway it had to mean something different from what Jack was getting at. Jack's words could open a chasm in a staircase, for Mikelis as well as himself, but the camera wasn't interested. Nevertheless, he did photograph his stairs, and caught the queer asymmetry of their plastered giddy winding round the stairwell. He showed Jack, who whistled. And you walk up those every day? Rather you than me, chum. And yet they'd served for years measured maybe in hundreds, their build was sturdy, they'd never fallen down, nor tipped off weary climbers. Though maybe they'd tripped

them. Maybe people had fallen down them, in fights, or
clumsily, or pushed. A lot of anger could fly about in several
hundred years. As photographed there was some evil intent
in these stairs. Or in Mikelis. Shapes was not what either of
them was about.

Jack never talked about being published; that wasn't a subject
that came up. He was a writer, he sat in a café and wrote;
Mikelis wondered if there were ever finished manuscripts, deep
piles of typescript parcelled up and posted off to editors, but
never asked. They behaved like travellers who happen to have
sat near one another in a train; they look out the windows
at fields of wheat, the distant towers of a cathedral, the villages
and towns where sometimes the train stops and people get
on and off, observing an old man with a bicycle who waits
at a crossing, children fishing in a canal, a broad river brimming
with mirror-coloured light in the dusk. All these things they
talk about, but they don't discuss themselves, or the train,
or the beginnings and purposes of their journey. Though
occasionally there is a glimpse like a label on luggage offering
a clue.

One day after they'd had lunch together in one of his cheap
restaurants Jack said, I need a walk. Counteract the *frites*.
They went down to the Seine at the Quai d'Austerlitz and
walked along its banks. The river flowed thickly in the direction
they were walking, carrying debris of chunks of wood and
branches. It seemed a natural sort of detritus, not the dirt
and discards of a careless city, not bottles and papers and plastic
bags but fragments that had come from farther away, from
some innocent pastoral countryside of shepherds and farriers
in villages and joiners practising an intricate craft. The river
bank was wide and quiet, the hum of the city was above them
and out of sight. A cold wind blew, but the stone walls and
pavement coddled the warmth of the sun. There were barges
berthed alongside. Some had geraniums, not yet flowering, and
lace curtains; their small paned windows allowed glimpses of
comfortable living rooms. Mikelis loitered in order to observe
the light inside them, the muted colours and patterns of the
lives they contained.

You are a voyeur by trade, said Jack.

Of course; aren't you?

Mentally, maybe, but not with your prying eye. I want to know, not see.

A man in a red and yellow jumper sat on a stool on the deck of one of the barges scrubbing sneakers in a bucket of soapsuds. A woman stood eating an apple, staring across the water.

That'd be a good thing to do, said Mikelis. I'd like to live on a barge for a while.

I did it for a year, said Jack. Plied the Seine in a sand barge. It's overrated.

Why?

Dull.

I'd imagine you'd be able to get a lot of writing done.

The shapes of things as seen from a barge are rarely conducive to writing, said Jack. On the other hand, young Mik could take his piccies.

Mikelis was silent. Again he wondered what Jack wrote about. Did he invent things? Create complicated structures that were limited only by his imagination? But then why live in Paris? He was suggesting that places mattered, that a barge on the river wasn't good. Jack must get something out of being here. Maybe there was a process, mysterious, chemical perhaps. Maybe the elements of light and air, the minerals in the buildings, the exhalations of the trees, the particular pollution of car exhausts all combined to make a kind of potion that you breathed in and that caused it to be a good place to work in. Mikelis pictured an imagination feeding off its surroundings but producing work quite different, like a worm eating mulberry leaves and spinning silk.

I'm beginning to think Paris is a terrible place to try to be a photographer in, he said. It's all been done before. It's stunning, it makes you want to grab it, but what can you do with it, that hasn't already been done? And as well you're a foreigner; it doesn't belong to you. Everybody wants to make it their own, but we're all interlopers.

They were coming up to the Pont de la Tournelle. Its golden stones spanned the river in a perfect shallow arch, across to the Île Saint Louis, and through this lovely curve Notre Dame could be seen.

Look at that, said Mikelis, camera to eye. Perfect. And so bloody hackneyed it's useless. I can't make anything of it. I'm not in the picture postcard business.

Don't knock the postcard, boy.

They were walking up the steps to the bridge. There was a strong stink of urine, reminding that the dark nights of these river places would be quite different from this sunny afternoon.

Nothing wrong with postcards, said Mikelis. They're just not my trade.

Here, catch this, said Jack. He was pulling his overcoat off, but it wasn't that he meant. He dropped it on the ground, jumped on the parapet of the bridge and stood posed for a moment like a fascist statue, handsome and boldly carved, then with a movement complicated as choreography turned and dived into the water. Mikelis got his camera back to his eye and began snapping. He leant over the bridge, laughing with the excitement of this mad act, determined not to miss any moments of it. He realised he'd lost Jack from the camera's lens and pulled it away to search for him with the naked eye; Jack was still lost. The river flowed, pale brown, greenish, carrying its innocent debris to the sea. Jack was nowhere to be seen.

Mikelis grabbed the overcoat and rushed down the stairs to the quay, skidding on the sour micturitic moss, shouting, Help! and He's drowning, He's drowning, in a voice squeaky as a nightmare. At first nobody paid much attention but then a woman walking an Afghan dog took charge and sent a passerby to telephone while she ran with Mikelis along the river bank, trying to work out where Jack's dive could have taken him. People began to gather, the crowd that always waits in the antechambers of violent actions, waiting for the spectacle to begin, ready in their desire for drama to turn any scene into a stage. They pointed with their fingers, murmured their rhubarb background of enquiry. Mikelis saw a dark shape turning like debris in the flowing water. He pulled off his own overcoat, shoes, camera, left them on the bank and jumped carefully in, feet first. The current was strong and the water cold, but both of these were familiar from the snow rivers of his childhood. He reached Jack easily enough, the momentum of the river helping him as it carried Jack along with it too, though he had to keep heaving himself out above its level in order to see where he was. But trying to swim back across the current with an unconscious water-weighted body was much harder. He turned him over and crooked his elbow round his neck in the classic life-saving method but Jack kept slipping and the water would slop over his face. It suddenly occurred to Mikelis that he wasn't going to make it, that maybe he should let Jack go and try to save himself. He didn't know anything about the Seine, whether it was treacherous. The Thames he knew people used for killing themselves, they dived off bridges, Waterloo Bridge was a popular one, and drowned in the cold and the black. He didn't know about the Seine, only the cold and the black heavy as lead liquid lead where gnomes swim in earth like fish in water . . .

◆ ◆ ◆

Maybe the police thought they were describing what had happened, but he didn't ever understand it. He'd come round, but vaguely, in an ambulance and could only ever imagine the process of getting there from where he was drowning; pulled out, no doubt, Jack too, though he didn't seem to be here in the ambulance with him. He had no notion of his rescuers: police, bystanders, the damp men now tending him, or the manner of their saving. The black water had swallowed up memory. The audience on the bank had seen the show but the chief actors knew nothing of it.

Jack they told him about. He was lucky, said a policeman sternly. He hit his head, on what we don't know, a log of wood I should suppose, there were such things about, and phht, out, drowned, done. The Seine is not always so kind to those who ask her favours.

Mikelis had to run these words through his head a second time to understand them, and then he realised that the policeman thought Jack had intended to kill himself and been lucky, succeeded. That all that monstrous swim back across the current had been with a willingly dead man. He said, No, no, that's not what happened, and tried to explain, but the policeman said, What? and went through it again in his heavy sarcastic voice. It was recorded as suicide, it was official, it was finished. No need to prosecute a dead man. The woman with the Afghan dog had seen it all. It was brave of Mikelis to try to rescue this person tired of life, but foolish. He'd had his luck too, a lot of luck in the river that day; his had been not drowning.

They showed him Jack's things: the fountain pen, cigarettes, lighter, wallet, black notebook. Everything capable of holding water was sodden. The notebook was a watery brown blur; the elegant sepia-coloured ink had run, not a word could be read. The spongy pages tore more easily than they turned. Yes, that body had owned these objects. Mikelis lay in the hospital for several days feverish and weak-headed; his own life seemed a fragile thing that might float away out of his reach and all his frantic swimming would not bring it to shore. Once he'd got a certificate for life-saving, but it would be out of date now. He'd been a child at the time.

There turned out to be a wife, who came over from England. She didn't seem to be surprised. It was bound to happen sooner or later, she said. Yes, she knew it wasn't suicide, not an intention at that moment, but doing suicidal things was bound to be successful sooner or later. She showed a calm melancholy grief, shaped by the satisfaction of seeing this episode, her marriage, some long dialogue with Jack that only a death could end, seeing it completed, with its own logic, unsurprising.

She arranged to have Jack cremated and collected his ashes in an urn. Mikelis was afraid she would ask him to go with her and sprinkle them in the Seine (it must be illegal, imagine the pollution if everybody did it) but she didn't. She asked him if he wanted any of Jack's things. He thought of the notebooks, the piles of black notebooks traced with sepia ink, the bundles of typescript waiting to be posted off to the publisher; he didn't want to find out whether they existed or not.

No, he said. I don't need any mementoes, any keepsakes.

I won't forget him. He looked steadily at Jack's wife, her capable grieving calm. He was a writer, you know. He wrote every day, in the café.

Oh yes, I know. I will do everything necessary there. There will be no problems in that direction.

Afterwards he wondered if he had seen compassion in her eyes. Would it have been for Jack, or him? For the non-existence of the black notebooks, or his belief in them? He wondered if he should have made sure of their yes or no, until he remembered that Jack had said he was a writer and that would do. Doubt was a choice that didn't have to be made.

Now Mikelis carries the death of Jack around with him as other people carry the photograph of a lover in a wallet. (Which Mikelis never did.) Forgetting it's there, often, or other times coming across it accidentally, looking at the secret smiling lines of the face. Does he love me? Do I possess him? Or maybe taking it out and examining it, holding it, with a little brim of affection saying, This is my dear one safe in my heart for ever.

He told Veronica about Jack, in those early passionate days when you long to give your beloved the gift of everything that has happened to you. He discussed his guilt. It was not my fault, he said to Veronica. I cannot see that I am to blame. It was Jack alone who did it. I would have prevented him. And yet, had I not been there . . .

There was always *and yet* . . . Whatever logic said, there was always *and yet* . . .

It was his nature, said Veronica. You have to see it as his nature. If not then, some other time, some other way.

As his wife had said: It was bound to happen, sooner or later.

But he didn't mean to die over it. He dived into a deep river; he must have expected to swim out. He liked being alive.

The risk was in his nature. It would have caught up with him, sooner or later. Veronica tightened her arms around him. You could even say it was a gift he had.

◆ ◆ ◆

When he developed the film, for camera, shoes, overcoat had

not got lost in the catastrophe, had gone with him in the ambulance and turned up plastic-bagged at the appropriate moment, and he always imagined the woman with the Afghan dog directing this, saving these belongings from potential petty thieves, so that several times he'd walked along the Quai de la Tournelle, hoping he would meet her, looking for the sign of the lolloping golden-haired dog, but he never did. When he developed the film it was to find that Jack appeared in none of the frames; there was not a single picture of him. Each shot had just missed him, each time he must have been just out of range; not even a foot, or a hand, not even a finger. But the pictures . . . there was Notre Dame, you could see its bones, the flying buttresses holding up the nave were thin strong bones like a powerful ribcage . . . They were good, these photographs, not hackneyed, not the familiar souvenir of tourists, the sad evidence of the impotent desire to possess. You looked at Notre Dame and you might never have seen it before; never had, like this.

It's a gift Jack's given him. After that, whenever a shot seems boring, dull, too safely in the footprints of others, and Mikelis remembers him, posed like a statue, the mocking skilful pirouette, the spring, the dive across and through that ancient flowering river- and city-scape, it can happen that he will make his picture work, that Jack's missing manic figure fills it with energy, the vibration of a presence that is there, just out of sight.

Gelatin silver

———————◆———————

Do you know why I became a photographer? Mikelis asked Dane. It was because of a word. When I was a child. I was looking at a book we had at home, pictures of Latvia it was, very arty, and I noticed the caption, after the bit telling you the subject, Fishermen on the shores of the estuary at Riga, something like that, and then it said, *Gelatin silver*. That was the word. Silver. The lands of the Baltic are bathed in silvery light, said my mother. And here it was. The light in the picture was just that, silvery. And I thought it would have been because of the gelatin silver, some amazing precious technique. By the time I found out that this was just the process, entirely everyday, the naming of the chemical means of capturing the image, started off by old Daguerre and his silver salts, well, it didn't matter.

That's why I've always loved black and white photography. Though when I was young we used to tint it. All those brides

with blue dot eyes and red bow mouths. Quite evil. Brides
. . . puppets in scenery.

There were long pauses in the old man's speech. Each time
Dane wondered if a word was needed from him, a kind of
triggering of the mechanism of remembering, but it could also
be in effect a sabotage. He waited, the tape recorder whirred
softly.

I wish I could have seen the Baltic, the silvery light. My
mother used to talk about it whenever she recalled her life
with my father. My father . . . it's funny how you think of
your father when you're old: patriarch, progenitor, all that.
And yet now I am old enough to be his father, his grandfather
even when you think of the age he died. Or maybe not, because
of course I don't know that. I don't know when he died. Just
that he was deported by the Russians in 1940, for printing
unapproved election material. What a crime, eh. They might
have executed him straight away, or he might have perished
on the long march into Russia, or survived for years in some
labour camp. I hope for the quick end, but I'll never know.

Mikelis pressed his fingers into his cheeks, like a sculptor
moulding. When he stopped his voice came out with a faint
wobble.

I didn't know him, either, you know. He was arrested before
I was born. And maybe dead. Perhaps I am a posthumous
child. My mother said I resemble him; I remember on my
fortieth birthday I looked in the mirror and thought, is this
my father I see here?

You know how there are great loves. The kind you read
about, so powerful that they demand to become stories and
belong to other people. That's what my mother had with my
father. Oh, she didn't talk about it, she just talked about their
work, what they did, in the two decades that Latvia was free.
She'd speak very flatly, very plainly; when I was young I didn't
see that if she'd allowed herself the slightest quiver of emotion
she'd have lost control, she kept her feeling locked up . . . you'd
have thought it was some savage supernatural animal, caged
and bound and gagged and cowed by the right charms and
amulets and fetishes. Like garlic and crosses and silver nails

and wooden stakes where two roads meet, not trusting just one to work.

I used to think that I would be like that and that when I met Veronica I loved her with that same savage passion. I'd think of losing her and stick pins in my fingers to change the subject of the pain. And you've seen how I photographed her. Silver gelatin, oho. Adoration, more like. Rose-coloured adoration. My eyes would water when I looked at them. Then I'd see them through these wavery tears and make the pictures look like that. We're all tarts and prostitutes, whores and sluts and their pimps too, blithely selling love to art. But that didn't kill it. She had affairs you know. So did I. I was jealous. That didn't kill it either. When it came to the point, neither of us wanted anyone else. We belonged. We just grew comfortable. Suburban love, undangerous. Did I make her happy? I irritated her. So she did me. Prosperity does that. Comfort. I couldn't bear it when she died. I miss her. But see how I talk about her. Melancholy. Elegiac. No savage beasts to be kept locked up. I think of that flat voice of my mother's: *When he got a new book of poems Janis would work all night. I'd help him . . .*

Of course there was my mother's huge anger. I never had that. I didn't want it. She tried to pass it on. We got letters from the people left behind, telling us about their lives *. . . Remember what our old father used to say, when the liberators had broken into our homeland. He said, from now on you will see nothing good, our golden age is over, the people will become like fish in the water and will swallow each other.* They were terrible, those letters, the old people with not enough to eat, their animals taken away, their land confiscated plot by plot, until there wasn't enough left to grow potatoes to keep them alive. *You squat like a bird on a branch and don't know when someone will come and chase you away again.* The thing was we couldn't help. Money would be taken and if you sent things like warm boots or coats the authorities would make them pay such huge customs duty that they couldn't afford to collect them.

My mother's anger would grow greater and greater, and she would lock my father's love away tighter and tighter. Her aunt wrote, deliberately making her handwriting shaky and almost illegible, as though she were a stupid illiterate woman, she who had always prided herself on her clarity of hand and mind, so the censors wouldn't be able to read it. She said: *Soon all the old generation will be gone, they are the ones who still remember the bright years of our nation's independence, therefore they are disliked by the regime and their extermination is facilitated in every way.* You could hear her heart breaking as she wrote. *And the children are turned to crime, the regime imports criminals in order to break down the morals of our oppressed nation and destroy all memory of the old ways.* It's genocide, my mother cried. Physical and cultural genocide. She copied these sentences out in her beautiful writing on white cardboard with coloured inks, she made texts out of them and hung them on the walls of our house. First in Latvian, then when she saw that I took no notice, in English. Against my will I read them; you know how you can't not read things, no matter how hard you try, but still I refused them, even as I got them by heart. I was a New Zealand boy and in my country we could buy enough to eat at the shop and what mattered was the cricket game at lunch-time and winning the best marbles and not losing your own and going to Billy Noble's because his mother had a refrigerator and gave you icecream.

Other kids had texts on the wall saying, *God is Love* and *The Peace that Passeth all Understanding.* Our house had: *We squat like birds on a branch* . . .

She made me promise never to go to Latvia, you know. Free Latvians were encouraged to visit, but it turned out to be very restricted. The whole country was out of bounds except for Riga and one or two resorts. They didn't dare let outsiders see what disasters they'd made in the countryside. Their relatives had to come to Riga to see them and that was difficult because they were afraid to leave the land. It might not be there when they got back. Tourists had to be in their hotels by midnight and were trailed by the secret police. I promised, I never did go, never saw the lands of the Baltic bathed in their silvery light. Even when everything changed, I still stuck to my word.

I think of her, in the small boat; she would never tell me about it, I have to imagine it, in that small boat propelled by love and fury, that's how I see it, and nothing silvery about the light, blackness and cold and the storm whipping up the waves, the *mare clausum* can be very violent you know, and this little boat, with her and me and the cousins, impelled by the force of her rage through the blackness and the storm, cleaving its path straight through to the New World.

And here we are. In the New World. Eva's been back, you know. It was just as my mother said. She hated it. I wish my mother could have known Eva. She'd recognise the rage. Eva's the Latvian-in-exile I would never be. As best she can.

The thrown pearls

◆

Newcastle, 1967

On Saturday Veronica and Martin were going to a wedding. At their age this happened a lot. The present was bought and she had a new suit.

She didn't know the bride; the groom was a colleague of Martin's. Doesn't she look lovely? he kept saying to Veronica. Yes, she said, though she didn't think so. The dress was too fussy, white velvet with fur and sequined embroidery. The bridesmaids' dresses were similar but red. Very cheering for a winter's day, said Martin. Veronica wondered if the bride were a virgin, whether she'd got good at sex or was about to start. She thought of the slow divesting of finery in some anonymous luxurious hotel bedroom. And after they were supposed to live together for the rest of their lives.

The bride walked into church to some Handel. Fabulous, said Martin. So much nicer than hackneyed old Here Comes the Bride. Fair fat and wide, muttered Veronica. The girl leant on her father's arm, both quite skilful at the step-pause step-pause process up the aisle that looked as though you really didn't want to arrive. At the end of the service they had the wedding march from *A Midsummer Night's Dream*, very pealing and triumphant on the organ. Superb, said Martin. Very nicely done, very nicely done.

By the time they got out of the church a man was directing the bridal party into shape for group photographs. It filled the steps so the guests had to walk round the outside. They formed a circle of their own, watching. The man was wearing a brown suit, with paler stripes, wide in the shoulders and the leg. Martin sniggered. He looks like a co-respondent, he said. A gangster, said Veronica. That's not a camera, it's a gun. Suddenly the man turned round and she saw that it was Mikelis. The brown suit had altered his shape entirely. He winked at her.

Probably just does something boring like selling insurance, said Martin. For the last thirty years by the looks of it. Veronica didn't think this very funny. Good heavens, said Martin. That's that friend of your parents—what's his name?

Mikelis.

Up close he was still himself, his smooth pale face, his round eyelids, his fair hair flopping. Hello, she said, standing, looking into his face. He smiled and looked at her. His hand smoothed the broad lapel of the brown suit. An ultimatum, from Neville, he said.

It's amazing, she said, not looking at it.

From Saint Vincent de Paul. He pronounced it in the French way.

Ah, she nodded. The latest from Paris.

Martin was beside her then and Mikelis took their photograph. Have to rush, he said. Back to the studio. What shall it be? Hymen's grotto? Or the red velvet *chaise longue*?

Veronica blushed and turned her head so that the brim of her hat hid her face.

Funny sort of chap, said Martin. That suit.

His boss said he had to get one.

It's absolutely hideous.

I think that might be why he bought it.

All the way to the reception Martin whistled the wedding march from *A Midsummer Night's Dream*. Great music, he said at intervals. He kissed the bride, toasted everybody in champagne, chatted up the bridesmaids and the mothers of the happy couple (he kept calling them that) and constantly told the groom how much he envied him.

He'll think you've got designs on Shirley if you don't stop, she hissed. But nothing could squash his exuberance. All this boisterousness made her tired; she'd have liked to go home early. They stayed to the end and Martin was disappointed that she didn't catch the bouquet, though the bride had clearly thrown it at one of the Father Christmas bridesmaids. I was sure you would, he repeated several times. The flowers were coloured with *chalk*, she said. Pink and blue *chalk*.

When they were going home over Memorial Drive, Veronica cried, Look! The moon on the water. Let's stop and have a look at it.

Martin groaned. Ugh. That's where the hoi polloi hang out. Necking in their horrible cars. Wouldn't it be much nicer in the flat?

There's no moon shining on the sea in your flat.

He pulled into a space on the cliff above the end of Bar Beach, where the rock platform was. A low wall protected them from driving over the edge.

Martin leant towards her, difficult in the narrow lumpy space of the Healey. She curled into the corner of the door, holding on to her handbag. Out of it she took her pearls in their box. He'd already asked her why she wasn't wearing them. Because they don't go with my suit, she lied. Now she was giving them back to him.

He didn't understand.

I just think I shouldn't keep them. They're too expensive.

That's my business. I want you to have them. Nothing's too expensive for you. We're getting married, aren't we?

Are we? Who says?

Oh come on, Vee. Everybody knows. You know.

I don't, she said, though she did. From the moment of the

pearls, no, earlier, she'd known Martin was bent on marrying. His education, his job, his car. Obviously the next thing he'd acquire was a wife. His intentions had been entirely honourable from the beginning. And acceptable. She pressed her hand against the walnut dashboard of the car. She was being dishonest.

Martin, I'm not ready to get married yet. This wasn't entirely true, either. I like you, I'm very fond of you. This was absolutely true. But I don't think there should be a question of marriage between us. Yet.

Why had she added yet? It was a cruel comfort. She put the box of pearls in his hand. I'd better give you these back, it's false pretences.

For a moment their hands bickered over them, both rejecting. Then she put them on the top of the dashboard.

I was going to take you to buy a ring. I saw a sapphire in Caldwell's, with pearls around it. I was going to say meet me at lunch-time, see what you thought. She was afraid he was going to cry.

He picked up the box off the dashboard, shook the pearls into his hand, opened the car door, jumped out and hurled them high over the cliff. They turned slowly over, luminous in the moonlight. They seemed to take a long time to fall, hanging in the air like a thread of moonspawn. That's where moons come from, she thought. They hatch out of pearls.

They were both too shocked to say anything. Martin started the car and drove her home.

Knowing

◆

Newcastle, late 1960s

Remember Dostoevsky, said George. Hardly anybody he said this to did, except Ivan, but it didn't matter because they couldn't get a word in anyway. George spoke beautifully. He had a pleasing voice and modulated it slow and fast, soft and louder, persuasive or hectoring. He could be indignant or full of awe. One of the things his mother had had in mind for him to be was a parson, and he certainly would have preached a good sermon. He used pauses, and people thought, in the next one I'll jump in and say something, but they never did, because the pause was as much a part of the speaking as the words were, and interrupting it would have been a rough thing to do. Remember Dostoevsky, said George, and it didn't matter if you didn't because he went on to tell you. That moment in *The Brothers Karamazov. I want to be there when everyone suddenly understands what it has all been for.*

Ivan wanted to say, Well, it isn't really Dostoevsky, is it? It's his character, the person he created, who says those words. But there was not a chance for that. George's pause quivered in the air, as uninterruptible as the flow of his voice. Then he went on.

When everyone suddenly understands . . . But when is that going to be? Sometime in the future? In the next life? Or will we have to wait until after the Resurrection? . . . Why not *now*? We want to understand *now*. It's too important to have to wait.

And that's the thing about this study I do. It offers answers now. Not faith. Knowledge. You don't have to trust in faith. You know.

Sometimes George did make converts. People joined the Order. Not his daughters. Not Ivan or Mikelis either, though they at least listened. Nor Martin, who slipped away. George didn't push. It had to be a person's own decision.

Newspaper

◆

Newcastle, 1967

Lickspittles. Lackeys. They're all the same these Liberal coves. George shook the newspaper as though it were one of them. If they're not just seeing dear old Betty Windsor passing by, then they're going all the way with some American hack. Haven't got an idea of their own in their heads.

Veronica wasn't listening. She was thinking of telling her mother that she'd be out again, with Mikelis. She'd wait until her father was gone, until she herself was going; kiss her mother, rush to the door, pause: Oh, falsely casual, Mum, won't be home tonight for tea, and off out the door. Not that her mother would question, say why Mikelis, why not Martin, who always comes to the house, having left a decent interval for showering and changing and the creation of an evening person scented and desirable, to be collected by an equally polished escort and carried away in a car as covetable as the woman it transports. Her mother would say none of these things, would say, Oh yes, and wait, and Veronica would see the space and want to fill it with explanations which would be too complicated and explain nothing. Better to rush off out of the space and leave her mother to her own thinking. Which would not follow her into a studio full of dusty looming objects waiting for a camera to turn them into the furniture of important moments. Where Veronica and Mikelis lay on balding velvet surrounded by these messages of bliss and achievement and shaped their own story among them. She sighed, for the innocence of parents and the simplicity of their expectations, and shook pepper into her egg, pushing it down with the spoon. The white was sloppy; she hated sloppy egg white.

Too much pepper, my girl. Not good for you. Destroys the lining of the stomach. George folded the paper and laid it on the table.

I love pepper.

Her father stood up and with his finger jabbed the photograph of Holt and Johnson grinning together. Look at that pair of goons. But then the country hasn't got an idea in its head either or it wouldn't vote for the beggars.

Mrs Gray brought his sandwiches wrapped in a cotton napkin and he stowed them in his small leather port. He put on his coat and hat and lit his pipe, tapping the top of the bowl with the matchbox. The rich fruit cake scent of the tobacco he mixed himself wafted into the room. This and eggs and toast were the smell of mornings in the Gray household, and everybody took them for granted. He kissed his wife and set out to walk to work; the pipe would last the journey.

Veronica put more pepper on her egg. Food so bland and pale needed pepper to give it a bit of life. She glanced at the folded paper. Underneath the grinning leaders was a small headline: *Unconscious After Cliff Foot Ordeal*. She read that a man had been found on the rocks at Bar Beach, suffering from a broken leg, broken ribs, concussion and exposure. Mr Ron Bourke, a fisherman, said he had been cutting cunjevoi with his companions when they discovered the man at the foot of the cliff on Monday morning. It was thought he had been there for twenty-four hours. Mr Martin Limeburner, twenty-eight, had not yet regained consciousness. His car had been found at the top of the cliff.

She saw the pearls turning high in the air, a thread of tiny moons wrenched angrily out of orbit, saw them falling slowly out of sight over the edge of the cliff. Martin had followed them. Martin who loved her and wanted to marry her. Martin had tried to kill himself.

The runny egg white curdled in her throat. She felt sick. Martin. Good old Martin with his conventional courting. She hadn't thought he'd take it so hard. There were other girls as pretty and nice as she, to grace the Healey, dine at Oliver's, celebrate the weddings of friends until it was time for their own. She'd expected him to be disappointed, of course. She hadn't at all understood him. She was the one he'd wanted; she, Veronica, he loved. Life wasn't worth living without her. And she'd been too shallow to see it. Had supposed him simply fond of her. It gave her a shock, to see herself so shallow.

Then she thought, did he mean it to work, or is this the result he intended? To hurt himself; to injure, not kill. Is he threatening, blackmailing, punishing? She pictured his death at the foot of the cliffs, where the waves splashed, the massive fleshy stranger among the intricate life of the rock pools. The crabs scuttling over him, the molluscs lifting their muscular feet to walk around him, fish patterned like stones nibbling at his fingers. His own in its way delicate life out of scale and clumsy there. Its function lost. Everything out of character, from the first furious throwing of the necklace high in the air, to the later meditated throwing of himself.

She saw his death . . . his death-wish, or maybe it was his death threat: he presented it as on a plate to her, a rich dish she couldn't refuse.

She ran out to the lavatory and vomited up the slimy egg, spitting and spitting to get rid of its clinging jellyfish threads. The taste in her mouth was the sea creatures her childhood had kept in glass jars intending to cherish, rotting.

I'm never going to eat another soft egg in my life, she said

to her mother. Always hard boiled from now on. She shuddered
from head to foot, all her flesh repudiating.

Mrs Gray was looking at the paper. Martin . . . whatever
can have happened to Martin?

I suppose he jumped off the cliff.

Her mother looked at her with narrow eyes. Martin?

Veronica shrugged. She thought of saying, he wanted to
marry me, but hearing the words in her head as they would
sound aloud she kept quiet. She said nothing. The space grew,
one of those spaces of her mother's which asked nothing, did
not pry, which her daughters could not bear not to fill. Veronica
began to cry. Her mother put her arms round her. He's young
and strong, she said. He'll pull through. She rocked gently
backwards and forwards. Veronica nestled into this little plump
woman, so much smaller than she was, but the comfort did
not really work. She knew her mother supposed her to be
crying for Martin, when her tears were for herself. She was
thinking I will have to marry Martin if I have allowed him
to love me as much as this. She could no longer go to the
red velvet couch that waited patient as an animal to carry
her and her lover away. That was what she cried for, and
her mother ignorant couldn't comfort.

She missed the bus and was late for work. Doctor McGovern
waited, impatient to begin the first IVP. The patient already
lay anonymous in a white smock. As she set up her machines
she saw her sallow cheek, her wiry grey hair. It was Aunt
Lily.

Lily and the washing

———————◆———————

Newcastle, 1941

Lily poked the boiling clothes
with the spongy copper stick. They bubbled, the steam rose,
the sheets whitened. She began to heave them out into the
tub of cold rinsing water, standing to the side so the boiling
water didn't directly splash her feet.

Joe came up behind her and touched her shoulder. She turned
and he picked her up and carried her into the bedroom. He
was freshly washed after the night shift, pink and scrubbed,
smelling of Sunlight soap. In the bedroom he stood her on
the floor in front of him. Even if he'd been speaking he wouldn't
have said a word. He took the pins out of her hair, pulling
its fine frizz about her face and neck, ravelling his fingers
through it. He undid her soapy apron, slid off her cardigan
with its rolled-up water-dabbled sleeves, her print wrapover
dress, her thick pink swami silk slip, her bloomers. He stood
looking for a while, then picked her up and lay her on the

bed, dropping her worn wet shoes on the floor, rolling her gartered stockings down and off. Then he removed his own clothes. Still he stood and looked at her, his eyes glittering, his teeth just plucking at his bottom lip, his mouth faintly turning down into a sketch of its old smile. He began to touch her, starting with her head, her eyebrows, the bones and hollows of her cheeks, the curve of her nostrils, her lips, her chin and curling ears. His fingers were gentle, quivering a little, slow; he watched them. Watched them move down her neck, her shoulders, the long silky hairs under her arms. Hold the mounds of her breasts, their globular weight, tickle the nipples. Stroke the little rolls where her waist had been. And so down through every cleft and groove and crease of her flesh, his glittering eyes watching, his own erection growing taller and stronger. She was not allowed to speak, or to move, though occasionally she gave a little involuntary ripple, but she could touch him with her eyes, let them linger on his curving mouth, the grey stiff hairs on his tanned chest, his sex. He spread her legs, his fingers moved down her thighs, delineating the little pads of fat behind her knees, the swell of her calves, pausing at the points of her ankles, holding the arches of her feet, her toes. By this time all her flesh hummed and sang, strung tight as a zither, longing for him to play any tune he would. Her juices ran, she felt them leaking down on to the counterpane.

He knelt between her legs, his fingers dallying now in the curls of her hair, dabbling in her moisture, straying inside. Once she had felt like a virgin on a stone and he the knife-wielding priest; she still felt like that but now with hardly any fear. She knew the only knife would be his penis; she couldn't wait, she couldn't bear it, she would have to grab him but still he held back touching and withdrawing till she wanted to scream with desire. Until he finally came in and she could wrap her legs and arms around him and hold him tight and still he teased, hardly moving, delaying him and her, penetrating and pulling back and she came and he laughed and she came again and still he played his pleasure and hers, the long zither notes vibrating in unison, the swelling organs flesh and music resonant with praise. Until the ritual was completed.

Afterwards he stayed in her arms, glittering eyes hooded, the stubble of his cheek prickling, his eyelashes dark on his worn brown skin. He slept and she kissed his face. She hadn't had a chance to put her diaphragm in. She hoped it wouldn't mean number six. Not with young Rick just started school.

The boiling washing waited.

Knitting

———————— ◆ ————————

George no longer thought of
Lily as the dusky-throated Tiger of their youth. After she
married Joe Sullivan he didn't see her for years. He was still
up north at the time of the wedding, that provided the excuse
for not going. He sent her messages when the children were
born, cards with notes for her, not Joe. Children. Six of them,
you'd think they were Catholics. Lily put on weight. She was
a big woman, still handsome, brown and weatherbeaten from
all the gardening she did. Great vegetables she grew. George
only ever went to her house when their mother was dying
there, and made sure it was when Joe was on the night shift
at the railways. He felt guilty about everybody being stuffed
into such a small place, but at least some of the kids had
left home, and the others were old enough to be quiet, not
like his little daughters. There were occasional visits between
the two sisters-in-law, who didn't always feel bound by male

feuds. The women thought cousins should know one another, that blood ties should be maintained, even when the effort had to be made by those who had no such connection themselves. And long past the days of any acquaintance between their children they continued to entertain one another to lunch and keep the family gossip flowing on both sides.

George still mourned for Victor. He couldn't give up the terrible vision of Lily married to him, and happy, and his friend. Joe made him sick. I don't know how Lily can stand the beggar, he said to his wife. It's a mystery to me. George gave the second Sullivan girl away when she got married; Joe refused to have anything to do with it. Anne walked down the aisle, step-slide, step-slide, on George's arm and when the minister said, Who giveth this woman to be married to this man? he replied in a firm clear voice, I do, and wondered what sort of a cove would let another man do that for him. Lily was beautifully gracious and behaved as though everything was just so.

Sometimes Joe didn't speak to anyone for months on end, he shut himself in the sitting room and lived there. They had to take his meals in on a tray; once, not liking the look of it he came out and dropped the tray upside down on the floor. When he was talking his voice boomed out: Lil, where are my shirts? Lil, what have you done with my book? Lil, what's happened to my cup of tea? Lil, who's taken the mustard? His eyes still glittered; his Irish tones could be thick and sweet as the strong milky tea he demanded each member of his family learn to make exactly right, those Irish tones saying How about a kiss for your uncle Joe, his words as physical as the act itself, sharing the moisture and the pressure of his curling red lips, but his eyes were sharp as glass piercing them, the girls turned their faces away. He was always so charming on those visits, he pressed them to take chocolates, cake, biscuits, glasses of port, but seeing Aunt Lily's eyes carefully looking away, you wondered whether it was all so jolly as it seemed. Uncle Joe looked at her, and urged and urged, the muscles in his arms were hard as rope, it wasn't really fun at all.

When he played Scrabble with his wife and unmarried

daughter he sulked unless he won; he spent a long time thinking and looked up other people's words in the dictionary. The women knitted while they waited for their turns. They weren't allowed to speak while he deliberated.

Veronica imagined the noise of the tin tray falling on the floor. The clang of it, the shatter of china and clatter of cutlery. It reminded her of the shunting, Uncle Joe was a shunter, in the dark a clashing of trains, a slow clanking clamour of them as they came together and parted. She loved trains because they meant holidays, they were lines connecting you to distant promise-filled places, but shunting was different, it was loneliness and danger and dark cold noise. Her father said I don't know how the beggar can stand it. You'd think he could have found something better in, how long is it, must be getting on for thirty years. Makes you wonder what can be going on in his head. Unless, George rarely let himself consider, so much was that the outside didn't matter. Mostly he thought, a cranky old coot.

He would never forgive him for taking Lily away from Vic who was dead now, some fool of a truck, some criminal cutting a corner on a dark northern road, Vic on the bike never standing a chance. Vic would be alive if Lily had married him, he wouldn't have been on that murderous night road, George wouldn't have lost a good friend, Lily would be leading a decent life.

Why did Auntie Lily marry Uncle Joe if he's such an awful person? Why does she stay with him? She should run away, Veronica said to her mother, who replied, Oh, he had a lot of charm. Still has, when he wants to. And besides, what else could she do? Where could she go? You get married, things happen. You can't undo them.

People get divorced, said Veronica.

It's not that easy. What about the children? A woman can't bring up children on her own, with no money. And anyway, outsiders can't always see what there is between people.

She thought, a lot of charm. And apart from that, quite different, there was sex. She had danced with him at Rick's twenty-first and knew that his whole body hummed with it. Those eyes: it was as though their glitter was the visible spark of the electricity that zoomed and sang through his whole body. When you danced with him, out there in public, the whole family looking on, you felt it prickling through your skin. What must it be like in private? She didn't like Joe and did not care at all for him giving her pricklings through her skin, but she could see that, if you did, well, it would be really something.

I reckon he beats her, said George, but she didn't think so. How could anybody beat Lily, so grand as she was. At the lunches, with finest china and heaviest linen and smart *Women's Weekly* food, Lily in her rich drawling voice spoke of Joe with such significance that she must believe it herself. When she described the doings of children and grandchildren she appeared the most fortunate of women. Lily called her sister-in-law Dear, and patronised her a bit, as though she were a young thing needing advice, although her children were turning out very well. But when she talked about them, and there was plenty to say, with Diana's tennis and Elinor's scholastic success, Lily took little notice, cutting in with remarks on how clever Anne's little daughter Robyn was, how good at football Joseph's eldest, though only five, and what a lovely girl John was engaged to. The Gray family—ironic that she was Mrs Gray and Lily wasn't—had always been arrogant. Lily had certainly inherited Ada's duchessy ways. Though she hadn't passed them on to Elizabeth, a girl tall like her mother but not shapely. She came to visit most weekends, bringing her knitting. It was from Elizabeth that the stories about Joe's silences and rages came; while her cousins were out at the beach or tennis or the pictures and George looked in only for afternoon tea, she talked to her aunt of her life at home. Afterwards you could see the secrets capering behind Lily's classy facade. What would she have said if she'd known! The two women sat at their handiwork and the soft murmur of their voices wove patterns of sadness and comfort around bodies bent over the intricate tasks. Purl one knit one slip one pass the slipstitch over. Purl two knit three slip one make one ... Elizabeth had beautiful hands, pale, long-fingered, with large oval nails, like the hands of a lady in a

Gainsborough portrait. They knew their way through the complications of the knitting pattern, turning white wool into a lace matinée jacket for somebody's baby, always somebody having a baby, without their skill needing to be thought about, leaving Elizabeth's mind free for the much more difficult job of putting words together. Her aunt watched the lovely sure movements of those fine white hands and thought how unlike knitting life was.

Webs

———————◆———————

We sit in our lives like spiders, and believe that the web about us is of our own spinning, but this is an illusion. It may appear to depend on that object, or this event; in fact the ravellings travel much further back— and will forward—than we are likely to observe. There are, for instance, and not just for the sake of the word-play, the Lancashire cotton spinners who emigrated early in the nineteenth century. There is the defrocked or perhaps simply truant Irish priest who dropped two 'o's from his name and maybe married but certainly impregnated a great grandmother (a number of times) and was not to be found when she and several of the children followed him to the new life in the colonies. Is still not to be found, though ancestor hungry descendants hunt through genealogical societies for him. Twelve-year old Emily who drowned in a well on a dark evening in 1872 while walking from a neighbour's garden to her parents',

Emily, her thread untimely cut, is there; in the descendants of her siblings sadness flickers a moment. And the memory of another well, in the Watkin Street house, a simple deep hole in the laundry floor, filled in early in the 1940s for the safety of a later child. But the de'o'ed priest? Who knows. Maybe he stowed away to achieve the promised land. Maybe he never left the Old Country, writing from the colonies by means of some subterfuge: sending letters with a friend to post back, maybe. Maybe staying home and fathering another line, parallel to and ignorant of the other. He was by all accounts a tricky charming customer. There are those alive who knew people who knew him.

O what a tangled web we weave/When first we practise to deceive, said Ada Gray to her children when she suspected them of dishonesty. What she meant was that beginning a course of deceit would enmesh them, entangle them, ensleave them, in ever more labyrinthine toils, coils, skeins, mazes of mendacity. *O what a tangled web we weave*, they admonished their own children. Not taking into account that the stickiest webs of all, the most inosculate and infretted, the most dishevelled and bedevilled, are self-spun, self-spinning, will ye nill ye, *nolens volens, bon gré mal gré*, through all the generations that came before us, and they hold us suspended gently turning in mid-air. Dependent from the matted mass that preceded us. The threads tangle and snaggle, you'll break them before you unravel them.

Unless you start at the beginning, at the very place where the furry filaments are excreted. Before the stories happen and twist everything about. Ada is a good point. Ada whose daughter Lily married Joe Sullivan, and bore him six children. The eldest was also Joseph, and then there were Elizabeth, John, Anne, Rick, and finally when you might have thought they'd stopped was Paul. Anne is the subject of one story; already the threads are beginning to mat together; it is necessary to keep a sharp eye on the line to be followed. Ignore Joseph, who worked for a carter and built up a trucking business that made him a modest fortune, forget John who went to sea and was last heard of in South Africa. Even Elizabeth, knitting as she plays

Scrabble with her father because he will not brook talk while he deliberates. Elizabeth, however precious for her perceptions, is an aberration. Follow only Anne. Though perhaps the up-turned tea tray clattering on to the linoleum of the dining-room floor ought to be remembered. Anne the fourth child, born in 1933. Lily again you might have thought, Tiger Lily, tall and shapely, with a long throat mole-spotted like her mother's, dusky-skinned and dark-haired. At fifteen years of age she could no longer bear to live at home, and left. Let her go, said Joe, on the only occasion he spoke of it. Joseph and John were already away. Anne got herself a job at a smart grocery store in the city, called Dean and Trethewey's. They sold ham of excellent quality, smallgoods, cheese, high class salmon and sardines in tins; George thought well of them from his old days at the customs agents. The girls wore frilly white aprons and caps; the customers could believe they were being served by pretty parlour maids. The work was hard because of all the standing, but there was the money to compensate. She got a room in a house in Perkin Street, so close she could walk to work, and to the pictures. There was a young man living in the same house, tall with slicked hair and blue eyes; Tony and Anne went to dances at the Palais. He was a traveller for Rawleigh's products and away sometimes, but they had fun while he was there. Bing Crosby on the radio sang of love. Soon they got married. George gave her away because Joe refused to have anything to do with it. Down the aisle she walked in white hail-spotted muslin and a picture hat. Later that year Robyn was born. Tony was away from home travelling a lot; one day he didn't come back. They were divorced, and after a while Anne married a man with four children, some older, some younger than Robyn. At this point Anne takes off into another set of stories, to do with the second husband, who collected gemstones and had built a large room in the back garden to accommodate them, and with his children, who had quite a range of problems not necessarily stereotypical connected with losing their own mother and gaining a step-mother. Robyn wished she could go and live with her father; sometimes she visited her grandmother and talked about him.

Something had gone wrong with selling the Rawleigh's products and nobody knew where Tony was, except up north somewhere. Robyn thought he might have become a beachcomber; she imagined him living by a white beach, unstreaked with coal, in an airy comfortable shack under some palm trees, collecting shells and rare corals, and quite rich from the treasure he occasionally found. Lily offered drearier details; he was probably working in an office, or a mine, and living in a boarding house in a dusty street, but Robyn didn't believe her. At school she looked out of the window and made plans to join him, which she imparted to her boyfriend.

At fourteen she got pregnant, and because she was under age there was a court case, carnal knowledge of a minor being a crime. Her boyfriend was eighteen and said he would like to marry her and be a father to the child, so the judge was lenient. The boy, called Steve Apples, was apprenticed to a butcher and doing well. There should be enough money to live on. Robyn was pleased with the idea of getting out of school. All her friends were extremely impressed with her marriage. Steve was thrilled when his daughter was born, and when Robyn wanted to call her Jade he thought that this precious name was just right for the child. When she was a year old he had her photograph taken at Neville of Newcastle, sitting on a marble table with a pull-along wooden duck in her lap. It was Mikelis who did the job.

Robyn still talked of going north. By this time Steve was a fully-fledged butcher and valued by his boss for his skill with the knife. He could slice the meat from the bones as clean as a whistle. He had long blond hair that curled on his shoulders and was very thin and even childish looking in an endearing way. His customers were fond of him and asked after the baby. He sharpened his knife on the steel to a thin curving edge, so it slid through the gravy beef and the chuck as though they were mince, and told his ladies how Jade was crawling and walking and talking. He repeated the delightful things she said.

But Robyn wanted to go up north, and they set out in their old Austin, with a tent, and drove along the beaches, stopping whenever they felt like it. This was nice for Jade, who had her father's attention all of the time; Robyn never took a lot of notice. In Murwillumbah they met some people with Kombivans painted with flowers who were living on an abandoned dairy farm growing grass and planning to be painters. They stayed there for a while. Steve's skills as a butcher weren't much use, since they were all vegetarians; he tried some wood-carving but found it too slow and crabbed after the swift gestures of the soft unresisting meat. One day Robyn disappeared. She left a note saying she was going to find her father. Steve stayed on in Murwillumbah. One of the girls from the farm looked after Jade, and he got a job with a local butcher. Time passed. Once he wrote to Anne about her granddaughter, sending her a photograph of the flourishing child, believing everybody must be as interested in her as he was. Anne didn't reply; this was because she was in hospital recovering from a nervous breakdown. The hippie girl, who was called Zoe, moved in with him, and was a good mother to Jade. He made enough money to buy a butcher's shop, in Grafton, and they moved there. Robyn had sent postcards from time to time to the household in Murwillumbah; mostly they said things like Peace. There was never an address. It would be possible to follow her career on its inosculating way, through other men, including a millionaire tax-evader and a member of parliament, other children, other jobs, but that is not the intention here. The butcher's shop in Grafton is the scene, now, and Robyn doesn't know where that is; or rather doesn't know that it exists. Anne should, since Steve wrote and told her; he thinks she ought to know where her grandchild is. But Anne never got that letter, since she'd moved out of the gemstone-collecting husband's house by then; he sent it on, but to a previous address. The new tenants left it on the sideboard for a while, intending to find out where to redirect it, but never did, and finally ashamed threw it away.

So, to Grafton and the butcher shop prospering and multi-plying into a chain of butcher shops, and Steve and Zoe building a large house and living in comfort with Jade and trying for another child, Jade not remembering that there was a mother before Zoe. They built a studio in the big house and Zoe took up painting again. Then Steve, at work in his latest shop, was electrocuted by a faulty meat-sawing machine; freak accident, said the papers. Inquiries would be made. None of which was much good to heartbroken Zoe. She couldn't bear to stay in Grafton; she moved to the Blue Mountains. A friend had an art gallery there; Zoe wanted to start a new life. She had plenty of money from the butcher shops and the house and the insurance, and bought an old stone cottage with azaleas and rhododendrons growing, a million spring bulbs in its green lawns, and central heating. Jade spent her early teenage years there.

Here again, there's a choice of the thread to follow. There's Zoe's, and Amelia's, the gallery owner whose life she joined up with, in more ways than one. And Robyn's is shooting out suckers, except that nobody recognised them, since she was now called Rob and had a different surname and was lean and leathery and wrinkled too, though not very old. She was famous, was on the television, on the news and interviewed in current affairs programmes, and photographed for the papers, as a passionate crusader for rainforests. The image of Rob Meletios appeared quite often in Zoe's sitting room, but Zoe did not recognise in her the lineaments of the sixteen-year-old who'd gone north to look for her father and never come back. Jade admired this weatherbeaten woman who lay down in front of bulldozers and chained herself high in the branches of doomed trees. She felt strongly about such things herself. She'd turned out very clever, to a prodigious degree, finished school at a precocious age and went on to Sydney University, where she read law and campaigned on women's issues. She violently objected to the term post-feminism because it implied that feminism was finished and had been replaced by something else, when in fact it was in its earliest stages and still had far to go before its basic goals were achieved. Her intention was to use her law training to these ends. Jade was tall and shapely, very like her great-grandmother Lily, though fair-haired like her father. Her boyfriend Eric was blond and tall too; they strode through the university in a rather powerful fashion. When Jade got pregnant, possibly through refusing certain kinds of contraception as exploitative of women's bodies, she refused to have an abortion, as was expected of her, and even though she proselytised the need for its availability. No, she said to Eric, I believe in rights, and in this case more strongly in this baby's right to be born than in mine to stop it. Well, if you're sure, I'm happy, he replied. Shall we get married? No, she said, but I'll toss you for her surname if you like. So they tossed a fifty cent coin, and Eric won. The baby was born two weeks after the exams, and Jade took him up to the mountains and played with him and fed him and read the books for next year's courses. Eric was there for a lot of the time. When term approached, Zoe said, why not leave Sebastian here with me? For she and Amelia were lovers, and thought a child for them to share would be a nice development of their relationship. So Jade came home at weekends, mostly, and everything went very swimmingly.

Zoe was one of those women you imagine became hippies because they looked the part, thin and pale with long straight hair and a head that seemed to nod on its slender neck, like a flower you'd have said if friendly, nodding and bending so the hair fell forwards across her face, and needed washing every day because it got greasy with all the pushing back. Amelia looked very similar. Are you sisters? people said. Zoe and Steve Apples had loved one another with the happy sensuality of children. Zoe and Amelia . . . but that's another story, another tangled web too intricate to begin on here.

Back to Jade, who continued with law and rights, passionately denouncing the dismissal of feminism as having achieved its aims. There's so much still to do, she cried. Sebastian with his double mothering flourished, nurtured upon every demanding toy the gallery had to offer. It had moved from its earlier elegant watercolour phase into crafts; sold pots and macramé, woodwork, weaving, knitwear, sculpture and home-made jams from all the artisans of the district. The rooms were full of the textures of wool and clay and the scent of dried dead flowers, and did a roaring trade from visitors who were seduced by so much productivity in such proximity. Men groaned, but their wives insisted they stop on weekend drives and holidays. In the evening was television, and Rob Meletios haranguing them, not knowing she was now a grandmother, Rob in her second bigamous marriage, so she believed but preferred not to think about, and ignorant of the widowhood which would have clarified matters. Rob and her husbands have children, his and hers and theirs twice over; all with names given them in the voluptuous moments after their births, when the power of naming seems the merest symbol of all the other powers invested in parents to make their children's lives fruitful and happy and good; names no concerns of ours, yet, or maybe at all. And no longer of Anne, the grandmother, who in the toils and the coils of another kind of nomenclature, the noble syllables of Serepax and Librium, Ativan and Valium, swallowed too many pills and killed herself, maybe on purpose, or maybe the prescribed dosage dulled her senses, as was intended, to the point, as was not, where she no longer knew what she was doing. Serepax and Librium, Ativan and Valium, deliver us; and they did.

Lily did not believe that Anne had suicided. She, who was stout these days and had trouble with her feet so that she never stood and hardly ever walked, was proud of Robyn on the telly and all her other grandchildren with their careers and marriages and the production of further batches of off-spring; it was almost hard to keep track of them all.

So there you are, up to the fifth generation, or counting Ada the sixth. You could write a thousand-page novel to get to this point; a block-busting, best selling, negotiating the mini-series in however many digits, retiring to the tax haven of your choice, unputdownable, RSI inducing, airport haunting novel. Instead of a neat little chapter of what, seven pages? six? simply to bring us to Sebastian, great-great-grandchild of Lily Sullivan, née Gray, son of Jade Apples and Eric Dane.

A fortune

◆

I am a man with three mothers,
said Sebastian Dane. This was in reply to Mikelis's question
about his parents. What were they like? he asked. Were you
loved as a child?

I am a man with three mothers, Dane said.

• • •

Amelia and Zoe and Jade. Maybe he was a man with no mothers,
if the name counted. There was never anybody that he called
Mummy or Mother or Mum but by the time he noticed that
it didn't matter. There was the wide bed with its fat quilts
and the two soft women who cuddled him in the night when
the Big Bad Banksia Men came up the gullies and along the
ridges, rattling the French doors in his bedroom, while their
hideous many-mouthed heads muttered and mumbled. The
women held him tight and stroked him, nibbled his toes and

fingers, kissed his eyes and ears and nose. You're safe here with us, they told him. Banksia Men can't get into houses with feather quilts on the beds. He knew that too, but it was nice to have it said again. He curled up against their warm bodies and the three of them slept in a soft safe cave.

In the day-time they also touched him, smoothing his hair, pulling his trousers up and his jumpers down, their neat deft fingers turning these actions into caresses. When they'd finished arranging him they'd lean back and admire him, then hug him and disarrange him again. They loved his smooth skin and his slippery blond hair that they stroked back, not expecting it to stay, just for the sake of doing it.

When Jade came it was like somebody opening a door on a cold night in a house where people sit reading and knitting and choosing chocolates out of a box according to the pictures on the lid. Close the door. Close it! Were you born in a tent? say the people safe inside the warm breathing of the central heating. The papers on the table lift, the curtains stir, the people shiver. And yet, in the opening, in this cold air that rushes in with the frosty scent of the starlight, the water and stone odour of the mountains, there are spaces and beckoning mysterious things. Until the heating breathes it in and breathes it out again, warm and calm once more. When Jade came it was like this. She breezed in and stirred things up, and then after a while all was warm and smooth again. Like her cheeks, cold from the mountain air, icy against kissing lips and cheeks, then after a while just like everybody else's.

She would sometimes come up on a train in the evening like a commuter and go back again in the morning, early. Eric never came on these quick trips, he waited for the weekends and brought the car. Let's wake Sebastian up and play with him, she'd say, and Zoe would laugh. You never wake sleeping babies, never. Let sleeping babies lie. You'd know that if it was you who got him to sleep. Jade would stand by his crib and watch him breathe, this mysterious self-contained little creature. Zoe got up in the morning dark and made breakfast so she could see her for a bit longer, and because she thought Jade didn't eat. Why don't you stay longer, you don't have to rush back, she said, but there was always something urgent back in the city.

Leila Kovacs is going to court this morning, to get her injunction. If I don't go she won't turn up.

So why should she, if she doesn't want to?

The thing about these women, said Jade, leaning forward over her coffee cup, is that they don't want to believe the trap they're caught in. You live with this man and he bashes you, and the kids too, but he's your man, you love him, you think you do, and where would you be without him, who'd look after you, and maybe it's your fault that he hurts you, and anyway he promised that it won't happen any more, it'll be all right, he's stopped drinking and there'll be money, and none of this is true but you believe it because it's the solution you want, the simple one. The proper marriage vows one. Last time Leila's bloke made all these promises so she didn't go to court when she was supposed to and next thing you know she's back at the refuge again and her little boy's got three cracked ribs and two toes broken and God knows what the bruises mean but he's lucky that's all.

The trouble is, Jade went on angrily, she doesn't believe she can manage on her own. She thinks that without a man she's nothing.

Can she? Manage on her own?

Of course. It won't be easy, but anybody who's lived in a household where rape and violence are the norm must find being on her own is better.

Rape and violence, said Zoe.

You don't know the half of it, said Jade kindly. You're still a flower child.

Of course I'm not.

Jade thought it was just as well Zoe didn't know more about life at the refuge. Women only came when there was nowhere else to go. Our women are at the bottom of the heap, remember that, said Sheila, who was in charge, and don't forget this: it's a shit heap. Jade wasn't so involved as some, since she was still at uni, she only went between lectures, to counsel women on their legal rights, but she knew the dangers.

Husbands who would rather kill their wives than lose them. Who plotted to bomb the homes of Family Court judges because they believed they'd taken their families away from them. A month ago a man had shot his wife, his four children—the eldest was eleven—and then himself because the woman had started to divorce him. The refuge had deadlocks on all the windows as well as the doors, and if a man paused too long outside they called the police.

I worry about you, Jade, Zoe said. You work too hard. You're so thin, you're running yourself ragged.

I'm strong, said Jade. I can keep going.

Don't let yourself get depressed then.

Jade laughed and tap-danced across the kitchen in her running shoes. Not depressed, she said, angry. But she was smiling, trying to leave the anger back in the city. Then she went soft-footed into the bedroom to kiss Sebastian goodbye, and he woke and she cuddled him for a moment. She felt sick with the knowledge that people hurt little creatures like him, held them against radiators or threw them across rooms, or whirled them round their heads until their brains banged against their skullbones and the damage could never be righted. Even knowing all the circumstances that might extenuate such acts, she still felt that there was some terrible foreignness in the humanity of such people. There were tears in her eyes when she took him out to Zoe in the kitchen.

As usual she refused a lift to the station and set off at a run with her bag on her back. Jade liked to travel light. Zoe took Sebastian with his milk and tea for herself and Amelia back to bed. She was worried about whether Jade was a bad mother. She wasn't worried about Sebastian, he was getting all the nurture he needed, but she couldn't help worrying about Jade's nature, that she could leave her baby to someone else.

Do you think she's maybe like her mother? she asked Amelia. Maybe the pattern's repeating itself. Robyn abandoning Jade. Now Jade abandoning Sebastian.

She's not abandoning him, for God's sake. I've never seen a baby less abandoned. Robyn was an entirely different case. Too young, needing a father herself.

Jade's those things too . . .

Not in that way. She's very mature. She loves Seb. She sees him pretty often. But she knows she's got to get her degree—her work's important to her. That's Jade, to be passionate about what she does. And she knows funny-pants here is in good hands—she tickled the baby's tummy, her voice cooed. Besides, it'd break your heart if she came galloping up and took him away to live with her.

Well, maybe it's because I don't want it to happen that I worry that maybe it should.

Live in the present. Amelia began to caress Zoe as she had the baby. Her fingers were gentle artful dancers across smooth skin, her lips made soft nips and tugs and pulls like a baby suckling. The bed hummed with pleasure.

The thing about Jade, said Amelia afterwards, is that she can love without needing to possess. That's a gift.

♦ ♦ ♦

If Jade had seen herself entering the house like a cold wind it would not have been as a brisk or healthy however frigid mountain breeze. The train journey from the city on the plain to the mountains seems like a voyage from one world to another, as though at one point a fissure opens between two orders of reality, so that were she to look up from her book at precisely the right moment she would see the quick dart of the train as it negotiated that passage. The image could have been of slipping through a mirror, not the skin of Alice's cheerful crazy-logical looking glass world but the poisoned mirror of Hans Andersen's Snow Queen story, which breaks and casts its fragments into the hearts and minds of ordinary people, to lodge there and twist them out of true. Its winds are breaths of despair that moan and wail through man-made wastes. On the other side of the mirror (and which one is the real one?) are the mountains, whose cold may be fruitful and pure, where a solid stone house is warmed with love and keeps a baby safe from the fates that dog those who dwell in the plains of the poisoned mirror. Jade sits in the train after a day at the refuge spent using all the strength of her will to protect women and children from the murderous intent of love gone wrong and holds tight to the thought of Sebastian happily far away from such harms. She loves him, and leaves him where he is. Goes to him, does not take him with her. It doesn't occur to her to say such things to Zoe or Amelia; it is only when she sits exhausted on the train that she has such thoughts. By the time she arrives at the mountains and the train has negotiated—the moment as always unperceived by her—the passage into the untwisted unpoisoned other world, she has recovered her energy and her spirits and gallops into the house, wanting to wake her sleeping child and play with him. She leans against the kitchen benches drinking apple juice, lifting saucepan lids, reading labels on jars and packets, telling bowdlerised stories about her life in the city, and forgets that Amelia and Zoe don't know about the transfer that has occurred.

In the train going back she takes out her books and works. She hasn't forgotten her fancy of the mirror world, thinks how one day she will catch the moment when the train slips through that fissure, that crack, that warp leading into the flawed *alter* world, but she has slept well, she is full of energy and hope. If she didn't have so much to do she might remember the rest of the Snow Queen story, how Gerda through strength of will and steadfastness saved her friend from his icy bondage, and then she could consider that fairytales are not often like life; the effort is there, the intention, the desire, but rarely are the results so clear and shapely. Ever after is too long for happiness; the best you can hope for is a moment of grace, and you have to be lucky.

Instead she's putting her mind to the law of trusts and successions. You don't get second chances at law exams. Sebastian is also in her mind, though she's not thinking about him; he's a small safe warm place and always there.

◆ ◆ ◆

Amelia and Zoe and Jade: the three mothers of Sebastian Dane. Amelia and Zoe: Mia and Zoo. Amelia's name came first, flattened into its barest undulations in the child's mouth. Meeya. The simple vocative for the mother-word common to all Indo-European languages, said Jade. Zoo was longer in coming and he learned a number of words before Jade. He pronounced it perfectly from the beginning. Mia and Zoo: Sebastian changed their personalities. They were not Amelia and Zoe, they were different women, were both more and less than the women of the given names. Jade was always Jade.

◆ ◆ ◆

When Sebastian was born, before they knew he was going to be their child, Amelia said, we must have his horoscope cast. Zoe replied, Oh yes, and I shall tell his fortune by the tarot cards.

Do you know how?

I used to do it all the time, up north. A gypsy woman, she was called Ruby, she taught me. You never forget.

She brought out a box of large brightly coloured cards, a bit limp and furry at the edges. They'd been wrapped in a cracked silk scarf.

We need a Querent, she said.

What's that?

The Querent's the person who's asking the questions of the cards.

Isn't that you and me?

It's supposed to be the one whose fortune it is.

Then it's Sebastian. Us asking on his behalf.

Okay. I'm the Reader, so you stand for the Querent.

She took the cards and shuffled them, slowly, rhythmically, stroking with her fingertips, rubbing with her palms. Amelia watched the familiar caressing movements.

Don't they get greasy, she asked, with all that handling?

You have to handle them. Get the feel. Communicate with them. Otherwise they won't tell you things.

She held out the cards to Amelia: Choose one. That will be Sebastian.

Amelia pulled out a picture of a young man, dressed in the red and yellow motley of a jester, with brassy bells and a pack over his shoulder. A little dog was pulling down his tights and biting his bare bum.

The Fool, she muttered, and looked at Zoe with horror.

Good, said Zoe. Excellent. That's man, on his journey through life. Possibilities of great spiritual power there. And creativity. The gypsies say he possesses the foolishness of God which is wiser than the wisdom of men.

I hope you're right. Amelia put the card down with a sharp pat; she might have been warning it to behave.

Zoe had her cut the deck into three piles, with her left hand, in the gypsy tradition. That's what Ruby said. She reversed the top card in each, turning the picture top to bottom, shuffled the pile from her right hand to her left, and then put them together again. She dealt them in a pattern of verticals and horizontals. Amelia watched, her head turned slightly away, so she saw through the corners of her eyes. Zoe's stroking fingers touched her hand, then began to turn the cards over.

The Page of Cups: a blond boy, holding a cup out of which rises a fish . . . The creative mind, said Zoe. A lover of the arts and a deep thinker.

Catching the slippery fish of thought, said Amelia.

The Three of Pentacles: a man painting in a church . . . he's artistic, spiritual, and what's more the card denotes *money* for artistic work.

Isn't this all a bit too good to be true? said Amelia.

It's not finished yet.

The Five of Swords: a victorious knight, holding the swords of his enemies . . . this card is reversed. It means a funeral.

Logical. Nobody goes through life without some of those.

The Hanged Man . . . Not what you think, said Zoe hastily. This is a rich and promising card. You see, he dangles by the ankle, and he has a halo round his head. He's a young man who sees the world with fresh eyes, he's creative, spiritual.

Everything's creative and spiritual, said Amelia. I expect he'll be a tax accountant. Or a bookie.

The next card was a skeleton, reaping crowned heads.

Death! No doubt that's death.

Not at all. Not Death, never say Death, the gypsies wouldn't dream of saying Death. This is a card of rebirth, the end of the old bad things and the beginning of a new life.

I can't cope with this. Amelia scraped her chair back from the table. Everything's so fantastically good. The good's good and the bad's good—it's got to be waffle.

Zoe looked hurt. I'm only just beginning. You have to juxtapose, find patterns, draw conclusions—but you've got to be receptive first.

Amelia stood behind her and began to knead her neck. All right, she said. Keep going.

You've lost faith, said Zoe. It's no good. She swept her hand through the cards. The significant pictures swirled in all directions over the table.

Isn't that bad luck? said Amelia.

How can it be? You don't believe in it.

♦ ♦ ♦

But not believing is not the same as taking no notice. The words are there, if they want them. Privately, each woman thinks: artistic, creative, spiritual. A seeker. When they see the little red baby with no hair and opaque blue eyes each believes that this good future is in store for him. That's the thing about babies. You look at them and believe against all evidence that this time the future can be got right.

♦ ♦ ♦

So Mikelis looks at Eva, and Lily at her six children, and Elinor at Blanche and Isabel, and George at his three little daughters, though by the time it is Veronica he is looking at, Diana is seven and it is already apparent that she is her own person, and she will make mistakes and he won't be able to save her. Nevertheless when Veronica looks up at him with large unchanged blue eyes he can think: This time . . .

Christening

——————◆——————

So far the mother, the wife, of the Gray household has been just that: Mrs Gray, a shadowy if supporting figure, with no life it seems of her own. Missus, Mummy, Mum, Ma; your mother; old girl, old cheese; sweetheart, love; so far she hasn't a Christian name, a given name, to identify her. Only titles.

Perhaps a Christian name will make her more substantial. Make her a person, not a role. She was given one, was given two, christened in fact, as a small baby, the fifth to wear the long elaborate gown that proclaimed to the world her mother was a skilful needlewoman, a woman gifted with the delicate household arts, so that her price is above rubies, her children rise up and call her blessed, and her husband praises her.

All that is needful is to reveal the name that loving parents and godparents, standing about the font in the church with the polished wooden roof (built by the family that gave its

name to the small mining township of Merewether because
it owned all the land on which it was built and did its share
of making the lives of its workers difficult) and observing the
ceremonies of the Book of Common Prayer of the Church
of England, gave her.

After many prayers and exhortations, the priest took the
child into his hands, turned to the godparents (one godfather and two godmothers as was necessary because she was
a female, the proportions being reversed in the case of a boy)
and said:

Name this child.

Her Uncle Edwin, who was the godfather, announced in
his clear firm voice, making the most of the rhythm and shape
of the syllables of the proper nouns it pronounced, the voice
which was the tool of his trade as a driver of lifts at Scotts
Department Store, Uncle Edwin announced:

Alice Louise (Louise being her mother's name, and Alice
because it was pretty).

Then, though the Prayer Book commanded the priest to
dip her into the Water discreetly and warily, he did not; but
simply poured the Water upon her, as was allowed if the child
were certified weak, which she wasn't, but the dipping was
no longer used, and said: I baptise thee in the name of the
Father, and of the Son, and of the Holy Ghost. Amen.

Had she died when a child she ought to have gone to Heaven,
for the Prayer Book says (though with a possible ambiguity,
it seems) that it is certain by God's Word, that children which
are baptised, dying before they commit actual sin, are un-
doubtedly saved.

Actual sin, eh? What can actual sin consist of? Everybody
who has ever lived with children knows that they are wicked
creatures, who with sweet evil smiles do what they know to
be wrong, watching sidelong to see how long they will get
away with it. But is this actual sin? There is a photograph
of Alice, standing on a chair and wearing a wonderful ruched
bonnet with points like a star; she's so shy she barely smiles,
just a faint quaver of the lips, and one foot turns timidly.
She touches your heart with the difficulty of the world for

children, even one so nurtured. Yet she'd have been naughty, sometimes; often; no doubt about it.

But she didn't die, she grew up, healthy, gentle, pretty, and married George Gray. And thereby hangs a tale. Some of which has already been told. How he asked her to marry him and she refused so he went up north to nurse his sorrow. Along with Vic his good friend and George survived but Vic didn't.

• • •

In a drawer in the Gray house was a white silk scarf, the kind that men used to wear with dinnersuits and overcoats over the top, that make you think of nightclubs and champagne in shallow cups and even of top hats though there was no sign of such a thing. It was crocheted in a fine bobble pattern and was of a stuff exceptionally white and silky, known as art silk. Elinor the second child of the eventual union of George and Alice thought this sounded very grand, until she found out that art was short for artificial. Did you make it? she asked Alice. No. Who did then? It was made for your father by Lizzie.

Everybody knew that Lizzie was an old girlfriend. Unlucky, obviously, since she didn't get to marry Dad. The scarf when looked at closely had a few mistakes in it. Lizzie did not seem to be so gifted in the housewifely arts as Alice, who dressed her children with the same public skill as her mother had shown. Poor Lizzie, thought Elinor, fingering the scarf. Not very successful in crochet or in love.

I wonder what she looked like? the Gray children asked one another. Do you think she was pretty?

Maybe she wasn't, said Elinor, since Dad didn't marry her.

They spoke about her in the past tense, like a story.

I'm glad, said Veronica. Lizzie's a silly name. Fancy having a mother called Lizzie.

They did find a photograph of her. Diana was rummaging in the desk drawer one day, in the way children have of reconnoitring the landscapes of their lives, for no reason but the sake of it, and found a yellowed snapshot in an old chocolate box that had pen-nibs in it, and a newspaper clipping about a bus knocking off a shop awning, and a flat leather booklet of the poems of Edna St Vincent Millay. Who's this? she asked. What are you doing fiddling about with that stuff? said Alice. Put it away. At once. But who is it? asked Diana. Lizzie, said Alice.

The sisters put the chocolate box back but kept Lizzie in a messy drawer in their bedroom and took her out from time to time and stared at her, the bold curl of her hair, the lace round the neck of her dress, her big eyes that flirted with the camera. She's pretty, said Veronica. I wonder why she's not in the album.

Perhaps you don't put old girlfriends in photo albums, said Diana.

Steve's there, Elinor pointed out.

They didn't ask Alice to explain why her old boyfriend rated the album when Dad's old girlfriend didn't. They knew from the way she said *Lizzie* that she wouldn't talk about her.

They smoothed out the bent edges of the unprized snapshot.

Dad reckons Mum chased Steve off pretty fast when he came on the scene, said Diana. Maybe Dad chased Lizzie off too.

So why's she not in the album? insisted Elinor.

Maybe she jilted him, said Veronica.

Maybe she loved another, said Elinor. Maybe they eloped.

I reckon it was Dad that jilted her, said Diana. He was pretty good-looking when he was young.

Maybe we'll see her in town one day, said Elinor. She could have married a rich man. Broken-hearted, turning to another who could give her money if not love. In furs, and wearing a corsage of orchids.

Let's look out for her, said Veronica.

You'd never recognise her, said Diana. She'd be too old.

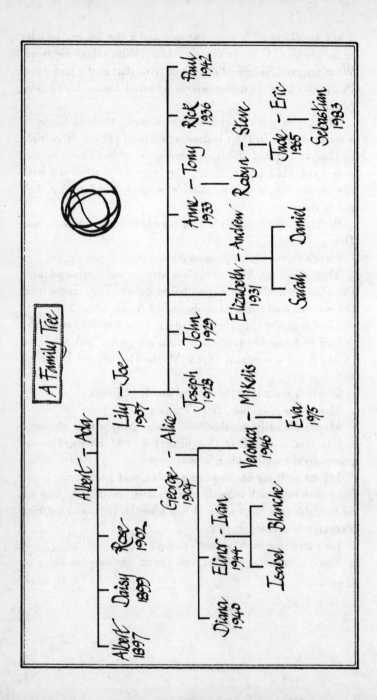

A Family Tree

The diary

———————◆———————

Having Alice come to school for concerts and folk-dancing and handiwork displays always ended in difficult feelings for Veronica. Her mother would discuss with her beforehand which dress, which hat, Veronica would go off to school glossy with anticipation of the beautiful mother who would swan in to see and bless her life at school, and then when she came it wasn't like that at all. The hat was the same, and the dress, and her mother, but not the beauty expected. It was as though the other mothers shifted the focus, somehow, and Veronica's looked odd. She stood shy, apart, and her mouth was glum. Or turned up in a smile more like despair. Veronica hated the feelings of guilt and disloyalty this caused her, and felt angry with Alice because it must be her fault that things weren't right.

It wasn't until much later, long out of primary school and its violent disappointments, that she understood why: when

Alice said, Oh those terrible school visits. I hated them. I always felt like your grandmother, not your mother. Stupid timid old gawk I was. Come off it, Mum, said Veronica, you looked terrific, perceiving what she hadn't known how to then, that the curious shift in focus brought about by the other mothers was the result of their youth. Not out of memory, she hadn't observed them then, but out of knowledge she reconstructed those laughing prospering flirty-skirted women with their growing baby boomers, that's what they were called now, all those hearty post-war children, and Alice weighted down by the Depression, and her postponed marriage. Postponed once by choice, a second time by necessity. Glum with the knowledge of compromise. Not even exaggerating when she saw herself old enough to be the mother of these mothers. Fifty knowing what thirty doesn't: when the hero and heroine ride off to their happy-ever-after in the sunset, the one certain thing is that it will get dark.

Veronica reconstructed all that and said, But you didn't look old, you've always looked amazingly young for your age. Which was true, now. Not for another twenty years, when it was too late to ask Alice anything, did she and Elinor discuss what Alice might actually have felt.

Do you think she regretted not marrying Father first time round? said Elinor.

She must've, surely. All that time wasted.

Yes, but do people think like that? If you let yourself regret huge decisions like that, well, maybe it's just so awful you don't do it. Regret it, I mean.

You mean, said Veronica, she'd have protected herself from even the admission that she wasted a good chunk of her life.

Well, she was always pretty serene. Except when we made her ratty, when we were kids. And—hang on, what makes you think she saw it as wasted? Perhaps she was glad she had all that time living the jolly single life. She certainly seemed to have fun. Going to Sydney for the opening of the Harbour Bridge, joy-riding in aeroplanes. Making fabulous clothes. I know she hated feeling dowdy and poor, when we were little.

Wish we'd asked her. We could know.

Maybe she didn't want us to, said Elinor. Maybe she would have told us, if she had.

One thing, if she had married him first off, we'd be a good fifteen years older than we are.

Yuk. Thank God she didn't. Selfishly speaking. It's bad enough being this old. Elinor pulled her face as though she could turn it into a girl's again.

Except we wouldn't be. We'd be somebody else altogether.

Maybe the boy at least one of us was supposed to be.

It's funny to think of George and Alice with a quite other family, said Veronica. Maybe six children, like Auntie Muriel, three boys three girls.

You can't really imagine it, can you? We're our parents' children. Nothing else is conceivable.

Ha ha. But why not? We have to imagine Diana dead.

She's still herself. Still alive for twenty-two years. Not never existing.

This is the received wisdom of Diana's death. The life to be celebrated, not the death to be mourned. They pause for a moment; it's a kind of black pit they don't care to look into in case it is all dark, no pinpoints of immortal life, or other incarnations. Even their father, at the end, could not always see that comforting brightness.

What about Lizzie? They've found out about Lizzie now. Lizzie's the one who had the rough time. George and Alice did after all get it together. Forty years' worth, after all.

◆ ◆ ◆

When George died Alice gave Elinor a fat little black-covered notebook. A diary. Read it, she said. Tell me if I should burn it.

It begins: *He has gone again—how empty is life when he is not here.* It's Lizzie's diary, Lizzie who knitted imperfectly a white silk evening scarf and was perhaps not quite as pretty as Mum, once. *Letters to My Diary* she calls it. It starts in April 1930 when she is boarding with some people in the country, away from the sea air, trying to get rid of her illness. Consumption, tuberculosis, though she never writes that word, only once a scribbled figure that might be a *t*. Twelve months the doctor tells her she must stay, and she can't bear it. Her Beloved comes to see her but the fortnights are long and so she writes her unhappiness in the diary so she will not be tempted to write it in letters to him. He's just left. There's 'corned horse' for dinner again and she *simply couldn't eat the salty stringy stuff and in the midst of trying to swallow the dreadful salty string I began to think of him and then a lump came to my throat and I had to get up and come into my little bedroom to pray for strength . . . And, oh, Diary, I did a sweet foolish thing. I went to the wardrobe and got his old grey 'strides' out that he leaves here with me and wears when he is here and I burried my face in them and cried and prayed and cried and prayed until I got strength enough to fight on again . . . I went back into the dining-room to get my 'sweets', but couldn't eat them, so gave dinner up altogether.*

She knows he would marry her *like this*, but would it be fair to him to be his wife in name only, even just for a couple of years while she gets better? And she is afraid she will infect him with the disease: *Last night—oh wonderful—how you loved me Beloved and how I loved you and yet even our sweet kisses are dangerous. You say not, but I know there is a risk and if you should catch it—Oh, I love you so, dear Brown Eyes and I don't half deserve all your goodness because I'm always—except when you are with me—so unhappy.*

Her dear Brown Eyes gives her a bag with her name painted on it, to carry the beads and stockings she sells from door to door when the weather is fine. And a portable gramophone— a secret he promises her, and she is disappointed because she hoped it would be news of a job in the country so they can get married, and her black despair comes on her. Then the doctor tells her she can get married but must practise BC, a little stranger would not be advisable in her state of health. Given this she can be a proper wife. She writes of her love and his and how he comes through a flood to see her . . . *On Sunday night Amy T. from next door over here visiting me and we were at the piano—she was playing and I was sewing at my fancy work and I think it must have been about 5.00 p.m.*

when I heard the gate click and my heart at once told me it was him! The sewing went flying and I sprang out of my chair and cried 'My heavens! It's Georgie!' And when I got to the window and looked out there he was looking up with his dear brown eyes full of love. It was still raining a little and he was in his big navy blue coat and he had the umbrella up. I rushed out and greeted him with: 'Oh Georgie dear, how did you manage it?' and he said with a sweet twinkle in his eye: 'Oh ways and means, Kid.' 'Kid' is his pet name for me . . . It turns out he's come first by train and then by bus through miles of water up to the axle of the bus and finally by train again.*

She longs for her wedding day—it's set for October—when he will give her happiness and health, and one day, babies. *Was ever a woman loved so*, she writes.

She has some oil she uses, which is good, later there's an inhalation that works well. She loses four pounds, which is bad, but puts it down to brooding and going off her food. She tortures herself with thinking she should give him up. And then he tells her how well she will get in his care. She pictures their life in the business they will have up north, with him and Daddy in the shop and her and Mummy in the house, and her commercial art lessons, and the piano. She gives up *the Membrosous for a few days because the old Lung has been feeling terribly sore today and I think perhaps I have been inhaling too deeply. And my right arm is hard to lift again— something that I haven't felt for quite a while.* Her bridesmaid is coming to visit her: *She doesn't know why I am not strong. I don't think I would like anybody to know only my near and dear ones. I may tell and yet again I may not. She might have guessed . . . I must shampoo my hair. I do hope it is a fine day and I will feel up to the job.*

Now there's a gap till after the wedding. Elinor takes a deep breath. It's like reading a book. She can't put it down. Lizzie is a good storyteller, even puts in dialogue. A bit of flashback too as well as her own addresses to her Dear Diary. Some days it blots and sometimes it's not very well spelt, and there are quaint devices like calling people Mrs B. and towns D-

(Dungog maybe, thinks Elinor; she doesn't even know this. N– is clearly enough Newcastle but where's M–, the place of the planned shop? Would it be Murwillumbah? That far away?) but the shape of her passion fills these pages in all its sensuous pain and trembling hope. She says, *How can I write of these things even to you Diary?* but she manages it. Oh yes, she manages it.

When she starts again after the gap, she's been married for five months (Elinor counts up, it's actually only four): *After all the sorrows I have burdened you with Dear Diary you are due for some joys now . . .*

Well, I had a sweet little Wedding! I shall always associate that happy day—21 October 1931—with the heavy sweet perfume of roses and my wedding night with the deliciously sweet masculine aroma of my G. (That last may sound a little queer, but I am sure it is something every bride knows.) . . . We went to K– [Elinor can guess this: it's got to be Katoomba] *for our Honeymoon, and the mountain air was glorious, although I didn't care for the mists much—seem to get down on my chest.* They come back home *laden with 'snaps' and mementoes of our happy stay.* She thinks that being happy and married and having her loved ones around her is doing more good than all the medicine in the world, and even the sea air is not harmful. They're living with her parents up on Glebe Hill, where the air is cool and fresh; they sleep on the verandah . . . *I find I must still rest a lot, but oh I'm so much better this year than I was last year, and next year I hope to be so much better than I am this year and so on until I am quite well and strong again. Oh I do want to get well again, so I can 'keep house' for G. and we can have a little house of our own and little—? Our idea for a little business at M– had to be discarded as things are too bad now to start out on any new ventures and anybody who has a steady job is considered very lucky so G. and Dad are sticking to there jobs like Oysters to a rock. Pop, by the way, has a new job. He has gone back to an old firm he used to work for years ago and it is a much easier job than his old one, although the wages are rather small.*

There she stops. The fat little book is not nearly half full.

In the back is a packet of photographs, airbrushed to angelic luminescence. Lizzie marrying in her *sweet white Georgette frock made long* and borrowed veil, looking plump and very pretty, blooming indeed (she several times remarks that she is surprisingly plump for her wretched condition, and thinks that it is probably the oil), Lizzie and bridegroom and roses, Lizzie and Maud the bridesmaid.

The last one is a postcard, of a grave, with a headstone in the shape of an open book, the pages separated by a marble tassel. On the left-hand one is written *Elizabeth Ivy Beloved Wife of George Edward Gray Died 11 August 1932 Aged 23 Years Omnia Vincit Amor*. The other page is blank.

◆ ◆ ◆

I don't really think you should burn it, says Elinor to Alice, giving her the diary back. It's a document. You know me, I always think you should keep things, written things, letters, whatever.

This is not what she means, but she thinks she should be a bit cool and practical, not show how moved she is. Her head feels dense and choked up, as though she has a bad cold.

What she is thinking is the terrible sad bravery of this little diary. Shapely as a fragment of autobiography. The ink on the page saying here I am, look, this is me, alive. Lizzie trying not to die. Trying to believe herself out of death. Lizzie managing not even a year, never anywhere near the little babies she wanted. But George managed them, he had his healthy brown-eyed children, and the least they can do for Lizzie is remember her. Shed tears for her. And keep her book.

He tried everything to save her, says Alice. Every medicine, every cure. He read books, studied everything he could find. You know your father, how thorough . . . I don't think he could believe that he hadn't been able to save her, not for a long time . . . he wanted it so much he was sure he could make it happen. He always said if he'd been rich she wouldn't have died. If he could have taken her away to a sanatorium.

And now the disease doesn't even exist any more, it's been wiped out.

• • •

In some ways Lizzie had the best of it, says Elinor to Veronica, after Alice is dead and the diary turns up again in one of the boxes of papers that are their legacy. Love and death. The short span of passion perfect for ever, not fading or souring or turning to habit.

Love-in-amber, says Veronica.

No compromises. No elderly comfortable affection.

Alice had the children, says Veronica. A long life and prized by her family. Which would you rather have?

Elinor looks at her. The passion. Why not?

It's easy to say that, now it's too late, you can't cark it at an early age. (There's Diana again. How is Diana's death different from Lizzie's? Lizzie saw hers coming, tried to fight it off. Diana lived to the last minute as though she had all her life before her. Which is better?) Anyway, says Veronica, I want both. I bet Alice had both. Look at these letters. Loveletters from George. Plenty of passion there.

They put Lizzie's book and the photographs on one side, to show their girls. Elinor picks up the photograph of the grave. He expected to join her, she says. It's kind of gaping, isn't it, that space never filled; the blank page. I wonder what's happened to it.

In the background is a rough wooden fence and a stretch of water which must be the Hunter River, there's some sort of mangrovey shore. Is the cemetery at Sandgate that close to the river? How long do people keep graves, and the records of them?

We should go and find out, says Veronica.

Maybe they will. One day.

• • •

Elinor can't stop thinking of the empty page on the headstone. It's a kind of betrayal, since in the first place it was a promise that he would join Lizzie one day, being in the meantime faithful to her. As soon as he married Alice that promise was broken. And there's another thing; that George, who was a bit of a dandy, who wore pince-nez and a signet ring with initials, who struggled through a flood for a chaste hour or two with the girl he loved, the girl he called Kid, that wasn't their George, their father, their mother's husband. That was Lizzie's George, and he is buried there; the blank page of the headstone is his grave too.

Dandy

◆

The Depression, George said. Always with a capital letter in his voice. Like the Flood, or the Diaspora, not needing an adjective to fix it in time or place.

His daughters were grown up before they realised that there were other depressions, and eventually they lived through one, televised this time with J curves and banana republics. Veronica who had that kind of mind imagined a banana bent at one end and the economy hooked on to it and of course the contraption wouldn't hold, how could a banana, however J-shaped, support anything? Let alone engender a recession-led recovery. But George's Depression, the one that stalked through their youth, was a mysterious act of anger and betrayal and decent coves let down. It stalked thrillingly but not finally threateningly; it was safely shut away as a story, it could do the girls no harm.

At least you'll never want for a job, said George, when Diana went to Teachers College. People will always need education. No danger of a teacher being out of work.

In fact they were, in the next depression. They trained, but nobody wanted them. But Diana didn't live to see that, and neither did George. His Depression never lost its capital letter, and he never quite lost his bitterness towards it. A decade and even two later, its memory was fresh as ever, and passions flowed from it.

George would be in his backyard working and so would Lew Jenkins next door. They'd moved into their houses at the same time, on the same bare and sandy blocks, with all the business of gardens to be made and no hope of paying anyone else to do it. They concreted paths and dug the sand out to two spades' depth, so when the good soil went in there would be no fear of the sand mixing up into it. They built low walls and lattice fences, George's with high latches to shut the little girls in; they planted vegetables, broad beans and mignonette lettuces and onions, tomatoes, beetroot. Lew put in roses and camellias; George stuck with beds of annuals, chrysanthemums, and poppies, and stocks that scent the already sea-salty summer evenings. There is a whole childhood in the scent of stocks on a summer evening by the sea. You put them inside in vases and very shortly the water stinks, but in the garden they are always sweet.

When the two men worked in their yards they'd sooner or later move near the fence for a chat, leaning on shovels or hoes, pushing their stained felt hats back—there was a progression of hats in men's lives, a new one which was the best one, an older one, and a really old one for gardening in, and every now and then they'd all move down a peg—and wiping their sweaty brows with their handkerchiefs.

While they talked about vegetables and the fertilisation of the soil it was all right, though they didn't always see eye to eye there and each thought the other had some pretty cranky ideas. But politics made real arguments. Lew went on doggedly asserting his views, while George would become almost speechless with indignation that a man could persist in such wrongheadedness.

What's a cove like Menzies going to do for you? You've been a miner all your life.

Menzies is a good bloke, said Lew.

Pig Iron Bob, said George.

Lew was older than George, and scrawnier. His arms were corded with veins. His voice was soft and lilting. He was still a Welshman when he spoke.

My father came out when I was a nipper, said George. To save my life, they reckoned. Pneumonia. You'd never guess I was a sickly child, ay? But not just that, I reckon; I reckon they were looking for a better life. Decency, justice, that kind of thing.

I was the one, said Lew. Fourteen I was. Went to Cessnock. Bellbird. Coal miners in my family since . . .

I know what it's like to be out of work, said George. Wouldn't wish that on m'worst enemy.

I'm retired, said Lew. Menzies is a good bloke. He'll look after us.

Stubborn as a mule, old Jenkins, George would say to Alice. And stupid as a donkey. The two men would always end up shouting at each other. They'd stamp off to opposite sides of the garden and dig furiously. Sometimes a prized plant would be a victim of their rage. At least the empty beds got a fierce digging over. George would still be angry when he went inside. How can he? he'd say, over and over. How can he? And him a miner. A miner and he votes for Pig Iron Bob.

But still another day they'd go at it again.

1932, said George. Oh a great year that. What were you doing in '32? I remember that bloke Thompson coming out here. A dingy town, he said this was. A city of bitter and out-of-work men. He was an Englishman but he could see that all right. Lazarus without a Christ, he called it.

You can't expect miracles, said Lew. He came close to the fence, the lilt and his voice quicker than ever, jabbing his finger. George never listened to Lew's arguments, he just wanted him to listen to his.

You and me, we're working men. We own nothing but our labour. We have to stick together on that.

See here, said Lew. I own a bloody sight more than my labour. He looked at his vegetables, at his stone-coloured weatherboard house with its brick porch and rainbow roof tiles, at his roses.

That's not the point, said George.

Lew went doggedly on. I vote for the bloke who's going to do the country some good.

You've only got to read, said George. See what goes on. Find out the facts.

Like the botanical gardens. That was the one that'd break your heart. 1868, as long ago as that, men had vision then. A large tract of land in Mayfield, low-lying, a bit swampy, had been set aside for a botanical reserve, and ideal for that purpose. Then, on the eve of the War, the first one, the government decides to sell it to BHP. George thought of the idyllic spot and the ordinary people who'd have enjoyed themselves there, the birds, the amazing birds, there were still some on the islands, like Kooragang, in the Hunter, even so close to all the noise and dirt of the industries. But the bosses didn't care about the pleasures of ordinary people. Treat them like machines, work them all hours, service minimal, as little as you can get away with, the machines probably better looked after and then chuck them away. Going to work in the ferry he could look across at the smoking chimneys and think of a botanical gardens there. How glorious it would have been. Of course you needed the smoking chimneys, chimneys mean work, a chance of employment, but not just there. The loss of the gardens summed up the whole huge breaking of faith between the might of governments and big business on the one hand and the impotent worker on the other.

And what's BHP ever done for the people of Newcastle? Nothing. Squeeze us dry and chuck us away.

There was another trick they played back then, the power hungry money-grubbing men. They dedicated land they didn't want, land usually too swampy to be of any use to them, the whole place was a swamp, on and off, thanks to the shifty Hunter estuary, they dedicated this land as parks and the area around it would be subdivided and sold as part of a garden suburb, the council drained and filled it, and people struggling to own their own bit of the suburban dream thought it was all being done for their benefit. Close to the Sydney Soap and Candle Factory, said the advertisements. The Gas Works. The Railway Workshops. And: Trains pass this land. So people found themselves living in the filthy lap of industrial Newcastle. All stink and noise and air you could scoop up with a spoon.

Aren't you glad you live near the sea? said George to Lew. At least the air's fit to breathe.

The southerly scoured it clean from time to time. Though, when Elinor years later brought the children up to visit, she was amazed by the black bities in their noses; at home in Canberra they were white, or anyway pale yellow.

When George tried to tell Lew things he didn't listen. Gradually the two men realised they'd have to stop arguing because all that came about was acrimony, never a chance of changing minds. No point in discussing it, said George to Alice, that cove's mind is set in concrete. Only after they'd stopped did they realise the fun there'd been in the arguments as well. Relations remained quite cordial, they were helpful to one another, but somehow not friendly. When George started learning exciting things from his studies with the Order, things that he wanted to share with others, he'd have made a good missionary if the Church'd had the right message, Lew turned out to be like the blokes at work. Not a matter of pearls before swine, exactly, but you soon got to tell who would be the fertile ground. However much his garden flourished Lew was stony terrain where the seeds of George's knowledge were concerned. But a hardy kind of neighbourliness still survived between them. They managed to agree on mending the fence that a particularly high southerly gale blew over. Excess vegetables were offered. Advice, sometimes, information on new fertilisers and such like, except that Lew was a more expensive gardener, he spent a lot of money on chemicals and seedlings, George had to be far more careful.

The Grays several times took the Jenkins's house at Rathmines for their summer holiday. This provided the girls with one of the idyllic places of their childhood, the placid little toy waves at the edge of the water, stirring the shingle, the lines of dry odorous seaweed fringing that, the thick green buffalo grass sloping up the few feet to the boathouse under the verandah; it was all child-sized, not like the rampaging ocean at home. Remember the Jenkins's. The place at the lake. A lucid space of feeling in the memory.

The house was a commercial transaction of course, they paid rent, no favours, for the fibro cottage on the edge of the lake, with its boat George used to row out in the dawn, fishing, or sometimes round the point to the general store, nearly as much effort as walking but you didn't have to carry the groceries, and enjoying the dip of the oars, the slide of the boat through the water. Diana was allowed to steer, using the rudder, Elinor had to sit still and not rock the boat, Veronica was too young to go at all.

For Alice it was all rather primitive and grubby and harder work than home. She wondered if the grubbiness of things belonging to people you know is easier to take than the grubbiness of strangers. Years later, when Elinor and Veronica raved on about those fabulous holidays at the lake when we were kids, she thought, I suppose it was worth it, for that.

Meanwhile the rest of the country seemed to think like Lew Jenkins. Enough of them to keep Menzies and those Liberal coves in power, time after time. Every election, hope: this time, this time. And always the cruel disappointment.

Ada Gray voted for Mr Menzies too. She was living on Stockton now, just down the road from the Boatrowers Hotel, not that that was of any interest to her, and Albert was dead and past temptation. Opposite the Boatrowers was the old Mission building, or rather the new one of 1913, the Chelmsford Institute it used to be called, where she had reigned over the sinker and tea cups before the Mission moved to Wickham when steam replaced sail and the Stockton mooring was too shallow for the new metal ships. Back to the old hunting grounds, ay Mother? said George, but Ada wasn't interested any more. She'd given up on the past. She was living with her granddaughter Anne and her baby girl Robyn. Tony the husband was away a lot travelling for Rawleigh's and Ada was supposed to be company for Anne but Alice, when they went visiting taking the bus the ferry and another bus or else a long walk right down the promontory, thought she was just hard work and bossiness and flirting with Tony when he was home, no good at all for a marriage said Alice to George, not adding, especially a shaky one. Alice insisted they never go for lunch or tea. It's too much work for Anne, she said. Alice hated making work for people, and as well not staying for meals meant she was safe from brawn. Not to mention tripe. She'd cook liver for George, cook it hard to make sure all the worrying juices were gone, with plenty of bacon to disguise the flavour, and make him butcher's brawn sandwiches occasionally, and her steak and kidney pudding was a triumph, but tripe she drew the line at. Lily did tripe in white sauce, with a bit of parsley that couldn't save the terrible whiteness of it. Ada often mentioned it. She spent a lot of time talking about food these days. And Mr Menzies. She thought he was a lovely man, so polite, such a gentleman. How could you vote for a political party because its leader had fancy manners? But George wouldn't talk politics with Ada any more either. He had determined to stop being indignant with her. And anyway he knew the answer. Had worked it out for Lew Jenkins too. It was snobbery. Vote Liberal and you proved you weren't working class. Vote Liberal and you proved you'd made it to the middle class. Even so he was amazed at the lack of logic. The ballot was secret, who knew that Ada Gray or Lew Jenkins made posh voting choices? Nobody who could do anything with it for them. Ada still lived on a miserable pension in a poky house kept on the remnants of a travelling salesman's wage, with a dunny out the back and a chip heater so violent you were scared to take baths. No wonder the country's going to the dogs, when a secret snobbery dictates how you vote.

George wore a white shirt to work, with a tie, a sports jacket; Harris tweed or a quiet houndstooth, rather than a suit, though he owned several, he carried his lunch, his book, his raincoat, his fruit cake smelling tobacco pouch in a small solid leather port. Attaché case was what you'd have asked for when you bought it. His daughters are looking at it now.

Still solid and not very shabby, though it must be into its second half century. Alice had used it for keeping photographs in, having pretty well given up on albums. They're trying to trace the narrative of their father's life, now it's too late to ask anybody who was there. All they have are objects, and little chips of memories. A leather collar box, monogrammed, a stud box, matching, a gold signet ring, a large round watch on a heavy chain for hanging across a waistcoat; it's monogrammed too. They belonged to the dashing Brown Eyes of Lizzie's diary, the dandy in blazer and flannels of the 1920s photographs. There's Lizzie's death, and the black hole of the Depression; Father up north. Where's north? Moree? Murwillumbah? Repton? What happened to the customs agents? No call for red salmon in tins from Canada any more, you have to suppose, retrenchments, cutbacks. Or did he, full of grief for Lizzie, throw it all in and go away, north as good as anywhere, not knowing that another job would be impossible to get, maybe not caring then? Refusing the susso, that they know, no self-respecting man took the susso if he could help it. Did he work on the roads, the terrible hand-building of roads that equalled dignified employment in the capital D Depression? Do they know this or have they invented it? As soon as you start speculating you forget where the truth once stopped. Or started. The man that comes back, up out of the black hole, and marries Alice, and fathers three daughters, the careful provider from the job he hated, he's no longer a glamorous figure, though he does go to Lodge in laundry-starched collars with sharp wings and black enamel studs. Elinor and Veronica feel sad about the dashing young man, forgetting that such visions always disappear, that they themselves are over fifty and not the pretty girls whom the likes of Martin Limeburner brought orchid corsages and took to balls but extremely offended they'd be if anybody felt sorry for them. Or maybe not forgetting, maybe mourning their own youth in George's, that is largely and so safely their own invention.

The New World, says Elinor, pressing the knob on the watch that makes its cover flip open. It doesn't go any more. Hasn't in all their memory of it. The Promised Land.

What?

I'm thinking of people coming here, like Grandfather Gray, and Grandma, looking for a better life. Do you reckon they found it?

I don't know that Grandma did. She was always awfully grumpy when I saw her. Of course, she was sick by then.

You know what she died of? says Elinor. Kidney failure. Brought on by analgesic abuse. Too many cups of tea and a Bex. Somewhat endemic in Newcastle, I believe. In the lower socio-economic classes, which means just about everybody. She stops talking like a death certificate and says softly: The disease of the poor and unhappy.

One or two things they know. Things that they got around to asking Alice, who was quite happy to open any cupboards she had the key to and let their skeletons dangle in the light of day. In her husband's family, anyway. And especially in her last insouciant days in the old people's home. So they know about Ada's bitter disappointment in Albert, who betrayed her with the drink, and got sent away and died reproached and lonely in Sydney. They've found a letter to their parents, elegantly written with a post-office nib dipped in ink, thoughtful, guilty, sad. Apologising between every line, and promising to be well again soon, he's got a brain tumour but it's responding to treatment, he'll be all right so long as he can keep going and keep improving, when he can he takes a walk down to the pool, this is at Manly, and depending on the clock has a brandy or a stout, and feels himself the stronger for it. It's anathema to Mum, he calls Ada, he knows that, but he needs the pick-me-up, he feels so much better, it's not drinking.

They know he died soon after, before any of them were born.

I think Alice rather liked Grandfather. He was always very sweet to her, she said.

I think she thought Ada would've driven anyone to drink.

You think they might have been better off staying in England? George might have died, and where would we be then?

We'll never know, says Elinor. One thing you can say, we're all right. I mean, prosperous enough. They pause to consider their upward mobility. Houses and cars and dishwashers and nice clothes and interesting jobs and bottles of wine when they feel like it; it's not the tightness of their childhood. Hand-me-downs of astounding ugliness and the sheer impossibility of peep-toe sandals and budgets as strict as a Victorian Baptist Sunday. But how safe is the new regime? Their own children may throw it all away.

Okay, says Veronica, but would we, I mean would their descendants, be any worse off if they'd stayed there?

Oh God, this is all too hard for me. Elinor stands up and does Tai Chi shrugs with her shoulders. Let's go and swim some laps, I'm seizing up.

They are after all over fifty and must not forget to exercise. Synthetic hormones on their own cannot keep the years at bay.

The launching

◆

Newcastle, 195–

They *that go down to the sea in ships, that do business in great waters*
These see the works of the Lord, and his wonders in the deep.

The soft knocking out of chocks had finished. The men stood around with their mallets, staring up at the platform where the minister read the service, high up beside the pointed sharp prow of the ship. Elinor held her father's hand. It was so very high, immense. From among the suited men a woman in a large hat stepped forth and said, I name this ship *Windarra*. At the same moment her silver scissors flashed, cutting through the ribbon, the champagne bottle flew out to smash against the bow, and the great ship began to move, slowly, slowly, gathering speed, faster, faster down the slipway. Elinor knew it wasn't the cut ribbon, the smashing bottle that set it off; her father had pointed out the man standing proud but unnoticed who would actually release the ship, held by one last slender tie, freeing it at the precise moment of the champagne hitting and exploding out in froth and glass so that it really seemed as though the christening wine had sent it on its way. Speeding now down the slipway, it hit the water with the aching splat of a belly buster, slowed, moved out into the channel, turned broadside on to the dock. Whistles sounded, and the works siren, with clapping and cheering from the men who had built it. What if it tips over, Elinor had asked at first. What if it sinks when it hits the water? It wouldn't happen, said George. They know what they're doing.

Will she sail off now, on her maiden voyage?

George looked at her, touched by this odd technical term in the child's mouth. Not yet, he said. She's not finished. It's only the hull that's done, that's what we've launched. Now all the inside fitting has to be done, the washbasins and the toilets, the tables and benches, the wood panelling. And of course the engines. A lot of work to be done, still. George knew because he paid all the bills for these things.

The tugs were moving *Windarra* into the wharf. She'd lost the grace of her glide down the slipway, had no power of her own in the water. Elinor was disappointed. She wanted the ship to set off immediately about its business in great waters, start straightaway seeing the wonders of the Lord. She felt the frustration of having to wait.

George often took Elinor to launchings. There were lots of boats abuilding, in those years, plenty of prosperous smoke in the chimneys: *Dongara, Karoon, Kootara, Townsville, Ben Shortridge, William McKell, Koojara, Illowra, Iranda, Princess of Tasmania, Bass Trader* . . . Not very grand boats: dredges, and tugs, ferries, coastal vessels, but when you stood on the ground and looked up at them they were mighty enough. Elinor was always moved by that quickening slide down the slipway into the water, it gave her a lump in the throat and she couldn't trust herself to speak. Even grown-up, when she saw such events only on the television, she felt her voice wobble when she spoke about them. Later, when her mother died and the two sisters had to sort out the family belongings, she found big glossy black and white photographs of some of these vessels in their moment of turning from engineering projects into living ships with names, genders, personalities; even, some people thought, souls. She kept them, though they were badly printed with spots and threads of dust, and she had no use for them.

The same river

— ◆ —

Mikelis liked to have Dane read aloud to him. He was particularly fond of the poems of A. D. Hope, who was back on his pedestal after some attempts towards the end of his life though only by certain young and iconoclastic poets to topple him. Mikelis's favourites were the eighteenth-century-style narrative poems with their classical wit; he thought that Dane's rather dry and deadpan though suave delivery was well-suited to their form. He also enjoyed the familiarity; he'd hear them over and over again. And yet each time there would be something fresh, something he hadn't noticed before.

I knew him, you know Dane, he said. I met him when he was quite an old man and I was commissioned to do some portraits of him. We'd often drink a bottle of claret together. He liked to know things; other people's skills and crafts and especially the science of them and the vocabulary always fascinated him. He used to write them down in notebooks. His dreams too, he always kept a record of his dreams. Said they were very fruitful. He'd have two or three notebooks going for different things. I expect they're in the National Library, one could see them. Unless he destroyed them at the end. I remember once he mislaid them and was terribly upset. It turned out he'd left them in a friend's car and they were quite soon returned but the panic in the meantime . . . Of course, there's nothing so precious as one's notebooks.

Mikelis paused. Dane recognised him going further off into memories.

Once in the days when I could still see well enough to read, I bought a book as one used to at airports, idly glancing over the titles to see if there was anything more interesting than what you'd brought along with you. It was a novel, and I don't usually go for novels much, but this one was by Jack Hawley. I read it, of course, every word, it was a kind of thriller, I suppose you'd say. His hero was a scholarly young man, he was writing a doctoral thesis, his field was philosophy, when he got caught up in a set of violent events. The writer obviously wanted to use the contrast of philosophy, of a person using his mind to make sense of the world around him, this tranquil and yet intense mental activity, and these violent events, which took place all over the globe as is the habit with thrillers. The action moved from Antwerp, to Riga, to Buenos Aires and then back to Europe, to Le Havre. Do you know what those cities have in common? Not easy to guess, is it. They're all estuarine cities, all ports on great river estuaries. So's Newcastle, of course; I was sorry he didn't put that in. And Christchurch is too, though it's not a port. I don't think the estuary business meant anything. It was just a pattern. He liked playing with patterns, the book's full of them, once you start to look you find more and more. For instance he gets involved with three women, Marguerite a French girl, she's the one he falls in love with; Peg an elderly expatriate Englishwoman living in South America, a black-sheepish heart-of-gold kind of person; and Greta who's a real villain, and as you see these names are all variants of Margaret, and yet again there seems no point in the pattern, it's just there. The plot unfolds through the seven deadly sins, ending of course in lust with the lovely Marguerite, just like those old James Bond movies. You felt that the writer was playing elaborate games with himself as much as with the reader, for how many people would read as carefully as I did and several times what was presented as just another thriller, one of those anonymous airport books as disposable as paper tissues were at the time. There was no biographical note on the author, for instance, and no identification of the book, just a line saying *This edition published 1983 Rooster Books*, which presumably implies other editions, though perhaps falsely. I tried to date it; Riga was post-Russian invasion but apart from that it was quite devoid of chronological hints, no mentions of governments and even the women's clothes didn't give anything away, just silk shirts, or overcoats, or jeans.

Jeans are well into the sixties, said Dane.

I suppose so. That still gives a period of nearly twenty years, possibly. Anyway, the book made a deep impression on me. There's a scene early on where the hero is visiting a resort near Riga, on the coast of the Gulf, and Greta, a stout and greedy though in her way handsome woman, is staying in the hotel and one already suspects up to no good. He goes swimming on one of those long pale yellow Baltic beaches, where the sand slips gently under the water, and he's walking out through this shallow area to the deeper water when he feels something bump against him, softly under the water, bump, in that slow languorous way that happens with objects floating under water, and when he looks down he sees that it's a man. His first thought is how ridiculous to be wearing a suit and dark red tie bumping about under the water like that, then he notices the eyes wide open and realises it's a dead body and of course he can't get out of the water fast enough. It turns out to be a curator from a museum in Antwerp which has just discovered that its famous collection of amber is missing. The question is, did he kill himself or did somebody else, and is he dead because he's guilty or because he's innocent?

Anyway, that body gently bumping around underwater,

that's how the book has often seemed to me. I'm idly going along doing something else, quite happily occupied, when along it comes, unexpected, making its presence felt with a sly and possibly sinister nudge; a bit of a shock and certainly a puzzle. Bump.

The young man whose name is Jacques (and is this another game that the writer, who remember is Jack Hawley, is playing with us?), Jacques Channel, is writing his thesis on Heraclitus, known as the Weeping Philosopher because his views on the nature of life as constantly changing, not to mention fleeting, were considered to be melancholy. (Always seemed quite logical to me.) Jacques' supervisor in this task is a middle-aged woman called Dr Patience Grange. Peg in Buenos Aires takes him to a nightclub called The Waters of Babylon where she divulges the connection between the amber mines of Hispaniola and the statue of Saint Margaret Martyr of Antioch that weeps tears of blood every 29 October, the feast day of Saint Narcissus.

Meanwhile Greta, whose profession is writing and illustrating children's books, a good job for a villain, has just published the story of amber, based on a legend. Listen to this. Mikelis settled forward and began to narrate. A tale within a tale. Once the Baltic Sea was warm and its shores were lined with thick tropical forests of vast pines, unknown today. Among them lived a race of kind-hearted gnomes who looked after the pines, which in turn loved their little owners. But one day cold winds bearing wicked giants came roaring in from the north and destroyed the gnomes. The pines wept bitterly, grieving for their dead friends. Their tears fell into the sea, transformed into the amber that to this day is washed up on Baltic shores.

I already knew that story, said Mikelis. Eva had it as a child. Anyway, this little legend is another vital clue. You see what tricks the writer is playing. What nests of clues he is brooding over. Leaving the reader to guess at which will hatch out.

But for me the final, the ultimate trick is the writer himself. Jack Hawley: is he my Jack who dived off the Pont de la Tournelle and accidentally killed himself? Or is he another

Jack Hawley who has absolutely no connection at all with
my Jack, except the not very amazing coincidence of possessing
the same name? And if it is my Jack, when did he write it?
Was it already published, in 1964 when I knew him in Paris,
had it already been parcelled up and sent away in a pile of
manuscript typed out late at night in an attic room in the
Rue des Fossés Saint Jacques? Or maybe even earlier, and it
was paying for his writer's life in Paris? Or was it the contents
of those small black notebooks which he wrote so assiduously
in the café called L'Ecritoire in the Place de la Sorbonne, the
notebooks carried away by his wife, as she'd promised she would,
and ordered by her into a final publishable state, the sodden
notebook and any bits unwritten filled in by her? A posthumous
work. Jack speaking from beyond the grave, the most valuable
of all utterances. That's why I read it so carefully, to look
for clues; I imagined I found them—shapes, said Jack; for shapes
read patterns—and then at other times I thought I was
imagining them. And that of course is my Jack too, with him
I never knew where the truth lay. He was a great liar; that
was what art was about, he reckoned, fabulous lies.

One thing: I said all those estuarine cities were a pattern
existing for its own sake, with no ulterior significance, but
there is this to be noted. Estuaries are not fixed: they shift
their banks, they silt up and wash away, they construct sand-
banks in awkward places. They've sometimes been more
dangerous to ships than the open sea. They are not ancient
creations like flooded river valleys, like the ports of Sydney
and Rio de Janeiro and Christchurch's Lyttelton, immovable
and immemorial. They are always in a state of flux, everything
flows and nothing stays. Said Heraclitus. People have to
construct dykes and sea walls filled with ballast to achieve
any kind of permanence at all, and even so they have to keep
working at it; stop paying attention and you could lose the
lot. Estuarine cities: they're right up Jack Hawley's alley.

Estuarine cities. There used to be a saying about Newcastle,
about a certain part of Stockton it was, where the harbour
had been made by building a sea wall and filling in behind
it. It was said that people from any country in the world could

walk there and be walking on native soil, because of the ballast that filled it being brought in sailing ships from all over the world. In one place it's rubble from the San Francisco earthquake. The ships'd come loaded with the stuff and take back coal. People would find dimes and cuff-links and bits of old typewriters and take them home and put them on their mantelpieces. Bits of San Francisco on their mantelpieces.

After a while Dane said, Would you like me to try to find out about Jack Hawley? Whether it was your Jack that wrote the book—what was it called?

The Same River.

Well, I could check the National Library, see if there's a copy with a biographical note; there must be ways of finding out if it's him.

No, said Mikelis. Don't do that. I like the puzzle. And anyway, I'm pretty well certain it has to be him. Most of the time.

You could be certain all of the time.

It might be the wrong kind of certainty. I mean the certainty that it isn't him. Why should I risk that?

What if I tried to find out some more of Jack Hawley's stories? Then I could read them to you.

I'll have to see, said Mikelis.

There might be other parts of the patterns filled in by them . . .

Mikelis was silent for a long moment. The thing is, he said, the detective novel is the most highly patterned of fictions. And the most comfortable. Because there are always solutions, it doesn't exist if there aren't solutions. And of course Jack Hawley does offer them. We know who the murderer is, we find out what happened to the amber. All of the threads are tied into neat little knots at the end, even if some of them are a bit slippery. You can't subvert the plot of a detective novel, if you do you kill it. But the themes, the patterns of apparently arbitrary choice, there's no solutions there, no explanations. Their mystery is inviolate. Mikelis's voice quivered. Inviolate. The word hung in the air, a strange shape as all words are when given separation and weight. After a pause he went on. And so it is full of unease . . . Have you ever read a book and felt it was written somehow at you? Latvia, for God's sake. Latvia. Why Latvia? And amber. You didn't see Veronica in her amber. Eva has it now, you know. She's maybe a bit fair for it, though it suits her well enough. But in Paris, when I knew Jack, I never even thought of amber. I knew my mother had some, that she wore it on occasions, but I never thought of it. It's all coincidence, I suppose. Everything's coincidence, one way or another. And everything that happens to us the most absurd accident of chance. And yet we want to believe in the patterns. So badly. So badly.

The cemetery

◆

Newcastle, 1968

It was some days before Veronica was allowed to see Martin. When Aunt Lily's IVP was over and she could take a moment to ring the hospital his condition was stable, he was resting, and was allowed no visitors. What about wives? fiancées? she thought of asking, but didn't because of staving off those roles as long as possible.

At lunch-time she walked up the side street where Neville of Newcastle displayed his wares. There was the wistaria grotto and the wishing well and the rustic seat, all those tawdry properties transformed by silvery mists of black and white film into mysterious landscapes; not real, not meaning to be, instead offering the comfort of artifice . . . We are pictures of the ideal, we are forms of the truth. Stray awhile among us. And now she was expelled.

Except for one brief excursion. There'd be a wedding, all the trappings. Martin would see to that. And Neville practising his art. Not Mikelis. She could trust him not to come. Which message of bliss will they choose to record their union? The wistaria weeps purple tears on her white satin sweetheart-necklined princess-panelled gown, the gnarled twigs of the rustic seat snaggle her veil.

She took herself away from the photographs, walking fast up the streets away from the town until she came to the back gate of the cathedral, and up the steps and through the neglected cemetery. Her father told stories of choir boys putting their fellows in underground tombs and all the naughty things they did to compensate for the holiness of their singing. She sat on a headstone; in front of her was the broad stretch of harbour and town, for the cathedral of Newcastle though nineteenth-century imitation is truly Gothic in its dominance of the city; there's nothing higher than it, the city never having been rich enough to go in for skyscraping. The harbour is at work, full of business and bustle and all so orderly. The portly sliding of the ships up and down from their berths, as stately as if on wheels, the invisible effort of the tugs that draw them on their way, the swarming of men on the wharves: it's all so habitual, places for everything and everything in place, all such hard work though from here it looks easy; so inevitable, so disciplined, and so much part of huge schemes of trade and agriculture and industry, of which each bit knows nothing but its own small role; and without choices except of the most minor kind.

It is exactly what being married to Martin will be like.

It's not often blue, this harbour. Its narrow estuarine mouth spits mud. Sometimes on sunny days it has the hard dark shining greens and indigos of metals. Today it is grey. The smoke wells out from the steelworks' chimneys and banks up with the clouds in the sky so that it's impossible to tell apart the towering dirty cumuli of man and nature. The sky hangs low with their weight. You have to see the smoke as a good thing. It means work, the gift of work and wages to the local men and women. A crystal sparkling sky to the north-west signifies disaster, in this town.

Veronica sat on her headstone and contemplated marriage

to Martin. There was a man in a grey gaberdine overcoat standing behind a vault, watching her. He walked briskly up, stopped just to her right, and exposed himself, pulling his coat back, his penis dankly dangling purple in the cold air. When she didn't respond he stood nonplussed for a moment, then wrapped himself up and went away.

The harbour at Newcastle is a serious place. The works of humankind come right up to its plain straight edges. Its plain straight edges are works of humankind: walls filled with ballast reclaiming swamp. The estuary mouth was never so sharply drawn. Its borders were fluid as quicksand and as untrustworthy. The artificial harbour has its beauty, if you know it, but its seductions are slow, insidious as comfort. Visitors and outsiders see only how industrial. But it functions, and is laboured over, livelihoods are made by it; these things are lovable.

When Veronica's brain finally saw the image of the man her retina had registered out of the corner of her unseeing eye, he'd gone. It occurred to her that this graveyard on a cold grey and now wet day was maybe not a safe place.

As it wasn't, in a sense. What happened was, she caught a cold and took to her bed, where her mother coddled her with pale peppery bone soup and fingers of toast and marmite. Mikelis came to visit her one evening and found her red-nosed and lank-haired beside the fire and not as enthusiastic as he'd expected about his marvellous news, that he'd bought a car. That was what he was saving up for, not a suit. It was a Morris Minor, he said, sort of green; well, it had been once. He'd bought it from a former headmistress of the girls grammar school. One careful little old lady owner, he said. One careful little old dragon, more like. That's probably what happened to the paintwork, she breathed on it. Her father gave the little chuckle which was all the laughing he ever did, his amusement was inside. What about some toast? her mother said. The fire's just right. Veronica started to cry. Her mother was worried. It was not like Veronica to give in to illness like this. Veronica went to bed, and George talked to Mikelis until late.

Their subject was suffering, the problem of pain. George's

choice, of course. He said the only way you could explain it was by reincarnation. People paying for the sins of a past life or lives through maybe many incarnations to come. Think of a Nero, what he'd have to go through, how long it would take to atone, said George. The mind falters, contemplating that expiation. And, on the other hand, think of a little kiddie, born with some terrible disease, mongolism or hydrocephalus. Or a young woman in her prime, struck down with polio. Did they deserve that, in this life? A blameless young woman, a newborn babe? Can you believe in a loving God, who sees even a sparrow fall, in the face of such evidence?

What about this war, said Mikelis. The terrible things happening to the people of Vietnam. The ordinary people, in villages. The children.

Ah yes, Vietnam, said George, and stopped. His pause wasn't rhetorical. What if he'd had a son, the right age? What if . . . daughters are a blessing at this moment. And at least the men they bring home are old enough to have missed . . . Yes, Vietnam, he said. It's hard to accept, the atrocities. And the young men, committing them; what are they laying up for the future?

Now? said Mikelis. I mean, this life or the next?

Exactly, said George. Both, you'd have to say. And as for the people, the innocent victims, their lives destroyed, well, it's hard to take. But if you see these terrible things now coming from something in a past life . . .

Isn't that maybe a bit too neat?

I don't know about neat. It's just. Better than random mindless evil.

So you think, asked Mikelis, that maybe a whole country has to suffer like that? Like Latvia, for instance . . . but no, that's not possible. It's never had the power to commit the kind of crimes that would need that sort of punishment.

No, not as a country. But maybe, as a set of individuals. Maybe your suffering countrymen are reincarnations of those very Russians or Germans or whoever they were that oppressed your people in the past?

Mikelis shuddered.

You have to see that there is a plan in all things, said George. Though maybe we can't always see what it is.

• • •

Veronica's cold went, and her state was put down to convalescence. Martin was allowed to have visitors.

Now she walked slowly along a corridor of the hospital. At the end of it was a tall window, offering a view of the sea, hazy because of the layers of spray that had been blown on the glass. At the bottom of it was a strip of sand, in the middle the waves breaking, and above the smooth lines of the swell. All the colours were milky silvery greenish grey in the winter sunlight. It was like a painting in the frame of the window. Monet perhaps, the salt haze on the glass the light he'd suffused it with. It moved, but so solidly it might have been the imagination believing the light the artist had painted, seeing it well and shine. There was nothing human in it, no people or boats, just horizontal bands of shifting light she knew were sand and sea, though in this frame they were abstracted far beyond themselves. Veronica had wanted to go to art school but everybody said radiography was a much safer career, even her art teacher who gave her good marks and said, Look at me, you don't want to end up like me, do you? She stopped when she saw the picture at the end of the passage, wanting to gaze at it, wishing she could turn what she saw into something she'd made, but a nurse bustled up, demanding that she do what she'd come for. Veronica's picture was just a window that never stayed clean because of the sea whose insistent salty vapours were destroying the hospital. What madness to build a hospital practically in the sea, people said. But what beauty for looking out on.

The nurse directed her to Martin in his bed in a ward that looked the other way, at the harbour and town full of human energy, and up to the yellow curves of Stockton Beach and the pines that hid the mental hospital. She was very fond of Martin, she must remember that, he was good company, they had a good time together. Marriage to him would be busy and fruitful, there was the harbour to prove it.

He lay flat with his leg trussed up, eyes closed, sad and pale amid the white sheets. She sat on a chair and looked at the way the mechanism of the bed was spotted with rust and waited for him to wake up and hoped he wouldn't just yet. She remembered how angry she was with him for doing this to himself, for offering himself to her like this, and by intention worse, presumably, since if he'd had his way it would be his corpse she was viewing. It would serve him right if she were to wish that it was. She sat furious and pitying him, waiting. This face on the gleaming hospital pillow would be the face in their own bed beside her through all the nights and mornings of marriage; this face already an older self, not the spicy-scented young man's face that smiled and promised. The curve of forehead where already his fine brown hair was creeping back was polished as a bone. Life with Martin would not be any more a series of outings; it was sitting and comforting, waiting and nursing. She wasn't the girl in the Healey any longer. She was a woman responsible for love. I've grown up, she thought, with a kind of melancholy pleasure; I can see the beauty of duty.

Martin opened his eyes. She smiled wanly and he looked at her with the milky vague eyes of a baby learning to see. She leant over and kissed him, he winced and she saw grazes across his chest and shoulder.

I've brought grapes. She laughed. People always bring grapes.

I couldn't find them, Martin said. I thought I saw them half way down but when I got there it wasn't them. And then the rocks slid away and I went down, I couldn't stop myself. I was sure they were there.

Veronica stared at him. Then she began to laugh and stopped herself and squeezed his hand. Don't worry, she said, it doesn't matter.

He looked at her like a child surprised. But I wanted to find them.

You're all right. That's what counts. You're going to be perfectly all right.

I reckon some fisherman must have got hold of them. Best catch he ever made, I reckon.

It doesn't matter.

Why do you keep saying that? His voice was querulous, he frowned as he turned his face towards her. She saw his cheek looking like a mushroom, puffy and speckled with grazes. They were real pearls, you know. Real cultivated pearls. Worth a lot of money.

Veronica saw an old man insisting, insisting: They were real cultured pearls, you know, in a voice that blamed all those who did not.

You should have insured them, I suppose, she said.

That's a thought. A good idea. Something to remember for the future.

Though of course, she went on, this time you'd have had to lie about how the goods were lost. I mean, you can't insure against throwing things away.

She saw a kind of puzzlement in his face, and realised that he wasn't thinking about the throwing at all, only about the retrieving; and then she saw that the responsibility of the act was becoming hers. It would be Veronica's fault that the pearls got pitched over the cliff, Martin's the bold and generous rescue. Even if it had failed.

I mustn't tire you, she said, touching his hand. Speedy recovery! She heard herself sounding like a get-well card.

She felt so light she could have levitated along the linoleum corridors, down the stairs, ducking under the lintel of the door into the street. Speedy recovery indeed. Martin needed no recovery, was still himself, the man she'd refused to marry, a man not only not throwing himself over a cliff but not throwing anything, obliterating that first rash divesting passionate act. His fine careless anger—things mean nothing to me without you—had been entirely undone and knitted up again into a crotchetty care for objects. She felt a moment of sadness for the elderly child that Martin had suddenly become, but that was immediately wiped out by relief: how much, how entirely, how absolutely she'd done the right thing. Martin could never be the man for her, need never be. Dear Martin, for making it so easy.

She went on levitating back to work, up and down the little steep hills of King Street. The sun shone; she could feel it warming her hair and under that her skin and deeper still her brain; she felt she might flower. At the top of one of the crests was a dress shop and in its windows black dresses glittering with bugle beads, tarty dresses short and tight and low, worn by leggy Shrimptonish dummies posing under arches of purple crêpe paper wistaria. She laughed aloud; a passer-by stared. She's going back to Mikelis, back to the studio and the balding red couch and all the tatty furnishings of bliss. She's unclasped the marriage pearls from round her neck, and her mind dances in tarty black dresses while the long legs of love flash like scissors through the daily silk of life.

Streetwalking

◆

Newcastle, late 1960s

When Mikelis asked Veronica
to marry him she said no. I've had enough of marriage, she
said.

Mikelis jumped up off the *chaise longue*. His face was that
of a man who steps on green grass and finds it's quicksand.
He spluttered, Whatever do you mean?

I mean the six I've had already, of course. What else?

(Four days of being mentally married to Martin could seem
like a lifetime. She'd done a lifetime's thinking.)

Was this a reprieve? Or was he still sinking? He frowned.

Naked men shouldn't frown, said Veronica. She draped herself
across the red velvet. Naked people should smile, like me.

You think this is a joke, he shouted, and his hurt was so
bare and needy she stood up and put her arms around him.
Held him tight. Safe from the quicksand. Or else joining him
in it.

I've been thinking about marriage lately, she said. It's such a show. The clothes and the presents and everybody watching. Horrible. Not us. You love me. I love you. Let's live together.

You mean, without being married?

Mm.

Mikelis began to grin, a huge grin, and grabbed her and danced with her. When they got to Hymen's Bower he pulled her inside, laughing, serious. We'll plight our troths, he said. The two of them stood, straight and still together, their bodies gently touching, a moment of calm passion so intense that each felt the thrilling in the other's flesh. Each was lightly encircled in the other's arms, and they looked into one another's eyes for a long time, knowing one another, feeling the air vibrating round these still bodies that enclosed so much emotion, and then Mikelis bent his head and slowly kissed her.

Sudden chill. The wistaria petals fluttered in a breeze from the thrown-open door. Do you mind! a loud voice shouted, and there stood Neville (of Newcastle). Veronica made a grab for her clothes but all she managed was her bra which with its lacy engineering seemed more naked than bare flesh. She tried to hide behind the fluttering pannicles of wistaria. If Botticelli had been around he could have made something of it.

Neville advanced, head poked forwards on his neck, hissing with rage: Decent people come here. Decent people. (The eees and esses shimmered with fury.) Unsuspecting people. Recording the holiest moment of their lives. And you bring whores and sluts.

Mikelis drew himself up, proud, cold. More so for being naked. Michelangelo could have made something of him.

This lady is neither a whore nor a slut. And there is only one of her. What's more, she's my . . . beloved.

This is a place for pure young women. The sanctity of the marrige vow is celebrated here week after week, and you, you despoil, you defile it. You taint it. It's sacrilege. I won't have the heart . . .

Oh, come on, Neville, what's pure about brides? If they're not pregnant it's not usually for want of having a go, you know.

Neville began to stutter in his rage. He gave Mikelis the sack. Tut-tut-two weeks' pay in lieu of notice. That calmed him down a bit. Get out! he screamed. And take your nasty lewd photographs with you.

It turned out he'd seen the pictures Mikelis had made of Veronica (quite ordinary tasteful nude shots, said Mikelis), had recognised the studio and crept back at night to catch them at it. It'd taken a few trips, which added to his fury.

I see you've been prying through my private work, said Mikelis. You deserve your fate. May you photograph brides forever. May you *tint* brides forever. He walked over to the door and held it open. Wait outside while we dress.

When he'd taken the pictures of Veronica he had said, Nobody will see them, they're just for us. And anyway, nobody'll recognise you. Veronica (and Mikelis? now she wondered) had not noticed the contradiction involved in these assurances at the time.

Mikelis strode around, collecting his cameras and folios of work. Veronica already dressed, her cherry wool coat wrapped tight around her, said, You're very dignified when you're starkers. You're like some classical person putting things to rights. Jupiter, do I mean, or Apollo? I think I'll do some pictures of you. I could fancy myself as a photographer of male nudes.

The male nude, said Mikelis. Just one. Me.

He came and put his arms around her. It was a strange feeling, her so thoroughly dressed and him naked. It had a wicked quality, exciting. He touched her clothed body and she his naked one and they both shivered with desire. Neville banged on the door. Get a move on, he shouted.

◆ ◆ ◆

They sat in the dim-lit Napoli drinking cappuccinos. Softly in the background swallows came back to Capistrano. Now they were both dressed the current of desire had lost its zap. Well, that's blown it, said Mikelis. We decide to set up house and kapow! I lose my job. And we won't have anywhere to go. Mikelis had a room in the house of a strict lady: no female visitors.

I'm sad about the red velvet couch, said Veronica. She mourned in silence for a while the old studio and all those furnishings of bliss. But no job doesn't matter. I've got a job, remember? Do you know how much I earn? We can easily live on that. And anyway you'll get work soon. Or you could set up your own business.

You need money for that.

You can start being itinerant. Go to people's places. Or in the street.

You still need a dark room, and all that. And publicity, advertising . . .

She leant over and kissed him. We're free, remember? We're together. Her voice murmured, darkly, as though she were hypnotising him. And think of all the money we'll save, not having a wedding.

I want to be a great photographer, you know, Vero. This bread-and-butter stuff, it's okay, but one day . . . do you know what Lartigue said? He said that there are cooks who pick cherries and make jam. I pick cherries but I prefer to eat fresh fruit. That was his approach to photography. One day I want people to say, Lartigue and Cartier-Bresson and Ballod.

What do you want them to say about you?

Mikelis paused for a moment. That he restored innocence. The eye is always choosing. It corrupts the camera.

Can you escape making choices?

Not in life. Choices should be made in life. Like this. He picked up her hand and began to kiss her fingers. But in photography . . . well, we'll see.

Do you know what I'd've liked to do? said Veronica, dreamy voiced from the hidden passion of Mikelis's finger kissing. In the studio. Turn everything round. Put the bride on the marble table with the ball, the baby with the bookshelves, the scholar in the bower.

That's subversion. Complete subversion. I didn't know you were such an anarchist.

I'm only beginning to find out myself.

When she told her parents she was going to live with Mikelis there was a terrible silence. George looked at her as though she were a changeling.

What sort of slap in the face is this for your mother and me? What does this say for the values we've given you?

A lot, said Veronica. Freedom and honour. Choosing. Not being a slave to society. After all, we're not religious. Our own promises are enough.

And what about respect?

There's stacks of that.

What sort of a man asks such a thing of a woman? George was wary, circling soft-footed this phenomenon, approaching it from all angles, as though sooner or later he'd find its weak spot, and then he'd pounce.

It's my idea.

George stared at her. You disgust me, girl. I thought you knew better than this.

Father, we love each other.

And what about when he gets tired of you? Ditches you? Soiled goods!

What about when I get tired of him? Ditch him!

It doesn't work like that.

Father, this is the sixties. People have evolved. We don't need outmoded conventions.

Look at your cousin Anne. Look at Robyn. Look at Jade. *Jade*, for pity's sake. What sort of name is that for an innocent babe?

Yes. Look at them. Some advertisement for marriage they are. What I'm doing is a damn sight more honest than getting married because you're pregnant.

And what happens when you . . . get that way?

The pill, Father. It's safe contraception that's changed the way we live. We're free now. Veronica looked at her parents. You and Mum were in love. You know what it's like. How pure it is . . .

I don't think you should speak of your mother in the same breath as what you're doing.

Alice's silence was a huger hole than ever.

George was saying words, softly to himself. Strumpet. Whore.

Scarlet woman. Fallen. Courtesan. Slut. Not at his daughter. Not name-calling. Rather as though trying them out for sound, size, shape. As though one day he might need them, and should get a little practice in first.

Veronica said, I honestly didn't think you'd mind. Which wasn't really true. She knew her father would hate the idea. By saying she didn't think he'd mind she hoped to make it happen.

They found a flat in Ordnance Street. Two rooms in an old house. Supposed to be fully furnished. If this is fully, I'd not care to see sparsely, said Veronica. At least we can choose our own things, not get stuck with the monstrosities great aunts think are good wedding presents.

Alice happened to have some new sheets and towels about and gave her those, and when she was shopping and came across things like nice coffee mugs she bought them. *Furnishing a love nest* was a phrase that often came into her mind. She liked the sound of it. The words nest and love were so full of good things. She thought of herself and George; a long time ago, perhaps they'd had one. In those old hard days, with the Depression still pinching and prying at them, and the War. Not the safety and ease of these young people. Living in sin was George's description of what was going on, but Alice saw Veronica's point; the only difference was the saying of words in church, and that shouldn't alter what was really happening between two people.

Elinor was full of admiration. I couldn't do it, she said. Too hard for me and Ivan.

Veronica remembered wondering whether she and Ivan were sleeping together, all that time when Martin was being so coy. Of course they were, looking back on it. Of course. It seemed silly even to have thought to consider it now. She said, That's not the hard part. For me and Mikelis it's easy. It's other people it's hard for. Are we a couple? Should they know? Do they invite us for dinner? It's quite funny really.

For Veronica it was exhilarating. Every morning she woke up and thought, I'm living with Mikelis, and felt a huge warm well of satisfaction, so that she reached for him and began to make love to him, and was nearly always late for work, until she started putting her alarm on half an hour earlier.

Mikelis was not in fact a person who needed encouraging for each new step, as she had feared on that first night in the café. In conversation he made objections but then he went and did things, and in imaginative ways. It was as though those conversations were with himself: bring up all the difficulties and talk about them, and then you'd dealt with them and could get on with the useful doing. He earned some money freelancing, and as a street photographer, though not many people bought these pictures. But they were the beginning of the series of photographs that he later titled *Streetwalking*. From this time dated the one of a mother turning on her child with a ferocious teeth-baring scowl, the child cringing, but not daring to take his eyes off her, large eyes full of such pure terror that in turn it terrifies the viewer. It was in Hunter Street, hot weather and frazzled shopping crowds. When Veronica saw this she said, You talk about innocence? About not making choices? Who are you kidding? The critics when finally it was shown mentioned Blakean visions, and bleak morality tales for our time. But in Newcastle at that time Mikelis was just a street photographer, and in terms of selling his wares not a successful one. People rarely liked the images he showed them of themselves. A bulging woman in tight skimpy clothes carrying a large bag, whose shape repeated her own shapelessness and staring with a kind of malevolent intensity at a suited hatted gloved pearled woman (Veronica recognised herself in the future of another life which, how gratefully, she'd rejected), neither of these ladies would have cared to pay money to perpetuate themselves looking like that.

Mikelis also applied for jobs. What about going to Canberra, he said. Why not, replied Veronica. A radiographer can get work anywhere. They packed the once-green Morris and set off for a new life in the capital.

So then her mother could say, Yes, Veronica's off to Canberra. Well, Elinor's down there too, you know. Yes, she and Ivan, they're buying a house. Alice might think about love nests, but it was easier not to have to explain them to nosy neighbours. A marriage and a house, they were safe topics.

♦ ♦ ♦

Good reason for Ivan and Elinor acquiring their own real estate. Canberra rents were huge. Just about everybody had a subsidy from their employer, it went with the job, but Mikelis hadn't realised this. All they could manage was a garage with a concrete floor and one tiny rug; the winter was freezing. Mikelis caught pneumonia. Then they rented a house in Forrest at a very good address but in bad repair. Their cat caught rats in the dining-room. They did the sums of all couples in that place at that time, and worked out that it was cheaper to pay off a house than rent one. If you were married, that is. Otherwise you couldn't get a loan. So they went to the registry office one day and tied the knot. Purely a financial arrangement, Veronica wrote to her parents. Was it? Do you feel any different, she asked Mikelis. No, of course not, he said. Veronica wasn't sure. It's a pity you can't stay free, she said. Love is more real when you're free. The morning exhilaration seemed to have leaked away. She felt that society had tricked them, trapped them.

We're still the same people, said Mikelis. This is just a convention, playing the game their way, so we can win. When they walked round the garden of the house they were buying in O'Connor he looked up at the gums that surrounded it. He tilted his head back and looked at the tall trees turning against the sky. The blueness of it, the turning trees, flashed in his eyes and made him dizzy. For a moment he understood the earth turning on its axis, the giddy pull of the sun, giving it a long rope but hanging on tight, the exciting controlled whirl through space. Veronica gazed down at the slender trunks rooted in the ground, the lumpy branches repeated under the earth, splitting it, wrenching out but held. Later she would plant daisies, day's eyes, pretty simple plants that bushed and blossomed among the roots. Mikelis would have chosen sunflowers, showy pushy creatures forever rubbernecking at the sun. Heliotrope, girasole, following the sun. Learning to look like it.

In this garden their cat would die, after a mighty battle with a snake. They would come home and find the two bodies entwined, for the cat killed the snake too. Veronica was upset; the cat had been their pet as long as they'd lived together. Mikelis said, with tears in his eyes, Look, what an epic battle. It could be the subject of a saga, the hero vanquishing the monster, but dying in the attempt. Beowulf, and who was it? Grendel, Grendel's mother, somebody. Veronica wondered whether this slotting of present unhappiness into a known art form, a story, a picture, perhaps diminished it; made it easier to bear by giving it a familiar shape but took away the grieving that ought to belong. Especially when the mode had to be mock-heroic. A cat isn't really an epic hero, she said. She wrapped him in a piece of white sheet and buried him. Mikelis dropped the snake into the grave. Buried with his trophy, he said. Well, what else can you do with a dead snake?

Shortly afterwards they went to the opening of an exhibition of his new boss's work, the usual bad wine affair of backs turned to the pictures and gossip. Veronica's photograph was taken and appeared in the social pages of the *Sun-Herald*. Mrs Mikelis Ballod, said the caption. She pointed this out to Mikelis: Look, I have turned into a different person.

Nevertheless she sent the clipping to her parents. She knew her father would like it. Veronica safe at last, and in the eyes of the world.

Twins

Newcastle, 1971

Elizabeth Sullivan surprised everybody by getting married long after the rest of the family had taken it for granted that she never would. Her siblings and cousins were long past the first bloom of that state. Several of her own nieces and nephews had beaten her to it. Some of them had stopped pitying her singleness and started envying it; they wouldn't have minded the opportunity to be their own person again. She'd taken up tennis and met a carpenter who had a good business remodelling kitchens, a widower with three children already grown up. Andrew considered that this was enough family for any man, but said to Elizabeth that every woman had a right to a child and she could have one. Just one; at their time of life that would be enough. Perhaps he thought that at thirty-nine she might be past it and this need be no more than a generous gesture from an experienced husband to his new wife. But Elizabeth's body having dutifully produced eggs for two and a half decades all to no avail seemed to jump at the chance to make something of them at last; a month after the wedding she was pregnant. Thin Elizabeth became all round and willowy; she'd always been as gawky as an adolescent and now she lost that gawkiness but kept the youthfulness. She sat with those beautiful hands of hers resting on her belly with a smooth Madonna air that made people think, Elizabeth's not bad looking, after all. Clever Andrew just happened to notice it.

Then she produced twins. A girl and a boy. Daniel and Sarah. After that her husband regarded her with a certain distrust, as well as a lot of respect. Here was a woman who could bend life to her will. He told the story to his mates: Talk about giving her an inch and she takes a mile. One kid I said. So off she goes and produces twins. There was a certain upper-handedness about it that was good for Elizabeth in the early days of marriage; it set her up as a woman not to be trifled with.

In fact it was a good idea, better than having an only child. Twins were homegrown playmates keeping one another amused. Andrew made plenty of money, the kitchen business was really taking off, he employed a number of men and had time to enjoy his babies. Lily lunched with Alice and boasted about their amazing exploits. With these babies to hand as well as three new great-grandchildren it's not surprising that she rarely remembered Jade, only sometimes in an insomniac early morning thinking of Steve and wondering how the child was, constructing worries about her well-being, but forgetting all about her in the busy hours of daylight.

The shooting

◆

Sydney, 1984

The theory was that Jade and Eric would drive up to the mountains at the weekends to see Sebastian, but in fact it often didn't happen because Eric had too much work to do, and Jade found herself going by train, sometimes just staying overnight, sometimes all day as well, when she could see Sebastian awake.

At this time Jade and Eric were living in Leichhardt, in a solid if rather musty old terrace with rooms taller than they were long and a tendency for being burgled until they persuaded the landlord to put bars on all the windows with deadlocks and security doors. Were they sharing a house or living together? It was house-sharing in that they had separate rooms and two other people in with them and the place was run along the usual lines of a group house. But they also slept together most nights. They treated one another with a certain politeness where their free time was concerned, and neither took the other's availability for granted. There's a party, they would say or, What about this movie or, Let's go round the corner for some pasta, but each was supposed to feel free to say no, they both had so many deadlines to meet. Jade and Eric are so civilised, said their friends. Who at the same time saw them as a couple, and this was partly because of their looks: both large, Jade with her great-grandmother Lily's tall and opulent figure, but harder and leaner, and not dark like her, fair like her father Steve Apples, a honey skin light brown hair fairness, and it is this hair which shows her to be somewhere a romantic because instead of having it cropped short as you would expect of a woman with her efficiency and instantness of being she wore it long and in a plait, or sometimes spreading down her back in shimmering plait-crimped waves. She's not pretty, rather she has a kind of beautiful plainness which is endearing as well as tough. If you wanted someone to spin shirts out of nettles Jade would be just the person to ask. She would not fear the stinging of her long brown fingers if it had to be done. And she'd know what you were talking about because Zoe brought her up on fairytales, and since she started law they haven't been supplanted by much else in the way of imaginative reading. Eric looks exactly the same, allowing for being a man, and his hair short. Because of their tallness they seem to look over people's heads, with their light-coloured eyes that don't falter or wink, and their expression of seeing further and better than most people. When they go out together they look so very much a pair that everybody believes they are one, and so do they seem to themselves.

Then, there are the assumptions. Certain things have been worked out, it is assumed that others will be. Eric graduated in the summer that Sebastian was born, Jade still has two years to go. When she has finished too then they'll go overseas. Will they take Sebastian? Why not? says Jade, we can't be parted from him for too long. It can be worked out. Perhaps Zoe and Amelia will go too. There's plenty of time.

In the meantime Eric will get a job. It's always been assumed that this will be in something like Legal Aid, some useful serving-the-cause-of-justice area. The other two people in the house were also studying law, and they all had friends, who dropped in and sat around the kitchen drinking coffee and talking about the profession they were planning to enter. There were arguments about what it meant, ranging from a shining-eyed idealism, the law as a great principle, through various theories of accessibility and helpfulness, to fierce personal ambition, from Jade in one corner with her desire to aid the ignorant and unfortunate, to Sean in another who intended to go into politics and become Attorney General and actually make laws, to Harold who planned to become a barrister and a QC in the $1000 a day or whatever it would be by then class. Over Nescafé they talked and there never was any doubt of the achievability of all these things. Eric was assumed to be in the same corner as Jade, except that he mostly wasn't present because he was shut in his room working, and eventually she did wonder how much she had made assumptions about him, and especially about people not changing, how they changed but didn't think to tell you, probably didn't even notice it themselves, so that you went on thinking things were as they'd always been when they were actually quite different, and this made her think carefully and nervously about the nature of assumptions, and that even when you did seem to share them exactly with another person you couldn't be sure that you both meant the same thing.

Eric was clever as well as hard-working and when he graduated he won the university medal. Harold who was in second year said, You can do something with that. I can see the dollar-signs flashing in your eyes, said Jade scornfully. Whenever it was Harold's turn to make a meal he did steamed vegetables. So did they all, but not so inevitably as Harold. Anything he could find in the fridge, all thrown together in a big Chinese bamboo steamer Zoe had given them when she found out what they mostly ate. Steamed vegetables, again. One day soon, Harold says, I shall never eat steamed vegetables, never one single time more.

Oho, says Jade. You'll get fat and unhealthy on rich man's food.

Jade, he replies, your argument is not logical. Your equations are false. Why not slender and healthy on rich man's food? On expensive fish and rare salads? His mouth gleams. Oysters, he says. I shall live on oysters. Washed down with the occasional glass of Chablis. I shall not only be wealthy and healthy, I shall be very very sexy.

Jade who never thinks about what she eats but grabs something she hopes is nourishing in transit from work to work, simply laughs at him. Harold sexy? Only if money seduces.

Harold was irritated when Eric went to work at the Legal Aid office in town. What a waste, he complains. Jade begins to see that he's quite serious about his greed. That when it comes to life choices it isn't a matter for the future, they're already made. At least in theory. She tries to argue in his terms. Don't you see that trying to make the system work for ordinary people is a buzz? What's money, compared to gratification? Even to her ears this sounds a bit feeble, which enrages her.

My poor Jade, Harold sneers. You're so naive. This enrages her more. After that she doesn't argue with him. She's believed in his affection, and that his materialism is more mannerism than intent. Now she wonders.

❖ ❖ ❖

Spring comes, and Sebastian is learning to walk. Men do not stop bashing their wives and children. The warmth is still pleasant, after winter, but there is in the air that hint of westerly dryness that foreshadows exams. It is weather hotting up for the last sprint to the finishing post of exams. Jade has been at the refuge and is loping up the path to the Fisher Library— she wears runners because she runs everywhere—when she hears her name called, and there is Eric, waving, no, beckoning.

I haven't got time, she begins, but he insists, is oddly insistent, draws her off to a corner of the lawn to sit in the sun. He's got a brown paper parcel, which he puts where his lap would be, if he weren't a man, sitting on the ground, cross-legged. Once having captured her, he doesn't say anything. Now she has stopped, she is actually glad to be sitting still for a moment, and beside him. She looks at the students, who seem to have fallen into a leisurely spring mood. They saunter, and pause, and chat, they have chosen to wear pale-coloured clothes, they are nearly all young, and handsome, they are picking life as though it were peaches on a tree, finished, ripened, without worms. Whose luscious flesh they can bite into with smiling well-grown teeth. Jade compares them with the women at the refuge, to whom life offers little in the way of fruits, a sour crab maybe, an apple riddled with the moth. Or if sweet it would be sure to find a hole in a tooth and make it ache. An immeasurable chasm would seem to separate these blooming university girls from battered wives. But in fact it doesn't. The same statistics encompass both. Jade knows the figures, knows that domestic violence is just as common among the middle classes, among the privileged, the wealthy, the educated. These women don't end up at the refuge only because money offers other options, not least the cover-up. There is a certain judge, not in the Family Court, of a higher rank than that, who is known for beating his wife. Cleverly. Where the bruises don't show. So far, the wife acquiesces. She must feel he makes it worth her while, murmurs Jade's informant, another law student whose sister works at a health farm. And don't forget love, says Jade, sarcastically, but truly. It is the most painful fact that they have to deal with, that they cannot leave love out. But with her women, money is a factor only in its absence.

Money, she says now, looking at the polished and gleaming students. It covers a multitude of sins. She grimaces. There's an original discovery for you.

Money, says Eric. Seriously . . . Legal Aid, you know . . . He's stammering. Clearly he does not know where to begin what he wants to say. Cheap justice will never change anything, he bursts out. Money means power and a law of your own and they won't give it up.

He's pulling off the wrapping of his parcel as he speaks, and it's a bottle of champagne, with two plastic cups.

Money means champagne, says Jade.

Well, says Eric, it's more the other way round. The champagne standing in for the money.

He's not very good at getting it open, first he can't untwist the wire then the cork is stiff and he pulls and pushes with no success. Finally it flies out with a sound like a shot and a similar trajectory. Jade looks at it with bemusement. The champagne fizzes out of the bottle and Eric tries to catch it in one of the plastic cups, which falls over, spilling the wine on Jade's feet. She finds the whole thing mysterious and irritating.

Just half a glass. I've got an essay to write tonight.

Well, says Eric, we're celebrating. I've got a new job.

Jade waits.

At Arden, Arden and Seemley.

Certainly Jade knows what this means. Just about the most prestigious law firm in Sydney. They are on the lookout for bright young men, it seems. Bright young people.

It's been in the offing for a while, says Eric. I had to think about it. You know. But I reckon that's the place to get things done.

Rich man's law, says Jade.

I know, we've discussed that. But the law belongs to the rich, Jade. You've got to get inside it to make it work for the poor as well.

She is hurt that he hasn't discussed it with her before making the decision. He understands this. He didn't because he knew what she'd say. He knew all her arguments; he could have their discussion on his own. He'd chosen to have it in his own head. And Jade sees all this and leaves him alone with his decision. His celebration.

Well, cheers, she says. Is this the way it's going to be in the future?

What?

Champagne all the way?

Of course not. This is just a little party. Now it's the hard work.

◆ ◆ ◆

It certainly was. Eric went off early each morning in one of his new suits and a clean shirt for every day of the week washed and ironed on Sundays. He came home late and worked later shifting paper. That was the office phrase. Shifting paper. He was hasty and excited, pent up. They spent little time together. Even weekends he had work to do and so still he could not often go up to the mountains to see Sebastian. You could say it's his future I'm working for, he said, but Jade laughed a rather ugly laugh and murmured, They all say that.

Our friend seems to be in the process of sloughing off the steamed vegetables, said Harold. Funny, I imagined it happening instantly: suddenly, no more, forever. I intend it to be like that for me.

In October Eric asked Jade to go to a dinner at the Regent. It's exam time, she said, I can't possibly. It's just one night, he urged. You don't need to drink at all, or be late. No, she said. And anyway I haven't got anything to wear. Not for the Regent. I'll buy you a dress. No you won't, I couldn't possibly let you. Why not? It'd give me pleasure. Wouldn't you like to give me pleasure? Wouldn't you like to look beautiful, in a glamorous dress, for once?

She thought, that means he doesn't find me beautiful, ordinarily, and was offended, and more determined not to go. I'm only happy in jeans, she lied.

Eric tried hard to persuade her. He badly wanted to appear at the firm's dinner with a partner he was proud of. He had the picture already: a dark red dress, very dark, low cut, with stiffish silky folds around the shoulders, a dress to rise up out of, and her hair shimmering down her back. Jade on his arm: such a brilliant couple. A man with a woman like that is a man to watch. Oh Jade, he said softly, I could make you the most beautiful woman in Sydney. You only care about a clothes-horse, said Jade. Eric got angry with her for being illogical. I'm talking about being a beautiful woman, he said, why bring in a clothes-horse—it's entirely irrelevant. Idiotic. Why be idiotic?

This situation repeated itself a number of times; working at Arden, Arden and Seemley involved a lot of socialising. When they went to bed together his breath seemed always to smell of wine. Jade thought it changed their lovemaking. She didn't care for it. For his part he found her smelling of garlic hard to take. He'd never noticed it before because they both ate cheap dishes of pasta and put lots of the stuff in the steamed vegetables but now it was sharp and strong. In surreptitious ways they turned their heads aside from each other.

Eric said, I hate to see you getting so tired.

Jade sighed. I disagree with you, so I'm tired. Great.

That's unkind. I worry about you. I think you're doing too much. Maybe you should give up your work at the refuge for a bit. Just till after the exams.

No, she said. No. Then, because she liked to see herself as an honest person, Well, yes, I am tired, but it's not anything I can't manage, it's not too much for me. It's natural to be tired.

Not for someone so young and strong as you, said Eric. He drew her into his arms, stroking her shapely body, ready to make love, but she was already fast asleep, breathing deeply, almost, you could say, snoring.

Another time, he said, Nobody's indispensable you know, Jade. They could do without you at the refuge for a bit, just until you get through the year.

Oh yes. I daresay they could. But could I do without them?

This time Eric sighed. He wanted to put her in a kind of private witness box and question her, to show her just how illogical her arguments were, but whenever he tried she wriggled out of it with more illogic. It exasperated him.

In March he suggested they move into a flat together. One of the guys at work was moving out of a very nice one-bedroom place at Potts Point. The kind that never gets on the market, always snapped up by word of mouth. When he told her the rent she laughed. Are you mad? I'd pay it, said Eric, I can afford it, all you have to do is live with me there. But she wouldn't have anything to do with it. She knew that living in a group house in Leichhardt wasn't a suitable thing for a young man with his prospects, but that was his problem. She had her principles. Next he said, Why don't we get married? Jade thought this was even less of a good idea than it had been before Sebastian was born. I never even get to talk to you any more, she said, what would be the point? Just that, he said, if we were married we would talk. She shook her head. What would we talk about, she asked. What colour to paint the drawing room? Which electronic appliance to purchase next? About us, said Eric, us.

For instance, he went on. We could get married and have Sebastian to live with us. After your finals, he said hastily. We'd get a nanny. You could go on with your career.

Great idea. Me working in a women's refuge and leaving my child at home with a nanny. Eric, have you any idea what you're actually saying?

I don't know, Jade. Your idea of a *mode de vie*. It worries me. It's so inchoate.

She flashed back: But it can grow. Develop into something. At least it's not a parasite. Not a tapeworm in the gut of the rich.

I don't know how you can say we never talk. We argue all the time.

Yes. Can you work out why?

In June Arden, Arden and Seemley offered him the chance to go overseas and he took it. The London office, what luck. He explained to Jade that he wasn't really failing to wait until she could come too, he was just going a bit ahead. She would join him after her finals.

My finals, she muttered. Sounds like a terminal illness. I'm going to heaven after my finals. What about you?

Oh, Jade. Do you have to be so frivolous? he said.

Oh, Eric. Do you have to be so pompous? she replied.

Yet still they hadn't got to the stage where they believed anything irrevocable had been said. They made love and were sad about parting, and out of the sadness came promises. They wrote letters. Descriptions of England, its people and institutions, on Eric's part, with equally detailed fancies of the life they would lead when she came over, scrappy notes run off the word processor to accompany Amelia's endless photographs of Sebastian, on hers. A young woman called Leonie took his place in the Leichhardt house. The end of the year came, Jade did well, perhaps not as brilliantly as she might have done had she not spent time at the refuge, but honourably.

Sebastian had his second birthday. Eric sent him a card and a set of cuisenaire rods. Followed by a letter for Jade. *I'm not quite sure how to say this*, it began, and eventually got to the point of mentioning a young woman whom he thought he might marry. Jade felt a terrible pang of jealousy and then wrote a letter back saying, *I am not surprised*, which she realised was the truth. *You went away a long time ago.*

Sadness is a kind of luxury, she said to Zoe. I've got a bit of time now, so I can enjoy it for a while. Then back to the real world.

Sweetheart, said Zoe, you don't have to be so practical. Grief . . . you can't organise it.

I suppose not. But, you know, if I'd wanted life with Eric, well, I could have had it. He gave me endless opportunities. I must have known what I was doing.

I sometimes wonder if we ever do, said Zoe. Know what we are doing.

Grief, said Jade. There's the person, and then there's the idea. The idea of Eric and me, taking on the world, changing it. Loving one another, of course, but in that context. And that hasn't been a reality for a long time. Eric's a rich lawyer now.

Do you mean he's sold out . . .

Oh, I don't mean he's corrupt, not anything like that. He just thinks like a rich man. You can't do anything for ordinary people when you think like a rich man.

Rich man, poor man, said Zoe.

Beggar man, thief, finished Jade. See what I mean? It's really a list of professions, isn't it.

And the person behind?

Ah, said Jade.

They were sitting on the stone-paved terrace, looking out over the mountain valleys, as blue as their name. Jade began to pace up and down, her bare soft feet wincing a little at the rough surface. When you think of it, she said, Eric and I, we could have been the classic trap. Thinking that love was enough, that I could make him the person I wanted him to be, that I thought he was once. I suppose I should be grateful that I didn't fall into it.

Zoe thought of Steve Apples, the way she'd first seen him, unhandily trying to carve a small animal out of wood, his baby daughter leaning against his leg. Steve with his fair hair curling down to his thin shoulders, his sharp skilful knife in the meat, under the smiles of his customers who always seemed to have something to stay and chat about, his soft hands, the way life might have been if he hadn't died.

Maybe Eric was thinking the same about you. That he could make you into the person he wanted you to be.

I never thought of that, said Jade. I guess you're right.

What about just accepting the person each of you is?

I don't think people do that any more, said Jade.

After the summer Jade got a job with Legal Aid, in the field of family law. She still spent her spare moments at the women's refuge. She went back to the Leichhardt house, to Leonie and her boyfriend and a nervous Harold who'd used up all his quota of failure, one more unit lost and he'd be thrown out of law. You could convert to an arts degree and become a schoolteacher, said Jade cruelly. It's a rewarding profession. They say. Though hard to get into. Or a public servant. Plenty of scope for ambition there. She still couldn't forgive him his greed, mainly because he'd been right about Eric.

A postcard arrived with a picture of him in pearl grey tails with a small bride hanging on his arm amid bushes of flowering May blossoms, and on the back a printed message: *To announce the marriage of* . . .

It was in May of the next year, when Sebastian was three and a half years old, that Jade was shot. She was shepherding one of her battered wives through the Family Court. The city was stuffed with cars and she had to park hers at some distance away. They walked back along the street and started up the stairs. The husband, his name was Gary Monahan, was waiting for them outside the building. Terri, he shouted, Terri, in a voice that was full of rage and pain like an animal uncomprehending its wounds, and when his wife turned, with Jade behind her and just a little above her, on the next step, he was pointing a rifle and fired at them both, swivelling the gun across and slightly upwards so that a hail of bullets moved over their bodies. Then he turned the gun round, awkwardly, the muzzle against his neck and his arms stretched out, and shot himself.

There were more than three victims. The spraying of the bullets had been indiscriminate, the steps busy with people. To bystanders a little further off it looked like a terrible massacre because of the fallen bodies and the blood, though not everyone shot was dead, and some people had fallen to the ground though no bullets had struck them, because they thought that was the right thing to do when someone is shooting at you.

Amber necklaces

◆

Canberra, 1969

Mikelis woke up on the morning of the first night he and Veronica had spent in the house that they'd had to get married to buy and knew that they'd done the right thing. The room was full of a nimble shifting light from the sun shining through a small grove of silver birches on the front lawn. He'd already taken pleasure in their slender white trunks and shivering leaves, and now they were offering their own special filtering of the morning light. He prodded Veronica.

Do you know what makes a good house? he asked. It's the way the light falls in it. This is a good house.

Mm, said Veronica, thinking she hadn't had enough sleep. They'd been working late at night on fixing the house, as well as at their jobs; this was Sunday and she wanted to sleep for a week. She turned for a snoozy cuddle but he was gone, into the sitting room to see how it looked at this hour.

They'd taken up all the carpets, which ranged in colour from hairy brown like a coconut to luminous nylon, purple in one bedroom and green in another, and found underneath fine ash flooring. They'd painted the walls white, needing a lot of coats because of the different bright shades they had to cover. The sitting room had had two lime green walls and a third pale beetroot, with a feature wall papered in a pattern of random bulbous shapes which when it was new had been called contemporary. For Veronica it had been an act of faith, buying into such ugliness. Mikelis said that underneath the hideous decoration were handsome shapes, and he was right. He stood in the early morning sitting room and looked at the oblique light shining on the white walls and the rosy polish of ash wood floors and the minimalist by necessity furniture and thought, We can be happy here. He got his camera, the better to see the shapes and spaces, the shadows, the angles and inclines that gave the room its being. These pictures were the beginnings of his fascination with the interiors he photographed all his life, these rooms that people loved and lived in, the people themselves never there, not in the flesh or its images, but the space belonging to them even more completely in their absence, as the shell of the oyster or the periwinkle or the mussel belongs to its owner, and how much more when the room-shells are a matter of choices made with passion or at least affection. He rarely used colour for these pictures, believing that in black and white the light was at its most illuminating. Eventually he published them in a book that was one of the most interesting and mysterious things he did; the reader of these photographs could gaze for a long time, contemplating the lives that these rooms were in the process of containing. Shabby rooms, they often were, and cluttered, or else bare, stark even; designers' rooms they never were. The fashionable lived-in look, Veronica teased him, and lived-in was what they were, though fashion had nothing to do with them.

But his own room was the first, and the light falling upon it, and him thinking, we can be happy here. And back in the bedroom was Vero, the white sheet pushed back, her skin pale biscuit colour and her brown hair spreading across the pillow, falling over the edge. He pulled the sheet further back to look at her, and feeling the coolness she stirred and turned, and he got back into bed with her, happiness welling into desire so that when he came tears ran out of his eyes for the whole pleasure of his life. Veronica looked a bit worried by this, until he murmured, It's happiness. Just happiness. She said, Remember the studio? Already constructing a history for them, so that they both recalled the messy room, the gas fire, the cold nights, the yellow light of the lamps and the shadows it made among the dusty shabby furniture. The red velvet couch. Hymen's Bower. The trappings of bliss.

Bliss has many trappings, said Veronica, surprising herself. This is its wholesome phase. Decadent was good, but I suppose wholesome is all right. She did look wholesome, with that smooth biscuit skin, like something a kind mother had lovingly baked. She made his mouth water. His gingerbread woman. Spicy and sweet. He began to nibble at her. I'm lucky, he said, I can eat my gingerbread and have her too.

This time they made love laughing, with games. Afterwards he said, Stay there, I'll bring us a wholesome breakfast, and came back with coffee and toast with tomato lavishly peppered, and a small box.

It's a housewarming present, he said. No it's not, it's an us-warming present. It's not a present, it's yours. They're yours.

Veronica wanted to laugh, until she saw that his muddle was serious. She took the box, which gave nothing away, being plain hard cardboard. Inside was tissue paper making three separate packets. Folding them undone, each packet, carefully, with the nervousness of the present-giver: what if she doesn't like it? In each one was amber. A long string of oval beads, a brown pear on a silver chain, and a necklace of chunks and flakes like toffee on a thread. She hung them one by one around her neck. Solemnly, in a ceremony.

Do you mind? asked Mikelis.

Mind? she said, incredulous.

I was scared to give them to you. That was why I didn't, before. Because of the pearls.

Veronica has told Mikelis about the pearls, and about Martin owning her with them. This amber is not the same. Why? she wonders later. Thinks carefully about the two jewels. Both have watery pasts. One is an irritant. The other a tomb: one of the oval beads contains a tiny long-winged insect, maybe a mosquito, a mosquito ancestor. One is animal, the irritated oyster building up its gauzy layers of secretion against discomfort, the other vegetable, an oozing gum dropping from prehistoric pines and fossilising in the earth, under the sea, finally washing up from drowned forests. But at the time she simply thinks, amber is not at all like pearls. As Mikelis is not at all like Martin. Things are and need no reasons. She sits up in bed wearing nothing but these three necklaces of amber and thinks of Martin, not-below-the-waist Martin. She giggles; even when she sits up straight the long string of oval beads reaches down below her navel. The pear sits between her breasts, the toffee chunks rest on their curve. She resembles an idol.

They are not of course new. They belonged to Mikelis's mother. Were worn by her as a young woman in Latvia, carried by her in a pouch strapped to her waist in that dangerous little boat crossing the Baltic Sea. Brought out on grand occasions in New Zealand; the women of the Latvian community liked to sport their amber. Left in her will: for my son's wife, and after that his daughter. A command.

Perhaps a virtue resides in them. This female ownership through the generations. Not the male power of buying with gifts but women handing on. Not as light as they seem, perhaps, and more than ornaments; weighted, freighted, with who knows what obligations. Fertility, for one . . . Veronica naked in amber necklaces is spot on for that role, but so far she's not got past the act, is blocking the consequences of it. Her sex is safe. The pill, as she proclaimed to her father, having given women control over their bodies. Provided they don't forget to take it. And fertility is just the future. What of the past? Not the millennia-dead mosquito, more recent lives than that. Amber is capable of being electrified by friction. It warms and is receptive, not like diamonds hard and icy; the warmth of its wearers is in the lustre of these beads.

For a moment they hang heavy round her neck. She remembers the grave fierce face of Mikelis's mother. A woman both clever and beautiful. What is she passing on with her not-so-frivolous baubles? Veronica is a wife, she is joint-owner of a house, she will have to behave, will have to perform. Her neck bends a little, trembles, then she straightens it and looks at Mikelis kneeling naked beside her, at his skinny milk-coloured shoulders and his blue eyes sharp with doubt and she loves him beyond bearing and holds him tightly so that the necklaces dint and dig into their skin but this isn't painful or irritating, it is the stony sharpness of desire, the prickle of otherness that makes them long more than ever to lose themselves in one another and know that finally they never will but still to go on trying.

And for this she will accept whatever the amber is asking of her. As she kneels in the bed with her arms around her husband.

Amber and Veronica. They go together. They like one another. They suit one another. From this point on Veronica thinks of her amber whenever she buys clothes, choses cream colours, white, black, brown, sometimes golden hues; with her brown hair and her biscuit skin and her eyes which Mikelis tells her are orbs of amber which he would write poetry to if only he had the language, and the complicated honey and toffee of her necklaces, she is a woman who has found a pattern for her beauty. Mikelis may remember the girl in the red flowered dress, but married woman Veronica is honey, gold and cream: not colour words, not even adjectives, but luxurious objects, for tongue and teeth and flesh to savour.

That morning Mikelis began the Amber Nude series, which were really the start of his fame. When he got to the stage of being able to photograph what he wanted and not what other people demanded, a long time coming still, he could look back and see that the amber nudes were the beginning of it.

◆ ◆ ◆

When fertility claimed them it was nothing to do with amber, though certainly with families, since it was a kind of legacy from her own grandmother. Veronica flew up to Newcastle to the funeral dressed very slim and smart in a straight black sheath with simply the amber pear on its silver chain. Doesn't Veronica look glamorous? said all her relations. Already her body was profiting from her error, or anyway omission, that in the grief or busyness of her departure she left her contraceptive pills behind on the bedside table, and was laying down juicy soft resting places for the lucky egg that if not yet fertilised soon would be. Eight and a half months later Eva was born.

Lithopaedia

◆

Canberra, late 1970s

Veronica was making a dessert of oranges; they had to be peeled and all the pith removed, separated into segments, sprinkled with brandy, and then a syrup of sugar and water poured over. Partly this syrup set into toffee, and partly the sweet acid juice of the oranges softened it so that it stretched into long sticky threads when it was served and eaten. She was making it because a friend, a bachelor with a sweet tooth, was coming for dinner. In the middle she became aware that she was bleeding, just a few spots, but disturbing because she was a little over four months' pregnant. She kept on making the dessert, because it wasn't effortful, but sat down and put her feet up on another chair. The books said a little spotting need not be a problem.

Eva woke up from her nap, with that grumpiness of a person called from a pleasanter place that comes out of children's day-time sleeps, and climbed into her lap to get used to the waking world again. The two sat, companionable and glum, waiting for Mikelis to come in. He could cook the steak and make the salad. The spotting stopped: as the books said, it might not mean anything at all.

But late in the night the spots turned into a flow and then a flood. A sharp pain woke her, and she found herself in a sticky puddle spreading across the sheets. The pain wrenched her body, the blood slithered. They had an old chamber pot painted with cabbage roses and gilt, the kind that comes with Victorian washstand sets, the jugs and basins and slopbuckets once necessary to bathroomless houses; now the useful had become the ornamental. She sat on that. Mikelis called the doctor. The blood slithered, the pain wrenched her body. Mikelis patted her sweating face with a cold washer, he held her in his arms and intermittently she leant on him, when the pain let her. The doctor came and called an ambulance. Good girl for using the chamber pot, he said. You'd be surprised how a lot lose everything down the toilet.

She was met at the door of the hospital in a wheelchair and pushed up to a ward. There were three other women in it, the lights and the noise woke them up. They turned and muttered. Complete bed rest, ordered the doctor. And I mean complete, my girl, he said. Not a foot to the floor. Bed pans and blanket baths. He was a good man, her doctor. Look at him coming out in the night to attend to her. She had quite a special relationship with him, he knew about her medical background, he treated her like an intelligent woman, almost a colleague. He didn't rush, he took time to talk, not pushing her in and out in three minutes but chatting, he was always passing on stories and gossip and information, curious medical facts which seemed to be a hobby with him. Telling them not because they had any relevance to her, but just because they were interesting. Like the old notion that gout was caused by too much port and claret: the suffering Georgian gentleman with giant bandaged foot propped up on a stool. Not true, he said; it was more likely the roast beef. That was the culprit. Plus heredity, our old friend heredity, stirring the pot as usual. Sometimes he told her private things, like buying the sportscar which he'd always wanted. Driving round with the wind in his hair. A bit long in the tooth for it, he said, but better late than never. His name was Kevin Merrilees and he was tall and handsome. What a dish. The other women swooned over him. He looks like Elvis Presley, said Jan in the next bed. Much better looking than that, said Mary. He visited much more often than their doctors, putting his head in the door, sitting on the bed, patting her leg, smiling and full of cheer. I wish my doctor was like that, said Mary. None of the other women were in for babies, they'd had hysterectomies and polyps off, things like that. The babies were in another ward.

Veronica obeyed everybody's instructions to the letter; she was as Dr Merrilees said, an intelligent woman and anxious for this to work. She lay in bed in a kind of daze, not wanting to read or watch television, as though her mind like her body was flat out resting, protecting the threatened embryo from mental as well as physical effort. She slid gingerly up in bed when meals came and drank her bed-time Aktavite like a good child. When Mikelis came to visit she hardly even talked to him, she who was usually so garrulous, smiling in a dreamy fashion and holding his hand while he told her about Eva and his housekeeping. Elinor rushed in with flowers and mad presents and all the gossip she could rake up; Veronica lay flat watching her. A pair of eyes on the pillow, said Elinor to Ivan, that's what she's turning into. The only thing that bothered her was her hair; the nurses wouldn't let her wash it. It smoothed back lank and sticky against her head. I feel so grotty, she sighed, but out of habit, and even when Mikelis brought his camera she didn't protest, just lay back with that faint wry smile.

At the end of the week the doctor came and said she wasn't actually pregnant any longer. She'd had a miscarriage. A spontaneous abortion, he called it; he always paid her the compliment of using proper terms. She wondered why he hadn't known, seeing all that in the antique chamber pot. Couldn't he tell there was no longer a baby inside her? People said embryos had perfect feet at four weeks. Why had she had to spend a week in bed saving something that no longer existed?

When she tried to find out the answers to these questions, not exactly asking them in any critical or accusing way but making statements like I thought it was all right, I thought the baby would be okay, and waiting for him to explain, he sat on the bed and patted her hand and said, Now don't you worry, you're a healthy girl, you and hubby can get together and start again in no time. We can't regret these spontaneous abortions, he said. Nature mostly knows what's she's doing. It's all for the best. A quick little curette and you'll be right as rain.

How right is rain? A damp drizzle out of a grey sky. The bitter beating storms that scour the silt from the soil and flood the valleys. Cold sleet wetting to the skin, to the bone, settling on the lungs: pneumonia. Tears welling up and running over like a leaky bubbler, crusting with rust.

She said, Can I wash my hair?

Of course. Get yourself prettied up for when hubby comes. No need to stay in bed now. We'll have you out and dancing on the town in no time. He stood up, tall and handsome, patted her knee, and winked, twitching his snubby nose in a friendly way at the same time. No worries, now.

There goes Veronica's dreamboat, said Jan. Isn't he gorgeous? I think I'll change doctors.

Later in the day sister came in and said no D and C after all, wasn't that good news? She could go home tomorrow.

Veronica wondered how this could be going to happen. She'd hardly moved for a week, by her own volition. She must have used up all her will on inaction; there didn't seem any left. Her limbs were made of lead, as though with staying still they had grown heavier and heavier; she couldn't motivate them. She couldn't imagine ever walking again.

One of Dr Merrilees' curious snippets of information concerned wombstones. He'd just read about them: medical history, fascinating stuff. Wombstones he told her are dead embryos which stay in the uterus and calcify. Of course, this was in the bad old days, before curettes and modern medicine solved all our problems. Some poor women could end up with a number of these wombstones; that is, if they had a tendency in that direction. Miscarriage after miscarriage, and the dead babies calcify into quite large stones and are a great weight to bear. And with them all bumping around in there it's impossible to have a successful pregnancy. No live children, just babies turned into stone.

Like the wolf and the goats, said Veronica.

Hmm? Of course, said Dr Merrilees, that was in the bad old days. Couldn't happen now.

She wasn't quite sure why he told her this. Perhaps he liked to share the pleasure of knowing odd facts. And out of a kind of pride, because life was better now; progress and people like him having so much improved the lot of women. Or showing off, expecting her to know enough to follow him. Or maybe more gruesome motives, she came to think. She reconstructed the pleasure of knowing that gleamed in his eyes into a more sadistic titillation.

Now Veronica turned her face to the wall. She remembered the story about the wolf who tricks her way into the house of a goat and eats up all her children. It's in a book belonging to Eva. The mother goat comes home and finds her babies gone. She weeps. She searches everywhere for them. After a while she finds the she-wolf asleep beside a river. Her stomach is seething. Like a cat a long way pregnant. The mother goat takes out her scissors and cuts the wolf open and there are all her kids. Quite unharmed. The wolf had swallowed them whole. The mother goat fills the wolf's stomach with stones and sews her up again. When she wakes up the wolf feels very thirsty: this is the effect of the dry stones in her stomach. She stands on the river bank to drink, but the weight of the stones tips her into the water, and she drowns.

Veronica began to make a fuss. She sobbed and wailed. She knew she was doing this, she was somehow watching herself at it, even making herself do it, but she wasn't controlling it, she couldn't stop. The baby was still there, she cried. It was turning into a stone, she could feel it, it was growing, she wouldn't be able to move. Calcifying, she sobbed, calcifying. The word came out in a long wailing shriek. Calcifying. A limestone baby. I'm going to drown. This performance, the desolation of her wailing, the nonsense of it, because nobody there had ever heard of wombstones and so they thought she was raving, the threshing of her body and the floods of tears that began to shake her, alarmed the nurses. Mrs Ballod, who'd behaved so well all week, so polite and smiling, so gentle, so hopeful; what had come over her? When they couldn't calm her down they called the doctor.

She's somewhat hysterical, he said. I think we'd better sedate her.

She wailed at him. It's growing into a stone. I know. I can feel it.

Mrs Ballod. You're upset. You must try to be calm.

What about modern medicine? What about a curette? You said a curette. This isn't the bad old days.

You don't need a curette. There's nothing there.

Yes there is. I've been a week saving it. It's there and it's dead and it's growing into a stone and it'll drown me.

She knew this couldn't go on. It was too tiring. But she couldn't stop yet. She was asking all the hard questions, not looking at anybody, twisting on the bed, crying out. They'd pulled the curtain and were fussing round, trying to calm her, trying to get valium down her throat, scolding her gently when she spat it out. Mrs Ballod, aren't we being just a wee bit naughty? Mrs Ballod, this isn't like you at all . . . When she was worn out, she stopped.

The valium, finally administered, stilled her body, not her mind. Not a good subject for sedation, the doctor said. She felt proud of herself. She'd behaved badly. Sometimes it is necessary to behave badly. It's an act of liberation. Exhilarating, like marching into a captive town and throwing out its oppressors. With bands and flowers cast in welcome and bottles of champagne spraying out bubbles and everybody singing at the tops of their voices and louder than all Mireille Matthieu belting out the words for it, *Paris weeping with joy*. Not that she'd got any answers, but she'd asked the questions, and that was her part, to ask the questions. If the others, the answerers, those who were supposed to own the information, failed to answer, that was their problem. And she'd made people take notice. They were a lot more careful of her now. Liberators might turn nasty, might become captors in their turn, might ravage and lay waste, pillage and burn and destroy. What pleasure, to pillage and burn and destroy. Stop being good. She lay with dazed body and galloping brain and sipped at anger like a cup. *Not like me*, she said to herself. How dare they. They don't know what I am, to be like or not.

The next morning Mikelis came and took her home. For a long time she felt worn out, hollow, empty. She knew perfectly well there were no wombstones growing in her belly, though sometimes she felt their phantom weight and hardness. But it had been true, often, for other women. For them it had been more than an odd medical curiosity. Lithopaedia: wombstones. *Litho* meaning stones, *paedia* pertaining to children. As if giving them a Greek name made them any easier to bear.

Kidnapped

◆

Dane who was making a catalogue of Mikelis's work came across a portfolio named 'Kidnapped'. Inside the photographs were all of staircases.

Kidnapped, said Mikelis. Ah, yes. That was an exhibition in Sydney. Late in the 1980s, I think. Or maybe 1990. People got very keen on photography about that time. There was a big exhibition at the National Gallery, I remember.

A lot of the staircases were sinister: vertiginous, shabby, decaying. They were not staircases you would trust. Some seemed malicious in intent.

That's the pathetic fallacy, of course, said Mikelis. Blaming the inanimate for our failings.

Quai de la Tournelle, said Dane. That's Paris, isn't it?

Yes. That's the one with the stone steps covered in treacherous urine-stinking moss, as I recall. I went back later and did that.

Later?

After Jack's death. The staircases were for him. That's why

the series is called 'Kidnapped'. The shapes of stories . . . the old man's voice trailed off.

Will you tell me what you mean?

'Kidnapped' . . . Stevenson's . . . the ruined staircase. It'd kill the boy were it not for the flash of lightning. Jack Hawley told me about it. Before he dived off the bridge and drowned. Mikelis sighed, tired of the labour of explaining. *You can't step twice into the same river.* Heraclitus said that, do you know? I don't know what the young know any more. For me Jack jumps over and over into that river, the Seine and behind him Notre Dame and the chestnut trees nearly invisible, but it's not the same river, *everything flows and nothing stays,* and maybe the river is me, maybe I am the river, and Jack eternally jumping. That's the moment of transfiguration. Transfiguration, he mumbled. Elevation. Illumination. As he said the words he was writing them with the pad of his finger on the table, making the polished wood squeak, speaking the words in slow syllables to keep up with the writing. El-e-va-tion. Il-lum-in-a-tion. The crossing of the body, that moment of life into death. I didn't catch it, not on film, yet the energy of that passing, that transfiguration, it's there in the pictures, in the absence of Jack. Find the ones of Notre Dame, the bones of its ribcage, you'll see what I mean.

I know the ones, said Dane. Tremendous.

It's Jack's transfiguration, not mine. I don't know that I've ever achieved it. You can't use words like that, not at the time, you can't even think in them, you'd make a fool of yourself and then when you're old and shameless it's too late.

I can use them, about you. Other people can. They do.

But I don't have to believe you, or them. I don't trust praise. If people knew what I know, they wouldn't praise me.

That's not the point, said Dane. They look at what you've made, not what you are.

The death of the artist, said Mikelis. Literally, soon enough. It's a pity I can't take my camera with me. Photograph the tunnel and the light at the end of it. That's what people always see, you know, when they die and then come back. Pity the words are such a cliché. Out of body experiences, they call them. The light, that's what strikes them. And why not. It's what counts. Is there light after death? That's the question. He heaved with laughter. I always preferred natural light when I took my pictures. But *no* light, neither in the eye of the beholder nor in that beholden, well, you're pretty much stymied.

Dane asked Mikelis about the photograph he had taken of Veronica after her death.

Did I tell you about that? Clearly I am old and beyond shame.

Dane watched his face wrinkle up. Now he could not see Mikelis did not control his expressions. As though his not-seeing was transferred to his companions.

Veronica, he murmured. Veronica dead of a heart attack at fifty-four. In the year of the millennium. What superstitions. What prognostications of hope. The turning of the century and of the second thousand years—what portents. What searching for signs. And instead my Veronica died. Perfectly healthy. His voice always flattened when he was moved, became matter of fact and dry. I photographed her on the chair beside the telephone. Who knows, had I been inside I might have saved her, instead of telephoning from the studio and thinking what long conversations she is having today, not going home, thinking Veronica has been on the phone all afternoon. Irritated. Typical gasbagging. Coming in and finding her sitting there. The receiver dangling and the dial tone burring away. Who had she been calling? Calling because she was ill, or just calling? I opened the door and came in, seeing her, knowing she was dead as soon as I touched her. Standing still for a moment. The weight of such a moment saves you from it, it's too large, too heavy; you can only slide around the edge of it. I went and got my camera. Photographed the misplaced receiver, her hand hanging down. Not until I'd photographed her death could I see it, my eye needed the photos, to know what it saw. I developed them. Got the light right. The dim hall. The mirror like steel. Hard. Nothing reflected. Didn't ever look at them again. Couldn't bear to. They're a record not just of that event, but of my presence at it. What I was capturing was my loss.

All my life, you know, I photographed her. When I first met her she was like a vase. You wanted to take her in your hands and raise her to your lips. All our life I photographed her. But I never caught her.

O yes, you did . . .

No inanities, please. I am not asking for reassurance. I'm telling you something. Listen to me. I caught moments, moods, sideways glances at her. None of those was her. If anything they were me.

But then, one can never catch anything, if that's true.

Yes, said Mikelis. His lips thinned in a bleak smile, a cold old man's smile.

It doesn't seem like that to me.

Perhaps you are lucky. Or innocent. Or stupid.

Dane in his turn made a hideous face, screwing up his eyes, twisting his mouth, clenching his teeth. It helped him relieve his feelings when the old man said things he didn't like. Never mind, said Mikelis now, as though he'd seen it. There's a box somewhere. An X-ray film box, grey. The photographs are in that. Go and get it.

It took a while to find and when he'd got it the old man held out his hand for it. The photographs were folded in tissue paper, he slid them out. On top was a notebook with a shiny black cover, which he passed to Dane. Veronica's name was written on the front page, and underneath that was the title: *A List of Things to be Borne in Mind*. The entries seemed to have been made at different times; the inks were variously coloured and the writing was sometimes small and neat, sometimes large and scrawly.

Read them out, said Mikelis.

Aren't they private?

Nothing's private when you're dead.

Dane read:

ITEM. Marie-Antoinette suffered terrible period pains, every month she was so ill she had to stay in bed for several days. So her judges calculated the date of her trial to coincide with her period. She was in such pain she couldn't follow the accusations nor make a coherent defence.

Dane stopped. Keep going, said Mikelis. Keep going.

ITEM. There is a fertility drug made of a chemical which is synthesised from the urine of menopausal nuns. Celibate brides of Christ going forth and multiplying, after all. In Italy. Why Italy, we might ask.

ITEM. Entry in antiquarian bookseller's catalogue: Clear Waters. Trouting Days and Trouting Ways in Wales, the West Country and the Scottish Borderland. *Blind-stamped cloth slightly rubbed along the bottom, the spine a little sunned, mild foxing.*

ITEM. Ayesha was the favourite wife of Mohammed. Her loss of a necklace under conditions regarded as suspicious is responsible for the seclusion of Moslem women, even to present times.

Dane paused again. Don't stop, said Mikelis. Why do you keep stopping?

ITEM. Sanitary napkins and tampons must not only be bought, they are very heavily taxed. Ditto the pads and adult nappies worn by incontinent women. All of course disposable. The catheters and bags used by incontinent men are considered essential medical goods, and are free.

ITEM. When some women miscarried the baby remained in the uterus and calcified. Some women could have a number of calcified foetuses inside them. They were called wombstones. Lithopaedia in Greek. It was impossible for such women to bring a pregnancy to term, they constanty miscarried, adding to their burden. Their only children were dead babies turned to stone in their wombs.

The anger, said Mikelis. *A List of Things to be Borne in Mind.* Borne in mind. They seem to be things not to be borne; things she found unbearable. I don't think I ever realised just how angry she was. Restless. Critical. Cranky. I knew all that. But not purely angry. With that kind of abstract power. When I read this I remembered my mother's rage. And now, Eva's. I wonder: is this rage a quality of women? Are they all so angry? And do men ever have it?

What about you? asked Dane, wondering how Mikelis saw himself.

Oh yes, I'm angry. But with me it's bursts, flashes. Not that abiding inexpressible rage. That fury with the whole world.

Dane wondered about himself. Annoyance, irritation. Not really rage. He thought about his mother, Jade. The sunniest of women. But rage was her life, her profession anyway, and that was her life. And Zoe, Amelia? In their scented gallery, cooking, knitting, reading, the music playing; not much anger there. Except that you could see them as deliberately opting out of it. They lived without men. Well, not counting him. Was that a contrivance to avoid anger? Their version of the old devalued hippy creed of Peace and Love: female homosexuality on a mountain.

Mikelis held his hand out for the black notebook. He put it and the tissue-wrapped photographs back in the box and closed the lid with a sharp tap. Perhaps you have led a life singularly free of rage, he said. Perhaps the gods smiled on you. Remember, in the 1970s? Well, you wouldn't, in fact, long before your time, there was a political slogan: *Maintain your rage*. Of course people didn't, not long enough, or hard enough. It's a sin, you know, anger, one of the seven deadlies. Lust, sloth, gluttony, covetousness, pride, envy, and the above-mentioned anger. All that pertains to man. And woman too. Though old age makes it easier to give some of them up. Live long enough and you could become quite saintly. Might manage to cross the bridge to a Muslim heaven; anyway, not over-balance into the chasm. Hope it's not a ruined staircase. And pray, not for the lightning flash but for the gentle glow at the end of the dark.

The cane

◆

Sydney, 1984

The Steps Massacre: that's what it came to be called. Named and made speakable. Bandied about with gory pleasure by press and public. Declaimed, denounced, deplored, dissected. To be consigned to living in interesting times may be a curse, but only for other people; the rest of us need their interesting times to save us from boredom. And when they suffer and die we are the more alive. The woman cooking dinner watching on the television the shrouded bodies lying in gutters looks down at her hands cutting carrots with careful slices of the knife and rejoices in the life of her own flesh. She slides the blade of the knife across her thumb and the faint pain of it charms her.

The massacre's victims missed most of the publicity, the public outcry, outrage. The dead were dead, six of them, and the wounded weren't reading newspapers. Nobody filmed it, not the actual action, since nobody knew it was going to happen, and the memories of witnesses, bystanders and victims are hazy. As were their perceptions at the time. Shouting came first. The name, bellowed in a voice like a hurt animal's, was it a man's or a woman's: Terri. Terri. Bullets spraying, a man with a gun. People falling over.

Jade on the step ahead of Terri, Terri beside her though that step behind, so when the noise came and the women turned, looking down to the right, full of fear but needing to see, Terri was, though slightly lower, in front of Jade and when the bullets sprayed she sagged back against her. Jade grabbed at Terri but she too had been hit and both women fell backwards across the steps. Their blood ran out of them. It is always surprising how much blood people have in them. Who would have thought ... Gushed may not be too strong a word, spurted even, bubbled. Then, once begun, flowed, quietly, like a river, flowing away and away. Forming a wide pool around them, dripping for a while from step to step, and then setting, crawling itself together into a thick red jelly, sticky and with the slightly brownish sheen of strawberry jam. Under the benign sun. The buzz of blowflies.

The little girl had been dragging on her mother's hand, skipping back down the steps as she went up them, as is the way of children, not satisfied with the ordinary difficulty of life. She seems to have been the focus of her father's aim, she the target he fixed in his sights, he moving the gun across to her mother but not upwards. This seems to be the explanation for Jade's not being killed, that the killer didn't shoot quite high enough. His bullets did not touch her head: her shoulder, arm and hip, but not her head. So she only nearly died.

A solicitor striding up the steps, two at a time, in the manner of a man importantly at home in his workplace, another man involved in a custody battle with his wife, a woman out doing the banking for a business on another floor, were the other people killed. Three more, apart from Jade, were wounded: a woman whose ex-husband had just ceded her his grand piano, in payment for her contribution to his household, a schoolboy on work experience, and a man on his way to his job in the canteen. They lay in hospital beds attached to bags of blood pumping back what had gushed out and wondered with varying degrees of success, why me? The woman with the grand piano had a further misfortune; her blood transfusion was infected with AIDS; she sat at the keyboard, as thin and sick as a camellia woman, playing mournful songs until she couldn't get out of bed any longer. Why me; why not: randomness is not a difficult principle to grasp.

Zoe invited the solicitor who lived next door but one in an equally old stone house with another thousand daffodil bulbs in the garden, to come to dinner, him and his wife. They often dined together. The massacre was now old news, except for those who had suffered from it. They talked about Jade. The Craigies knew her from a child. I expect she'll be giving up this Family Court business now, said Donald Craigie. Cranky set-up, the Family Court.

I wish she would, said Zoe.

I'll ask around, said Donald. I think young Farfroe's on the lookout for someone.

That'd be marvellous, said Zoe. She'd begun nursing a secret desire to settle Jade nearby in a safe job and also young Farfroe didn't have a wife. It'd be nice for Seb to have his mother close. And why not a father? Zoe had nothing against men. Her hair fell across her cheek, her eyes widened up at them, she flirted. Only so far, of course. They had partners, so did she.

Wills, said Donald. Wills, and the odd gazumping. That's about as high as passions run round here.

What about Agatha Christie? said Coralie Craigie. Wills are always leading to murder in her books. More than anything else.

Agatha Christie is hardly life, said Amelia.

It all happens in sleepy little villages. Just like this.

Oh no they're not, said Amelia. Those sleepy villages are like nothing on earth.

Well, anyway, said Coralie, you'd have to say that the Family Court is an unsuitable job for a woman.

Oh, I don't know, said Amelia. Would getting shot have been any better if she'd been a man?

Farfroe was interested, but Jade was not. Nearly dying hadn't changed her mind about the sort of job she wanted. It changed her body; the function of her right lung was a little impaired, and she was likely to be stuck with a limp, quite a charming mannerism in a young woman, though not so good as the bones grow older and frailer and earlier injuries nag away at them. It changed her spirit too; her anger which was the force behind her work had been exuberant and full of energy, now it was deeper, harder, more steadfast. As though the old blood that had flowed out across the Family Court steps had taken her old anger with it, and the transfused blood, concentrated and enriched, filled her with a thicker kind of anger.

Come up to Leura, said Zoe. There's a job there, it's a good one. You like the mountains. And Seb, of course.

No, said Jade, banging the bed with her fist, the undamaged arm. I couldn't possibly stop now.

She had been wounded by the misery she was trying to alleviate, and this made her all the more determined not to give up, not to be beaten, but she had learnt its power, and knew how much it was to be feared. It had lodged itself inside her, in the weakness of lung and leg, she couldn't ever forget it. And wouldn't forgive it. She went to counselling, she knew you have to work through the pain, the grief, not to mention the failure to save the woman in her care, must not let these things fester in the mind any more than you do wounds in the flesh, but the anger, no, I'm keeping the anger, she said to the counsellor.

On one of her antique shop forays Amelia found a cedar cane with a carved silver handle in the shape of a duck's head. A solid man's walking stick and just the right size for Jade who was tall. How distinguished she looked moving fast still but with that faint skewing of her gait, intriguing in one so young and deftly made. My old war wound, she said grimly, and at meetings she would sit, holding the duck's silver neck in her hand and beating her cheek softly with it, and slowly; an odd sight, the duck pecking, or exhorting, or imparting secret things with his beak dinting in to her cheek. It was quite heavy, that silver knob, you could have fetched somebody a fair blow over the head with it, but there was no evidence that she saw it as a weapon. Sebastian, for his part, regarded it as a good friend, who could save his mother from being lonely when she was away from him. He did not miss her so much as worry that she would miss him.

Fruit

◆

Canberra, early 1980s

When Eva went to school Veronica took up her old trade of radiography. She'd stopped the moment she knew she was pregnant. At one stage she'd worried that it might not have been soon enough, but she saw no sign of any damage. She hadn't planned to get pregnant; she'd gone to her grandmother's funeral, leaving of course in a hurry, and forgotten her pills. Though there was a choice, in that she hadn't stopped having sex. Maybe that was a kind of dare. Which had been taken up. She quite approved of this. There ought to be something accidental in the conception of children. Not too much planning. No human intervention. Some people have high intelligences. Some have small waists. Some can bear children. It's natural, and a gift. IVF programmes made her angry. It's flying in the face of nature, she said. Sooner or later revenge will have to be taken.

Her grandmother was ninety-eight, a straight spare woman

who walked with a stick and was deaf, but suffered no other physical or mental failings. Everybody expected her to live to be a hundred, because she was healthy and ate well and insisted on knowing everything that was going on in the family. Then one day she walked around her back garden, came inside, sat in a chair, and died. What a wonderful death, said everybody. What a good way to go. Full of pride and admiration, as though it were the old lady's doing, a good death topping off a good life; as though here virtue were being rewarded.

When Veronica discovered she was pregnant, she saw a neatness in it, but only of idea. An old woman dies, a child is conceived. She didn't see any other connection between the two, did not believe in the spirit of one in the other, though her child was a daughter; it was simply the neatness that pleased her. And she was sad that her grandmother never saw Eva. There were a lot of other great-grandchildren, but Veronica wanted her to have known this one.

The baby who miscarried had been planned. Two years after Eva. To be a playmate. To be born in the spring: a winter pregnancy, a summer infancy. None of the insouciance of Eva's conception. Maybe that was why it failed. Altogether too unrandom. Man proposes, God disposes. Even if you don't believe in God, this is a saying of import. She still felt the dry stony weight of the wombstones in her belly when she thought of that lost child. She never could bear to think of another one growing there. I can't conceive, she said to herself, not even the idea of another child. If Mikelis minded, he never let on.

So Eva grew up with the grave charm of an only child. With the colouring for it, white skin, that turned blue as milk in the shadows, long pale hair in a plait, big grey eyes that you could call candid. She was a child full of secrets, but her eyes were candid. She was polite and used to elders; good at conversation and solitude. Fond of reading, an activity Veronica never cared for much. She, poking about the house in her restless fashion, would look with puzzlement at this small calm mouse of a child curved over a book, note with impatience the way she never heard a thing that was said to her at such moments, and took pride in the admiration of schoolteachers for the bookish little girl. Eva's self-containment confirmed her mother's decision to have no more children.

Len came into the rooms to have his ribs X-rayed. He'd slipped over in a café and crashed on to the back of a chair. Perfectly sober at the time, he said, when he saw her expression. Something spilt on the floor. Tiled floor, very slippery. He said this with dignity, but she saw his eyes sparkling. His skin was brown and his shoulders square. When she touched them to position him for the X-ray she felt a humming in her fingers. When she looked at his solid chest with its triangle of curly black hair she saw it not as a covering for bruised or broken ribs, a covering which it was her job to deny and make disappear, but as his flesh. She touched him again, he was not at all in the right place for the X-ray. The pads of her fingers just for a moment curled into nails. Wanting to try out with their sharpness the density of his body. She looked in his eyes and blushed. When she walked back to the machine her hips swayed, the skimpy white fabric of her uniform stretched taut across her bottom. Her bottom seemed to have a life of its own. As she got older it grew rounder, the rest of her body stayed the same. As if it did all the plumpening and thickening and filling out of middling age, while her shoulders and waist stayed slender as ever.

At lunch-time, sitting in Mario's, she was not surprised to look up from her coffee and see him standing in front of her.

Still frequenting cafés? she said. You must be a glutton for punishment.

Oh, I am, he said. Definitely. A glutton for punishment.

He sat down at her table without asking.

◆ ◆ ◆

Len made love as though he'd written the sex manuals. He didn't ask her what she'd like, he knew. Whenever they met they fell upon one another like hungry animals. They almost never used their mouths for communication in words. They drove in cars or hurried along streets and up stairs speechless with lust and as soon as they reached privacy began devouring one another as they dragged off their clothes. Veronica dressed for speed of undressing. Uniform knickers sandals. Sometimes he'd wait for her on a rug under the willows thick by the lake; she'd run from her car, her dress already unbuttoned, not even saying hello, not *saying* it. They never went to cafés or bars, they couldn't stand the apartness. The waiting. In lifts he'd put his fingers inside her and she'd feel swollen and ripe, a fruit ready to drop from the tree should he not hurry up and pick her. Her mouth was pulpy and full of juice, it could no longer remember how to shape words. This was the period of Mikelis's photographs of her sitting on her bottom like a luminous pear with her knees under her chin, the chin resting on them and her mouth pouting, her hair tangled. It's a picture of paradoxes: a predatory fruit which eats as well as being eaten, and also of words like insatiable satiety. Her face is no longer that of a girl, it no longer blooms, and now she needs them he no longer uses silk filters, but her bum is more splendid than ever.

What does Mikelis make of this? Apart from famous photographs. Veronica is so full of desire it overflows on to everyone around her. She picks up Eva from after school care, breathless, running, late often; at home she goes straight to the shower—work was filthy today—and emerges wearing a rose-pink Indian shift, her long hair wet; she rubs at it with a towel which she puts down in awkward places as she wanders about the house. She pours wine in goblets and piles up grapes on silver stands, puts pâté on a plate with a long French stick, unwraps cheeses, brings out oysters, smoked salmon, baby tomatoes, cuts into the green flesh of avocados. When Mikelis mentions having a cooked meal she says, Hot food is so boring. She looks at him over the edge of a wineglass, then dips a strawberry into the red liquor. I can't stand food that is mucked about, she says, spreading pâté on bread for Eva, shaping crescent moons of melons. Her smiling teeth nibble at olives blue-black as squid's ink. She smells nectarines before she buys them, and apricots; each one must have the right rich odour before she'll put it in her bag. There's a kind of zipping hum in the air, like lightning meandering about; it's as though she needs all this soft round food to soak it up. You can bite into a nectarine or a grape and zap, out it comes, burst and prickle in the mouth. The sharp bones of chops, the glazed edges of steaks, the dense weighty meatiness of sausages would be out of place in this atmosphere.

She shakes too much bubble into Eva's bath and laughs as she piles it on the little white body. She wraps her in a heated towel and sings, Dance for your daddy, my little laddie, dance for your daddy, my little dear. He'll have a fishy upon a silver dishy, Ooh dance for your daddy, oh my little dear. And Mikelis thinks, wherever shall I get a fish from?

She goes to bed and flips through fashion magazines, staring at pictures of languorous women in glamorous clothes. She identifies with the intense complicated artifice of them. Her face is hours' worth of painting, her shoes are jewelled and her brassières silk, she smells of L'Air du Temps, L'Heure Bleue, Je Reviens. When Mikelis finally gets in beside her she reaches out and draws him to her. Every night they make love.

Mikelis remembers Veronica's words when she was forced into marrying him. Her shotgun marriage, she called it, no not shotgun, machine gun, cannon, Big Bertha Bureaucracy fixing its sights on me. No marriage lines, no mortgage, simple as blackmail. And apt, when you come to think of it: both chains around your neck forever. She said, I think you should be faithful to your lover because you want to be, not because you've been obliged to marry him. You're my lover, I don't want a husband. And yet she's turned into a wife, and here she is a loving one, night after night her voice murmurs words to him. She is not irritable. He is taking pictures that please him; not satisfy, but please. He can work hard all day and half the night, take all the photographs he wants of Veronica-equals-desire and make love to her. Mostly he thinks no further than this. Why inquire why restless Veronica is become languorous Veronica? Too much to do. Mikelis is as little interested in conversation with Veronica as Len is, if for different reasons.

Of course she and Len had sometimes to use their mouths for talking. To say tomorrow, or Friday, the willows, or the

flat. Or not tomorrow, not Friday, not till next week. How
soon? Too long. Five o'clock. Lunch-time. Half-past nine.
Words the base currency in more florid transactions.

One day Len said, I've got to go to Sydney. She frowned.
How long for? He kissed her disappointed mouth. For always.
For now. The firm. I can't not go. Come with me. They strained
together. Fucking for them was always trying to swallow one
another as entirely as possible. Come with me. Sweetheart,
come with me.

She didn't even think of not saying no.

◆ ◆ ◆

Veronica conceived a passion for soup and began boiling up
big pots of bones, chopping vegetables, piles of eye-pricking
onions, carrots, celery, earth-scented turnips and cabbages
sweet as nuts, adding herbs and barley in handfuls. Rib-sticking,
Mikelis called these soups, when she glared at him. The days
were getting colder, the leaves falling sadly from the trees.
No shelter in the willows now. It was weather for tracksuits,
not rose-pink Indian cotton shifts. She didn't write to Len
nor he to her. She grieved for him. When she thought of him,
a sad slow shiver dropped through her mind like a dying leaf.
She and Mikelis still made love, a statistical 2.6 times a week,
unlanguorous. Yet loving.

The shellgrit gatherers

◆

Merewether, early 1980s

Eva as a child visiting Grandma Gray found Latvia in the encyclopaedia, which had belonged to Grandfather when he was young. She often looked at these books because as well as having pictures of real things they told legends and stories for children. Like 'Tales the Woodman Told', about a lynx with wings, or Androcles and the Lion, or the adventure of Sir Lancelot, the Ninth Diamond, and the Lily Maid of Astolat. Grandfather let her look at his books, which were precious, provided she sat on the floor and lay them flat in front of her, turning the thick shiny pages from the top right corner so they didn't crack or wrinkle. The encyclopaedia was called *Cassell's Book of Knowledge* and had eight volumes, in blue covers with gilt patterns and odd words on the back: BOA to CON, or FLO to ISIS; Latvia was in ITA to NAV. This is what it said:

Latvia or Letvia—'the land of the Letts'—is a new name that

*has appeared on our maps since November 1918; it comprises
most of the former Russian province of Courland and Livonia,
and lies between Esthonia and Lithuania on the Baltic Sea. The
Gulf of Riga makes a deep indentation on the west coast. Much
of the surface of the country is very low, and there are many
marshes and peat bogs; but part of Livonia consists of wooded
hills, picturesque deep valleys and charming lakes. Latvia is
mainly an agricultural country, but the people are passing from
agricultural to industrial life. This new republic, which is a product
of the World War and the Russian Revolution, has an area of
about 25 000 square miles and 1 900 000 people.*

*In the thirteenth century what is now Latvia was a part of
the territory conquered and Christianised by the crusading
Teutonic knights. It was added to Russia by Peter the Great,
and remained a part of that country until it was established
as a separate republic in 1918.*

Eva showed it to Mikelis. There was a photograph, too,
so blurred it consisted of swathes and blotches of light and
shade, no edges at all. The caption said: *A peasant woman of
the new republic of Latvia laden with her household provisions,
making her way home through the deep snow.* The bulky
kerchiefed woman had a yoke over her shoulder bearing the
weight of two great buckets. A strange choice of illustration.
She could have been anywhere. Any peasant, anywhere. Not
the words though. The whole thing gave him a queer feeling.

Is, he said. It *is*.

What is, Daddy? asked Eva.

Latvia. Don't you see, it says Latvia *is* an independent
country. It's still in the present tense. Here, shut up in this
book, it's still going.

You can't step twice into the same river, says Heraclitus. But
here, for a moment, in this book, you could; just for a moment.
Here in this book his mother is still collecting Dainas, his
father is running his printing press, the new republic is passing
from agricultural to industrial life.

When this book was made, Eva, he said, your grandparents,
not Granny and Grandfather here, but my parents, were still
living in Latvia. I wasn't even born at the time . . .

And so Mikelis began to tell Eva the stories of her Latvian parentage, the stories he'd rejected once, but had after all absorbed. His mother stood beside him, but only in his head; it was too late for her to see him tentatively nurturing Eva as the child she'd always wanted; he searched his memory for the tales she'd told him.

Like Lacplesis, the Bearslayer, the human child suckled by the she-bear, found in the forest by a prince and brought to his castle where he grew into a strong and cunning boy, who inherited the throne and became a great ruler. Found in the forest, thinks Mikelis now. Hardly found. Revealed to these careless courtiers, them taken to him, by a she-bear whom they'd just shot full of arrows. He finds himself worrying about this she-bear, bleeding to death but not giving up, staggering through the forest, falling over but getting up again, keeping going, by some amazing force of will making herself not die until she has brought the blood-sportive prince and his fellows to the child not only not of her blood but not even of her species, and not until she has offered this marvellous gift to both child and prince allowing herself to die of being shot full of arrows out of royal fun. It occurs to him that the real hero of this story is the she-bear who understands love in its purest form and Mikelis hopes that everyone in the story knows it, but judging from the way it's been handed down nobody even notices. He makes sure that Eva sees what is going on with the she-bear. Then on to the dutiful history of the gifted child, and Mikelis wonders if he should make him grateful to that magnificent foster-mother, as well as law-giver and warrior and at least wise enough to set up a council of wise-men to be guardians of the sacred scrolls kept in the Castle of Light on the shores of Lake Burtnieks. Only of course to have the key stolen by the treacherous Black Knight, and maybe he wasn't in his mind grateful and maybe this is the punishment for the failure of love, and the sinking of the Castle of Light into the waters and him having to spend his life in the depths of the River Daugava fighting with the Black Knight is just what he deserves. He wishes he'd thought to ask his mother all this, maybe the bear-suckling—and what does the name Bearslayer mean, in the context?—is some kind of warrior-type Ancient Mariner figure and when he learns the meaning of love he'll be able to restore the Castle of Light and make Latvia free. But it seems more likely that everybody just forgot what was owing to the she-bear and the Bearslayer is the only hero anybody has in mind.

That's what my mother used to call me, he says to Eva. *My little Bearslayer*, she'd say. I thought she wanted me to dive into the river and fight the Black Knight and get the key back.

Could you have, really?

Well, I don't think so, says Mikelis. After all, I live on the other side of the world now.

Could the Bearslayer be a woman? Eva asks.

Mikelis thinks. Why not? he says. Latvians have always thought their womenfolk could do anything they put their minds to.

• • •

Later in the evening, when the heat had gone from the sun and the crowds home, leaving only a few board-riders and fishermen and people who walked briskly along the hard damp sand, Veronica and Mikelis and Eva went down to the beach. Veronica had taken up swimming, she wanted to do some laps in the baths. Eva had a dip, then she and Mikelis wandered among the rockpools, drawing one another's attention to the shells, weed, anemones. It was a kind of game. The tide was out, and the pools were full of warm water. They squatted on the edges peering quietly and carefully, catching creatures unawares. When they looked up the waves of the returning tide breaking on the edge of the rock platform were much higher than themselves. They looked up at the green surge of water that loomed and rolled and broke into cascades of foam, and it seemed like a tidal wave that would bear down on them, obliterate them, but by the time it reached them it was a little frill of chillier water that eddied briefly across the pools and was swallowed up. Mikelis stared up at these walls of water that here at this moment came to naught and imagined being in a small boat and no safe shore to tame them.

Did I ever tell you, he said, of your grandmother's escape from Latvia, when I was a small child . . .

They walked home through the late yellow light of the sun turning the sea haze into a nimbus round them. Where the sand was damp along the edge of the water there were two women with plastic spades and a bucket scraping up shellgrit. An elderly man wearing a hat and an ancient suit shiny and worn past the memory of its original shape stood and watched them. They bent over on stiff legs so that their clumsy flower-dressed bottoms lifted in the air, and slid their shovels delicately over the surface so that they got just the top layer of grit, without the sand underneath it. That'll give you double-yolkers, said the man, smiling over empty gums. Mikelis had his camera out and them photographed before the scene could shift. Afternoon, they said, looking up, and Mikelis grateful for the picture started a conversation about chooks. Do you have Rhode Island Reds? he asked. White Leghorns? Bluff Orpingtons? The two women laughed, straightening up and pushing their hands into the small of their backs. Just chooks, said one. Good little layers, but. The man said, Nothing like your own eggs.

Then they really had to hurry home in time for tea. George did not like it to be late, even when there were visitors. Even retired he was set in his ways, still said, System and order, that's the ticket. It wastes the best part of the day, said Mikelis. I know, replied Veronica. When we were children we'd have tea on the beach, bring a picnic and have it in one of those summer houses up on the hill. I don't see why we can't now, but they never will. Well, Father never will. Mum would.

Did you do that often?

I don't know. It seems now like one of those things we always did. But maybe it was only a couple of times; maybe even only once. You know how happy memories multiply. She said this in such a melancholy voice that Mikelis stopped and looked at her.

Eva running ahead jumped on a bluebottle to pop it, tripped and touched the sting. Ssh, said her mother, don't bellow.

Mikelis hoisted her up and gave her a piggyback, Veronica
sucked up gobs of spit to put on thé sore place, and they
galloped home as fast as possible.

• • •

He got a good collection of pictures out of that summer. A
child squatting and peering into a rockpool while behind and
it seems above looms a great wave of curling water, on the
point of crashing down upon her, so that you catch your breath
in horror for the next moment. Veronica in her swimsuit, edgily
eyeing the water in the manner of people about to dive in,
her round head in its rubber cap repeated in the shape of the
whitewashed hut where the pumping machinery for the baths
is housed. And his favourite, as well as everyone else's, *The
Shellgrit Gatherers*, the two ungainly women delicately scraping
their spades, and the old man watching them, while the low
light shines through the sea mist. As always Veronica marvels
at the way pictures seem to find Mikelis; he walks along
Merewether Beach with his family and here is this scene offering
itself. Out of time: it could be the Depression or the 1950s,
it doesn't announce itself as the 1980s that in fact it is. Simply
the three figures, the task, the space of the beach, and the
way the light falls on ordinary lives. Illuminating, says one
critic, illuminating ordinary lives, but that is not right, it
implies that the light, and in that particular sense of giving
meaning, comes from outside, whereas the point is that the
radiance belongs to the people in the picture. Knowing that
it is the product of the evening sun and a sea mist doesn't
change anything; these people own their radiance.

Hospitalising

Newcastle, late 1980s

Veronica Ballod sits in a train travelling north. She has forgotten that once trains meant connection with glamorous places, so that whenever she saw or heard one her heart yearned to be on it, going there. Not staying here. Or rather, she hasn't forgotten, she remembers it as a fond desultory fact, long past its use-by date. Train travel is a chore now. Planes are what is glamorous, planes to Europe. The destination, if not the vehicle. The cities of home are known.

Then, after Sydney, she recalls it again, in the gut, where memory counts. She looks at the backyards sloping down to the railway line, the grass as green as an Irish bog, lush, mowed, but nothing cultivated, the fences reduced to sheaves of palings, the morning glory vines gobbling everything, the sheds for wood and junk, the clotheslines, sometimes a tree. Not gardens: these are backyards, private spaces of earth and air open to the view of every passing train passenger. She is a child again, coming from the coast where the trees hunch dry-leaved against the gales, and this is where exotic begins. Going now the other way. Back.

The house was dark and very cold. Living in Canberra you forgot how cold Newcastle got. Here the wind didn't slice like a knife, it roared in from the sea, blustering, it picked up the frail houses in its teeth and shook them. They groaned, cracks opened, they shuddered with draughts and eddies of air. People said their roofs were filled with sand, tonnes of it blown in on these winds; that sometimes the ceiling couldn't hold and collapsed with killing weight on the occupants, unless they were lucky enough to be out. Though Veronica knew of no specific examples. She couldn't remember when she'd been on her own in this house before. With the groaning of the timbers and the roaring of the wind she could have been at sea. In a vessel unseaworthy and likely to founder. Like the old Tin Mission, shaking off its anchorings, setting sail, out past Nobby's, a danger to shipping as well as itself. How far did it get before it sank? Did anybody know?

She prowled around the house. It was late, but she didn't feel like going to bed. She opened cupboards and drawers, not looking for anything, not looking at anything. Simply registering. The button box. The string in the coffee canister. The soup tureen of recipes in the kitchen cabinet whose glass doors rattled, so when you crept past it too late home you held your breath, tested the floor, but still were not alway successful in not setting them off, the glass doors transparent and sliding, more modern than the open-out colour-stained and leaded kind, but they'd've been quieter. Not this sort of late-warning system. She jumped up and down in front of it. The noise of the rattling glass was very loud inside the hollow shell of the roaring winter's night outside. She checked the board in the hall, the back-up trap; still the same long-drawn creak. Though Father had a number of times crawled under the house to try to fix it. When you stood on it and it sounded and you froze, you understood how ineluctable fate was: when you took your foot off it, it would creak back into place again. However long you waited. Like the second boot.

You would think of the noises that alerted others to your presence, now, when there was nobody to hear, nobody to care.

It was strange to look at other people's objects when they weren't there to temper your gaze. These things that when their mother was at home belonged to her daughters too, but in her absence proclaimed themselves her possessions. And the other things that in the busyness of daily life went unexamined. Over the sideboard was a blown-up photograph. *Ships at Stockton NSW, c.1906* said the caption. They were sailing ships, no funnels, with powerful masts and crosspieces and all the careful tracery of ropes, the sky of the picture full of their shapely pencil lines, long diagonals, sometimes cross-hatched into ladders, and horizontal loops and somewhere, though they were not to be seen, would have been the men who knew what they all meant, who could unfurl the sails, lower and raise them, turn them so they caught the breeze or slipped through the gales. Here they were moored several deep to the wharf. Graceful boats, with curving prows and strong bowsprits: George would have known the names, barques perhaps, barquentines, schooners, windjammers, and their cargo: it was coal, wasn't it? Since she was a young woman, when George brought it proudly home and hung it from the picture rail (not at all Alice's idea of a work of art) she'd seen this picture, and never thought to ask. And look, figureheads, curved women white against the black prows, arms crossed, draperies fluttering back, or perhaps it was wings. At the sign of the Flying Angel. Breasting the waves, breasts to the waves: angels and ministers of grace, keeping safe.

They that go down to the sea in ships, said the psalm. *These see the works of the Lord*. What it particularly meant was, the violent ones. The furies of the Lord. In weather like this Nobby's would have flown the flag, Bar Dangerous. Meaning that trying to enter the harbour could wreck your ship. Witness the approaches sown with carcasses. The bones of fifty ships lie on the Oyster Bank alone, this shoal of shifting sands where anchors do not hold. Vessels would be lost and all the people in them, within sight, a stone's throw people said, of calm water. In one place there are five in a single heap: *Wendouree, Lindus, Colonist, Cawarra, Adolphe*, one on top of the other.

What could you do when the harbour, the port, the safe place was too dangerous to enter? Wait in the roads until the storm abated. Hope not to be cast on the rocks. And even when you were actually in port, it wasn't always much safer. When the winds blew, ships thrashed about at the wharves, at those berths three and four deep, damaging themselves and their neighbours, or broke free of their moorings and collided in the congestion, grounded, capsized.

How calm it is in the picture. The frozen moment. Twilight perhaps when the light has clarity but not warmth. Two horses graze. This photograph is a Grecian urn of perfect forever. At this moment, entirely safe. No gales can touch it.

And the men, not to be seen: maybe they are off at the Missions to Seamen just across the wharf—in 1906 still the old tin building—falling in love with the pretty lasses. *Forever wilt thou love and she be fair*. No. Not all of them, anyway. She's never noticed before. There are men in the photographs, not down on the deck where she'd been looking for them, where the finely planked lifeboats hang, but high up, in the rigging, perched on yard-arms, where the sails are partly furled. Tiny figures. They seem to be looking at the camera. Perhaps they are actually posing, for the photographer standing just where she is. On the grass, with his shuttered telescoping apparatus taking their picture. The horses are blurry round the edges, and there is a figure that looks like a little girl running across the grass, smudging her space, in the time the shutter was open. Maybe the ropes are so clearly delineated because they too moved as the picture was being taken, occupying more space than the eye could ever perceive.

Veronica remembers Mikelis saying how he loves the solemness of faces in old photographs. Because the picture took a while to take, not the split second as now. As though that time necessary imparted your real face, not just the fleeting image of it; its substance, its character. As though a bigger chunk of your life had been captured.

Thinking of Mikelis makes her feel lonely in the empty house. She goes into Alice's bedroom, and that's worse. Her mother is so much not there, in this room as it's always been, in the immemorial placing of objects: the pink china basket with a china rose on the side, the pincushion stuck with hatpins, the cut glass lidded bowl where Alice keeps now little poems she cuts out of the paper, ornaments and trinket boxes which her daughters once gave her and now find hideous, which Alice still treasures. It's orderly, no evidence here of the accident, the emergency departure.

She's well, the hospital says, she's resting, as well as can be expected with a broken leg, not a light thing breaking bones at her age, but she's doing well. Veronica thinks of the hospital on its headland, its lighted floors like the decks of an ocean liner, it too breasting the stormy night. She doesn't want to think of her mother slipping over in this lonely house. Lying with doubled up leg a day and a night. Needing the neighbour to notice the paper not brought in. So frail a hold on life and safety: the neighbour noticing the paper. She was wandering a bit, said Josie, the neighbour. She kept talking about the Japanese. Something about them having blocks of wood for pillows. They're lucky, she said, they have blocks of wood for pillows.

◆ ◆ ◆

Alice's room in the hospital looks across the green park where the helicopters land, to the sea that way. She sits propped up in bed, not close enough to the window to see what happens on the ground with the helicopters, but able to observe brief moments of their rise and fall, when the swift blades of the rotors chop the silence into chunks that tumble their noise into the waiting hospital. Just as well. The helicopter means damage and fear. Saving people, perhaps, but after what disaster.

Alice wonders how she feels. Do you have any pain? the nurses ask. If she says yes they give her some pills. Sometimes she says yes, sometimes no. There is a pain, there is always a pain. She can't grasp it. She isn't sure it should go away. There hadn't been pain on the bathroom floor. That was a black space, and no pillow. Even the Japanese who don't have pillows have blocks of wood to rest on. With a pain you know you are there. It drags at you, holds you in place. You won't float off into black space, out into that dangerous air where the helicopters chop the silence into chunks that tumble down and bruise the ears. Alice has had plenty of pains in her life, but has never got into the habit of taking pills for them.

There are four women in the ward. Near the window on the right is Marie Dare. No one ever visits her. She says in a clear voice: I am bored. I am so bored I am counting my pills to pass the time. She shakes them into her hand and counts them back one by one into the paper cup. She gets to seventeen. In fact there are only nine. Nobody but Marie Dare knows this is a joke. She pours them out again, counts. This time she gets to twenty-five. Pours again. To pick them up and swallow them she feels in the palm of her hand. She is almost blind. Miss Dare she is, though most of the nurses call her Marie. Or darling. When they breeze in and take you by the hand. Are you all right, darling? they say. Oh sweetheart, all your bedclothes are on the floor. They bustle and smile and put a shield of friendly energy around the old women. Who flourish briefly, until the nurses swirl off to the next ward.

Near the door on the right is Doreen. She has a startling beauty that the ruin of her old age only makes more poignant. Her hair is silky white ringlets and her eyes summer sea blue. She is a woman out of a drawing-room comedy. She needs to make conquests all the time. She tells stories out of play scripts; the other women hear them over and over, see them being polished, see the art with which she offers herself. She adores men. Men are always right. She dotes on her grandson, her granddaughter is okay, some of the time. Her daughter can do nothing right. It's always the wrong nightie, or she's late, or too soon, or hasn't remembered the curlers or the book or the bedjacket she ought to have known her mother would want. For sons and sons-in-law there's charming petulance and flirtatious demands. She has always been charming and beloved, little girl to old lady. The darling of daddy and uncles and then of lovers, husbands, and now of sons and lovers.

Doreen tells stories, she woos, she croons, she manipulates. Darling, she says to the nurses, sweetheart, the sheets are wrinkled, the light's too bright, my head hurts, I have to have a cup of tea. Her endearments are the velveting of her iron. Alice takes mild malicious pleasure in noticing that she is deserted by syntax and betrayed by grammar. In Alice's family people have always spoken well, even if they weren't much educated. No yous or ain'ts. Marie Dare wishes she'd shut up. She's sick of her whingeing.

In the left-hand bed near the window is Betty. She has a visitor who sits on a chair beside the bed. From time to time they have a conversation though they don't look at one another as they speak.

—Did you sit in the chair?

—Yes. I sat in the chair.

—Yes. I used to sit in the chair.

—I sat in the chair for quite a long time.

—You don't want to get cold, sitting in the chair.

—No.

—You've got to watch you don't get a chill.

—I wouldn't want to get a chill.

—Shouldn't sit in the chair too long.

If Doreen is illiterate Noel Coward, it is Pinter writing Betty and her friend. He's coached them in the delivery too: slowly, slowly, slow down! Pauses: the strength is in the pauses. Make your audience wait for the next word. It's as if the words are musical notes, and they are gentle jazz musicians, trading slow improvisations.

—They're lovely looking kids. That youngest kiddie.

—Yes. Lovely.

—A real little beauty.

—She's always kept them nice.

—Yes. Lovely. A real credit.

—Lovely things she puts them in.

—Yes. She looks after them. Something lovely.

—Mm. She looks after them. They're a real credit.

—Her mother was good like that.

—Yes. She liked things nice.

The hour is nearly up. Time for one more.

—The Chinaman's wife, she had a stroke.

—Oh.

—Yes. A stroke. On Sunday.

—The Chinaman's wife.

—Yes.

—She had a stroke, did she.

—Yes. On Sunday.

Alice sits in her bed, on the left-hand side near the door, and watches these performances with the interested eyes of a child. You can see the serious and rather worried small girl she must have been. But she's enjoying the shows, happy to let the spectacle unfold around her. Alice never wanted starring roles, never sought the limelight. But she's about to offer a performance of her own. Out-of-town daughter paying a visit.

♦ ♦ ♦

Walking through the hospital Veronica found again the Monet painting of the window at the end of a corridor, the bands of green colours, sand sea sky, hazed in the light of its own spray and by the salt-encrusted glass. Just as when she'd come to visit Martin. All the people in all the years who'd passed through this hospital, and still there were windows like Monet paintings. This was a different floor from Martin's; she imagined them ranged one above the other, a series, like haystacks, or waterlilies. This was their winter phase, greenish and subtle; in summer it would be primary blue and yellow, with people, maybe the red sails of windsurfers. Dufy cheerful.

When Veronica came into the ward all the women watched her walk up to her mother and put her arms round her, fearfully, shocked by the frailty of her bones. She sat by the bed and held Alice's hand, bending over, resting her head, pretending to rest her head, on the tiny bony shoulder, so that her mother wouldn't see her eyes filled with tears. The hand was as soft and cool as always; it released a memory of all the years of her mother's touch. And the feel of her cheek as she kissed. Her mother's famous complexion, famous like an Austen heroine's for its rosy pink and cream colours but fine too, the texture as well as the colour of rose petals, fresh and fragrant soft as they. Wrinkled now, the petals creased and crumpled, but still fine and cool.

Veronica's tears were not entirely for Alice, they were for Veronica's looming loss of Alice. Of course she worried about her mother, the pain, the terrible black space of the day the night the day, lying on the bathroom floor, the jostle and prod and pry of death too close and neither of them knowing how to talk about it. She wanted her mother comfortable, happy, unanxious, and she wanted her mother. Alice was sitting up in bed like a small girl who'd lost hers and Veronica wanted to be her child again as well as a competent grown-up person looking after her. She thought there are no grown-up people. No one to make it all right. No mothers any more. We're all children. Except the nurses who do it as a job. In miserly little parcels.

A nurse came in. This is my daughter, said Alice, with pride. The nurse dispensed pills in paper cups. She talked in a very loud voice. Why does she shout, whispered Veronica. She thinks everybody's deaf, said Alice. Nearly everybody is. I'm glad I'm not.

It hadn't ever occurred to Veronica that being able to whisper at your mother was a luxury.

Doreen called out to be introduced and when Veronica was leaving she came over, took her hand, kissed her, all heartfelt goodbye, doing her best to add Veronica to her circle of admirers. Watching her trying to appropriate her daughter Alice thought of all the people Doreen would have made jealous throughout her life, all the people who'd have watched in impotent rage as she stole their lovers, children, husbands. Suppose that everybody had somewhere a kind of spirit figure, a sort of alter ego voodoo doll that kept the scars and bruises of all the kicks blows scratches stabs that people had thought against them; what a mess Doreen's would be.

You're so lucky, she said to Alice, to have such a *kind* daughter. Her voice wistful, her eyes teary.

In the corridor Veronica met Helen Murphy who'd done radiography training with her. Helen used to be in demand when they had practical inspections because she was thin, it was easy to find her bones. You didn't ask people with cushions of fat hiding their skeletons to be your patient. They'd stayed Christmas card friends and Veronica sometimes looked her up when she came to Newcastle. Now she was greatly pleased to see her.

What are you doing here? they both asked, delicately, in case the reasons were bad. Helen's face went wan, and out flooded words.

It's my mother. She's broken her hip. But that's not the real problem. The trouble is, she doesn't remember anything. Not anything. Not even that she's broken her hip. She keeps trying to get out of bed because she thinks she can walk. She doesn't remember that she falls over when she stands up. She forgets that she had a cup of tea a minute ago. I suppose she knows who I am, I'm not sure about that, but when I go out the door she doesn't remember I've been. I go to the nurses' station and back and she behaves as though she hasn't seen me for ten years.

Veronica felt a pang of gratitude for Alice's intact mind. Helen went on with her story, down the stairs, across the car park—she was giving Veronica a lift—in the car, over coffee at the Merewether house. Her mother had been living with her, until the broken hip, physically well enough but needing constant vigilance. Having no memory, said Helen, it's a living death. She isn't herself any more.

She'd been in the lavatory when it happened. Had forgotten her knickers were down around her ankles, had stood up and tipped over. Against the door, so they couldn't open it to get her out. Helen had huge dark circles under her eyes, where the skin had an opalescent bronze sheen. It would have been quite beautiful had people admired that kind of thing. Veronica thought of the days when her skinny bones had been in demand by radiography students. She'd be even more useful now.

I wish she'd die, said Helen. Not for me, I don't mean for me, I think I don't, I mean for her, she's not herself, what's the use of going on living when she's not herself. Hurting and miserable and not even remembering why or that this isn't how it always is.

Nobody tells you how to deal with these sorts of things, said Veronica. They tell you how to have babies and how to bring them up and what to do when problems come with school and teenagers and stuff, not always useful but at least it gives you something to go *against*, something to help you work out what might be right for you by rejecting, but your parents and getting old and death maybe . . . you're on your own.

Yes, said Helen. I suppose nobody knows. Who knows about death? I don't. And I don't believe people who reckon they do.

◆ ◆ ◆

Veronica sorted out photographs and took them into the hospital for Alice to identify. It was a kind of pastime, it hid the fact that there wasn't always a lot of conversation to make. But important too, if the pictures were to be a record. Alice's remembering was faultless and fast. Veronica wrote the names of people and the places and if not the dates the periods of them on the backs. They laughed and talked about them, both ignoring the darker meaning, that this had to be done before it was too late, and the information died with its owner. *When a person dies a library dies*; this is a Black American saying that Mikelis read in the newspaper and liked to quote, but Veronica did not say it aloud at this moment.

There was an envelope of sepia snaps gone yellowish, and their bottoms were cut off. The figures were reduced to heads and shoulders; girls in lacy pin-tucked pale pretty dresses presumably and hats that dipped at the back and framed bright-eyed faces. They were Alice and Lily, Nell and Rose, with Vic and George. Some were just Alice and George, side by side, their heads at conscious angles. They were just as recognisably courting photographs as others are wedding photographs. The time was 1927, and some years later Alice had cut them off above the waist because she thought the dresses looked silly. Veronica had always scolded her for this, because in her eyes the fashions were beautiful, much more so than the dull clothes of the next decades. I suppose you're right, said Alice, peering at the fine needlework of the top halves, they are pretty, but just afterwards, you know, those shapeless dresses and the waists round the hips, they made you look like the side of a house, and we just thought, how could we have worn such things.

Oh Mother. You thought you could change history, cut it away, wipe it from people's minds. But you can't you know. Veronica produced another envelope: Alice had missed these, they hadn't been doctored. There they were, the no-waists in full glory, and droopy hems dipping down to little pale leather curvaceous shoes.

Louis heels. Alice smiled, pleased. See, how broad in the beam we looked, she said.

But gorgeous.

Sixty years. Silly things we were. If we'd known then . . .

My God. What a horror. It's just about the only good luck people have. That they don't know what's in store for them.

Do you think it was so bad? Alice spoke with a kind of mild curiosity, as though she were gossiping, which didn't deceive Veronica.

Oh, I don't mean it was bad. Not to live through. But if you saw all your life spread out ahead of you, well, you'd quail. Don't you think? It's dealing with one thing and then the next that makes you able to cope. And getting older, and . . . not wiser, but more used to it.

Until there aren't any more things left to deal with. Or only one.

Veronica squeezes her mother's hand. She thinks she means death, dying. This is her chance to speak of these things, as received wisdom has it, to be open about this final fact of life, not leave her to face it alone. But she is scared, she doesn't know how, she hears clumsy words, dangerous, clanging in the air between them, she can't take the chance. Instead she dodges. Well, you're not there yet, she says. Still a million things to do. She picks up the faded photographs of the long ago young people in their fancy clothes.

The background seemed to be a framework of skewed and rusty metal. Where are you exactly? asked Veronica.

That's the *Adolphe*, said Alice. The wreck of the *Adolphe*. She was lost on the Oyster Bank, oh, before I was born. You could get to her from the Stockton Breakwater. It was something people did on Sunday afternoons. You took the ferry across and walked along the Breakwater to the *Adolphe*. She'd been a beautiful boat. French, George said, a windjammer, I think. But just a shell by then. Filled with concrete.

What a way to spend Sunday afternoon. Getting all dressed up to go and stroll on a wreck.

Taking the air.

Wasn't it rather melancholy?

I don't remember. It was what you did. I do recall George and Rose having a terrible argument, though. But they were always doing that.

◆ ◆ ◆

After a fortnight Veronica had to go back to Canberra. Elinor drove up the day before, and Veronica handed over to her. She'd talked to the woman who specialised in geriatrics at the hospital, a tall severe clever person. She had a number of young doctors, registrars and students, working with her; they were warm and friendly to the patients and their relations. They touched the old people with gentle hands, rested their palms on their shoulders, even gave them hugs. It seemed a good thing that they found their charges lovable. There was quite a lot of scope for them to practise their speciality; Newcastle had an ageing population. Dr Pulowski was strict, she would not offer hope where it wasn't due. Alice was doing as well as could be expected; she is an old woman, said Dr Pulowski. Veronica reported all this to Elinor. Every day the families of patients try to catch the doctors and ask how things are going, there might be news, a change, an improvement of course is what they want, and they need to be sure that the doctors keep thinking of them.

When visiting hours were over the sisters went to the Italian restaurant in Islington. Over dinner they caught up on their own news. Elinor was trying to work out how to get back to France to write a book with a woman called Flora Hart whom she'd met when she was last there, a book about women's lives in the seventeenth century, from the lady of a castle down to the scullery maid. At home afterwards at the Merewether house she opened a bottle of wine and they sat at the dining table. Veronica told the story of the woman with no memory. Even animals remember, she said. They remember what they need to know.

This night wasn't stormy, the sound of the sea was very quiet in the night air, with no wind racketing about. Just the endless muted breaking turning breaking of the waves. The sea is calm tonight, said Elinor. The women felt the house full of melancholy, they were aware of finitude. This house and the family life in it which had for so long been available for them whenever they wanted it was slipping away. Alice breathing lightly in the high hospital bed made an adult cot by its raised chrome bars, Alice's thin breath was the fraying thread that held it.

They sat slumped over the table with their heads on their hands and sipped the wine. They didn't want to talk about what was happening. Elinor reached over to the bookcase and took out the copy of *Quo Vadis* that had sat just there for forty years and more. It was the first adult book she'd read, at what age, eleven, twelve, ten, and she still remembered her excitement, and the respect, and the revelation: so this was a real book, the richness, the detail, the sheer quantity of matter in it. And the world was full of them. You could hardly believe such luck. She wouldn't reread it now, probably couldn't even if she tried, certainly hadn't watched the lurid old film that turned up on the telly last year. She preferred it to remain safe in its past. *Quo Vadis*: whither goest thou? Into a life of reading books.

Beside it on the shelf there was a colouring book kept at one time for grandchildren of an age for that sort of thing. Alice never throws anything away. Only a few pages had been attempted. Elinor went to the bookcase behind the door and got the oblong biscuit tin which held the coloured pencils, dozens of them, worn short and many of them blunt. She opened the book and began colouring in a picture on the right-hand page. Veronica went to work on the left, sideways on, because she was sitting round the corner of the table. They sat concentrating, getting the strokes all one way, not slipping over the outlines. Now and then one would rub a large area of colour with the pad of her finger to smudge it smooth, though this needed care not to go too far. When they were small children Father had screwed a big green metal pencil sharpener to the bookshelf. Now when a pencil was too blunt or broken they went and sharpened it. After a bit nearly all the pencils were freshly pointed in pale sweet wood and colour.

The pictures were quite finely detailed. *Flower Fairies of the Spring*, the book was called. Veronica had Hawthorn and Elinor's was Briar Rose. There was a wide range of colours possible because the pencils were remnants of many sets: Derwent, Cumberland, Lakeland, and so it was possible to get subtle shades and nuances. Elinor had her tongue between her teeth. They took only occasional sips of wine, and their conversation was small trails of words across the concentration of the colouring-in. Every now and then one would sit up straight craning her neck back and slitting her eyes, head on one side, to judge the effect of the whole. Frown perhaps, add more colour, darken, fill in, shade more evenly. It was late when the pictures were finished and they could go to bed.

◆ ◆ ◆

Next morning, in the train to Sydney, a shabby and crowded electric commuter train with no room for luggage, Veronica's carriage was travelled in by a dwarf, a man with a withered arm, another with a limp, a girl with one hip twisted. Sitting opposite her were a girl and her mother both with speech impediments. The girl had a baby. They talked to one another and to him in soft honking ululations of sound that were a distant rhythmic echo of sense. Veronica couldn't understand them. The baby said Dadadadad very loudly.

The train to Canberra was emptier. She read a magazine, looked out the window, dozed. There'd been a lot of rain. The ground was a swamp. From beside the line a heron took off, its legs hanging, its wings not yet in rhythm. A bundle of fencing, wire and posts, lay beside the track. A yellow dirt road stopped, or maybe it was beginning, at nowhere. She read a bit, and looked out the window again. A grey heron took off, its legs hanging. There was a bundle of fencing beside the track. A yellow dirt road. She dozed, opened her eyes. The ground was green and swampy, a grey heron took off. Fencing wire and posts lay in a bundle. The yellow dirt road stopping or starting. She sat and stared out of the window, waiting for the images to repeat a fourth, a fifth time. Perhaps the train was in a time loop, perhaps it would run through this circle forever, the same heron lifting, the same bundle of fencing, the same lost road. Forever; or until the loop was broken, the journey to somewhere resumed. She wondered: if you perceive a time loop, does it exist? Or does it by definition depend on being come to, each time, afresh and ignorant, so that the previous moments offer no message, nothing is learnt, each time however often repeated is the first time.

She stared at the green swampy grass by the track and then after a bit the train came to Bungendore with its painted wooden station. If they had been travelling in a loop, they seemed to have broken out of it.

Desire

◆

Desire, said Mikelis. Do you
know what it is that everybody desires? It's desire. They desire
to desire. When you lose that you're as good as dead. Or a
saint. Or approaching nirvana. When, all passion spent and
not just the passion but the faintest odour and expectation
of it, we will dewdrop slip into the shining sea.

And no, that is not where I am at because although I no
longer desire to desire I can remember what it was like to
do so. I remember Veronica in her red-flowered dress and the
way she walked through the salty Christmas air. In the pride
of her youth, with her slender waist and her rolling hips and
her coiled brown hair with the curls escaping. She owned the
street. She swung along on her red-sandalled feet and she owned
the whole world. The breeze off the harbour and the Christmas
bush on the barrows and the crowds of people shopping, the
cranky buses . . . the world and all its wants in a woman. Oh,

you hear me mooning on in my old man's way, but I tell you, Dane, I knew then what desire was. And in the studio, the bald velvet and the dozy gas fire . . . she did too. That's why she didn't want to get married. She knew you can't make desire legal.

And making it habitual; that's pretty much as bad. It's not the legality that does the hurt, it's the daily business. And it's forever being corrupted, diluted, polluted. For me the perfect moment, the absolute, was seeing her walking down that street in another town and that other country the past. When I talked to her, touched her, fucked her . . . never again the pure *zap* of the first moment.

That's where the affairs came in. Mikelis gave a kind of burping chuckle. His fingers tapped on his knee. Oh, ho. Jealousy, you'll be thinking. Passion's other face. The leer and the tear. The mask that smiles and the mask that moans. Jealousy was good fun too. Veronica also desired desire. And in affairs she found it. Snatched and grabbed. Awkward, secret, hurried. But in the spaces in between she flowed like honey. It took me a long time to see it and even after I did I couldn't always manage to keep hold of it, but sometimes I could believe that those affairs were a kind of restoration, for me, of that first pure moment. Another man's urgent fresh passion, and hers for him, and there, briefly, was my first moment of desire.

She loved me at those times. Perhaps best of all at those times. As I did her when I was fucking other women. The jealousy made our connection, Veronica's and mine, I mean, raw and exciting, unhabitual, hard and unhappy and important. The quotidian was dull afterwards. She was never interested in serenity, Veronica. Never got old enough, I suppose. She certainly wasn't in any dewdrop frame of mind when she died.

Dane thought that at this moment Mikelis wasn't either. He was tense and taut, the quirky bones of his skinny fingers snapped, under the polished arch of his skull his brain buzzed as anxiously as ever. More, probably, because that was the only part of him that functioned still in its old way.

That was my father-in-law's idea, he said. He liked that image, that the end of human life—and it might take you many lifetimes—was to become like a dewdrop on a leaf, round, transparent, purged of all selfhood, able to slip off its momentary resting place and be lost in the vast ocean, become part of its substance, water joining water.

Was he a Buddhist? asked Dane. Isn't that a Buddhist idea?

Probably. He was a Rosicrucian. They're very eclectic. Get ideas from everywhere. Ecumenical, you might say. Why not? There are many versions of the truth. He had another way of putting the same thing, that the perfection of human life is absorption in the infinite, as a ripple dies away on the surface of the Nile. He chuckled: When, I suppose, you no longer care whether it's the same river or not. A ripple; what does it know of the river underneath, on which it so soon loses itself? Odd, when you think of it; the Egyptians were absolutely obsessed with the individuality of the self; all those embalmed bodies and entrails in jars and household goods and models of servants so you could be as entirely you in the next world as you had been in this. No turning into a drop in a bucket let alone a river for them.

Did you go along with your father-in-law?

I listened. For years I listened. His daughters wouldn't. They'd got adept at never settling in his presence so he couldn't pin them down with his words. But I liked hearing him. He was a person who thought all the time. His mind was a busy place. He had this boring job and this busy mind. Always looking for meanings. Always answers.

His own father was a lay reader with the Missions to Seamen. At the sign of the Flying Angel. The good news of eternity. Saving sailors from drink and lechery. Only he drank too much and got dismissed. George was a choirboy, saw the Church of England from the back and wasn't impressed. Not with the Rosicrucians either, in the end. When he retired and was living on the pension, not much money, he wrote and asked was it possible to belong for a reduced rate, after all his years with them, the advancement and so on, and they wrote back and said no. Just a form letter, not personal to him at all, they didn't seem to know him. He decided they were mortal men, flawed, not manifestations of the Divine Mind, not

Illuminati, not anywhere near absorption in the absolute. Not actually very friendly at all.

Mikelis shook his head. I don't think I'm a dewdrop person. I'd rather be me crossing the bridge. Risking getting pitched into the chasm below because I hadn't been good enough. Not just moral-good but talent-good. You know, like the Bible and the talents: did I work hard enough at mine?

There can be no question . . .

I'm questioning, aren't I? Was I a good enough and faithful servant to my talents, that's the thing. I reckon that's all that'll save me from the pit.

Not faith but works, said Dane daringly.

That's good, said Mikelis. But actually I'm not hopeful of that either, I mean of there even being a bridge, let alone anywhere on the other side. Paradise, with houris. Veronica in her red and white dress and forever that first moment of desire. And would I want it? It only works because it's a moment, it has a context of non-desire, absence of desire, to make it work. No. Paradise is a problem.

But one thing I reckon: life that has once been is always. Death can't stop it or change it—death isn't retrospective. That life—Veronica's, George's, Nero's—still *is*. It's in the past, but it is.

Dane thought of Mikelis's photographs. Clearly, if you made something important, worthwhile, that went on, there you were in it, but he didn't say this because he didn't think it was what the old man meant. He imagined his irritation: That isn't it at all. Artefacts, they're themselves, not me. Don't confuse us.

Dane looked at the old man leaning back in his chair. Trembling with the buffeting of his busy mind in a frail body. The bridge, if there was one, seemed very near. He turned the tape recorder off, picked him up and carried him to bed. He stayed up, making himself a cup of coffee and typing up the day's tapes. There was quite a wad of observations now, playing round the meaning of life and art. Dane was getting more and more excited by them. He saw them as notes to a book of collected photographs; discrete observations, like *pensées*. As Mikelis said, it was the work that counted.

When the tapes were transcribed and the hard copies printed out and stored away in their file he took a pad of onion-skin notepaper and a fountain pen with blue black ink. *Dear Eva*, he began, then stopped. Ought he to be so familiar with her given name?

The pole

◆

Canberra, 1986

In the middle of the day the light falls straight down and is harsh. In the high country there is much less air between land and sun. But in the early mornings and evening it falls aslant; things look different, and possibly more themselves. Perhaps they are seen in a new light. It's the shifting moments that are interesting, of the day and of the year when winter turns to summer and back again; in spring it is often disturbed by wind, you cannot see the light for the violent concussion of the air, but autumn . . . the best Canberra autumns seem painted, not just for the colours of the leaves but because of the stillness. They are held in a long unbreathing moment which might last as long as a painting. But here and now it is winter and still, waiting for the twilight, for the frost to come down and the mist to curl into the valleys, round and round and squat in the best hollow, like a cat in a sleeping baby's cradle.

Veronica likes Canberra evenings. She stands in the kitchen of her house in O'Connor and looks across to Mount Ainslie where the westering light is turning the hill rose pink. It is not a colour to be photographed, it would look like a trick, though Gauguin could paint it in that particular vibrant colour he uses for hills and horses and coral strands. Veronica stands washing lettuce; it gets very clean as she watches the rose-pink light on the hill. Mount Ainslie it's called but it's only a hill. Shallow and symmetrical. The hills of Canberra surround the city like breasts; some people say this is what the city's name means. Though there seems to be no mythology attached, no vision of a generous woman sensuously spread, offering her nourishment to an abundance of sucklings. But there's plenty of affection the other way.

Veronica is rather surprised to recognise it. She's a sea woman, from the coast. She's never expected to get fond of a too cold too hot inland city.

The soup is bubbling on the stove. Now she's finely slicing cabbage, to put in as Mikelis walks through the door. She likes the cabbage crispish. The soup is to warm him; this is one of his pole days. Veronica looks up from the chopping board; the pink light has gone, it's almost dark, the aircraft warning light on Mount Ainslie is glowing red, the beacon flashing green and white, swinging its long tunnels through the misty air. Mikelis should be finished by now, he always does before dark.

One day shortly after he'd began this work he came rushing home in the middle of the morning and began to hug her, she could feel him trembling. He began to touch her skin with avid hands. He was behaving like a person who'd got a sudden uncontrollable attack of lust and had to take it out on the nearest available willing creature. He'd have done it on the kitchen floor, but she managed to draw him into the bedroom. His love-making was urgent, nervous, did not think of her; afterwards when she held him close in the rather motherly way that seems to follow such self-centred sex, he said, murmuring in her neck, Oh Vero. I nearly killed myself. He tried the feel of the words in his mouth again: Today I nearly killed myself.

Are the pictures worth it, says Veronica. Do you ever ask yourself that? Great pictures, dead you?

Both recognise the rhetorical and impotent nature of this remark. Mikelis simply smiles contentedly and goes to sleep, until a loud ringing on the studio bell reminds him that he has an appointment to do a portrait of a middle-aged female writer, who wants him to make her look interesting. Perhaps the odour of lust will help, he says; no time to shower. She can look quizzically at him, a writer ought to look as though she's making up outrageous stories in her head. He'll tell her this, about the outrageous stories.

♦ ♦ ♦

Once a week Mikelis drives to the top of Mount Ainslie. He parks his truck beside the tall pole that supports the aeroplane warning light, unfolds a ladder and sets it up on the tray of the truck in such a way that it hooks on to the iron ladder that is permanently attached to the pole. When he climbs both ladders he reaches his camera, which is set in a solid brass periscope case to prevent it from being shot full of holes by vandals' rifles. Once a week he has to change the film. He's supposed to attach himself by means of a safety belt, the kind that telephone linesmen wear; on the day he nearly killed himself he forgot. He felt himself slip and thought, It's okay I've got the belt. Then he remembered that it wasn't done up. He caught himself in time. Saved himself. What really frightened him was that nearly-not-remembering that the belt wasn't done up. Everybody he knew was talking about their brains going. Alzheimer's disease was a kind of sub-text when they said this, and mentioning it seemed to push it away; if I can talk about it I haven't got it sort of thing. AIDS for the body and Alzheimer's for the brain; one was sure to get you. At least they didn't use aluminium saucepans at home.

Veronica put it down to foolhardiness. Pity you so easily overcame all your phobias, she said. A bit of healthy terror could be quite useful.

At the beginning Mikelis had been so afraid of climbing the ladders he could barely do it; he took a long time to crawl up, hanging on for dear life, he told the story afterwards, the word dear very round in his mouth. His legs trembled and he sweated. He was so clumsy with fear that he didn't think he'd ever manage to change the film. He stood at the top of the ladder for a long time, hanging on to the brass casing. He felt like a robot with stiff claw hands and nobody knew the commands to make them function, and even if they did the rigid fingers would not be able to obey. The circuitry between thinking and doing had seized up, he had to open it up stage by stage. By concentrating on each separate step of the process of opening the submarine case, rewinding the film, undoing the camera, taking out the film, closing the camera, stowing the film in the bag around his neck, he was able to keep the fear at bay, but when he'd performed all the tiny acts involved, reciting them to himself as he did so, all the tiny acts that normally he'd do without noticing, then he inadvertently looked down at his shrunken truck and the fear sprang on him again and shook him until he was dizzy and sick. As though the pole were describing wild arcs across the sky, and one of its trajectories would fling him over the horizon. He felt his brain bursting with the effort of controlling it, bringing it back to stillness, so that he could gingerly climb down to safety.

✦ ✦ ✦

The camera on the mountain looks across the dome of the War Memorial, straight down the pink gravelled strips of Anzac Parade (military gravel, chosen for the crunching noise it makes when marched on) across the lake to the old, and above it on a decapitated hill, the new Parliament House, its goal. This is called the land axis. Five times a day, every three hours, between six in the morning and six at night, for all the years of its building, the camera is photographing the process.

A curious thing about the pole is that it moves. It sways. Not the sickening wild swoops of Mikelis's early panic: a precise and measurable movement. First thing in the morning it's cold, even in summer there's the small hours' chill of the high country, then when the sun rises one side is warmed, so the pole sways. At different times of the day the photographs have different perimeters. Mikelis has aligned the camera so that the symmetrical blocks of offices at the bottom of Anzac Parade are in the lower corners; he uses their windows to register the image.

When the new Parliament House is quite finished, he will create a moving film of the burgeoning of a building. Like those shots of flowers opening; this will be a monument growing.

Over the years there'll be more than 10 000 photographs. A lot will be rejected; sometimes there's nothing happening. Only those that show a progression will be used.

He's already been doing it for three years. Now he's used to it. He's forgotten his old fears. He makes jokes about it. Erudite ones, he's become fond of erudition as he grows older, is always reading, queer books, Veronica calls them, picking them up in fingers like tongs, dingy books, dun books; she scans the borrower's sheet in the back, nobody has taken them out since 1952, she says, or is it 1928? If he's bought them second-hand she says, No wonder their owners didn't want them, they had the good sense to get rid of them. Her shoulders prickle, Mikelis teases her for judging books by their covers, she becomes more irritated. She only likes books with pictures, art books sometimes, or else magazines, the glossiest ones, *Vogue, American House and Garden, Belle.* Mikelis suspects her of wanting to change her life by coloured pictures. Whereas he is a storehouse of odd facts in odder words. I am Mikelis the Stylite, he says. I sit on my column and regard the world. Only part-time at the moment. But one day, who knows, I may decide to stay. Lower baskets for you to put my food in.

Only lettuce leaves, said Veronica. You've got to lead an ascetic life. That's the point of pole-sitting.

Oh no. Juicy red stews and bottles of wine.

I won't do it, she said. I'm not feeding anybody up on top of a pole.

Once at a party he was telling people about his camera on Mount Ainslie. I am Mikelis Stylites, he began saying.

Oh, interrupted a woman. I thought your name was Ballod. Veronica laughed so much she had to hide in the kitchen.

◆ ◆ ◆

Partly she laughs because she's worried. Her fears have not been conquered like Mikelis's, they stay with her. She has not the skill of doing to overcome them, she can only stay behind and worry. Mikelis not only makes pictures from up his pole, he has himself dollied all over the site by a crane. When he does aerial shots, he takes the door off the plane, he gets a better view like that. Veronica can't bear to think about it, but her subconscious mind retaliates with a juicy nightmare or two.

Like this. There is a sign on Mount Ainslie which says it is 842 metres above sea level. Veronica has perfected a dream in which she sees Mikelis falling through every one of those metres, plus the height of the tower, falling slowly, turning over and over, like Lucifer thrown out of heaven, and she runs and runs but she can never get there in time; when she reaches him there is only a small amber amulet half-buried in the sands of the Baltic. She wakes up with her heart beating so fast it nearly suffocates her, but she can't bear to tell Mikelis the dream, she always pretends she can't remember.

The night of the day he came home and said, I nearly killed myself, she dreamed it again. This time the amulet has turned into a gnome who's dead and she's added a small pine tree squatting in the sand beside him, weeping amber tears over the gnarled little corpse. Mikelis holds her tight. He makes love to her, not thinking of himself this time, and afterwards his mouth and eyes curve in a glittering smile. I'd much rather die like this, he says. Veronica doesn't know it's another of his erudite jokes.

◆ ◆ ◆

Mikelis has read in a novel by Günter Grass that amber dissolved in a hot liquid is aphrodisiac. Against impotence a most potent tool. He imagines himself in his old age dropping Veronica's beads, one by one, night by night, into goblets of hot spiced wine. And who will be the partner of these amberous lusts?

Fortunately, the question does not yet arise. The beads are safe on their string, Eva may get her hands on them yet. Veronica is still his amber woman. And he can still climb to the top of his pole.

He's proud of this skill. Not bad for an old man like me, he says. He's forty-six. Lively as a young goat, I am. Positively capricious. He has to tell Veronica what this means. More queer words. Young goat, she says. Old goat.

◆ ◆ ◆

Isn't it dinner-time? says Eva, coming into the kitchen. Veronica looks out the window. It's completely dark now. The green and white beacon is struggling to flash its tunnels through the mist, the red unwinking light is almost invisible.

Not till Mikelis gets home, she says. What's the time? He should be here any minute. It's all ready, when he comes.

Eva leans against her mother, eating cabbage off the chopping board. I'm starving, she says. Eva is at the end of her childhood, she is still a child's shape but there is evidence that this is about to change. Not too soon, hopes Veronica. She would like her to stay a child as long as possible. Her experience is that later children have a better time of it. Less is demanded of them. Next year is high school, easier to manage without adolescence as well. She is so much always hungry that Mikelis claims she is eating her way into womanhood.

Get yourself a glass of milk. Veronica puts olives in a dish, and cheese biscuits. She pours herself some wine, and they sit and watch the television news. They see two lots of news, the political commentary begins. Eva curled up against her mother is hungry again. Veronica is disquiet. Where is Mikelis? He's never this late. She goes to the kitchen and stirs the soup, slices some more cabbage and gets cheese out of the fridge. She gives Eva another glass of milk. She puts the cabbage in the soup pot. She looks out the window; the beacon is making hardly any impression now on the mist. Mist? Fog. She turns up the heating.

Finally she gets her coat, scarf, gloves, hat. I'll just pop out and see if he's okay, she says to Eva. You stay here. He'll probably be home before I get back. She remembers a torch, and takes the doona off their bed.

She has to crawl along the road up the mountain. That's what it is now, a mountain. In the dark and the fog and the worry. The road winds, the visibility is barely beyond the car's bonnet. There should be no other traffic on the road but it's the unexpected that makes accidents. That's what she always says to Eva. Accidents are accidental. Like kids in a car expecting the road to be empty.

It's clearer on the top of the mountain, the fog and the woodsmoke are pressed down into the valley by the cold. Still she crawls along. Luckily. Her way is blocked by what looks like a heap of scrap metal. Can it be Mikelis's truck? It's reddish. Driven over the small but dangerous cliff that forms a sheer drop around the plot where the pole stands. Here is another shape for fear to inhabit. Mangled metal. She gets out, holding the torch; she seems to be running across the flinty ground, it's not a nightmare, her legs however they tremble obey her but she doesn't want to arrive, to see by the meagre light of the torch what that pile of metal will offer her. She's running, running, running, when she hears a voice, high, hollow, wispy as the mist: Vero . . . Ve-er-o-o . . .

I thought you were never coming, says Mikelis. She's driven the wrong way round the mountain's steep little nipple, is propping up the ladder against the pole, limbs chattering with cold and relief. It won't reach the bottom rung of the permanent ladder where Mikelis squats, waiting. You'll have to extend it, he says, and she's so clumsy she can hardly manage it, but then he's down and she's hugging him. You silly old goat, she says, you silly old goat. His face is as cold as death.

He wants to go and look at the truck but she won't let him. I suppose you're right, he says. I did hear the crash when it went over. Tomorrow, daylight, there'll be time for all that. She wraps him in the doona. Lucky I got you that thermal underwear, she says, with faint malice, for he'd demurred, was not sure thermal underwear fitted his image of himself. Yes, she says. Lucky.

So, how did Mikelis come to be up his pole, without a ladder and his truck a mangled heap on the road another cliff below? Well, he must have forgotten the handbrake, no, he'd have remembered the handbrake, forgotten to leave it in gear then, and after a bit it had started to roll, and that would've dislodged the ladder, that was the first he knew of it, a sort of jarring, and the pole swaying, and he looked down and there was the truck, this small dark shape, creeping backwards, in a sort of stately way, but getting faster, back down the track, veering in a curve and finally tipping over the cliff. Quite a clatter.

He didn't tell her how scared he was, how the pole swooped its wild arcs of terror across the sky and all the furry yellow lights in the valley swung together and collided. No, he just went on, reasonable, explaining, how far away the ground was, and the spikes, girdling the trunk like an iron maiden. Imagine sliding down that, he said. What a hug she'd give you. I kept thinking of Mikelis Stylites, and how that joke had come home to roost. He gave a long hoot of laughter.

I should have left you there, said Veronica. Passed up baskets of lettuce leaves. The occasional radish.

I tell you what, said Mikelis, it'd've been different for those old pole-sitters. They actually sat on the top on platforms. There was quite a lot of space, maybe even furniture. A small stove, and some books, probably. Blankets, I bet. Quite comfortable, compared with clinging to the side of the bloody thing. You could do it here, of course, there's a platform on the top, it's even got a fence around it, like a lighthouse, and a trapdoor opening on to it. Just that it was fastened with monstrous great bolts and padlocks.

Clinging to the side sounds very suitable to me. They had to keep making things harder, those guys. Getting more and more ascetic.

I wish you'd shut up about ascetic. It's not my scene. Soup and red wine, that's me.

In bed that night she said, How did you know I'd come and get you?

Oh, I just worked it all out, by logic. You always worry when I'm up my pole. You're an intelligent woman, ay. I knew you'd think it out.

Ah, she said. And do you deserve me?

Television

———◆———

The scene: the windblown porch of Parliament House, finished now, anchored by its pole like a paperweight. The West side, the Senate side. Just outside its heavy doors. Caution: Heavy doors. Take care when opening. If you are too frail to push those doors open, you have no business here. A young man is holding a microphone at the face of a woman. She is spare, lean, there is nothing about her to flutter in the freezing breeze, not hair or clothes or even a scarf, certainly not a skirt. Her body is slender and her age unclear. Her face is tanned, not as in browned by the sun though that is part of it, but as leather is tanned; like a smartly polished old shoe, seamed, dark, impervious to the elements, and the inanities of the young man with the microphone.

The date is something like June 1995. The wind is blowing from Brindabella snows.

Well, says the woman, I got a bit tired of roosting in trees and copulating with bulldozers.

Interrupts the young man: Did you think you were getting a bit old for it, perhaps? Liked the idea of a more restful life?

Young man, says the woman, you are a reporter. It is your job to report. Not manufacture. Did I say old? Suddenly she throws her hands back, then her body forward, and turns three cartwheels across the porch. The camera is caught unaware. I expect you lost that, she says, and does it again. She's had plenty of experience at getting herself in the telecam's eye.

She shakes a finger at the staring young man. Still limber, you see. No. I did not say old, I said tired. As in sick and. The process was not efficient enough. The grass roots was a good idea at the time, but I thought I'd have a go at doing a bit of moving and shaking from the top. Not of a tree. For a change.

Is the Senate the best place? asks the young man. In tones too late conciliatory. You can see from the pinching of his face that he knows all the televiewers will be laughing at him, at that moment in the future when his cartwheel-provoked discomfiture is shown on the screen. Didn't he know he wouldn't win? Somebody should have warned him.

The woman folds her arms, puts her head on one side, and bites her bottom lip at him. I think you can leave that to me, she says. Hours later, on the seven o'clock news, the viewers laugh. Too right, they say. Leave it to Rob. She's a character, she is.

The young man closes off, falsely dignified: That was Senator Rob Meletios, who took her seat in the House today. We'll be watching the Rainforest Crusader, as she gives up bulldozers and takes on the Senate. Will her raunchy defiance work there too? Or will she find the men a tougher prospect than the machines?

◆ ◆ ◆

The second millennium is drawing to a close. Society practises its solitary rituals. Family-nuclear. Individual. *Where one or two are gathered together in my name* . . . and every night, all over the country, in ones and twos, maybe occasionally a four or a five, people do gather. In the name of TV, pronounced, as Jehovah is JWH, minus the vowels, out of respect. What is the power of this community of spirit? When how many people, or rather, what percentage—it could be computed, however unreliably, by checking the ratings for that particular day—when whatever this proportion of the population collectively sighs at a fleshless Ethiopian child, frowns at the balance of payment figures, winces as the man jumps to his death from a burning building, laughs at a silly reporter: what is the effect of this concatenation of joint emotion? These collective exhalations, groans, sighs, laughs: how do they reverberate through the atmosphere? Would a god's eye view see them as pulsing through the starry mists of the universe; as puffs, ripples, farts, whatever? Do they together wash against the stones of the stars and wear them away; could enough of them rock worlds on their axes and tilt time out of true? Maybe they are as powerful as prayer, whatever that means.

Certainly quite a number of people saw Rob Meletios on the television that night. Sebastian, for instance, in the old stone house in the Blue Mountains. Amelia sitting in a chair knitting one of the multi-coloured jumpers she will sell in the shop for a lot of money. Zoe lying full length on the sofa drinking a dark red liquorous herbal tea called Rêve Exotique. Sebastian at the table drawing—was this the artisitic creative self finding its expression?—drawing a large picture of the Battle of Britain: more than half a century on its goodies and baddies capacity for infinite intricate detail still providing endless hours of tongue-protruding occupation for young boys. He claimed to have done all his homework. All three were keen greenies and Rob Meletios was a hero. They laughed with pleasure when she turned her cartwheels. They didn't know she was Sebastian's grandmother. If Zoe had ever thought her face looked a trifle familiar, it was not out of any connection with the sixteen-year-old girl who'd lived for a while on an abandoned dairy farm near Murwillumbah some thirty years ago. People are always finding other people's faces familiar and never knowing why. And Amelia had never seen her. Sebastian wasn't on the lookout for a granny. Zoo's and Mia's mothers, and come to that if they felt like it Zoo and Mia themselves, were all the grannies a twelve-year-old needed.

Elizabeth watched the programme because Rob had rung her and told her it was on. Elizabeth saw quite a bit of her niece, and did a lot of listening to her. From being the one who talked, to Alice as they bent over their knitting, the stitches so much easier than the words she tried to find for the awkward misshapen unregular ideas that bumped about in her head, Elizabeth had become the one who listened, to her own children, to Rob's, to Rob herself. She still looked like a madonna, not the girl of the paintings nursing her baby in a rose garden, nor yet the grieving mother of a pieta, but a pleasant comfortable matronly madonna. Still knitting; she listened most carefully when she knitted, her Gainsborough fingers all by themselves turning white wool into lace: at this moment a matinée jacket for her daughter Sarah's baby, to be born at Christmas. She lived on her own now; she was a widow, Andrew had had a stroke while up a ladder checking the alignment of a kitchen cupboard, still working though past the age of needing to, and falling killed himself, while Daniel, Sarah's twin, was at Cambridge, on a scholarship; the family cleverness coming out. Fancy Joe's grandson at Cambridge, reading philosophy.

Veronica saw the interview, sitting in her kitchen eating biscuits and cheese and red wine for dinner, because Mikelis was away. She knew Rob was her cousin, first cousin once removed, Robyn of the long ago carnal knowledge case, because she had met her at Aunt Lily's funeral, the year before. She's a bit of a ratbag, she told Eva, whom she called from her bedroom where she was writing an essay on *The Mayor of Casterbridge*, but you have to admire her. Did you see cousin Senator Rob on the TV? she asked Mikelis on the telephone next morning, but he only caught a glimpse, in the hotel room where he was getting dressed to go out for dinner with a young woman he had begun sleeping with. She was an editor at his publishers and wore black stockings with short skirts, really short, barely covering her bum; he loved short skirts. Though he was less keen on the clumpy lace-up shoes that all her generation seemed to wear, Eva too, Doc Martens with thick soft soles, what healthy feet these girls would have in their old age. If they didn't get seduced by stilettos in their middle years.

So who's not watching? Well, not Lily, of course. Nor Joe her grandfather, who would have been ninety-seven now; and not George, nor Alice; nor Anne, unless we suppose that there is television after death. If there were, would it be in hell, or heaven, or merely purgatory? Take a poll, Morgan or Gallup: I bet opinions would be equally divided as to its location. It's a pretty neat device, whose presence or absence could be equally heaven or hell, depending on the viewer. Even more devilish, perhaps, hell is television for those who hate it, and no television for those who love it, while heaven is the reverse.

Jade is a favourer of absence. She never watches telly, not since her long convalescence when she sat like a vegetable and waited for her mind as well as her body to heal. If you want news, the radio is more reliable. Pictures are tricky things. They concern themselves with the sensational, not necessarily the significant. Jade believes that the words that caption them are not honest in intent. Besides, she hasn't got time to sit in front of the idiot box. She'd rather spend it puzzling out the knots the twists the tangles the ravellings of family life and Family Law. Family Law and family lore: trying to sort out that lot takes her every waking moment. And stalks her dreams too. But were she to have seen the interview it would not have occurred to her that Rob was her mother. Sometimes, sitting on the train that carries her from the plains to the mountains, closing her eyes in exhaustion (missing as always the slide through the crack, the fissure in the mirror, that brings her out of the daily warped world into the charmed loving one), sometimes, in this undemanding train, she ponders the curious fact that she who spends her whole life on families gone wrong should not know where her own mother is. She knows about the sixteen-year-old girl who set off north to find her father. She doesn't hold this against her; she's seen too many sixteen-year-olds with babies to cast any stones. She does wonder if the girl Robyn ever did find the missing daddy; the odds are pretty even that the outcome isn't likely to have changed her life in any dazzling way. She thinks that one day she might go and look for her, and she also thinks that maybe she is better off as she is. She sees adopted children burning to know their 'real' mothers (the inverted commas are hers) and feels sad that simple biology should be so seductive. It is Zoe that she loves, and Amelia. In the nature–nurture debate she would choose nurture every time. She remarks that mothers do not seem to search so assiduously for their lost children as those children search for them.

And yet, were Jade to appear on television and Rob Meletios to be watching it, her mother would know who she is. Robyn never did find her father. She found a lot of other people, some her father's age, who mostly resisted her attempts to turn them into father figures. After a while it occurred to her that what she had to do was find herself, that she was the only person she could entirely depend on not to fail her. It was in the rainforest that I found myself, she was fond of saying, with an ironic snort. And of course it was there that a lot of other people found her, and it is always good to have the reassurance of third parties. Solitary self-finding is hard work, best left to saints.

She did a lot of thinking in the rainforest, and one day it was suddenly borne upon her that in searching for her father she had lost her child. The simplicity of the equation: she felt sick. Until then she'd managed to see leaving Jade as something that had to be done, something unavoidable, an absolute; now she realised it had been a choice. She hired a private detective and he traced Steve Apples from the farm at Murwillumbah to the butcher shop in Grafton. She went down herself, looked through the plate glass window and remembered how she hated meat, the redness and glisten of it; stood outside the big house and thought how she didn't really like suburbs, the neatness of houses in rows, the blindness of curtained windows; watched long-haired Zoe walk a little girl home from school, Jade in a cotton dress and round hat, how could she be old enough to go to school? That was not so simple as a house, or meat. She walked a long way, thinking. Jacaranda trees not so conducive as rainforest.

She stayed in Grafton for three days. She lurked in Zoe's street, sunglassed and droopy hatted, to see her and Jade going to and from school. The little girl was one of those never-still children who dance on the spot and walk six times as far as the distance they cover, like dogs off the leash; she was good at cartwheels too, in her lolly pink shorts in the front garden. Jade was so happy playing with the young woman that Rob's chest burned with envy and she wanted to go up to her and say, Give her back, she's mine.

She didn't do this. She went back to the rainforest and thought about Jade and found a bit more of herself, a bit that said, Oh shit, face up to it, Jade is happy where she is, with her father, she always was happier with him, and the mother he's found for her, and it's your part to leave her there. What right do you have to turn up like a bad smell and bugger their lives? She didn't go near her again. The camps of the protesters were no place for a child, anyway. She had love affairs, and a baby, she could have got rid of it but thought of Jade and didn't, a boy this one, named Forest, met Mick Meletios, married him, got on the television, became famous, had two more babies and as well there were the children he already had. She married Mick because he wanted to, wanted a real wife with his name and the words said in church. Fuck that for a lark, she said when he asked her. Get married? Jeesus. Only she'd fallen in love with Mick, and he was so keen she couldn't refuse him. Real quiet, then, she said, you and me and the kids. But of course the local telly station got wind of it and sent a reporter. Mick was news in his home town. *Millionaire haulage magnate marries hippie* wasn't something that happened every day. It wasn't entirely true, but very rich doesn't have the same ring as millionaire, and only Mick still thought of himself as a truckie. He didn't take kindly to the publicity. He wanted to pitch a nosy cameraman into the hedge but she stopped him. Gently boyo. We need these blokes. Fucking mongrels and all, we have to have them on side. She performed for them, casting melting glances at Mick, kissing him so he forgot anybody was watching. All a bit grotesque, Elizabeth thought, what a circus her niece had got herself into, but Lily enjoyed it. The energy. The sex. The freedom. Lily thought of her own life. She'd had some of those things, sometimes. Not often enough. Was that what you lived for, so the next generation, or the one after that, could have the advantages you missed? Why shouldn't it be your generation with the advantages? Lily thought back to the early days, when Joe came on the scene and she was a tall long-throated girl, George's Tiger Lily, and the future was full of bloom and promise; it was as easy to imagine herself inside Robyn's skin as to remember what it was to be that girl. The past was like snapshots; you could look at them, and wonder, or laugh, or sigh, but you couldn't be them. At least the television moved and laughed and sighed for you. That was something her old age had that Mother's hadn't: television. How Ada would have loved it. Ada whose sad feet finally opted out entirely, leaving her chair-ridden, and then the disease eating away. Television would have offered some amusement. Better than visitors racking their brains for conversation. The terrible well-meaning boredom of it. At least I'm still mobile, thought Lily, comfortably watching the television, following the rise to fame of her granddaughter Rob Meletios the rainforest crusader.

And now she'd stood for the Senate, and got elected as a green independent, and Canberra here I come she said. Her friends were fascinated by her private and public vocabularies, her neat switching between the two. Occasionally uneasy: would she slip up?

◆ ◆ ◆

Rob would have meant the cartwheels across the porch to be symbolic, an up-you image of how easily she was going to bowl her way into political life. Her enemies had different intentions. Certain entrepreneurs into whose works she had thrown some rather painful spanners. *Bodies against bulldozers*: those other bodies that owned the bulldozers would not easily forgive. They dug for dirt. She had not been in Canberra a week before she was in the news again. Headlines in the evening tabloids: *Search for Newcastle Butcher. Where are you Steve?* The snubbed reporter on the telly: *The hunt is on tonight for Newcastle butcher Steve Apples, who Senator Rob Meletios married back in 1965, when she was just a girl, and then deserted. The question on everybody's lips is, did she divorce him? Or did she marry husband number two without shedding husband number one?* It was juicy stuff; no sign of a divorce anywhere.

As she came out the weighty door of Parliament House he pushed his microphone in her face again but she merely smiled, and twirled her hands in imaginary cartwheels before his nose. He stepped back and she jumped into a car and drove off.

Bigamy? That was the next headline. A question mark to avoid libel. Mick asked Rob was it true. Search me, she said. He shouted, Don't you know? She shouted back, How the fuck would I? Haven't seen him for thirty years. Whatever. Probably is. Mick was beside himself. How could you? he said. I don't understand you. It was perfectly easy, she replied. You wanted to get married, we got married. So what if I'd done it before? Fucking stupid habit. Doesn't mean anything. Love does, and being honourable, not some silly bugger muttering out-of-date words over you. Witch doctor stuff.

She didn't tell Mick about the carnal knowledge business, or Jade. Time enough to deal with that if the press got hold of it. So far they were content with the bigamy. Rob smiled, her brown skin breaking into a thousand cheerful wrinkles. Was she bluffing, people wondered.

Ivan grinned when he saw the bigamy report: Rob's at it again. Veronica laughed: Bigamy now, ha? You have to hand it to her. She's an idiot, said Elinor, it won't do her career any good. Zoe gave a shriek, and clapped her hand over her mouth. Sebastian said, Apples? That's Mum's name. Common enough name, by the look of it, Zoe said. I've never heard it anywhere else, said Sebastian. Well, you have now. Jade didn't react, since she wasn't watching the television again.

I'll make some tea, said Zoe. From behind Sebastian's back, she made urgent beckoning signs to Amelia. In the kitchen she whispered, I know who she is now. Rob Meletios. She's

Jade's mother. Sebastian's grandma, for heaven's sake. Rob Meletios is Robyn Apples. She threw herself in a chair and began to giggle wildly. Robyn Apples.

Then she's no bigamist, said Amelia.

Golly, no she isn't, said Zoe. Should we tell someone?

Who?

The press?

But they didn't need to. The press ferreted it out for themselves. Steve Apples was dead. Senator Rob had been very much a widow. Shame on smear campaigns.

Going from the city to the mountains on the train, Jade sat with her eyes shut and pondered the question of mothers. Her policy of do-nothing justified, since the knowledge had come without her seeking it. But mainly she was excited. She hadn't expected to be so lucky. Well, Rob, she said in her head, picturing that small furious figure, furious and funny, capering about on the television and making fools of her adversaries, as far back as she could remember, maybe there is something in heredity after all. Nature as well as nurture.

She should have kept up the cartwheels.

The kangaroo

◆

Canberra, early 1990s

Part of Amelia's share of running
the gallery was keeping in touch with the craftspeople who
supplied it. Sometimes she went round in person to see what
her old clients were working on, and to find out new ones.
One day she decided that Sebastian should go with her. It's
time we broadened his outlook, she said. We'll take in Canberra.
Seb's never seen the nation's capital.

They set off west. First of all to Hartley, where a man
made carvings out of old apple wood. He'd lived on apple
orchards all his life, had grown the fruit for a living, and now
he turned the no longer useful trees into artefacts, making
a virtue of the gnarling, the twisting and knotting. They sold
well; people straightaway wanted to touch them, they touched
and were hooked, they bought them and took them home and
put them on coffee tables and said to friends, Go on, go ahead,
touch it. This is a good thing, the old carver said. The natural

oil of human flesh polishes wood and makes it glow. Just like people, he would add.

After Hartley they passed through Lithgow, the first industrial place Sebastian had ever seen, and he was shocked by the greyness of it, as though all the beauty of green growing things and the carved coloured shapes of rocks had all been rubbed away leaving only grey powdery earth and rusty junky buildings. He was glad when they got on to Bathurst, which was flat, but recognisably normal; he'd have liked to build it with Lego, pink Lego making the buildings, with cream patterns on them, and clock towers and columns. Here lived a woman who painted on silk, cushions and scarves, in colours like Smarties melted and rubbed together. She lived in Bathurst because her husband taught at the university, and she was discontented. It's so provincial here, you can't imagine, she said to Amelia, who laughed. What do you think Leura is? Not provincial, said the woman. And there's Sydney down the line.

After the silk woman they stopped at a motel because Amelia disliked long drives. They had a room with a bed in it each, both the same, and a bathroom. Mia made herself some coffee with a little electric jug and they had a hidden fridge with orange juice in it for him. Sebastian liked this neat set-up, and going to the restaurant to have dinner; it was the first time he'd read a menu for himself and chosen what he wanted to eat. Can I choose all by myself? he asked Mia, and she replied, Yes, now you can read you can choose.

The next day in the car she said, Here, take the map, you can be navigator. She showed him the red road they were to follow, and the white dots of towns. Just make sure we're on the right track. He looked at the names: Carcoar, Mandurama, Lyndhurst, Cowra, Noonbenna, Koorawatha . . . for somebody who hadn't been reading for long they were difficult letters to organise into words, until he got to Young. Why would a town be called Young? What would happen to it when it grew old? I've always supposed it was named after a person, said Amelia. Mr Young. Whoever he was. So what would happen when Mr Young got old? It's just a name, Mia said.

The map reading turned out to be quite easy. The names came up on signposts, Amelia pronounced them, and there they were on the map. They had to be careful at Cowra, not to take the road to Grenfell, way off to the west, but even that was easy not to do. One of the towns on the wrong road was called Bumbaldry. What sort of place would that be? He wondered what it would be like to live in a place with a rather rude name. Bumbaldry.

That day they visited two potters, one of them gave Sebastian a small bowl glazed a deep shiny blue, and a furniture-maker, whose work Amelia found too clumsy. She decided to give herself a treat and go to Boorowa where the antique shop always had something good. The gallery didn't sell antiques, she liked to buy them for herself. It was late when they got to Canberra and found a motel, so they called room service and ate sandwiches in bed. That way they could be up bright and early and go out first thing in the morning.

When they got up it was early all right but not Sebastian thought very bright. There was no sunshine, just a quiet silvery light. It was cold and somehow watery. The world could be underwater; the smooth grey sky above them could be the surface of the water and they underneath it; above would be the noisy world of colour and sun shining. Like a pool with coloured swimsuits and people screaming. If you looked hard enough you might see someone dive through it. Let's go somewhere interesting for breakfast, said Amelia, so they got in the Volvo. Even the roads seemed quiet and empty, theirs was just about the only car. Slugabeds, that's what the people of Canberra are, said Amelia, and Sebastian repeated, slugabeds, several times in a growling sort of way so he could enjoy the feel of the sounds in his mouth, until the word started to be nonsense. A strange collection of sounds that didn't mean anything any more.

They were travelling along a wide street, with quite a lot of traffic lights, which made them seem to be stopping and starting in a sort of dance, not for any reason of traffic except that once there was another car to let pass. This is Limestone Avenue, he read from a sign with big letters while they were waiting at a red light, a long time it seemed. Then he saw it, in the side street up to the left, loping along, easily, but covering the ground fast, getting closer very quickly. A kangaroo. Loping down the middle of the road, past the houses, the garbage bins lying loose where the men had thrown them. Look, he whispered, gently touching Amelia, as though he might frighten it away. The light turned to green and Amelia started the car moving, then stopped again; the kangaroo was still loping down the road. Would it know about stopping at a red light? A car came up in the left-hand lane, fast, catching the green light; the kangaroo kept coming. Suddenly it saw the car, propped, skidded. Sebastian saw the car speeding past, the kangaroo falling over. No, he cried, not wanting to look, but seeing this scene happening for a long time in front of his eyes that kept on seeing even though he didn't want to. The car rushing past, the kangaroo checking, skidding, falling over. Then the car was past, and the kangaroo was lying on its side, its legs kicking as though it were still galloping along, but clumsily, out of rhythm, not able to get any grip on the air. It's hurt, whispered Amelia. By this time the lights were red again. She was scared, but thought she ought to move the car, pull over into the side street, what could she do for an injured kangaroo, but she couldn't just drive on and leave him there in pain, she ought to stop and see and maybe ring up someone. A vet, or the RSPCA. By the time she'd decided that she had to do this and the lights were green so that she could get out of the middle of the traffic lanes and turn left the kangaroo's kicking had made contact with the ground and it had scrabbled to its feet and was loping back up the road, the way it had come. So it couldn't have been hurt by the car, or collided with it, after all. It must have just skidded, through stopping so suddenly. They were both suffused with relief, they turned to one another with beaming smiles of pleasure. It was the morning's gift, that the kangaroo should be safe, and bouncing along on its once-again powerful legs in the right direction, towards the hill and the bush where it must have its home.

That was Sebastian's memory of Canberra: the sight of the

kangaroo coming down the hill, the fear of the car speeding past and it falling, the delight when it got back to its feet and made off up the road in the clear grey underwater light. They did a lot of interesting things after that, breakfast in a café and visits to more potters and a weaver who showed him how his looms worked and a woman who made paper by hand, except she used a number of neat little machines to do it, and a photographer with round eyes who sat him on a stool and made a picture of him, saying I'll send it with the prints, it's just for fun, but it was the kangaroo he remembered, like a film he could play in his mind, the details always there and exactly ordered. When people made jokes about Australian cities having kangaroos jumping down their streets he smiled; it's true.

The red car

———◆———

Sebastian added the kangaroo
story to his repertoire of drawings. There was the hill with
the street curving down, the traffic lights, the speeding car,
the animal with its legs in the air. He sat at the dining table
drawing it, carefully, line after line. When he showed it to
Zoe she didn't understand it. It's lovely, she said, playing for
time. There's the Volvo, she could say, because he'd written
its name on the back, and what a steep hill, and then seeing
the bare-branched trees, It's Canberrra, isn't it, but he had
to tell her about the kangaroo and the car not running it
over. Sebastian spent a lot of time drawing. At first they were
very proud of him, and thought he was not just precocious
but probably a genius. The pictures had a kind of medieval
quality, of things being there because the observer knows they
are, rather than because that's how they are seen. Spatial re-
lationships did not interest him, what he drew was power and

meaning. You could tell who counted in his drawings, and what; they were visual parables. But the thing was that as he grew older his drawing technique didn't get any better, and whereas they could heap lavish praise on a five-year-old, from the ten-year-old they expected more skill, more craft, and his odd little parables of power seemed clumsy, out of perspective and out of kilter. He still drew as much as ever, but Zoo and Mia got into the habit of saying, How interesting, instead of, How marvellous, and setting him little tasks of drawing things exactly how they are, the table with the vase of flowers, the trees by the creek, the horse out of a book, which Sebastian would sometimes dutifully set out to do or shrug and ignore, but either way his drawing remained the same; beautifully carefully badly drawn schemes of his own observed world. Tell me about it, Sebi love, they learned to say, and listened gravely, nodding. Very interesting. Jade pinned them up on her walls and was troubled by them and took them down again and kept them in a folder in her filing cabinet.

His schoolwork had similar qualities. He was studious and it was meticulous, but somehow it did not connect with the subjects in hand. At first Zoe and Amelia were puzzled that this child of brilliant parents should show so dim. They talked it over in bed at night, over and over, what could have gone wrong, until they managed to remember that neither of them was a genius and was it something they valued highly anyway. Happiness is more important, they said. Sebastian is not ambitious. They recalled the tarot fool with his bum out of his pants wandering around the world getting wisdom. Jade wondered how he would get on in life if he wasn't clever, the people she knew all were and made their lives out of that, as lawyers or judges or doctors, materially if not emotionally making them work, or else they were completely stuffed, they suffered from having no control over their existence or anyone else's and hurt the people they cared for. They were full of rage at their powerlessness and that was where the violence came from.

Sebastian's drawings covered larger and larger sheets of paper. Then one day he just stopped. They weren't any good, he said, when asked.

What do you think you might like to do? When you've finished with school, I mean. Jade asked this question with trepidation. She didn't want to appear to be pressuring him, to be fussing in any kind of establishment way over careers. On the other hand, Sebastian was almost seventeen, school would finish with him soon. She looked at his report printouts; they gave no clues to his abilities or interests. All passes, and clichés. A quiet and studious boy. Sebastian works well. Sebastian is a hardworking student. Serious. Conscientious. All of them a calm acceptance of mediocrity.

I don't know, he said. I'll have to see.

Maybe he should come in with us, said Zoe. In the gallery. I suppose he could take it over eventually.

Yes, said Amelia. That's a good idea.

But both women spoke doubtfully. They weren't far into their fifties, they were full of energy, the gallery flourished, there was nothing they needed from Sebastian. He was so dreamy, there seemed no energy for getting things done.

He's a kind of passionately passive person, said Amelia. They were sitting at the kitchen table one winter day. Through the French windows they could see Sebastian in the garden. He was looking at things, the lichen on a rock, the bunched leaves of a peppercorn tree, the stone table with its pattern of mosaic chips. Studying them. It's as though he's absorbing them, said Zoe.

It wasn't just the natural world he regarded like this. He did the same in the High Street, with the shop windows, and in the supermarket, the piles of tins and packets, looking with the same meticulous care he'd have given a silver birch or a Rembrandt. He often caught the train to town and stayed with Jade in her house in Newtown; he took buses around the city and in the evening they ate in Thai restaurants where he observed the other customers. He was a nice boy to be with, not handsome but pleasant looking and giving off a great sense of goodwill. There wasn't much conversation and little wit, though a quirkiness that could make you laugh; you realised with a certain surprise if you were his mother and anxious, that you'd enjoyed yourself with him, you'd had a good time though you couldn't say why. Jade who'd just broken angrily with her lover of some years, a surgeon with a requisite wife deep in the North Shore and a cold cruel wit that sharpened itself on her kinder one and made their conversations into exhilarating bouts with winners and losers, was baffled by her unexpected son. Jade in her thirties is more beautiful than ever, leaner, and lined in the way of handsome women, delineating the shapely bones beneath the skin; men fall in love with her. Why has she stayed so long with the unrequiting surgeon? She has reservations about families, thinks that hardly anyone should embark upon children. Most likely not even herself, blithe in her ignorant youth, believing she was doing the right thing by the innocent unborn child. Certainly not in her middling and wiser years. Married men mean safer sex.

Maybe he's gay, she says to Zoe and Amelia. I mean, he has got some good role models.

She quite likes this idea. Gay men seem to have happy lives, she notices. Good times, anyway.

Well, yes, so why should he be shy about saying so? demands Zoe.

Jade gives Sebastian a serious talk about sex. AIDS may not be the terrible scourge it once was, but still care must be taken. No substitute for condoms.

Sebastian listens with his sweet attentive manner. I'm not gay, Jade, he says. He's got a girlfriend. He names a small plump sparkly girl who lives up the road.

Whatever do they do? wonder the three women. They haven't even been aware that the two spend time together.

I suppose they walk around and look at the world, says Amelia.

Maybe he listens to her talk, says Zoe.

Both feel a momentary pang of guilt for the closed-in circle of their lives, which they've all three accepted makes a safe little nest for the beloved child to grow in, but maybe could be seen as not taking a lot of notice. Not being very percipient. Only momentary, this pang. They remember how much they love him and cherish him and worry about him, and take comfort. You can't expect to own a seventeen-year-old boy.

◆ ◆ ◆

Then there's his father. Eric had stayed in London for a number of years, returned to Sydney and then gone to New York. He was a partner in the grand old firm now. He came back to Sydney again and moved into a house he'd bought in Bellevue Hill. He was no longer married to the May bush bride of the postcard sent to Jade. His new wife was American, of impossible tallness and slenderness. You looked at her and marvelled. She had been a model and possessed the wide full-mouthed face of the new world dream woman, healthy and wholesome with good child-bearing cheekbones. The staircase of the Bellevue Hill house was studded with working photographs of Tilly, where her beauty was of a remoter kind, the black-and-white glamour that an enamoured camera creates by reassembling its subject's elements into another artefact, where fashion becomes a matter of a rag, a bone and a hank of hair. The differently dazzling colour shots of her covers for *Vogue*, *Harper's Bazaar*, *Elle* and such decorated the walls of the downstairs sunroom.

Both wives are childless. Eric wanted to do something about this second, medical science could work out why, he wanted her to go on an IVF programme, he could afford the monstrous fees, but Tilly wouldn't, she didn't like the ethics or the invasiveness of it. It's my body, she said, huddling her arms round its thinness that looked more likely to snap than bend. IVF programmes don't care about women. Besides, there are more than enough babies in the world. Why don't we adopt an unfortunate one?

You know that's impossible, said Eric, who'd got into the habit of talking to Tilly with the exaggerated rationality of one explaining to a gifted child. The world may be full of unfortunate babies, as you call them, but none of them are available for adoption. It's one of the paradoxes of modern life.

It can be done, said Tilly.

Not by any legal means, said Eric.

Is this the moment after all to worry about legality? asked Tilly, and Eric was offended.

When they were settled into the Bellevue Hill house they gave a housewarming party and invited Jade along with quite a lot of the rest of Sydney. She went with the surgeon, when they had one of their last great fights. She had no real conversation with Eric, but agreed to meet him for lunch. She gazed at the house, and remarked to the surgeon, Is he wanting to show me what I've missed out on? He replied, Money talks; you could have done worse, and Jade, thinking of her own friendly little house in Newtown where the sun shone through the leaves and warmed the wavery-paned glass windows of her kitchen, replied, You poncy bugger, you know, I'm more glad than I can say that I'm not going to see you ever again, and that was how the fight began. She was still feeling martial when she met Eric.

You look fabulous, Jade, he said. She'd not stopped dressing in jeans, but now her shirts were silk and the runners had turned into exquisite expensive leather shoes. She'd grown cynical about the ability of her economies in clothes to change the world. Eric eyed the way the silk dipped and swelled across her body. You know we never should have parted, don't you.

Shit, Eric, I hope you're not going to say anything more like that, or this is likely to be the shortest lunch you've ever had. She began to push back her chair, squeaking over the worn polished boards of the You Beaut Brasserie, which had once been a suitcase factory, in Chippendale.

Not if you don't want to, he said quickly, and began to ask her about her work, but hardly listening, and it turned out that he wanted to talk about Sebastian.

He's going to school in the *mountains*! High school! I thought you'd have sent him to a decent school at least.

Jade raised her eyebrows. This plus her silence was a strong sign of fury, but Eric didn't notice. What about his results? Is he getting good marks? Medicine/law type marks?

Quite mediocre. On the low side of mediocre. Barely-getting-a-job-in-a-shop type marks. Her voice was as smoky as dry ice.

Eric was appalled. He fumed and questioned. Jade gave short cold answers. After a while Eric noticed. He tried to conciliate. I thought he'd be bright. Like you and me.

Well, he's not. He's not at all like me, and I imagine he's even less like you.

What are we going to do about his future? Eric asked, and Jade gave a shriek of laughter. We, she said. She tipped her head back and grimaced at the ceiling. Finally she said, You leave me speechless, because she suddenly felt too tired to try and explain to a person capable of saying these things what was wrong.

Eric was quiet for a moment. He began to eat salad in large bites. Then he said, Could I meet him?

Why not ring him up, at the gallery. Ask him. I'll tell him you're going to.

On reflection she thought that Sebastian ought to see his father. Eric was boiling with plans; they might appeal to the boy; the three women didn't know what to do with him, perhaps this man of power with the glitter of London, New York and Sydney on his shoulders might find the right offer.

It turned out to be going to live in Bellevue Hill with him and Tilly, and Eric pulling strings to get him into a really good school for his last year. Poor Tilly, said the three women, then Jade supposed they might get on quite well together. Orphans of the storm, she thought, and wondered why. Lucky Tilly, it might be. Sebastian thought he should have a go, try it out. Is it a bribe, he asked Jade. What might it be a bribe for, she said. To be his child, I suppose, said Sebastian.

Jade thought about this. Well, you are his child, really, aren't you. Nothing can change that. But whether you love him, hmm. Giving you things won't buy that.

Did Eric know this? In January he came up to the mountains in a little red car with an electric hood that went up and down. For Seb. He'd need it when he got down to Sydney, to run about the city. And for going to Jade's, and visiting Amelia and Zoe, which he'd obviously want to do occasionally. Not depend on that dreadful train.

The train's safer, said Zoe.

Oh, we'll make Seb a good driver, said Eric.

It won't be Sebastian, it's the other drivers who'll be the problem. That road's deathly.

You can't live your life worrying about death, said Sebastian.

The women looked at one another with hopeless mothers' eyes. They realised they were in the presence of a moment that had been snuffling round for a while, for years maybe, for all Sebastian's life, of course, the moment when he would take his life into his own hands, maybe entrust it to others, untrustworthy people, heedless. A moment that could no longer be kept at bay by any act or will of theirs; they could watch, warn perhaps, but not keep him safe. To them across the hood of a shining red car came the hard knowledge of every parent: the only thing to be done is hope.

Sebastian walked around the car, studying it. He might have been entranced, so completely did he give himself to looking at it. Eric straightaway offered him a lesson in driving it; he seemed to pick it up quite fast. He could make it go quite neatly by the end of the day. He obviously has a natural bent, said Eric. When Jade heard she was disgusted. A red car? A convertible, no less. How obvious can you get. She wasn't rich. Her presents to Sebastian were intended to appeal to his intelligence. Seb had been right about bribes. But would he continue to see it?

Amelia and Zoe were gloomy when he went to live with Eric and Tilly. Why go now? muttered Zoe. We've always offered to send him to school in town, he could have boarded, or lived with Jade. Why choose to go now?

Who knows, said Amelia. Children that age aren't rational. They don't have long-term logical plans. They just do what seems a good thing at the time.

It didn't occur to either of them that he might have been doing it for their sake. To offer them some shape and purpose in his life.

I'm thinking of us, of course, said Zoe. Missing him. But him too. I hope he's happy.

They found it hard to find out. Sebastian was vague, seemed

unable to tell them anything about his life in the city, at school or at home. It's okay, he said. Everything was okay.

❖ ❖ ❖

In August Sebastian disappeared. Eric telephoned. No, he's not here, said Jade. He wasn't in the mountains either. The school had no idea. The police weren't very interested. Teenagers were always disappearing. It was pretty well symptomatic for the age. An argument at home, and off they went.

There were no arguments, said Eric. He was very happy. We all got on wonderfully well. We'll circulate the details, said the police. He'll no doubt turn up somewhere, sometime.

It's not good enough. Eric lost his temper. He wasn't used to feeling so powerless when dealing with the law. A humble client to it. Not to mention idiot children who threw away their lives, wasting their chances at good results when they were just within their grasp, plotting a course straight for the gutter.

Impotence doesn't suit you, said Jade.

Impotence! shouted Eric, and banged down the phone.

After a while he started saying, He won't get far. He hasn't got any money. Not to speak of.

Jade began to laugh. I bet he has, she said. I bet he's sold the car.

She was pleased to think that Sebastian might still surprise them.

He wouldn't do that. He loves that car.

That's why he'd do it. People don't always want things to be easy.

Whatever do you mean?

Jade nearly always felt tired when she had to explain things to Eric. God, she said. If I was a client of yours wouldn't you work harder at understanding what I was talking about? I'll try to be monosyllabic. Sebastian loves his car. If he has to sell it in order to escape, then he might think that such a sacrifice makes him deserve to escape. Do you see what I mean?

I'm not sure that I do, said Eric.

Sebastian's departure

◆

Newcastle, 2000

Sebastian left for school one morning with his other clothes, the jeans and shirts and sweaters and sneakers that he thought of as real clothes, in his sports bag. As usual he drove in his red car. However awfully school loomed up, getting in the car, even to drive there, made his skin prickle with pleasure. He stopped at the park round the corner and changed out of his school clothes, which he planned to leave behind in the public lavatory, but then thinking they might incriminate him he decided to take them with him and drop them off the Harbour Bridge, which would be much more fun. That was how he chose his route, north over the Harbour Bridge, so he could chuck his expensive tailored uniform over the edge and into the water and watch school and the whole dreary business of his education cast away with them. But as soon as he got on to the clattering steel span he realised that the traffic would carry him across stuck fast in his accidentally chosen lane, and he wouldn't have a hope of getting near the edge, so he kept going north waiting for the next chance, until he got to Mooney Mooney and pulled off the road there and threw them over the concrete wall. He put stones in the pockets so that though they caught the wind and filled with it they fell directly down like the parts of a dismembered body, and for a moment he thought someone might stop and apprehend him for murdering someone but nobody took any notice, and then he thought I am murdering someone, Sebastian Dane hopeless schoolboy gone to a watery grave, and here he was a man who now would be called simply Dane starting off in a new life. He hadn't a clue what it would be but for the moment it was driving north. How far? Newcastle was what the signposts were offering and suddenly the phrase came into his head, *Steve Apples, Newcastle butcher* from all that time ago on the TV, and him saying that's Jade's name, and finally Zoe telling him that Steve Apples was his grandfather who'd died and left her with Jade a little girl to bring up, so really Zoo and Mia were no relation, though this didn't seem to change anything. Steve Apples his grandfather from Newcastle. So he zipped along and turned off the highway into Merewether because he liked the sound of the name. May your weather always be merry he said to himself, and stopped at the hotel and asked for a room and stood at the window looking at the sea stretching from right to left and far into the distance with the afternoon light sparkling on it so that it seemed as though it were boiling away in sharp little points, and looked and thought, I'll stay for a while. Being miserable was one thing, another was the world getting on with itself. He still had his sandwiches from school and was going to throw them away since he was no longer the person they were meant for, but then he remembered he didn't have much money, so he ate them. Afterwards he walked along the beach, a long way, looking out to sea and closer in at sand and long sharp grasses, walking past the rock platform and along a curious curved concrete path that looked like an old pipe and saw more beach stretching to distant headlands and on the land side wind-bitten bushes hunching in to the lie of the land, walking so far that when he turned back the bright winter day was coming to an end and the sun's rays shone in bands through the thick sea haze, so that he seemed to be walking through dense yellow light. When he got back to the pipe the water was washing over it in curt business-like waves that made you glad they were still quite small; he had to take his shoes off and roll up his jeans and even so they got quite wet.

He was entranced by this new landscape. None of the three women he'd lived with were much interested in seashores or beaches. The mountains were what they loved. This yellow salty sea light was different from the blue eucalyptus haze of home, just as the sharpness of the sea wind had a different quality from the stony mountain breeze, so that the interest of it all comforted him in his misery and he was glad he was going to stay.

◆   ◆   ◆

The first thing he did was sell the car. It drew attention too easily, he could quite quickly be traced by it. And he needed the money. He went to several dealers and even so thought he was probably being ripped off but still he got a lot for it. Cash, he asked for, and the piles of notes were thick in his hands. Then he had to work out what to do with them. He didn't have enough identity papers to be able to open a bank account so he bought a money belt but just the same carrying wads of notes was uncomfortable. Then he thought of the hotel safe and left it there. So he was free to walk the beach in shorts and a sweater and not have all his worldly goods weighing him down. He was sorry about the car. But the bus service worked quite well. This was what he said to himself. A pity about the car but the bus service is good. He didn't allow himself to be heartbroken; a new life will not work if it starts off with too many broken hearts.

He went into town and wandered through the shops, climbed the hill to the cathedral and looked down over the port, took the ferry to Stockton and walked along the breakwater. There were still some old wrecks, rusted and unrecognisable, incorporated in the stone walls. One was a skeleton sticking out into the water, you could walk out along its rattling plates and girders and feel the suck of the sea deep and greedy at it; the sun shone and the water was blue and only gently heaving but you could feel what it would be like, the danger, in a storm and no land near. Nearly a century ago now; the boat was solid enough to last as a wreck all that time, but not strong enough to save itself being wrecked in the first place.

He walked miles. Across to the other side of Stockton, the river side, where there were some fishing boats tied up, and over the channel the steelworks whose main job in life could have been the creation of new skyscapes. You could watch it for hours. Sometimes he went so long without talking to anyone that his tongue felt stiff in his mouth, like a stuck hinge that would need to be oiled before it could function again, and then he'd give it a bit of a warm-up, talking to himself in solitary places where the wind grabbed his words and tore them to shreds before anyone else could catch them.

He wrote a postcard to Mia and Zoo and put it in an envelope. He expected them to know he'd run away because of the car being gone too, they'd know he wasn't kidnapped or killed, but he wanted to tell them he was okay. Around the pub he kept an eye out for someone who was a traveller, and picked on a woman who got out of a car with dresses hanging on a hook in the back seat and went into the bistro to have a meal. She ordered a number of dishes and a bottle of wine and was sitting staring into the fire and pensively drinking it while she waited for her food to come.

Excuse me, he said, are you travelling far?

At first she was cold, staring at him in a what-business-is-it-of-yours fashion, and then when he offered her his charming manners she warmed a little. He'd worked out a story, rather feeble, but partly true.

I want to get in touch with some friends but I want to surprise them too, it's for a birthday, so I don't want them to know where I am, so I wondered if I could ask you a favour, could you post this letter for me? Somewhere not here, would you mind?

The woman laughed. That sounds like a tricky idea, she said. What about Murwillumbah? Or maybe Grafton? She took the letter and put it in her handbag.

It didn't occur to Dane that she might forget about it, or not bother. In fact she took it out of her handbag and put it in her car glove box, and then rummaged for maps, and the letter got shuffled to the bottom, and she didn't find it until nearly a year later. It was not for another three months that Dane's family got a message from him, and that was on a card Marcus posted in Sydney.

◆ ◆ ◆

He met Marcus on the beach. He came down in the mornings in a wetsuit and went surfing. Normally Marcus wouldn't have talked to somebody who wasn't a surfer and quite likely not even then but he was curious about Dane being always there. He was intrigued that he lived in the pub and they got into the habit of having a drink together in the evenings. Marcus accepted that Dane didn't have to do things like surfing to be quite interesting. Marcus was an architecture student who lived in a small wooden house round the corner in Ranclaud Street. It was one of a number his father who was an engineer had bought at a good price after the earthquake. He'll develop them one day, said Marcus. But in the meantime he lets me have this one. Beats the family mansion any day. Marcus whose surname was Limeburner seemed to do more surfing than architecture. One day he pointed out the family mansion, on Merewether Hill overlooking the city and the ocean, an enormous three-storeyed place with a pointed pediment and pink and blue latticed arches. Hideous, isn't it, said Marcus. Hopelessly embarrassing for a student of architecture. In fact I normally never admit to it, he said, eyeing Dane with a certain surprise. By the way, how can you afford to live in this pub, on the dole and all?

It was occurring to Dane that living in the pub was more than he could afford, so he said, Well I can't really. I have to look for somewhere else. I like it round here, though.

I've got some slob sharing with me at the moment. Why don't I throw him out and you could move in instead?

Marcus organised this, not quite so cruelly since it was the end of the year and the guy was going anyway. Dane found himself peeling off notes with less frightening speed. Marcus said, How come you're living on the dole in this time of economic upturn? You should have a job, my lad.

That's rich, coming from you. A professional student! Professional surfie, more like. Rich daddies, they've got a lot to answer for.

I shall astound everybody by graduating one day. And besides, being the child of my parents' declining years . . .

What's that got to do with it?

Nothing at all. Arriving in the world when they fondly believed their childbearing years were well and truly done . . .

Gives you the right to spend twenty years getting an architecture degree.

I am the Benjamin, the golden-haired boy, or is it white-haired? The apple of their eye. Eyes. Marcus got oratorical on beer. Dane wondered if he were telling the truth, or the opposite of it. When he met Marcus's mother Gemma, a tall weather-beaten woman who spent her days playing golf and appeared briskly fond of her son he still didn't know. She seemed quite prepared to let him get on with his life as he would. Even a bit bored with him. But maybe she doted. She shook Dane's hand and seemed quite pleased to meet him as she said and got in her car and drove off to her golf game. He thought of Jade, and Zoo and Mia, and a huge well of sadness opened in his chest. He wondered when he could go back to them. He hadn't let himself have this thought yet, had been living his daily life and not considering tomorrows until they were todays. Now it had trickily twisted into his brain, thanks to Gemma Limeburner, and he couldn't put it away. He pictured going back . . . School. The gallery. *What are we going to do with Sebastian?*

Well, he'd done something with Sebastian. Chucked him off a bridge, drowned him deep in Mooney Creek with rocks in his pockets. But of course, replacing him with Dane still didn't answer the question's meaning. There it was still: what is to become of this boy? Man. Or, what is this man going to do with himself?

It was very clear. When he found the answer to that question, then he could go back.

Marcus had surfed all summer and worked enough shifts as a barman to earn the funds to maintain his lifestyle and gone through three love affairs but now the new term loomed he looked like doing some work. Textbooks littered the house. He kept dramatically pulling himself together, unsprawling out of armchairs, pushing himself away from the table, refusing further beers, and heaving gusty sighs, saying, Oh well, back to the drawing board and actually slouching over to this elaborate affair that now filled the living room, when he became quite absorbed in work. The summer was evidently over. Dane had done some shifts at the pub too (Marcus told him how to lie about his previous experience in order to get taken on), and had flirted with girls but hadn't fallen in love with any of them. With Marcus reformed he was back to being on his own.

He bought the paper and read the job advertisements. He tried to picture himself doing these jobs, as he sat at Marcus's crumby breakfast table eating yoghurt out of the pot, but the pictures never worked. He'd start off with a storeman or a bricklayer, then he'd find himself watching his feet walking along the pipe beyond the baths. Or a shop assistant: that would get him into town, crossing the high level bridge, on to the wharf and the ferry to Stockton. Or there were things like accountant, or surveyor, or engineer, that needed going back to school and getting into university and years of study; he just skipped them. Far too heavy a weight on the brain. All the jobs that were in his range had no pictures for him. Morning after morning he slid his finger through the columns, spooning up yoghurt with the other hand; any images offering quickly turned into other things, things that had nothing to do with making money or earning livings.

After the jobs he read back through the features to the news. He liked the features, the notes about the Lord Mayor, who was a woman, the photographs of ships and traffic accidents, the accounts of all the doings and happenings of any possible interest, which were really a graph of the hopes and fears of the city. The fate of the Norfolk Island pines in King Edward

Park. The insidious earthquake damage still appearing. The opening of schools, or their closing. The long-running acrimony over the old hospital site. And people. The city's children distinguishing themselves, or suffering tragedies. The newspaper dwelt lovingly on the city's inhabitants.

Like Neville of Newcastle. There was a picture of an old man with a lot of white hair. Retiring at last, in his eightieth year. *I have looked at all of Newcastle through the lens of a camera*, says Neville of Newcastle.

The article burbles on. A recording angel, the reporter calls him. Attendant on all our most joyous moments, the christenings, the engagements, the weddings and graduations, perpetuating the family in portraits, capturing our civic moments, our hours of glory and occasions of pride. How fitting, if melancholy, that his last task should be the immortalising of this year's crop of graduates as they pause for a moment on the threshold of their destinies.

Wonderful stuff. A new young cadet galloping off with the purple between his teeth. But Dane isn't taking much notice of this. He keeps going back to that remark of Neville's: I have looked at all of Newcastle through the lens of a camera . . .

Neville is in the telephone book and easy to find, the small side street actually a paved pedestrian mall, the stairs to the first floor lined with portraits, a varnished door into a large room with lamps hanging yellow and round in the dusk. It's not the glamorous business he's expected; perhaps the newspaper article was an act of piety rather than of truth, an obituary not waiting for the old man's death. In fact the place is like a junk shop. There's furniture standing round like a herd of exotic beasts, familiar with one another's company but not exactly fraternising. A red velvet couch, the wooden parts worn but the velvet plushy new. A carved chair like a throne. A short wall of gilded books. Some sort of bower hung with flowers of dusty coloured silk. Dane's hardly started looking at all this, and hasn't he seen it somewhere before, when the white-haired old man of the picture comes out of an inner room, nods, and says, How can I help you, young man?

I want to be a photographer, says Dane.

Fathering

◆

Are you gay? Mikelis asked Dane. This was in the early days of their association, when he often spoke sharply, rudely. Dane accepted this brusqueness as a test he had to pass.

I don't seem to be. Why?

No reason. Just that nearly everybody is these days.

Not me.

You sleep with me.

Yes, but I don't make passes at you.

The old man suddenly giggled. I suppose I've left it a bit late to try. Sad to think of all the things you'll never do . . . be . . . see . . .

Quicker than the giggle he was becoming melancholy. To distract him Dane said, I think I might be the father of my dad's daughter. That makes me my daughter's brother and she her father's sister and him his daughter's grandfather.

It sounds grotesquely incestuous.

It's not. Well, only in some dead old Church of England rulebook way.

Very well. Explain. I hope it's a good tale. Not too unedifying.

The more unedifying the better, I should think. You don't want anything too dull.

The old man grunted. Dane turned off the tape recorder. Well, my father . . . my mother Jade didn't want to marry him because he was turning into a rich lawyer so he went off to England and took up with some posh sort of girl (How salutary, said Mikelis) and then they divorced and he married Tilly who is American and I hardly saw him until I was seventeen and then I went to live with them in Sydney in my last year of school.

Calm down boy. Less breathiness.

Dane thought of Tilly and took deep breaths. Tilly who'd been a fashion model and who was thin like a child, sometimes, with skinny arms that made him sad, and other times was a rich warm woman. Who could be both things in such speedy succession and even sometimes at once. He wondered how on earth he'd started to tell Mikelis about Tilly.

Well, I was going to school and I hated it, not my sort of thing, rich kids spoilt rotten and the work, I couldn't cope with it, and Tilly saw that I did, hated it, I mean, and when I came home in the afternoons she'd make cups of tea and sit and talk to me about how it was. Eric never came in till seven or eight. That big-time lawyering takes a lot of doing. She wasn't very happy either because Eric wanted her to have a baby and she didn't seem to be able to and she wouldn't go on an IVF programme. She said that if love can't make babies nothing should. Dane smiled. She also said that her body belonged to her and she wasn't going to have a whole lot of strangers fucking about with it. Anyway, they had a lot of arguments, her and Eric, because of course he blamed her because there was me to prove he was all right, it obviously wasn't his fault that they weren't having a baby. Tilly didn't have a job or anything and we'd sit in the afternoons drinking tea and talking, you know the way you do, the meaning of life and everything, and one day she opened a bottle of champagne and poured it into these tall glasses and then she kissed me and that was it, really, we were making love in the afternoons as well as talking . . .

A classic seduction scene, said Mikelis. Was that your first time?

Well, except for this girl in Leura, but that wasn't anything like Tilly. Dane was silent, Mikelis could feel him thinking about her. He spoke sharply.

Get on, boy. Not the end of the story yet, is it?

Well, Tilly was quite clever, and she helped me with schoolwork, so I didn't come unstuck the way I really ought to have done, I mean I scraped along, being a conscientious student and a hard worker and all those things they say about you when you're no good but your parents are paying massive fees, and of course Eric wasn't pleased because he wanted a miracle but at least nothing blew up.

◆ ◆ ◆

Dane remembering could feel those autumn days, the year turning with the leaves in the stately old garden of the Bellevue Hill house, the freshness of the air and the nights drawing in as the winter approached. The fire lighting the room and Tilly naked on the rug in front of it, her smooth skin and the furry tickle of the rug, the slow rise of the bubbles in the tall wine glasses and the leisurely long drawn murmur of their conversation. That was bliss, he thought, those moments, I can look back on them and say, that was bliss. He tried the word out loud, thinking this is a word I've never said before.

A real fire, was it? said Mikelis. Not gas.

No, real logs, massive, in this huge fireplace. The whole place was like that. Colonial baronial, Tilly called it.

Get on, said Mikelis.

Those times are funny. You don't think about the end of them, you know they're going to have one, they can't possibly go on in the same way, but you don't think about it, until afterwards you look back and see that something had to put a stop to it, what did or something else.

Mikelis snorted. You do try the patience, he said.

Well, what happened was that Tilly got pregnant. She didn't tell me at first, she waited to be sure, but after the second month missed she told me and then she told Eric. She told me that she was sure it was my baby, but naturally she didn't tell Eric that. Everything changed. He sort of got besotted with her. She got careful. He came home earlier from work. Tilly somehow pulled inside herself. Went frail, but not in the old way. She sort of turned into a piece of china, precious, it might break, and there was Eric wrapping plastic bubble wrap around her. I thought she'd suffocate. But I couldn't do anything, just watch them at it. I couldn't stand it. I said let's go away together and have our baby but she looked at me as though I was going for her with an axe. I've never seen such alarm. I couldn't do that, she said, Eric thinks it's his, and of course it might be, it's not impossible. Of course it's not his, I said, you know that as well as I do, it's my baby. Suddenly she goes all pale, and says in this small thin voice like a kid shut out in the cold, You wouldn't ever tell, Sebbie, would you? Promise me you never would. And of course I did promise her, how could I be so nasty as to not, but I couldn't stay there any longer so I just got in the car and drove away, didn't leave a note or anything, took some clothes of course and my money which wasn't much and drove away. Looking back it was a pretty awful thing to do, not tell anybody I was going, but at the time I didn't think of that, I was so miserable I didn't give a stuff about anybody else, and anyway I reckon Tilly'd have known what was going on except of course she couldn't say anything. And of course she was right, the baby could've been Eric's but given what we were up to I reckon it's pretty certain that she's mine. The odd marital fuck wouldn't have stood a chance beside what we were doing. Remember that about love making babies. I don't know that Eric loved her. Of course he did in a way. He valued her. As though she were some incredibly gifted work of art. And anyway I reckon all his sperm went into making money.

So there you are. That's how I'm the father of my sister. Etcetera.

Have you seen her?

Years later. You can't stay disappeared forever. I went back and made my peace with Eric. He wasn't madly interested by then. Back to the heavy lawyering and Tilly drinking tea in the afternoons with Catherine. My little sister, she made a great fuss of her being. Funny thing, I thought she looked just like Jade. My mother. Colour and hair and the shape of her head. But then the thing was that Jade and Eric were always said to look alike, brother and sister Zoe reckoned. And I suppose you could say she had Tilly's thin bones. Very polite, she was, very well brought up. I sat there drinking tea and thinking this is my child but I couldn't get too excited by it.

Fatherhood needs to be cultivated, said Mikelis.

Fishers of men

◆

Stockton, mid 1990s

The view was straight across the river to the steelworks. Immediately in front was a small plot of wasteland beside a derelict factory, with sticking out from the bank a number of jetties, humpty-do the way jetties should be, the planks rattling and skewiff, doing their job of linking boats to bank. The boats shabby too, but quite efficient, fishing boats mainly. Then across the broad sweep of the river to the BHP, a spectacular view, even beautiful, with its lights and fires and clouds of smoke that with sunrise and sunset, all the angles of sun and moon, the darkness of night or day, the movement of wind and storm, change colour and pattern and shape and are a source of endless contemplation. Alice who always felt a little sorry for people who lived in Mayfield or Waratah or anywhere not close to the beach and clear air, sits for hours at her window just watching the scene in front of her. The river changes too, with the tides and the weather and the angle of light, a friendly small-scale change, it's mostly smoothly rippled and greyish coloured, not showy and grand like the sea.

Sometimes she sits in the day room and looks through the front door at the courtyard. She stares vacantly in front of her. Poor thing, be better off dead, thinks a young woman visiting her grandmother, a garrulous old lady who laughs in a cracked voice at jokes she tells, mainly about her desire to get to the Boatrowers and have a few beers. The young woman doesn't know how intensely alive Alice is. Her legs are frail, she can take only a few steps with the aid of a walking frame. She no longer looks in the mirror. That wrinkled whiskery face isn't her own face, inside her head. Inside her head is where life is. The body has failed but not the brain, not yet.

In the day room there's cups of tea, heavy china milky tea. She's never cared for milky tea but that's how it comes here; she likes hers pale and weak. In her room she makes it like that. Clear amber-coloured liquid. And the cup white porcelain but outside the colour of toast brown to yellow with pink roses and green leaves calling in at Mother's you like it helpless don't you Alice, now she's started drinking it after all, hot and pale in the thin cup hideous in some ways pink and green and yet you're fond of things you've used all your life unpacking it out of the box from Anthony Hordern's it's like Christmas they always said, one time a doll for Alice yellow hair and the clock tall clock on the mantelpiece with etched poppies on the glass case of the pendulum brass tick-tocking back and forth and chimes Westminster chimes they were like the clock they got for a wedding present, that stopped though Elinor says she will get it fixed hard work nobody has chiming clocks and not clockwork clocks these days. Turn it off George for goodness sake says Rose coming to stay keeps her awake, so then not sleeping you can't hear the quarters, halves three-quarters and then count the hours comforting in the sleepless dark. Mother's clock Muriel took it her children will have it now. Was the toast-coloured teaset the same year there were a lot of parcels, boxes and boxes ordered from Anthony

Hordern's catalogue smart Sydney things there in the pictures one time candlesticks just like Christmas everybody said. Only two cups left now and their saucers maybe a cake plate. Elinor might want them she likes pale tea in a thin cup. Whistle kettle time to make the tea Earl Grey teabag George never would have teabags in out pale tea hot in a thin cup.

You bought things and people gave them to you and sometimes you inherited them and they accumulated in a house standing in the rooms filling the cupboards so many things dust them wash them can't be bothered using them then you die and they all spread out again and accumulate in other people's houses Mother's teacups Grandfather's clock Muriel's children Muriel's grandchildren and Alice's, not Nell's her things spread around now other people's children and her ashes over the headland sunny day over the cliff the water down below the ashes in the air grit on the wind the cindery air from the steelworks maybe a spectacle but pretty filthy dirty work dangerous like the railways shunting and such a racket in the dark old Mr Gray and Joe Sullivan too all his life shunting on the railways dirty work. George at the dockyard can't see it from here know where it is just down the river past the steelworks flowing out to sea and there's the dockyard closed now no more ships no more jobs dirty work better than none. Rusty red iron ships berthed at the steelworks clumsy tubs not like the sailing ships that tied up here George's sailing ships graceful's the word though he got no further than rowboats oars dipping in smooth rippled waters and the little craft shooting along the regular piston effort of his stroke producing the effortless glide of the boat along the dark river and Alice with her hand dipping in the water oily it looks the picnic in a basket trees crowding down is she remembering the moment or the photograph . . .

So the performance of the steelworks goes on, sun and clouds and light and smoke, and Alice sees it and does not see it. Her mind is a little boat gliding effortlessly back through all the long twisting complicated river her life has been until now, meandering along tributaries, little crooked creeks, nudging into sticky swamps and mangrove flats and mud, floating over

billabongs and anabranches, a boat in which she by choice
embarks and a metaphor of a journey because she does not
stick in the mud or get trapped in the billabongs, and every
now and then she looks out at the broadened harbour-forming
only imperceptibly moving stretch of water where her life is
becalmed now. She loves her mind and the quick neat way
it threads through all the old memories; she is very happy
not to be dead with all that going on.

Sometimes matron drops in for a chat, she pauses smiling
and waits until Alice comes back from wherever she has been.
Sometimes matron would like to ask what is going on in Alice's
head; she wonders if it is a putting of her life in order, a working
out of what it has all meant. If matron were to think of an
uncrude way of asking, Alice could tell her, no. She is simply
observing. Present and past. She has never been much interested
in meanings. George was the one for that. Alice kept her eyes
wide open like a child's, gazing at life coming to pass.

She knows that the place she is living in is the site of the
Missions to Seamen before it moved to Wickham across the
harbour, first the old Tin Mission that washed away to sea
and then the red brick hall that was demolished to make space
for the natty unit she lives in now. The chapel remains; one
day soon she'll go to the ceremony reopening it, mended and
refurbished after neglect and the earthquake. Such a pretty
chapel, Gothicky turrets and a spire, a polished wooden roof
and eleven stained glass windows telling the stories of Jesus'
mission to sailors and fisherfolk. *I will make you fishers of
men, fishers of men, fishers of men. I will make you fishers of
men if you follow me.* That was old Mr Gray, until he took
a drop too much and the church dropped him. Lay members
being meant to set an example against drink, not for it. Poor
Ada. Ada was there when the chapel was built. Was there in
the leaky old building whose ratty floor was awash at every
high tide anyway, on that night of torrential rain and roaring
gales when the water rose knee high and the floor lifted and
the order was given to abandon ship. Was one of those ladies
carried by the young sailors through the raging torrent to
safety. All the young sailors had been picked up by the new

launch, the *Ada* (not really any connection except coincidence, sad for Ada) which had ploughed its way through the mountainous seas in the harbour, going from ship to ship, finally assembling some eighty men and boys for tea and service. A useful disaster, finally, since it got rid of the old Tin Mission for good and all and they could build a new one, Ada making cakes to raise money, five years it took. Alice knows all this, Ada told the stories often enough. They were her golden age. Near enough to eighty years ago now.

George didn't touch alcohol because of his father. A glass of wine when they went to visit the girls, but that was in his old age and he'd never choose it. Ada was strong minded in that way too. Alice always thought of George being like his mother, nicer of course, more loving, but arrogant too, self-willed, wanting his own way. She used to think some of his father's meekness wouldn't have gone amiss. But of course he was like his father, the fisher of men. She can still hear both men intone the text from Revelation: *Then I saw another angel flying high overhead to announce the good news of eternity to all who live on earth* . . . each giving it his own meaning and George's eternity not so simple nor so Christian as Albert's, the Kingdom of Heaven is within, you must find it for yourself, said George, but both loving the words, both voices quivering with the power of them.

It is all a ruse to fend off death says her son-in-law Mikelis. Religion, love, alcohol and art: they are what we put between us and the reality of death. It is not words that Mikelis covets, but images. She smiles to think of Mikelis desiring to picture forth angels which of course he has done but only at secondhand after they were already images in stone or wood. It's the first-hand he longs for; Mikelis in the next life camera to eye snapping the heavenly host.

So now here is Alice ending her days at the sign of the Flying Angel. The home knows its history, it uses the medieval woodcut style long-trumpeted angel as a logo on its newsletter and publicity. Does she see a pattern in all this? A mild interest mainly. If it had been Ada, now, that would have been a neat sort of loop, in my end is my beginning, but for Alice, it's a curiosity, it sets her mind off on one of its elaborate trails through her winding streams and smelly backwaters. Randomness. That's what it is. Interesting.

Alice sitting at her window drinking tea there's a little plane flying up the river looks like the shark spotter hardly the season remember the joy ride when was it 1928 or 1929 she and Nell took with their brothers driving in the car that used to be a hearse blue plush seats big as a drawing room out to the airport at Broadmeadow paying their money up in the plane like a big moth really noisy what a view better than a mountain all dressed up silly it seems these days those long-waisted dresses they did make you look like the side of a house if you weren't careful and summer coats over Nell was quite substantial in those days not like the end when she couldn't eat couldn't eat wouldn't eat and the brothers and their wives Alice too not Muriel not really up to it no longer herself went to visit her in hospital and said what do you fancy tell us what to bring you and she said custard or chocolates but when they brought them she never could not even taste them. Not substantial then bones in a bag of skin like paper and there she is gliding across the piece of wasteland be a park one day prefer it empty more honest somehow stooped back dowager's hump white hair in a fuzz round her head. Nell arthritic but quite speedy come back from the ashes thrown over the headland. No she isn't of course she hasn't that isn't Nell not a ghost from the ashes a person in a dressing-gown pale blue and gliding with a clumsy gait through weedy grass and worn stony patches pausing under the tree giant tree opposite the Boatrowers hiding behind the trunk peering back at the home nobody about though cars pass swiftly along the road down to the bridge across to Kooragang then to the mainland and into the city no punt now cars have to go by the bridge takes quite a while but at least no delays not like the punt queued up for miles.

Alice now watches the woman as herself, her own thoughts forgotten. She pauses under the tree, looking up and down the street and back at the buildings whose glassy windows shine in the feeble afternoon sun and give nothing away. The river flows coldly, there's a niggling wind lifting the pearly plastic bags that litter the wasteland, the smoke from the steelworks wells up in lurid gleaming clouds, maybe it's steam, maybe. Alice can see the tension in her stance, she's like a runner ready to shoot off the mark when the pistol sounds. On your mark get set go. And off she goes, across the wasteland to the edge of the water. There's a jetty that sticks out, turns in a square and comes back to the land, and in the far side of the square is a little metal bridge you can move aside to let bigger boats in, only a dinghy could fit under it. The woman in the blue dressing-gown walks out on to the jetty, you can see the planks wobbling and there are no rails to hang on to, moving fast and awkward but balancing, round to the start of the bridge where she pauses for a moment, this does have a rail, her hand on the rail and then steps off into the water. Her blue gown floats around her then wetting sinks with her.

What should Alice do? Press her buzzer? A nurse will come, but to Alice, not the woman. Open the window? Shout? Who to? In fact she does nothing, considers these things, but rejects them. The woman is making a choice, she has a careful plan, that was in the tension of her figure under the tree. Why should Alice try to stop it? Sometimes old people want to die and it can be very hard if the body is strong. The spirit ready to go but the body hanging on.

Maybe still. Drowning doesn't seem to be happening. The woman's head seems to be showing above the water. And already there's been a shout, a man is running out of the Boatrowers ducking past a speeding car and another follows him. They're out on the jetty pounding along the planks, one jumping in, it's not actually that deep, waist high perhaps. He's pulling her out, the other man drags her up on to the jetty and now it's general alarm, people dashing out with blankets, wrap her up warm in silver paper, a stretcher comes and she's carried into the hospital wing of the home.

Alice is sad. Such a careful plan, it ought to have worked. It's terrible that the water should not do its share by being deep enough to drown but how could you know? The fishing boats that berth there seem sizeable enough, for small fishing boats; they must have a shallow draught. Poor woman. Alive when she wanted to be dead.

But in fact it's not so bad as that. Alice asks matron, who tells her, no point in beating about the bush with Alice. She does die. Pneumonia. At three o'clock in the morning. Pneumonia, the old people's friend, they call it. Coming in the lowest darkest hours of the day to carry off those who don't need to go on living any more. Alice smiles. So it was a successful plan after all, she says to matron, smiling with her child's eyes and her shy little mouth.

Religion, art, alcohol and love, says Mikelis. Alice thinks of suicide. Maybe suicide is something else that people put between themselves and death.

Career

◆

Newcastle, 2000

Dane hadn't known he was going to say to Neville of Newcastle, I want to be a photographer. He'd taken the bus into town, crossed the street, walked up the stairs without any plans beyond his moment of arrival. But when the words came out he wasn't surprised. They made good sense. They would lead on to the next thing.

You're a bit late, son. I'm finishing up here in a couple of weeks. And I haven't taken an apprentice on in years.

Oh, said Dane.

Unless you want to *buy* the business. The goodwill'd be worth a lot, of course. Not to mention the equipment.

Are you selling it?

It's been on the market . . . the old man paused, Dane could see him thinking, could practically hear his brain shifting into commercial gear. I've had a lot of offers, he went on. No problem in people offering *money*. But when it's a lifetime's business, and so close to a man's heart . . .

I can see you'd need the right person, said Dane. You wouldn't want to trust it to just anybody.

You're right there. The old man was looking cannily at him.

I'll tell you what. Why don't I come and work with you for these last couple of weeks. You wouldn't have to pay me, he said, and Neville relaxed. You could see if you liked the look of me, and I could see if I had any talent. Then we could decide what was the best thing to do. Um, could I ask, um, what sort of price you had in mind?

Neville named a figure far higher than the sum Dane had got for the car, a lot of which was gone anyway. He looked at Dane craftily and must have seen his face falling. Of course, it is open to negotiation. There's always arrangements to be come to in these things.

So Dane went to work with Neville. There wasn't a lot of it. The old man didn't come in until the afternoon, and went home about four o'clock. There were occasional clients. Some people wanting passports. An elderly widow getting engaged. Several grandmothers brought in cute little toddling children, to be sat on a table with gilt mouldings, holding a marble-patterned ball. The grandmothers knew all about it, kneeling with creaking legs out of camera range to hold the baby on. I had my daughter done, said one to Neville. Over thirty years ago now. She looked lovely. A pink dress with rosebuds. Lovely with her dark curls. I remember you remarked, what a wonderful head of curls for such a little girl. Maybe you recall . . . But even the grandmother seemed to realise that was unlikely. Well, as I say, over thirty years ago now. I was beginning to give up hope, you know. Thought I might be doomed to have no descendants. She smiled. But, as you see, it's turned out well. Of course, they do leave it late these days. With their careers. I look after Melinda three days a week. Nana comes in handy. Although I'm not as young as I used to be, she said, as Melinda arched her back, rolled over, and tried to dive off the table. She was wearing a denim skirt with lace frills and braces, and a red gingham shirt with more lace frills and the whole thing came apart with the lunging around so she needed to be tucked and patted back into shape which was quite a difficult job for Nana given Melinda's muscular wriggling. Neville didn't have much small talk, Dane noticed, just concentrating on getting the camera in the right place. Lucky it was on a stand, the old man's hands were rather shaky.

Melinda was still bucking around so that the braces fell off one shoulder and she was half way out of her skirt. Shall I hold her for you? said Dane, taking her from the grandmother. It was the first time he'd held such a small child and was amazed at the terrible energy coursing through the little body. She needed a lot of holding. Then she went absolutely rigid and started to roar. Her stiff body leant away from him in terror. Nana made soothing noises, got the clothes into order on the little ramrod shape, and took the child back. She stopped yelling immediately, and Nana put her on the table with the ball. She got a tissue and wiped her cheeks dry. The child looked up at Dane as though he were a monster that she was only just safe from, her mouth pursed and her eyes wide open. The resulting photographs were quite successful, the child's eyes huge and glittering with the tears left over from the previous moment's crying. Dane wondered how much luck was involved in the taking of pictures.

The flocks of graduates didn't eventuate, though there were four or five. No weddings. Video killed the wedding business, said Neville. They don't last, you know. Video film, give it ten years, fifteen, it's gone. Nothing left. Still, lasts as long as a lot of marriages, he cackled. Yes, the video camera, got a lot to answer for. He suddenly realised he was talking to a potential buyer. Of course, you can't beat the calm and majesty of a real studio shot, and there's people still as know it. There's always a market for quality.

But not here, Dane was beginning to think. Not any more. Not now.

Neville couldn't teach him very much. His photographs turned out all right, but he was not able to show or tell Dane what the processes were. But nevertheless he learnt a lot, working for him. He came in to the studio first thing and had the place to himself all morning. He examined it. Neville had been a man of meticulous filing, and had not entirely lost the habit. He'd kept card indexes of clients, cross-referenced to filing cabinets of proof sheets and negatives and notes on cameras, lighting, and all the technical details of shooting, developing, printing. In theory Dane could have reproduced them all exactly. If he'd wanted to. Who would've? There was a terrible repetitiveness about these photographs. Skilful they were, professional, charming, and all the same. 1949, 1999: fifty years and nothing had changed. Neville was a kind of one-man factory. How could he not have got bored with taking the same photograph over and over? Even the shots of local landmarks, the Town Hall, Nobby's, the Civic fountain, the foreshore development, the earthquake damage: Dane held a shot of Nobby's in one hand and one of a baby on the table with a pull-along duck (1951) in the other and thought, there's not any difference.

Nevertheless he investigated everything. He studied the cameras, checking them off against Neville's filing notes. There were a lot of old trade magazines and journals, none later than the early 1970s, Neville seemed to have given up by then, but he'd also never thrown anything away. The articles were of the same period as the cameras. By observing Neville, and practising, and collating the records with the articles, he taught himself to take pictures. And develop and print them. He photographed the studio. He liked its weird furnishings better without people in them, he moved them round in different patterns, made large-scale still lifes out of them. He used up a lot of film experimenting and was sometimes pleased with the results. Was always pleased with the feel of the camera in his hands, against his eye, always excited when he saw the way things were, different and yet much more themselves, through the camera's lens. He ransacked the whole place, looking for anything that might inform him.

On top of a cupboard he found a box thick with dust and inside it a folder of photographs without the usual details of

client, date, technicalities. Though they were clearly taken here
in the studio. Black and white, of a pretty girl, shapely, nude,
though quite chastely so. She had long brown hair and a habit
of hiding behind it. Maybe shy of her situation. In one she
lay on the velvet couch with her back turned, showing her
nice cello-shaped bum, much the same picture as Velasquez
and Goya painted not to mention countless followers with
brush and camera. It was interesting, though, it didn't look
like a cliché. In another the young woman sat on the marble
table, her legs neatly crossed to hide her private parts, looking
up from under her lashes and holding the marble-patterned
ball. Dane laughed, because she looked so much like the babies,
except for being naked and adult.

These photographs seemed different from the usual. Of course
they were the only nudes, but was it just that? The last one
showed the same woman, sitting in the carved chair, wrapped
in brocade and twisted round with long garlands of roses. The
pale flowers damasked in the fabric glimmered against the dark
wood, the woman did not smile, her skin was like a pearl.
It was a romantic picture, glamorous, mysterious. It raised
a whole stack of questions in the viewer's mind. Who is she?
Where has she come from, what is she doing, what does it
mean? Why is she looking at me like that, out of her bindings
of garlands of roses? What next? Dane realised that mystery,
the sense of more to be known, more worth knowing, was
the quality missing from Neville's work, and which he without
recognising it had valued in his own shots of the unpeopled
studio. Why, if Neville could do this sort of thing, had he
stopped? Because he hadn't taken these pictures, that was why.
Dane had grown up in a gallery, he knew that people's works
of art are their own, however modest or clumsy, jumpers or
pots or ink and wash drawings of the Three Sisters, and from
looking at this folder of photographs he learnt that camera
work is the same. That was why they weren't catalogued and
labelled in the system, they weren't Neville's.

One morning a woman came in, rather upset. She'd had
a fire in her house, fat catching fire on the stove, a big pot
of it for cooking chips, her husband was very fond of chips,

nobody hurt thank goodness but the kitchen destroyed and the family room beside it, not destroyed entirely but ruined, the contents burnt before the fire brigade could come and get it under control or else spoilt by water, and the thing was they'd lost the photographs, including the albums of wedding photographs, and she'd come to see if just possibly there was a chance of getting copies. It was a while ago now, 1968, but still the longer ago the more you treasure, you need the memories the further the past, don't you? she said, and Dane's eighteen years politely agreed with her. Though of course she said I understand that Neville might not keep so far back.

Certainly Neville had them, Dane could find them for her, and she smiled with satisfaction at the faded proofs of her bridal self. He did do a good job, didn't he, she said. Though come to think of it, of course, it wasn't Neville of Newcastle in person. No. It was a man in a brown suit. A very strange suit as I remember it. I was a bit put out at the time, we had thought we'd've had Neville, but as it turned out we were very happy.

Dane wondered if the man in the brown suit had taken the photographs in the folder. The dust on the box could have been there since 1968. He told the woman to come back in a week and the prints would be ready. Ours were tinted, she said, but Dane was not sure about that aspect of things. When Neville came in he told him about the request. The old man was smug. People are so careless. You'd be surprised how often it happens. Lucky it wasn't a video, ay? No second chances with video. Not even a first chance for all that long.

When Dane asked him about the man in the brown suit he said, Oh yes. That fellow, what was his name? Had to let him go. Nasty piece of work. Had some floozy here, taking pictures in the nud. Never liked pictures in the nud, meself. What self-respecting man wants to look at that sort of thing? Art photography they call it. Hah. Porno-photo-graphy I say. What was his name. Never came across him again. Never bothered with an assistant after that, either. More trouble than they're worth. Most of the time. Speaking of which, what about the business?

Have you got a buyer yet?

I thought you were keen.

Well, the problem is, I don't think I can afford it.

I said we could negotiate. I tell you what, you name a price. A fair price, you name it. Cameras, equipment, studio, goodwill.

Is there that much goodwill? I mean, there aren't that many customers.

All the goodwill in the world, boy. Cabinets full of satisfied customers.

Yeah, but I'd need them to keep coming.

Well, you see them, don't you? Steady stream.

I wouldn't've thought . . .

Of course it's up to you to make your own way. I can't do it for you when I'm gone.

Can I ask you something? said Dane. Why are you retiring? Why don't you just keep going?

Mickerliss, said Neville.

Pardon?

Mickerliss. That fellow's name. The shots in the nud. Foreigner of course. Went to Canberra, now I come to think of it. Last I heard.

Dane had put the box back but not the folder out of it. He doubted Neville would miss it. Judging by the dust. He wrote the name Mickerliss on a piece of paper and put it inside the folder.

◆ ◆ ◆

Neville's retirement was a nebulous thing. There didn't seem to be a moment when it was going to happen. The newspaper article had implied a cut-off, a glorious career coming to a full-stop, but it seemed as though he could go on for ever with his trickle of clients. A couple of weeks he'd said and it was already two months. His health was all right, he was shaky but in control of his medium: today's photographs still alarmingly like those of fifty years ago. Dane was learning a lot, teaching himself a lot, about taking photographs but wasn't any closer to earning any money. He had an inspiration. In the mornings he went out into the streets with a camera

and took people's pictures, handing out Neville's cards after
he'd done so. Some people threw them away instantly, others
shook their heads and wouldn't accept them, a few smiled and
put them in their pockets or handbags, but nobody got in
touch. Dane found himself with a file of photographs of strangers, anonymous strangers; he looked at them and wondered
about their lives. They were like characters in a play, whose
plot they knew and he could only guess at. The more he looked
at them the more sense he got of the mysterious and interesting
stories they inhabited. Even though they were simply people
with mostly closed faces walking down a street.

Finally Dane found out why the old man was retiring. A
letter came. Neville hardly ever got any mail. Dane got this
one out of the box and looked at it, wanting to open it, wondering if he counted as secretary, and deciding that he did.
It was a final notice of expiry of lease. The old crook, thought
Dane. He'd have sold me this as a going concern, and look
where I'd be.

You could still take the furnishings and the cameras, said
Neville. And the goodwill. Set up your own place somewhere
else. Name is everything.

Neville the Second, said Dane. He looked at the carved chair,
the *chaise longue*, the twiggy seat and noble table and antique
ball, the wishing well and the faded flowers of what he'd just
discovered Neville called Hymen's Bower. Scrapheap stuff,
every bit of it. He had all he wanted of the studio's tatty
furnishings on film. Cruelly he said, Look Neville, your goodwill is the fading memories of a few old customers. They
wouldn't survive a change of place and owner. But the cameras
were interesting, not new, but good. He knew what Neville
would have paid for them, they were in his old journals.
Depreciation? Appreciation, Neville said. You don't get quality
like that these days. Seeing Neville as a wily old crook made
it easier for Dane to bargain with him, and anyway he felt
a gratitude that didn't mind paying more than they were
probably worth. Neville had introduced him to photography,
by being written up in the paper and then by being there.
A master letting the novice sit at his feet. In Japan an intending

potter has to do menial tasks for years before being allowed to approach the art. Neville hadn't kept him at arm's length or made him do dirty work, or hidden his skills from him.

And at the end he was generous. You can take that stuff if you like, he said, pointing to the dark room. Might as well see it to a good home. He gave him boxes of film too. Neville was going to walk out of the studio and away from photography. I've done enough to last me out, he said.

◆ ◆ ◆

Marcus watched with interest all this stuff turn up in his house. He was keen on photography himself, had the latest, well a year ago it was, in reflex cameras brought back by his father from Hong Kong. He liked to take pictures of buildings, to study their shapes and shadows. He could turn out his own prints, there was a dark room in the basement of the Limeburners' house, which made a point of having everything. Except a tennis court, there wasn't enough flat land for that, what a blow. But there was a pool, partly cantilevered, partly hollowed into the hillside, so it was like swimming in a grotto when the weather was hot. In winter it was heated by solar power. Dane who was used to living in old houses that put character before wizardry was impressed.

Dad won't mind you using the dark room. He likes things to be used. He never does any more and I hardly do. Marcus was getting quite involved in Dane's career.

Freelance, that's the way to go. Even better, set yourself up as a photography consultant, find a catchy title, charge astronomical fees and people will think you're brilliant. They'll flock to give you their money.

Oh yeah, said Dane.

But the freelancing was a good idea. He bought all the new photography magazines he could find and digested them. He bought a notebook and divided the pages into two columns, on the left expenses, on the right income. There was a considerable discrepancy but at least the right side had some entries in it. He sold single shots from time to time. Once he got a commission. You need a portfolio, said Marcus, and a CV.

What's that? asked Dane. You've got no training, said Marcus. No degrees or diplomas. You've got to offer some sort of evidence of capability. There's the photographs themselves, said Dane. Not enough. You've got to get a good-sounding CV. Marcus helped. He was a great enhancer of the truth. Marcus's father liked his work and gave him the occasional job. And one day he won a prize, which did wonders for the plus entries. Though he did consider whether you could count a prize as income. Then he decided you could, you just had to make it a regular event.

Before another year had passed the right and the left had achieved a shaky sort of alignment, which was beginning to be necessary. There wasn't much of the car money left.

Ballod

◆

It took Dane eight years to work out that the author of the photographs in the folder he'd lifted from Neville of Newcastle's studio was Ballod. He knew his work, of course, had read too many journals not to be familiar with it, had seen exhibitions and prints in collections. But it wasn't until the National Gallery rehung its Amber Nude series and he saw again that lovely pear-shaped bum that he began to make the connection. At first he thought simply that it was the same model, but knew there was more than that. He went home and dug out the folder, which he'd put in the back of a filing cabinet and half forgotten. He looked at the photographs, the silky light, the way the camera dwelt upon the woman; they had to be by the same person. He remembered the fire woman's man in the brown suit. They were round about the same period, late 1960s, early 1970s. Found the scrap of paper with Mickerliss written on it, and worked it out.

Ballod didn't use his given name, but it had been on the biographical panel accompanying the photographs. Mikelis Ballod. He looked up every thing of his that he could find. He fell in love with him. He wanted to go and work with him.

After eight years his own career was okay. He'd stayed in Newcastle for much of that time, waiting until his right-hand columns consistently exceeded his left before going back to his three mothers, saying, Guess what, here I am alive and well and living in Newcastle and earning a living. Oh, so you are still alive, great, said Jade. How kind of you to keep us informed, but almost immediately admitting that she'd known that all along. Pretty well. So had they all. How? The car. They discovered he'd sold it, where. Eric had traced him. The really hard work had been making Eric leave him alone; he was all for haling him back home into another version of the old life. Jade had been passionate in her arguments for not interfering, and Tilly had joined her. He needs to make it on his own, you have to give him the chance, people have to be free to choose, Tilly said vehemently, and Eric somewhat amazed by this liaison between the two women gave in. He kept an eye on the boy just the same and knew what he was up to. He's playing power games, said Jade, and Tilly replied wasn't he always, that was the way he lived, he no longer knew he was doing it. Why not assume affection? Because for so many years it hadn't been convenient. Affection is suspect that starts at seventeen years old.

Dane wasn't sure whether he felt more guilty or less that they'd known where he was all the time. Sebbie love, how could we have managed, not knowing whether you were all right? For a bit he felt that their having known about him finding himself a career meant that somehow they'd done it, they were responsible, not him, but of course that was non-sense. Anyway, it was rather good being able to be Sebastian sometimes, and bask in the love of his three mothers. Not Tilly, though, who was being offered as number four. You should come and see your stepmother, son, said Eric on the telephone, but it was some years before he stopped making excuses and went, and met his little sister Catherine.

Newcastle was his home. The place where he worked. He and Marcus had done a series of architecture books, not amazing sellers, but solid. The most successful was *Earthquake*, a pictorial essay on the changed and unchanging faces of the city. On the strength of that he acquired a house, a little terrace near the beach, sturdy enough to have survived more than a century of head-on buffeting from the sea winds, and you could see Nobby's and a bit of the Stockton breakwater from an upstairs window. He got plenty of commissions. Had travelled, quite profitably. Had lived for four years with a woman who he thought was going to be a wife for life, but turned out not to be. She went off with a man who ran a chain of video stores and liked going to nightclubs. He thought, I am twenty-six, I need to do something more, and suddenly there was Ballod for him to become obsessed with.

It took Mikelis a while to accept him. I can manage, he said. I have managed alone for all this century and I shall continue to do so. But in fact he wasn't managing at all well. The house was a mess and he didn't eat properly. Meals on wheels came but the food didn't interest him, he just picked at it out of a dim sense of duty. There was no family nearby; his sister-in-law had gone to France and his daughter was in Rome; they thought he was still the healthy man they'd last and only a year or so ago seen. The word *retinopathy* had never passed between them.

Dane simply moved in and took over and quite quickly even so curmudgeonly a person as Mikelis had become began to enjoy the difference. He even told him he was good with injections; I suppose it's a luxury I should be grateful for, he said. Not too painful needles may be more than I deserve.

At the beginning the old man's eyesight had not entirely failed. He was still taking pictures. What I am about, he said, when he'd not only accepted Dane but discovered the pleasure of talking to him, what I am about in these last years is the communication of my darkness. You see these photographs: they're a record of my going blind.

And there was a process to be observed. A fuzzing, a hazing, a simplifying into light and dark. A shaping of the elemental, the primitive, a reduction to an essence. Dane wrote words on sheets of paper; he did not feel that he had the right description yet. They are not clumsy work, he wrote, not mistakes, or a failure of technique. They are exactly right, and they are powerful. As the blindness encroached further Dane would take the pictures for him, following Mikelis's instructions, aware of how weird they were, but never interfering. And he took care of the results, filing them away in the system that he'd observed from old Neville. Mikelis having made them didn't care, it was the act that counted with him. In the years since Veronica's death there had been no ordering of his work. Stuff lay in dusty teetering piles about the studio and every now and then suffered a paperslide, when it would be shuffled back into a heap again, but of different composition.

The communication of my darkness, said Mikelis. The irony was that with his blindness his pictures became more and more light, until finally they were full of it. Dazzling glowing brilliant light. Blinding light. A vision. The road to Damascus, ay, said Mikelis. I wish it were. Not all of us achieve our Damascus.

Maybe some people show others, said Dane.

Oh, you are full of handy comforts. Not the least, verbal. You are like a mother distracting her child with new words. You sing them and chant them and charm him with these new sounds with their new meanings. *Archipelago*, you say, *invertebrate*, *commandeer*, *voluminous*; and the child is entranced. You forget I've got an old and dogged brain and when its teeth sink in, well, it's too tired to prise them out.

You're tired with not eating, said Dane. I'm restoring your strength. Nourishing you. You're just run down.

And you will wind me up? Don't you know that clockwork is obsolete?

This sort of conversation seemed to have an invigorating effect on the old man, briefly at least. And Dane could feel the affection in his niggling. But the building up wasn't working, or maybe the disease was just working faster; Mikelis was getting more and more frail. Then one day when Dane brought him his most recent most dazzled photographs he said I can't see them at all. Not the darkest glimmer. I shan't take any more pictures. Write finis. Full stop. The end.

After all, he said the next day, it's been more than fifty years. You have to know when to stop. And he shook with laughter more robust than his skinny body could quite manage.

Then he began to talk to Dane in earnest. Or rather it was not so much to Dane as from himself. Dane occasionally wondered what he'd got into, but not often. He was too busy, ordering and cataloguing the Ballod *oeuvre*, planning a retrospective exhibition, he wondered if it would be too much to call it Blinding Light: The Road to Damascus. Recording and typing up the old man's utterances. And doing some work of his own. He worried about this. Would all this unadulterated Ballod start influencing his own work? It was one thing to learn from the master, another to be tainted by him. Dane saw things very differently from Mikelis, he had to struggle to keep that view while absorbing what the old pro had to teach. Am I as good, have I the capacity to be as good, was the octopus-tentacled question that would keep slithering into his mind, but he was an at least good enough craftsman to push it out again. You have to hope, if you're an artist, that one day you'll get somewhere near as good as you want to be. It'll only ever be somewhere near, never there. Mikelis knows this. It's the most terrible thing about having to stop: you have lost the chance that the next thing you do will be the truly marvellous one, *opus mirabile*, the real justification of a lifetime's work. To have to say I have done all I can could break your heart.

On the other hand there is a kind of cracked gaiety about Mikelis now. I'm retired, he says. I'm taking things easy. I can stop trying.

Dane is learning not to say, You needn't try because you've already done it. You've achieved it. *It*, the old man will quite properly sneer. What's *it*? Instead he asks questions. Tell me, he says, and the old man does. As though now he's stopped doing, he can talk. Who for years would not: You have my pictures, he said, you do not need my words. Or: There are the photographs which you will observe are already another

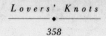

thing and far removed from the objects they claim to picture, why would you distance yourself even further by talk which is a making of artefacts about artefacts?

Now is the time for words, and Dane is recording them all.

The mirror of art

◆

Down behind a filing cabinet Dane found several large white cards, bent and shabby, written on in the black copperplate script of Mikelis's palmy days. One said: *The exclusive taste for the True oppresses and stifles the taste for the Beautiful.* Another: *The photographic industry was the refuge of every would-be painter, every painter too ill-endowed or too lazy to complete his studies. This industry, by invading the territories of art, has become art's most mortal enemy.* The last phrase, *art's most mortal enemy*, was shadowed with red ink, so it jumped off the cardboard at you.

What are these? asked Dane. These signs. These sentences about photography.

What? said Mikelis. They were sitting in the studio at the bottom of the garden as they often did on hot days because it was cooler than the house, its ceiling tall and shadowed and the trees outside blocking out the sun. For the same reason it was freezing in winter. Mikelis lay back in an ancient leather chair, like a lizard with his vital functions half suspended. Dane had to describe the cards a number of times and read the inscriptions twice before Mikelis understood what he was on about. Oh yes, he said. Yes.

Well? What are they?

Sentences, that's good. Life sentences, ay. Mikelis chuckled. Once he set his brain to work on something, it functioned very smartly. It was just a matter of getting him started. I wrote them out, ooh, when we first built the studio it would have been. Copied them out of a book I was reading. What's-his-name. Baudelaire. I forget the title. It should be on the shelves somewhere. One of those queer old books I was always reading, according to Veronica. I had them pinned up on the wall for a bit, but she made me take them down, reckoned they'd put the customers off.

You can see her point. He doesn't seem much of an admirer of photography, your Baudelaire.

No? No. I suppose not. Have you read him? What do the young read these days? You should.

I'll have a go, said Dane. He had a sketchy notion that Baudelaire was a long-ago poet. French. Something about evil. Flowers? He scanned the bookshelves, he'd already looked closely at them, though not so as to register unknown specific titles. But he'd examined the old books, observed the weight of them, the leather and cloth bindings, the inky scented old paper, the gentle foxings, the blurrings of edges, had even read at some of them. Here's something by Baudelaire. *The Mirror of Art*. Is that it? Yeah, it is. I can see where they came from.

There were bookmarks and in these places portions of the text were highlighted with a turquoise marker pen. Dane read out: *Since photography gives us every degree of exactitude that we could desire (they really believe that, the mad fools!) then photography and Art are the same thing. From that moment our squalid society rushed, Narcissus to a man, to gaze at its trivial image on a scrap of metal.* Great stuff. I mean, really good indignation. But do you believe it? Why put it on the *wall*?

Mikelis shrugged. Who knows? I am my mother's son, I

suppose; she fastened texts to her walls. Perhaps I found them salutary. Or thought they induced humility. Maybe I felt I needed to protect myself with irony. It's a long time ago. You, Dane, a young man, may have more notion of why the young man I was then did those things than I an old man have now. Then again, maybe not.

Dane thought that anybody who could construct such sentences as Mikelis was so artlessly proffering still knew what he was doing. When he'd worked this one out he said impatiently, Yes, but do you think what Baudelaire says is true?

Do you? Mikelis was turning back into a lizard. It was clear that he wasn't interested in Dane's answer. The young man propped the texts up against the wall. The white cardboard was cobwebby and grubby and bent, though not eaten, there were no silverfish in the studio. The words were as clear as ever. 1859 was the year Baudelaire had written them; they still had a querulous freshness. Dane left them around for a while, realising that they made him feel uneasy. Marcus was always on about the importance of creative unease to an artist. Maybe that was the point of them. To niggle and needle and stop you feeling secure.

He kept questioning Mikelis. Do you really believe that, about photography being art's most mortal enemy?

When I was young I thought a lot about art, the old man said. Then when I got older I just took photographs. I was much happier. Read Lartigue about picking cherries.

Dane has. He's still uneasy. He's realising words can say whatever they like. Whatever they like whenever they like. So where's the truth? In my heart I know it, he says to himself. But what if he knows different things at different times?

He stuffs the sentences back behind the filing cabinet.

Alice reading

◆

Stockton, mid-1990s

Y ou could take a slice out of
Alice's life at just about any point and find her reading. All
her life she sewed and knitted, crocheted and embroidered,
keeping the devil well and truly at arm's length with her busy
hands, but a day without reading was a day without savour.
On this occasion she is reading a book she found in the library
of the retirement home. It's a whodunnit, not her favourite
kind of book, she sometimes gets impatient with the fiddly
plots, that's not why she borrowed it, it's the name, it's called
The Same River. It recalls a book read long ago, by Rumer
Godden, whose title was *The River*, she remembers it because
she never forgot it, it was that kind of book, and now she's
come to finish her days by a river, a river's end, she's interested
in books about rivers, and there's a lot in this one, including
one in Latvia, which is interesting because of her son-in-law,
and then there's the amber, just like Veronica's, but it's taking

her a long time, she sits at her window to read and instead it's the stories inside her head that take her attention, and the book slips flat in her lap, unheeded. She stares at the wide channel of the river that flows past her window, and follows the stories in her head.

The letter to Eva

———◆———

Dane took out the pad of onion-skin note paper, the fountain pen with brown lacquer patterns. Dear Eva, he wrote. He looked at the way the lines wavered faintly over the bumps in the paper. Dear Eva. That was the right form of address. He couldn't call her Ms Ballod. Not after all those other letters, Mikelis's letters, indeed, but the words formed by him. He thought of the way writing to people made them belong to you. You traced the letters of their name and there was the connection made.

He got up and went to the door of Mikelis's bedroom and stood quietly for a moment, listening to the faint shallow puffs of the old man's breathing. Listening for intermittence. Mikelis had forbidden him to write. No, he said. It's not time. His sleeping breath sighed in, then out in that faint exhausting puff. Dane went back to his letter.

He wrote in a kind of formal parody of the letter he had

always imagined writing, saying that she might be surprised
to hear from him, but that in fact he had been in the habit
of writing letters to her for some time though on her father's
behalf, that now he was writing himself and against the old
man's wishes, because he believed that it was time to tell
her that soon might come a telephone call, informing her . . .
here the brown lacquer pen sliding over the delicate bumps
in the paper not like onion skins at all really, he thought
of writing these words on the fleshy dense skins of onions
and how the pen would sink into their aromatic thickness
and the ink run and stain, not this delicate sliding grip, the
pen paused wondering about the next words . . . informing
her . . .

Mikelis believed that death would not come without a
warning, but Dane could tell that each of these exhalations
of breath considered being the last, that the little sigh as the
next went in was a sigh of regret that the machine had to
keep going, as though the body had its own desire and its
own will and did not care as the mind did still to keep on
functioning as long as possible, was prepared at a time of no
attention being paid to pack it all in.

That was what would be known as a good death, the moment
unmarked, sleep in an instant becoming death, no alarm, no
warning to set the mind grappling to fend off, to hold on,
no panic or pain because no perception.

. . . informing her that her father was very frail, that quite
soon perhaps there would be a telephone call to tell her that
his life was failing, or had failed, that Mikelis believed that
there would be time to let her know, *let her know*, how unfraught
with action the phrase was, to let her know of this but that
he Sebastian Dane did not.

He sealed it in an envelope, stuck on stamps at the fastest
rate and a sticker to point this out, and walked down to the
post office. There were faxes and satellites and phone links
sounding as near as next door, but letters were for life and
death. A ritual. He stood for a while with the envelope poked
through the slot but still in his fingers, waiting for the moment
when it would drop and be out of his hands. Plop. A soft

metal echo from the walls of the box. A papery thud on the other missives in there. Out of his hands.

It occured to him that maybe Mikelis intended to die without disturbing Eva. But that wasn't what he said.

Back at home he listened to his breathing. The sigh in, the faint exhausting puff out, the pauses when you waited to see if this hiatus was the final one. Not yet. He got into bed, slowing his breathing to the rhythm of the old man's. One breathing willing the other. Like a swimmer pacing, or a runner.

◆ ◆ ◆

Eva came. She telephoned to say she was on tomorrow's plane. Dane could wonder if it was the alacrity of fear or affection or even boredom with the place she's in, a desire to exchange her present situation for another. But Dane is good at love, being a person who grew up with it, his cynicism is only a jaunty outer jacket required by fashion and actually quite good at keeping cosy what's inside. Dane believes that it is love that is bringing Eva home.

The photographer's daughter

◆

Was Dane disappointed when
he met Eva? All the passengers streaming off the plane and
finally only one unclaimed and tentative. After all, he did know
what she looked like, didn't he? The photographer's daughter:
who better documented than she?

And yet standing watching the disgorging passengers he
realises with the beginning of panic that he has too many
pictures. There's the busy little girl of her mother's snapshots.
There are wedding photos, wearing a hat of such high drama
he cannot recall the face it frames. There's the angry Eva
of the Latvian politics letters to her father, with their black
and jabbing words, the third and fourth pages indented with
the first's furious script. A mind's eye vision, this one. Playing
the cello, crook-kneed and head bent, hair like a tent. Madonna
and cello, Mikelis called these pictures. Washing up in a cloud
of steam. Rubbing noses with a black cat, white head black

cat. Reading in a whole range of rubbery positions. Mikelis's photographs are the reverse of mug shots. You'd never recognise anybody from them.

And what about the opulent Italian beauty whom once he imagined, with feral hair and furs stirred by large gestures, a woman who demands admiration and leaves no room for more intimate emotions? And the matter of women resembling their mothers; she might be a new Veronica, stepping along and owning the world in the ghost of a red-flowered dress. Or like Jade, tall and loping. Or Mia and Zoo with their flower child faces and falling forward hair. Or Tilly's exquisite thinness. Or dark-eyed Linda whom he lived with for four years.

He was behaving like a man with a wardrobe of women, trying them out for size and shape and colour on all those who came off the plane and none of them fitting, and why should they, why fit Eva to a hand-me-down? Trust her to be herself, and straightaway recognisable.

She came through the doors with an unpurposeful step, gazing round, expecting. She was a small woman, fair, and deftly made. She wore an unbulky down coat in a silvery pale brown colour which was exactly the same as her hair, and underneath black trousers and a jumper. Suitable flying gear. When the edges of the coat parted and he saw that she was wearing a pear-shaped piece of amber on a long chain he was certain he'd chosen the right person.

They met and shook hands. She had to look up at him. Her eyes were silvery too, but grey rather than brown. He remembered Mikelis's words, the shores of the Baltic are bathed in silvery light, and him saying that his mother looked at him with eyes like Latvian lakes, as best he could imagine them. Eva must have inherited her grandmother's eyes. Her hair was smooth against her head but falling in silky strands as she moved, her cheekbones were wide and flat, with the same thin Northern skin that Mikelis had before the ruin of his age and health, pale but pinkening with cold and nervousness.

She doesn't come across as pretty, none of that look-at-me-aren't-I-amazingly-put-together air that grabs the gaze of the beholder. When you know her you no longer think this. She does look like her father. And something of a waif. Dane supposes that she doesn't look like her mother because he knows Veronica through Mikelis's words and pictures. But in fact she does. Eva is Veronica as waif; she will move you not by beauty but by vulnerability. Which explains her rather closed and crisp manner; she doesn't want to be taken by the world for a waif. Next thing to a wimp. Will not allow an accident of appearance to betray her. She is thirty-six years old, a woman who must make things work for herself on her own. Dane feels quite nervous with her. His usual gazing is met with a frosty stare.

What luck there's weather and journeys. How grateful people are for answers to questions they don't really care about at all. Who's interested in whether the flight was bumpy or slow or fast or late, the food unspeakable, the weather muggy or cold, yet what delight to listen to accounts of all these things. For then there is conversation, not silence, entertainment, not dullness, as Dane generously offers her the chance to talk about herself, which for most people is the pleasantest thing in the world.

But Eva is tense. What about Mikelis? He has not been told she is coming. Dane has decided on *fait accompli*, no warning, no time for worry or complaint. Both fall silent. Each imagines some grotesque version of Dane's bouncing into the house, crying, Guess who's here! He's frail, you know, says Dane, to reassure them both that it will be done delicately. Well, frail, but he's okay. He seems to be able to go on being frail for quite a long time.

Why didn't he tell me? asks Eva, though it's not really asking, she knows the answer as well as Dane. I imagined him so flourishing, his letters so lively and him a master of technology, all that clever word processing, I should have guessed, he wouldn't have anything to do with it in the past you know. Copperplate script. A fountain pen as modern as he was prepared to go. I should have known. Why didn't I know?

He didn't want you to, remember, says Dane. He was very keen that you shouldn't be burdened . . .

That's the point! Why think it a burden? How dare he choose how I would feel about it. Why shouldn't I want to come more than anything in the world?

He thought you had your life over there . . .

My life! Do you know what I do over there? I do translations. I'm good at it, I do them well, I'm in demand, I make enough to live on. I do one job, then another. There's no continuity, no certainty, no security. Oh, so far they turn up more often than I can do them but there's no guarantees. I have no family, no lover, well sometimes lovers. How important is all that as a life?

He thought you loved living in Rome . . .

So I did. But maybe I also love him. And there are other cities.

I take photographs like that, says Dane. One after the other. Producing them and hoping that they work. You could get neurotic about the future. What if you stop being able to do it?

You're a photographer too?

Dane nodded. He said, Is Canberra one of the cities?

What?

One of the other cities that there are.

Oh. Once I'd have said no, no way. Couldn't wait to get out of the place. But maybe.

◆ ◆ ◆

Mikelis lived for a week after Eva's return. His manner was grumpy and niggling when first he was presented with Dane's accomplished fact, but then his joy was too much to pretend against, and they hugged one another and cried. Canberra turned on one of the painted autumns which it manages every now and then, day after day of stillness under the warm bright gaze of the sun. The season in its turning seems to pause: maybe there is no need to go on to the next bit. The light shines through the transparent brilliant leaves: perhaps they will continue to hang there, poised, not falling. The world is freeze-framed, and only an occasional quiver reminds you that the machine won't allow you to hold the picture still forever.

Then Mikelis died, and the season resumed its running. Death came in the lowest hours of the new day, when it's still deep night, that time which is always nearest to death. When it only needs a short step, a quick pluck of the bony finger. He breathed out and didn't breathe in again. Dane didn't notice the exact moment. In the morning his body was cold, and so was the day. Rain blew like rice against the windows and the tremulous bright leaves were dragged from their branches and whirled briefly in the air before being pounded into a sodden dun mass underfoot.

• • •

Nobody takes photographs at funerals, said the old grandmother, and that's true, but Dane did. Nobody sends invitations to funerals either, there's just a notice in the paper. The funeral directors take care of all that as part of their large fee. Mikelis has left instructions: in the cemetery at Woden, beside Veronica, with few words and some music; if his friend Gilbert who plays jazz trumpet is still around then that's what he wants, loud and cheerful. Eva and Dane are unprepared for the number of people who come, people who did little in life, recent life anyway, the part Dane knows about, turn up in droves to pay their respects in death. It's been obvious from letters and requests that a lot of people knew him, now they've come to see him safely put away. Cross off that person, we've done him, says Eva in Dane's ear. Unkindly; their motives are in some part grief. For somebody. There are square metres of flowers curling up in the freezing gale, and squads of people shrinking into their coat collars as they listen to the notes of the trumpet that try to soar but are chopped up by the cold wind. The sun shines out of a purple sky but there is no warmth in its livid stormy glare. Dane photographs the whole thing.

He doesn't know who most of the people are, and Eva isn't much better; people she's never seen before come and speak to her. Directors of galleries with capital Gs and critics and newspaper people, academics and politicians and fellow artists, former students, local admirers, neighbours. Some say their names with the luminous modesty that expects recognition. Eva hasn't a clue. She shakes their hands and says thank you. Even relations are doubtful; her cousins she knows, but not their husbands or children. Apart from them if any of the family are still alive they're mostly too distant to come. (She and Dane have not yet worked out that they are second cousins twice removed.) The person she really cares for, her Aunt Elinor, went to France two years ago and hasn't yet come back; she's in a very busy later middle age, Elinor. The story of the consolation she and her brother-in-law were to one another in their widowhoods, some years ago now, is unknown to Eva, and Dane too. Mikelis did not tell him everything. It's certainly not the only secret this grave is burying.

There's a lull in the wind, the notes soar from the trumpet, the sunlight glitters upon its brass bell shape. Light without warmth. A good life, says a man in a velvet-collared overcoat. Thank you, says Eva. She stands beside Dane with her hand through his arm. He wasn't very old you know, she whispers. It would've been a good life if it had gone on for longer.

They mean he did a lot, says Dane. He did, you know.

She turns her face to his shoulder, he can feel her shivering and gulping, and puts his arm round her. After a minute she lifts her head and is her old self-contained self again.

The wake was to be a glass of wine back at the house, probably nobody much would come but dozens do and they have to send cousin Blanche's husband up to the shops for some more cases of grog. It turns out to be a great party. Everybody is being reminded how good it is to be alive. At first they drink to Mikelis's memory, grateful to him for bringing it, this goodness of life, to their notice. After a while they just drink. The next day they won't know whether they've got hangovers, or whether it's their own mortality that fingers them. Especially the eyeballs, just behind, the round solid jelly part. The morning after of grog or grief.

Somebody takes up a collection and goes and gets pizzas and brings casks of red wine as well. Both Eva and Dane are bemused to find themselves hosts to this convivial gathering. I suppose the best thing to say is that Dad would have liked it, says Eva. Would he, really? asks Dane, and this moment is the saddest of the whole day, because he realises that he did not know this, or all sorts of similar things, that whatever the memories Mikelis offered him Dane never knew him when he was full of life and health. The past is another country and old people no longer live there.

Yes, says Eva, he liked parties. Both my parents did. Even at the age when most people had given them up they used to have wonderful ones. I remember one time cleaning up and Dad saying that they hadn't broken any glasses because when people dropped them there was no room for them to fall to the floor and smash. They liked a lot of people.

By the time everybody's finally gone they're exhausted and go straight to bed. The mess can wait. Dane gets into the big bed he shared with Mikelis but before he can dwell on this melancholy thought he's fast asleep. But then in the small hours, the subversive hours, he wakes up and has another much grimmer thought.

This was the thought he had. Mikelis's death: had bringing Eva hastened it? Would he have lived for another week whenever she'd come? Was he in waiting to choose his moment knowing exactly what he was doing? Dane was examining this thought from all its angles when Eva pushed his door open. Dane, she whispered, can I come in with you? I'm cold.

There's nothing so warm as a person, she said. She told him about waking up and having a terrible thought. What if Mikelis knew exactly what he was doing? Knew he would live only a short time after she came and was postponing that until he was ready? So her coming has in fact precipitated his death?

Oh no, said Dane. We can't know the hour of our death. Mikelis any more than anybody else. And how could we take the risk? What if he'd died three days ago and you'd still been in Rome? It would have broken our hearts.

Yes, she said, on a little sigh, and went to sleep, and Dane lay awake for a while with this small hot sweet-scented round person in his arms, and sighed too, and went to sleep. In the early morning they woke up, and there the other was, what pleasure, and why refuse more? Dane found out that being a self-contained person may be because there is a lot to contain; Eva wasn't cool or dry or sharp when she made love. Not at all the smooth woman quite a lot older than he who made him a bit nervous. Nor a waif.

After this further excitement they wrapped themselves in one another's arms and fell asleep again. But just before he dropped off Dane had a funny thought about Mikelis, a kind of dream thought. It was as though the old man his bedfellow for these last several years had turned into his own daughter. Out of his death made himself into a gift for his young friend. That was silly. But as he really went to sleep he heard that rich old voice say, You could marry her, when she comes.

He could, at that. If she wanted to. And who would have made it happen?

◆ ◆ ◆

Eventually they got up, and cleaned up, threw away all the plastic cups that had served their guests—*their* guests, the funeral had instantly coupled them—and washed the glasses, feeling like people who have been ill but are now convalescent, Mikelis's death lying heavy but comfortably inside them so that they were rather fragile, at the same time as they felt the exhilaration of the health to come. But after the party was cleared away the prospect of future and more creative housekeeping made them anxious. It was a bitter day, no sun and sleety rain. Dane made a fire. But it was Eva's house now, and decisions hung in the air.

Dane said, I've got this little place, it's a terrace. In Newcastle, near the beach. Would you care—how formal he sounded, making this proposal—would you care to take a little holiday there? Before you have to decide on what's to be done in the future, whatever? I like the sea in bad weather, and it's never all that cold. Blow the cobwebs away.

The end

◆

$\mathbf{B}$y the end of this chapter it will be the end of the story, or rather, the stories, as much of them as is going to be told between these covers. They themselves will keep on going.

There is no single person who knows all of these stories, and these stories are a very small part of what there is to know.

Remember where they started.

Ada and Albert Gray, who would have loved each other once, leaving England to save their second and only surviving son's life. Albert's job the message of salvation to those whose trade is the sea . . .

Halina Ballod sailing in storms across the Baltic to save herself and her son from the death of the spirit, if not the body . . .

Going, coming, to a new world, to the colonies of old mother

England, to Australasia, Océanie: other places have names for what are in fact two quite separate and foreign countries, Australia and New Zealand. Places to live, like any other, being what people make of them.

◆ ◆ ◆

Life is not a rich tapestry. Its shapes and colours are not delineated in tidy threads, rather in a human eye view anyway they're a matted tangle like water hyacinth in a river, beautiful possibly and charmingly named, but what a pest. But okay, you want to stick to the tapestry idea, maybe the definition of God is seeing the right side, the front, while we mortals have to make do with the reverse, the back, the knots and tangles and rough ends, and work out the pattern as best we can.

So many threads, and so few chosen: George but not Daisy (who was Daisy?), Lily but not Rose, not Elizabeth's but Anne's descendants though not her siblings, so few threads chosen but even so, what a tangle. And apart from those lost or ignored there's the threads snipped off, of course all are snipped off sooner or later, but some more violently and untimely, like Diana's or Lizzie's or Jack Hawley's, others disappearing and impossible to pick out, like Elinor's daughter or Rob's or Dane's Catherine, and we don't know where they have their ending but man that is born of woman and woman too is always cut off in the end.

◆ ◆ ◆

Two emerging, for a moment clear: Eva and Dane. But only because we are stopping at this precise moment. Soon theirs'll be as ravelled as their forebears'.

So, can we have a happy ending? Bring them together, the not-so-young lovers, plight their troths, send them into the sunset to live happily ever after?

No. Happy endings can't be prescribed. Did Ada and Albert have a happy ending, her furious and triumphant pouring his booze down the drain? Him oyster-eyed shunting trains in the clanking night? Both dying alone, ill, in different unhomely cities. But they did have a happy beginning. Most people do. Just for the moment there is smoothness and clarity. Eva and Dane may have their happy beginning. Everyone deserves at least one. What they make of it, what sort of muddle and tangle and matted mess it turns into, stitches dropped and fabric cobbled, is not of concern here. Here and now there are two threads fine and free, and the pattern, for the moment, is a lovers' knot.

Thea Astley

Vanishing Points

I feel I am a lot more warmable to than Clifford. Clifford is my husband. Well, that's a misuse of a term as well. There's nothing husbanding about Clifford, even though we are legally tied. (That word should be spelt with an 'r'.) . . .

Thea Astley, Australia's most acclaimed and awarded writer, presents two novellas which sweep the reader on sentimental journeys towards an ending rather than a beginning.

Julie Truscott, a seemingly ordinary housewife, and Macintosh Hope, a disenchanted academic, each flee from lives they cannot control. The balance of their flight is destroyed by Clifford Truscott — Julie's real estate husband and the rapacious developer of Mac's neighbouring island.

In *Vanishing Points* Thea Astley is at her best.

'. . . an ebullient wit and unflagging comic energy.'

Helen Daniel, the *Age*

Minerva rrp $14.95 pb
ISBN 1 86330 186 0

Rosie Scott

Feral City

It was a dangerous [time] . . . I was suddenly and irretrievably in
the presence of the past, Lin's old car, blue foxgloves in bloom by the
rushing white-bouldered rivers, a long trip we made once through
the light-filled landscapes of the south . . . At the moment of seeing
all this I became blind and deaf to everything else. It was the first
time since I'd come to the city that I'd allowed myself to taste that
sort of memory. Never mind that I was roaring down an unknown
road loaded with the tools of a new trade, condoms and soup,
clean syringes, on a mercy run to bring in lost city souls from
the dead . . .

Feral City is the city of our future, its centre a wasteland peopled
by addicts, violent gangs and the homeless. In a gesture of defiant
optimism, two sisters — one a warrior, the other a survivor —
open a bookshop in the heart of this decaying city. Their bizarre
and moving story mirrors the fragile balance between defeat and
courage.

   With the passionate imagination we now expect from her, Rosie
Scott presents a future shock which is alive with imminent danger.

'At its best, Rosie Scott's writing is reminiscent of the work of
Colombian genius Gabriel Garcia Marquez.'

Ken Spillman, the *West Australian*

Minerva rrp $14.95 pb
ISBN 1 86330 182 8

Susan Johnson

Flying Lessons

In the early 1920s in a small town in north Queensland, Emma James, daughter of an Anglican family, disobeyed her bigoted father's wishes and married Sam Lubrano — a Catholic and son of an Italian immigrant.

And so begins a story of the heart.

In the 1980s Ria Lubrano, singer of advertising jingles, leaves Sydney without a trace, journeying to the tableland town in search of her missing brother, her roots and herself. She believes there is a meaning in the past that will bring purpose to her life if she can but reach back across time.

Through Emma's and Ria's stories, Susan Johnson weaves a moving saga of family life and the passions that pattern our identity.

'. . . a knowing and feeling author whose text sweeps along, intriguing and engaging the readers . . . [Susan Johnson] writes of her own context with such appealing strength and . . . searching critique . . .'

Stephen Knight, the *Sydney Morning Herald*

Minerva rrp $14.95 pb
ISBN 1 86330 078 3